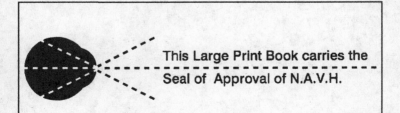

This Large Print Book carries the
Seal of Approval of N.A.V.H.

ROBBING THE PILLARS

KALEN VAUGHAN JOHNSON

WHEELER PUBLISHING

A part of Gale, a Cengage Company

Farmington Hills, Mich • San Francisco • New York • Waterville, Maine
Meriden, Conn • Mason, Ohio • Chicago

Copyright © 2015 by Kalen Vaughan Johnson.
Map of Nevada County was created by Maria E. Brower, author of *Gold Rush Towns of Nevada County*.
Map of Nevada City was created by Kelly Michele Bryson
Wheeler Publishing, a part of Gale, a Cengage Company.

Wheeler Publishing Large Print Western.
The text of this Large Print edition is unabridged.
Other aspects of the book may vary from the original edition.
Set in 16 pt. Plantin.

LIBRARY OF CONGRESS CIP DATA ON FILE.
CATALOGUING IN PUBLICATION FOR THIS BOOK
IS AVAILABLE FROM THE LIBRARY OF CONGRESS

ISBN-13: 978-1-4328-4751-7 (softcover)

Published in 2018 by arrangement with Kalen Vaughan Johnson

Printed in Mexico
1 2 3 4 5 6 7 22 21 20 19 18

To Gary—my best friend, confidant, and dearest love of my life. Your unwavering faith in me in all things is such a gift, and I am blessed to be your wife. Thanks for your steadfast support, for prodding me into new adventures, for Kristin, Kelly, and Matt, and for shared laughter.

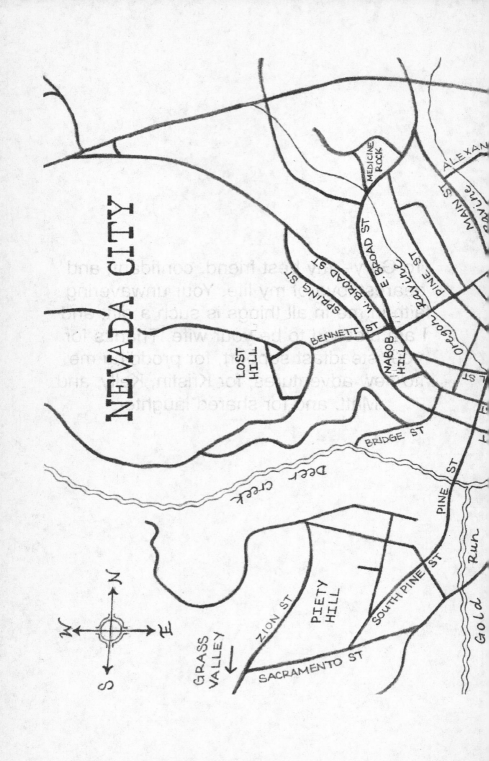

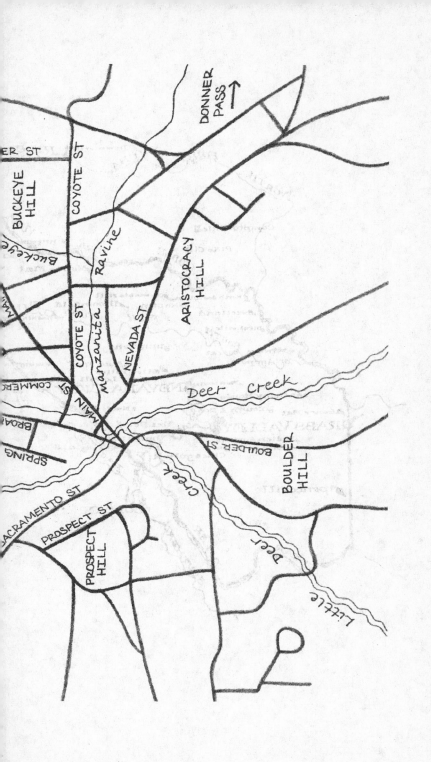

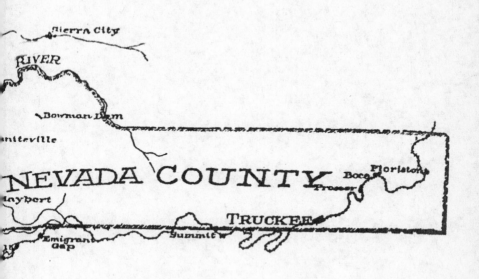

ACKNOWLEDGEMENTS

It is with heartfelt gratitude that I thank the gracious folks of Nevada City for sharing the secrets of its past, making this historic jewel such a pleasure to visit. Thanks to Nicole Dillard for digging out the perfect out-of-print books, to Allan Rogers for sharing over one hundred years of treasures from the Odd Fellows Hall, and to the dedicated staff of the Empire Mine in Grass Valley. From their combined knowledge and love of history, special nuggets were gleaned to give life and depth to the more broad-sweeping research.

Thanks also to Casey and Angela Stone of the Yolo Land & Cattle Company for the tour of your beautiful ranch and your commitment to the environment.

Special thanks to author Maria E. Brower for the use of her map of Nevada County featured in the book and on the cover. Also, thanks to my daughter, Kelly Michele Bryson, for creating the Nevada City street map.

My appreciation goes to Kimball M Sterling auctioneers for the photo of the unique silver-headed cane.

Lastly, and affectionately, thanks to my dad, Richard Vaughan, Sr., for sharing with me his love of history and books and for enthusiastically reading every draft of this novel.

PROLOGUE

Greenock, Scotland — 1840

Thundering groans of equipment surrounded him. He stalked down each aisle, glancing between rows of furnaces, cooling troughs, and rail carts full of sugarcane. Cloying odors of processing cane filled his nostrils. A visibly thick vapor concealed the object of his building rage. Nothing deterred the tall, burly boy. He pushed back rusty-red curls sticking to his brow from steam and sweat as he rounded a corner of hogsheads neatly stacked in pyramid form.

He caught sight of a storeroom door falling to a close. He quickened his pace and yanked the door open. "MacFie!" he bellowed.

A finely dressed figure at the end of the room inspected a tower of wooden cases. The man turned slowly, fingered his silk cravat, and glared as the sixteen-year-old strode towards him.

"Don't waste my time," MacFie called, giving a dismissive wave. He turned away. "Tell your brother he's got two weeks off to recuperate; that's the best I can do."

Clapping his hand heavily on the shoulder of the retreating man, the youth spun him around. "Ye've bullied Lachlan for the last time, MacFie."

The paunchy man in the lavish brocade coat struck his hand away. "You're forgetting your place, Laddie. Thugs, the whole lot of you, all except for that frail excuse of an errand boy. He needed work. I gave it to him. Be grateful."

"Grateful? He earned his wage fair enough, and ye treated him like a slave. He got the back of yer hand if ye were in a passing temper."

"My family's owned this refinery for generations. Yours? Lowly ship rats. You'll address me with respect. Get out before I call a constable."

The tall lad's pale-green eyes narrowed. "A constable? Ye need a constable? Ye don't want ta cuff *me* the way ye do Lachlan? That last shove ye gave him shattered his leg when he fell from the platform. He'll be a cripple the rest of his life! *My* family should be calling the authorities, if we didn't know they were already in yer pocket.

14

Come on; let's see what kind of power ye have over a man instead of a wee boy."

"I wouldn't sully myself with dirt such as you. You're nothing. And your brother's sacked. How's that for power? Perhaps when I see him begging on the streets, I'll toss a coin in his cup."

A roaring pressure in his ears overtook his senses. Light-headed, he recoiled his arm and hit MacFie's jaw with such impact the man sprawled off his feet. He heard a sickening thud, a sound like a melon hitting rock. His vision cleared. MacFie lay on the floor, eyes wide and mouth gaping. A dark puddle coursed under his head where it had struck a crate's corner.

He doubled over, staring in disbelief. Glancing quickly around the quiet storeroom, the lad darted for the door. He threw it open, releasing the noise of equipment into the room. He saw no one. James pulled his collar up around his face and fled.

CHAPTER 1

Nevada City, California — March 1866
Charlotte stiffened with the first toll of the bell, the ever-present threat of cave-in surging to life with one note. Pushing her way into the street, she saw townspeople rush from shops and homes, grabbing shovels, axes, and levers as they sprinted for the mines. She found herself running with them, her throat aching from tension, preventing her from swallowing, almost from breathing. Each clang threatened as she raced franticly along the wooded path. "Not Da, not Da, not Da," her mind chanted rapidly, chiming in with the sound of her feet striking the ground and the bell pealing the alarm.

When she arrived, sweaty and struggling for breath, a dry, earthy mist began sticking to the dampness on her face, hair, and arms. A crowd formed at the mouth of the mine. She darted amongst men shouting in confusion until she reached the front. She heard someone yell, "Number nine has collapsed!"

Clouds of dust spilled forth from the cavernous maw. Men covered in dirt, their features barely distinguishing their identities, stumbled out coughing.

She recognized Clancy as he spit the grime from his mouth and swiped the same from his eyes by rubbing his face against his shoulder. He dragged an unconscious man. "Nine's down; over a dozen trapped," he called as he approached the foreman.

"How many injured?" shouted Miller.

"Three more by the entrance, hit by rubble. One with a broken leg; another got a chunk of scalp hangin' loose; the last got bumps and scratches."

"What about them that's trapped?"

"Not sure. We hear voices, not much else. We won't know 'til we break through." His wheezing came in short gasps and he spit again as he lay the man down. "It's nearly a half mile in."

She watched as Sean Miller bounded on top of a nearby rock to stand above the gathering crew. "All right, let's organize teams to dig and move debris! Pritchett! Grab those men there around you and start hauling out timber and smaller rock. Get the shovels; clear the area for the boulder busters. Everson! Take those men with the picks and start swinging at stone like the devil's after your own ever-lovin' mother! You boys over there . . . get down to the creek and haul some water up here! Let's move!"

As rescuers bolted to position, three injured were carried out. Charlotte stood with her hands clasped in front of her silently praying. Someone slipped an arm lightly over her shoulders.

"It could be a long wait," Althea breathed.

Charlotte nodded, gazing ahead at the mine. Althea's son Justin darted past them, a shovel in hand.

Althea continued, "I brought medical supplies with Lodie in the buckboard. Rather slow going with half the town flocking to the path on foot. Your father rode off on horseback at first warning." She gave Charlotte a squeeze. "He wasn't in there when it came down, but I imagine he was first to arrive."

Not reassured by Althea's comforting words, Charlotte whipped around and cried, "But it's *still falling*! He's no safer now than when it hit."

In the distance a man screamed in pain; a bone poked cruelly through his flesh. Charlotte blocked out his screeching, searching the faces of men scrambling to the liberation effort. A towering figure emerged from the billowing gloom, covered in dust. Her heart danced a syncopated beat. "Da!"

James's hawkish eyes raked the crowd until he found her.

Relief washed over her, awakening her from the stupor of anxiety. She ran and flung her arms around his waist, burying her head in his chest.

"Thank heaven you're all right!" she exclaimed.

"Whatever is wrong with ye, girl?" He pushed her roughly away. "Can't ye see there are injured ta be tended ta? And here ye stand? Doing nothing!"

"James!" Althea stepped forward. "She's worried sick about you!" She stood behind Charlotte, placing her hands gently on her shoulders.

"A fine thing! Standing here idle and useless when men cu be dyin'," he fumed.

Charlotte's eyes filled with tears.

"She thought one of them might be you!" Althea raised her chin.

"I'm na raising the girl ta stand around being afraid of fear." He looked squarely at his daughter. "I'm fine, lass. Whether I'm standing before ye, or buried in ore, yer place is helping the wounded. Twisting yer

20

hands helps no one. Live or dead, I'll *always be* one of the last out. I'll na be rearing any faint of heart. Now, get over there and be of some use."

Charlotte bit her lip and lowered her head as she moved past her father. She heard Althea chiding furiously, "How could you be so cold?"

"This world is cold," he said flatly. "She has ta learn the most important person in the world ta her can be taken in a blink of an eye."

"I think she's learned that already," she snapped.

Startled, Charlotte turned to see James stare angrily at Althea. She watched as his eyes softened with pain. Charlotte threw back her shoulders as she listened to his words.

"And she has ta learn ta survive it. She can only rely on herself. There may come a day . . ." he broke off abruptly. "I'm needed within." He turned to leave.

"Compassion, James. She needs your strength."

"She needs ta build her own." And with that, he left.

James paced as he scolded, his heavy boots resonating in a measured way against the timber floor. The men still coated with chaff from the cave-in assembled in the school-house.

"Ye got greedy."

He stopped. He glared at them. "We've always worked together ta avoid this very thing." He resumed striding in his attempt to walk off mounting anger.

"How many? Put at risk today? Because ye were foolish." He shook his head in disgust. "Robbing the pillars, yet again," he muttered loudly. "It's bad enough ye've torn up the entire hillside above the city. Trying ta get ta the last little bits, and when ye cu na reach far enough down, ye tried ta cheat yer way out, grab the last few dollars as ye backed out of there. The most dangerous tactic there is . . ."

"Easy for you to say, James, now that you're out," Clancy grumbled.

"Not so out that I did na come running ta pull yer arse out of the hole. I don't appreciate the opportunity ta leave my daughter an orphan yet."

"It's still ours to do with what we please," called a man from the crowd.

"Then don't expect the rest of us to pick up the pieces!" yelled another.

Infuriated opinions burst forth, men demanding to be heard. Frustration, fear, desperation, and need, all commanded a voice on the floor. James noted Lodie leaning against the back wall with his arms folded tightly. His friend's tall, hunch-shouldered form represented an authoritative presence as he took stock of clamoring viewpoints. Lodie shook his head at him, and James knew his friend wondered how to bring the multitude of voices to accord. Trouble had been building, layer upon layer. The prospect of unity dissolved in the melee as miners stood up howling accusations and townspeople retorted. James decided to let them exhaust themselves in their bawling. He saw Lodie fix fatigued eyes on him as he headed for the doorway, abandoning them all to their quarrels. James held his gaze — an unspoken acknowledgement passed between the two as he departed.

After dinner, James sat alone on the porch of his small farmhouse, eyes closed, trying to take in nothing but the choir of crickets. He heard the door close behind him, and Althea's soft voice as she handed him a cup. "I thought you might like a spot of tea."

He looked tiredly into her English fair face, her pale blue eyes and flaxen blonde hair swept properly into a tight coil at the back of her head. Gratefully, he accepted the steaming mug.

She settled into the rocker next to him, wrapping her hands around her cup to absorb its warmth. The faint scowl on his brow invited her question, "What happened out there today?"

He let loose a heavy sigh. "Desperate measures that did na pay off." He blew on the hot liquid. "Stuben and Clancy, who should know better — tried ta rob the pillars."

She looked puzzled. "Sorry?"

"Times for any man picking from the streams are gone. They're all exhausted. It's why I cashed out. We all got used ta having some luck with no more than picks and long toms. More and more hours ta collect less and less — and then divide that amongst hundreds showing up every day ta have a go. Squabbles over claims, tempers flaring . . . aye," he flicked his wrist as if swatting away problems.

"About the time I bought land and horses, the vagabonds moved on. The regular boys discovered diggin' a bit in the high ground above Nevada City, and that kept them profitable for a while, didn't it? Not so much as when we began, but enough ta make a living. Well, they tore up the whole damn hill."

Althea sipped her tea, then pondered aloud, "I always wondered why you quit with money yet to be made." She smiled wryly. "You, who saved every penny preparing for years to start your perfect endeavor."

"Nothing's ever perfect." He chose to ignore her teasing. "At any rate, the diggings began ta slow down except for odd pockets of flakes and ore. So the geniuses from other underground mines decided there had ta be more below the surface, and partially right, they were. So they sank shafts down ta the lower depths ta get ta more gold loaded gravels — only much of it's deeper than the shallow shafts they put there in haste."

"What on earth was the rush? Why didn't they build it more properly if this is their livelihood?"

"They meant ta reorganize and rebuild after they got a better look — if they found some sort of mother lode. But so it was, the gold was thinly spread throughout. Heavy work, that is. Hours spent with pick and shovel were na amounting ta enough ta sustain them. But they would na give up, afraid ta walk away — and then there was all the talk."

Althea nodded. "The company mines. I've heard it, too. No one wants to give up and let a company make a go of it when they could not."

"Sometimes only operations with money can get the job done. At least that creates jobs with wages. If . . . the boys don't antagonize the buyers, they cu make themselves damn useful, if not indispensible. At least that's what ye hope for."

"But what caused the accident today?"

"They adapted an old coal miner's practice — the most dangerous one. Once they grabbed all their rickety supports allowed, they went for broke ta get every last bit. As ye work yer way along the vein from the end of the line up ta the front, ye try and tap out the pockets of anything ye can see, including yer stone supports as ye back out."

Althea's eyes grew large, understanding now as James made motions of chiseling out above his head. "They *tried* to get the roof to cave in?"

He nodded. "Trying ta control it as they go — as sections collapse, they sift through the rubble and move it ta the front, as if ta sweep their riches right out the door before they close it. Trick is ta retreat ta the next section before the last gives way. It's a big wager they'll all hold until ye're done. Trouble is with so many running bands of granite, ye can't tell when ye'll start a run

26

ye can't stop."

"Robbing the pillars," she breathed.

"Impatience and greed. Destroying the very things working ta sustain a man."

"A very American attitude." Althea smoothed her skirts primly and straightened her posture as if calling forth her English fortitude. "It's certainly indicative of California. They haven't our traditions to fall back on."

"They haven't our limitations of class and caste, either. At least what ye earn by the sweat of yer brow is yer own." James shook his head. "Those boys were far too eager ta snatch the rewards without looking for the hook. There's no shame in earning an honest dollar for wages, ye know."

"Ah. Speaking of that." Althea tugged her shawl tightly around her shoulders to fend off the cool night air. "I'm traveling to Marysville tomorrow to deliver a gown. I'm expecting to find orders piling up. I wonder if I might take Charlotte with me?"

He shrugged. "Justin and I can manage. I've a few supplies I'd like her ta bring back. Nevada City is a wee slow in keeping up with necessities."

Althea rose. "Well then, I'll see you all at breakfast. Good night."

"And ta you." James watched her graceful

form cross the courtyard to the small cabin where she and her son Justin slept. She was a good woman, he mused, his Emma's best friend. Their children had been born within eleven months of each other. Althea was reserved, dutifully firm and unwavering, and yet there was a lingering sadness about her. He supposed it would always be so.

He closed his eyes and sank into the rocker. No one asked how he came to be close by when the mine had fallen, and he was glad. Lodie had summoned him.

James brooded over their conversation in The Silver Moon Tavern. His friend was a big fellow with a calm and measured way, slow moving — as if the muscles hung too loosely on his large frame. Unflappable as Lodie appeared, James immediately detected something odd in his demeanor. Perhaps it was the sudden disappearance of his irrepressible smile.

The mood had grown heavy as Lodie dispensed with family pleasantries and sighed, "It's not going well out there, James. This town is teetering on the edge of an exaggerated prosperity reaching its natural end."

The rusty haired Scot had remained silent, thoughtful. Lodie waved his arm, pointing towards the hills. "You can see

28

they've turned the mountainside into a giant prairie dog village full of holes!"

"Aye. It's a slim way ta be making a living without backers. They need heavy equipment ta even put a dent into what's left. The small mines are dying out."

Lodie lowered his voice. "They're being bought out."

James leaned forward. "By whom? I have na heard tell of it."

"And you won't. Not yet anyway. Nobody knows. Some say it's the Empire Mine. Others say it's a group out of San Francisco — bankers or some such bunch."

"I don't keep up with operations of the well-ta-do." He sat back. "In any case, there's good solid work out there ta be had. Some folks are smart enough ta move on and take advantage of it. Empire needs men; North Star is going strong, all the way ta the Bloomfield. Others could get on with the hydraulics — it isn't the dragon they think it is, ye know . . ."

"Yes, you and I know that, but I'm not still out there and you've only got one foot in. They'd *all* be doing better on a wage now than scraping dirt around, but they're afraid of a company taking charge of their future. They think they're giving up on the dream."

"It takes more than a dream; it takes a

plan. We put our time in there when we needed ta. The dream has faded away, Lodie. We've gone round and round on this."

"Now it's time to act. Our neighbors, our friends are scattered like chaff on the wind — no direction. We need a united front. It's time for a union."

"All right, help organize them ta be sure; see that there's talk between them and owners. I can see that."

"No, James. I'm asking you to step up as local union chief."

James stared at him incredulously. "Och. I'm na even workin' the mines anymore. I'm only supervisin' a bit of blastin'."

"Even more reason it should be you. This is a community stand. Our businesses are driven by the success or failure of the mines. We — you and I — have a foot in each arena: my store and your farm. And you . . ." Lodie gave a knowing look. "You know better than most what happens when a few wealthy families take over. Some prosper for awhile, but it's the town it'll choke."

"Why not yerself, then? Ye're the voice of reason."

"They'll listen to me, but they'll follow you. You're the man to bet on in a fight."

James sat back in his chair and scowled.

"My fightin' days are over."

"You didn't get here alone!" Lodie pounded his fist on the table. "We supported each other in the beginning. Have you forgotten? A lot of us — you and me in particular — we've done better than most. Like it or not, we owe it to the rest of them."

"I don't see any askin'. Against all advice, each go their own way."

"You're a righteous man, James — one with ideals. Men notice these things. But you don't back down when threatened, either. They respect you. Frightened men need a leader, a shepherd, if you like. If we give 'em a logical path, they'll take it."

James stared sullenly at the table, irritably spinning his beer mug.

"I'm asking you to think on this. It's only a matter of time before the utter lack of civic order leads to disaster."

James had leaned in to counter, but the pealing of a distant bell silenced him. Both he and Lodie froze, as did everyone in the Silver Moon. When the firehouse bell echoed the cry a moment later, all leapt to their feet. Bursting through the doors and into the street, men scurried to their wagons and horses.

"Take my horse, James!" Lodie had shouted. "I'll grab tools and bring Justin in

the wagon!"
And he heeded calamity's call.

CHAPTER 2

Grass Valley, California — April 1866

The man with the silver-headed cane was late. It was an honor to be included in the inner circle, and here he was, out of breath, and hopelessly without excuse. The gloom of drizzling rain dampened his spirit and caused him to consider if he really belonged. Perhaps it was too soon. If he pushed the mare harder, he risked the splatter of mud on his clothing. Appearances mattered in these circumstances.

He arrived at the deserted mining office and dismounted. The door opened and a guard nodded for him to come inside. He swung the silver-headed cane out in front of him with an air of bravado he did not yet feel. The cane's original owner was a man to be reckoned with, and he hoped to conjure up the same steely confidence by leaning on it.

He removed his cloak as he followed the

guard down two ill-lit levels of stairs and a maze of dingy, narrow hallways. The walls were slightly damp and gave off a musky, earthy odor. This level contained nothing but former workrooms used to store and sort ore. He squinted to see a cramped entrance, a barely discernible door in a far corner. The door's windows had been blackened. In fact, as he glanced back down the hallway, an entire row of blackened interior windows lined up like a jack-o-lantern's missing teeth. These portals of observation were no longer needed to thwart the pilfering of profit. The guard knocked twice, quickly. At the sound of a latch being drawn, the man took a deep breath, and set his face with a look of unapologetic distinction.

The room, plain and nearly void of furnishings, was dimly illuminated. The speaker proceeded without a hitch, fully engaged in oratory as the man entered.

"After all, gentlemen, what is it we are exploiting?" boomed the enthusiastic voice. "Only greed. It seems logical for theirs to be channeled appropriately to feed ours."

A mild chuckle arose from the assembly of men in well-tailored suits seated in a semi-circle. The speaker glanced up, acknowledging the new arrival, and nodded towards an empty chair. He took his place silently amongst them as the speaker continued.

"What are we taking from them, really? Once they have taken care of their basic necessities, there seems a need amongst them to squander all else on vices of proximity and choice. Gambling. Whiskey. Women of ill repute. Oh, I grant you, they came as we did — with big plans. They are as children on summer holiday from school. Freedom! To do as they please. And they do. Without regard or forethought for their own futures. They mean to look into that . . . someday." The orator shook his head, affecting a concerned air. "Much like a man on his deathbed . . . only beginning to consider his place in the heavenly realm."

As late as he was, the newcomer found himself immediately drawn to the charisma of the speaker. Young, sharp, eloquent, and savvy. Momentarily startled, he recognized the bearded man sitting next to him. Indeed, as he glanced discreetly around, he saw an impressive quorum representing most all the giants of industry — banks, railroads, mines, shipping, freight. He shifted uncomfortably in his chair, leaning heavily upon the silver-headed cane.

"In every society . . ." the orator pontificated, "there is this stratum, this station of men who live only for the moment. They lack the education and motivation to move their community forward to the growth and development that improves the lives of their families." He paused, allowing the gathering to reflect upon the plight of their fellow man.

"Think . . ." began the speaker in a solicitous tone, "what can be done for the public good with control of these mines in our hands, under our direction? Proper streets . . . railroads . . . profitable businesses. Governing of resources in our mining towns is key to our state's advancement. It is the opportunity for *our* city to grow in stature in the eyes of the world. Temporarily displaced miners will prosper by our leadership, by what we create for them."

He walked slowly towards his audience as if joining them. "They'll need advocates," he said more softly. "They'll need leaders with power and money behind them."

He stopped behind the chair of his colleague with the silver-headed cane and placed hands on his shoulders and stated, "Political careers . . . are made from opportunities such as these."

The orator turned with renewed vigor, pointing his finger in the air. "Few fortunes are made in the hands of the simple minded and are more likely recklessly lost. A sophisticated hand creates a society caring for the needs of all. That's what we seek to accomplish here, gentlemen. I ask you, with the advantages available to us — how can we not step in? How can we not lead them to greatness?"

The authoritative, bearded gentleman seated in the first chair remarked, "Local city officials are paid for service such as we provide, yet they have not the power, acumen, or reach for that matter, to bring such vision into being. We are successful businessmen. Our efforts in governing this massive undertaking, while setting aside our own endeavors, need to be compensated accordingly. We are here to amass a conglomeration of power."

"Exactly!" cried their host. "If this business does not prosper, if we do not prosper, then Sacramento does not move forward. Any city not moving forward is moving backward. We have already lost the state capital once, gentlemen. I do not intend to see that happen again."

Nods and murmurs of assent echoed down the line of seated men.

For the first time the speaker smiled, a dark and dazzling smile. "Each of us possesses a unique purpose . . . skills, connections, backing. We each hold an essential element for what we hope to accomplish. Roll up your sleeves, gents. We have details to work out." He made a grand gesture towards yet another locked and bolted door behind him. "Shall we adjourn to the war room?"

The swarthy speaker of the event produced a brass key from beneath his Savile Row–cut coat and removed the hefty lock. He pushed the heavy door open, nodding for his staff to enter. Two men carrying long poles tipped with wicks moved quickly around the room, lighting the hanging lanterns. With a sweep of his hand, he ushered his guests into the massive chamber. Oil lamps posted around the room at regular intervals cast an eerie glow against the sooty tinted glass of the windows. The war room was impressive. This elite assembly of men gazed in wonder at their covert surroundings. The man with the silver-headed cane entered last, stepping just inside the entrance.

The orator proceeded to follow when a short, portly man grasped his elbow. The man's bushy eyebrows raised in irritation as he hissed lowly, "Where the devil is Burke?"

The smile vanished from the speaker's

face as he answered in hushed tones, "He assured me this was a priority."

"His presence is essential!"

"The support of his office is essential. His *actual* contributions are limited. We'll simply have to make our apologies . . ."

The portly man interrupted angrily, "He's of little use now. Changes will have to be made . . ."

"Father, our guests . . ."

"Quite right." The portly man collected himself. He nodded with a strained smile at the man with the silver-headed cane watching the exchange from the other side of the threshold. The man tipped his head in reply and wandered uncomfortably away, though still within earshot.

"What about him?"

The swarthy man smiled and lowered his voice. "*He* is useful on so many levels . . . position in the community, connections . . . you might say he's my new project."

The speaker stepped in to address his guests. "This is a secret room, gentlemen. Only a handful of employees know of its existence." His voice took on a hollow sound in the vast space.

Men filed in around him, craning their necks upward to see the cavernous ceiling nearly eighteen feet up. The sound of their footsteps reverberated on the cold stone floor. Rusted iron ladders led to a catwalk nearly halfway up the closest wall; hundreds of labeled pigeonholes spread across its expanse. There were two mammoth oak conference tables, one at each end of the immense room, and the two staffers moved to light three enormous iron candelabras placed every five feet along the tabletops.

"The nearest wall is covered from floor to ceiling with slots containing maps of land parcels and legends of mines and tunnels. Some we own, some we intend to, and some belong to competitors. The library wall on the far end contains literature on every mining practice and problem known to the civilized world. And, finally," he turned, ". . . here we have a masterpiece of genius. Follow me."

He led them to an alcove at the far end of the room. There, a massive scale model dominated, portraying a labyrinth of levels, tunnels, and rooms. The man with the silver-headed cane stared in awe at the detailed representation of both current and future Empire holdings.

"This," the orator gestured theatrically, "is the Empire Mine. What you see on the surface is many mines, many miles apart." He turned to face the structure. "But what this model shows is how they connect — a complex network of tunnels both horizontal and vertical. Tunnels you see in black now exist. The red ones . . . are where we are going. Small independent mines we are in the process of securing will feed this network through the proposed tunnels. With the development of square set timbering, we will clean up old played-out property, make it safe and chase the vein wealth down." He paced dramatically in front of the structure. "Over three . . . hundred . . . feet . . . down, gentlemen."

Murmurings arose from the gathering. The men wandered up and down in front of the model, admiring its complexity and scale. Before he was diverted from his speech with questions, he continued. "I present this to you to demonstrate our ability to back new innovations, to stay ahead of the game — ahead of our competition. We will drive the industry where we desire and we will drive the profits. Empire is not merely a name, gentlemen. Empire is our destiny."

CHAPTER 3

In the beginning . . . There was gold
1851 — The MacLarens Arrive

John Sutter constructed a sawmill using waterpower on an unprecedented industrial scale. When his endeavors turned up more than expected, it brought on a surge of miners and fortune hunters transforming the Sierra Nevada from a lonely mountain range inhabited only by native tribes to 100,000 gold hungry sharks from all parts of the globe.

San Francisco burst through its borders, and the city of Sacramento was born at the joining of the Sacramento and American rivers. An entire civilization arrived at the heralding cry of "Gold!" The yellow harlot, a cruel and selective mistress, left thousands seeking new occupations when savings ran out and dreams were dashed. The best livelihoods belonged to those who outfitted the hopefuls.

The valley's metamorphosis transpired callously quick and, north of Sacramento, towns sprung up as if planted by seed. Ranchers pushed herds of cattle and sheep to the perimeters. Epidemics unknown to indigenous tribes so decimated their numbers that they fled for safer lands. Nearly fifty miles from the capital city, Colusa and Marysville sprouted up on the heels of the gold rush. Colusa staked its claim west of Sutter Buttes beside the Sacramento River. East of the buttes, Marysville nestled on the Feather River, the great tributary of the Sacramento and the Yuba River — whose headlong journey surged from deep in the Sierra Nevada. Marysville grew as an important transport town for goods and services to and from the northern mines.

Steamboats became a common sight. River oaks once lining the banks of waterways were felled to feed the furnaces of transportation and industry. Millions of dollars in gold shipped each year from the riverine town to the U.S. Mint in San Francisco. Marysville prospered, replacing its miners' town of tents with brick buildings occupied by mills, iron works, and factories. Socially, it boasted of churches, schools, and two daily newspapers.

Conveniences of the bustling town lured

settlers, weary of desolate plains and hardship, to its comforts. Such were the nearly forty men, women, and children who ventured out with James MacLaren on his trek west. Five covered wagons began the expedition in Boston, more joining outside farm towns in Pennsylvania and Ohio.

James chose oxen, the hardiest and most reliable of beasts, to haul his family to his vision of the Promised Land. Others favored sure-footed mules for the pilgrimage, averaging sixteen miles a day following behind the great lumbering brutes. In the driest parts of the journey, wagons kicked up great clouds of alkali on hot and dusty days, making walkers look floured and fit for frying. Canvas roofs protected their households on wheels, lined inside with pocketed cloth walls stuffed to overflowing with any useful household item — bushel bags, feather ticking, candles, medicine, dried provisions, buckets, ladles, tools, and turpentine. Cherished furnishings filled excess space, barely leaving room for passengers in need of rest. The bone of contention in the MacLaren wagon arose when their former Boston employer gifted Emma with a spinet. James considered it a ridiculous thing, wagon space being precious. Emma fought for it, stating her contentment to remain at their present jobs in Boston. James grumbled, "She beat me so with the knowledge of this, she might as well beat me with the instrument itself."

Lodie Glenn and his young wife, Matilda, grew up on farms in rural Pennsylvania as childhood friends turned sweethearts. They lived a fine life, a settled life, with a steady rhythm and few surprises. Like his immigrant grandfather, Lodie harbored the inclination to discover what else the world had to offer. The first step of his journey introduced him to a kindred spirit in James.

For James, a moment of desperate rage had instigated the jump from Scotland to England, to Boston, and finally California. His calculated wanderings from Scottish riverfront to the underground worlds of iron, silver, and coal in Northumberland mines helped him determine he was a lad meant to spend his days above ground. Once he felt safe enough to seek work out in the open he spent several years in service at the stables of the Vernon estate in Lancashire, methodically making his way closer to Liverpool and his route to America.

At trail's end, their wagon master proceeded on to San Francisco while their caravan gathered in camp on the Yuba River east of Marysville and west of Nevada City.

Upon arrival in Marysville, James Mac-Laren noted with alarm the look of enchantment in the eyes of Emma and Althea, a look shared by all the women in their party. The comforts of town beckoned, but did not fit his plan. By his preliminary explorations, James determined settling close to Nevada City the more logistical move. Nevada City's tents far exceeded buildings, proving social livability to be in its infancy.

Near the Yuba River, their tight knit circle of wagons formed a community while they made decisions, acquired land, and secured jobs. Some intended to homestead; others had trades to ply. But all hoped to stake their objectives in the goldfields.

Althea Albright favored this time of day, as the women prepared the evening meal and children of all sizes ran in every conceivable direction. She smiled at the sounds of their youthful laughter and shrieking, giving busy mothers sufficient indication of their whereabouts. Water jug in hand, she strolled back from the creek, where she had organized the older children to draw water in pails and sent others to gather firewood. She encouraged them to stop and give chase to the little ones at play, stoking their energies when possible. Althea considered exhausted children a blessing.

46

Her friends gathered where most household decisions transpired — around the cook pots and the fire. Althea approached her childhood alter ego, Emma MacLaren, kneading and cutting dough. Emma reached for the Dutch kettle to set the biscuits to baking and pushed back an errant lock of dark hair with a floured wrist. Althea nudged her to look up from her task to observe their youngsters. They chuckled as they watched Justin, Charlotte, and Ella Louise tumbling down a grassy incline, performing their best somersaults. The hillside was colorfully littered with cloth caps and calico bonnets abandoned by children seeking freedom from restraint.

"Ella Louise! Put down that there stick before you put your eye out!" shouted Lucille Speeks to her daughter.

Ella Louise halted as if waiting for further instruction.

"Put . . . it . . . down!"

The child dropped the stick and stalked away as if all the fun vanished from the game. She plopped down on the ground and hugged her knees, sulking.

"Honestly, rollin' round with a sharp stick, a beggin' to poke herself or somebody else . . ." Lucille muttered as she went back to cutting up potatoes.

Althea laughed. "They never think when they're having fun — and here, they have endless space for it. There's an advantage over Boston. I still picture my Justin venturing onto those plains to stare in amazement at land fanning out all the way to the horizon. He looked so very small . . . like an acorn hidden in the expanse of an old oak tree."

Emma sighed. "True enough; the streets of a busy town are no place to play. Ah, but I miss the house."

"Oh, indoor plumbing! Don't get me started. But fancy gaslights — that's what I miss most. Flip a key in every hallway. I had forgotten what dark was until those first nights with the lights of the city miles behind us," Althea added.

Matilda Glenn teased. "Pampered things you were! It's good I never got used to such luxuries. You'll learn to rely on the stars soon enough."

Althea snorted. "Ha! If you can call waiting on lords and ladies hand and foot pampered!" She walked over to turn the haunch of venison roasting on the spit. Smoky, spiraling tendrils of aroma danced tantalizingly on the air as fat dripped and hissed when it hit the flames.

"It's city life I truly miss," she yearned.

"Rows and rows of wide, redbrick houses, gardens, and squares. Carriages of fine people splendidly dressed — that didn't hurt my business, I'll tell you. I learned more about fashion and flourish and the skills to pull it off in Boston than I could hope to learn in years in our little village in England." Althea wore a faint smile. "I watched ships from exotic places coming to port in the Charles River. Oh, and the markets! So lively! I doubt we'll find the likes of those goods out here."

Matilda made a face. "What a dreamer this one is!"

"I hear tell most any goods you like come on in San Francisco. Sacramento, too. And then right up them rivers to Marysville," Lucille piped in before asking, "I don't reckon you'd be willing to help us with our 'fashion and flourish'? Your clothes are right pretty, Althea."

"Makes them all herself. You should have seen the gowns she used to make for Mistress Doyle. Althea made her look like a queen." Emma beamed, a hint of longing in her deep-blue eyes. "It was a grand house . . . stately and beautiful. I was most content there. Good honest work and allowed me plenty of time with the children." She looked up at said children and, with her hand cupped to the side of her face, called out to them, "Come wash for supper, all of you!"

Althea noted Emma found it difficult to break up the jocularity of youth, as they hardly seemed to notice, or hear above their own noise. Her gaze drifted to Ruth Cleary. She was a rather large woman, with a rather large voice. Her sons and daughter, all in their teens, had found spare time from their chores. Ruth would fix that. She stepped in shouting loudly, "Max! More wood set by this fire! Mary! There are plates to be put out on the table! Bertram! Chase those children to the creek. I suppose none of you are hungry?"

Ella Louise had recovered her mood and giggled as she rolled herself down the embankment with her friends. Bertram, arms spread wide, ran zigzag patterns to herd them all in.

Emma called more insistently to the rogue tumbleweeds, "Charlotte and Justin! Come in now; you'll both be complaining of itchiness from rolling in that grass!"

Althea laid a hand on Lucille's arm in passing. "I'd be happy to help you, of course."

"Oh, thank ya kindly! Boston sounds

heavenly. It's a wonder you ever wanted to leave."

"Almost didn't. I suppose Mistress Doyle thought I never would — Emma and I worked for her mother in England; grew up on their estate, actually. She was kind, allowing me to work on my own as well as for her," she stated stiffly. "I educated myself in my profession and saved a little money — a fair bit of independence for an indentured ladies maid."

"There musta been lots of nice men in Boston for a young widow to meet up with?"

Althea lowered her eyes, but not before noticing Emma's sharp look directed at Lucille. "It's far too soon," Emma bristled.

"I'm sorry. I didn't know . . . how or when it happened," Lucille replied, flustered.

"It was a drowning. It isn't my story to tell," retorted Emma.

Lucille remained frozen to her spot, held by Emma's stern gaze, as Althea walked briskly away. Matilda followed her to the end of one of the wagons where she stopped, staring out towards the mountains. Althea said softly without turning around, "I wasn't ready for such things."

"Lucille didn't mean anything by it, dear."

"Yes, I know. Sometimes I'm not sure if it

51

hurts more when people ask or when they don't."

"You're so lively. It's hard to imagine there wasn't a pack of men following after you," Matilda soothed. "Justin is such a beautiful child. I see a lot of you in him . . . Does he look much like his father?"

Althea noticed Matilda peek quickly back as if to make sure Emma was not there to box her ears. Althea smiled. "Emma's very protective. I guess we always have been of each other. It's true I don't talk about it much. Somehow it seems like giving away the little bit I have left of him." She fidgeted with her apron. "I try to hold on to what I can."

Matilda placed a comforting hand on her shoulder.

Althea hesitated. "Though, Mattie . . ." She slipped her hand in her pocket, pulled out a small silver frame, and held it out.

"Lo! He's a handsome devil. Why I do see a bit of young Justin there! Does he take after him in other ways?" Matilda stopped abruptly. Emma appeared behind them as they huddled together. Matilda straightened and changed the subject, peering back beyond the camp. "I think I hear the men folk arriving."

Only Althea saw Emma's piercing recogni-

52

tion as she stared at the daguerreotype and then looked up accusingly. Althea felt her cheeks grow warm.

"Not my story to tell," Emma repeated as she brushed past to retrieve the water jug.

Matilda stammered, "I didn't mean to be nosy . . ."

"It's all right. Sometimes a question gently asked is kinder than looks of pity. It's bound to come up again."

"Well, then," declared Matilda, "you may count on the rest of us to be as shielding as Emma. It's nobody's business."

Noise at the site increased as men drifted in from various outposts. Some ventured far afield to inspect land, pinpoint water sources, and check mining locations. Most plunged into exploration of mining pursuits. They sought out conversations with locals in taverns and general stores in Marysville, Colusa, Yuba City, Nicholas, and Nevada City. They compared notes and stories, landscapes and terrain, soil and weather conditions. The women scurried to feed the children so they might listen to hints of their future.

James stood in line behind Matthew Cleary as he doused his head in a water bucket, splashing about, taking a quick birdbath in preparation for supper. James

53

stepped up for his turn as Matthew wiped his hands on his pants and launched into details of his day.

"Well, friends — I kin tell you a bit about local manners. Don't come on a feller working a claim unless you make some noise. Some of 'em are a touchy lot. Pull a gun on you faster than you can shout halloo."

Tim Speeks concurred. "I heared a lot in town 'bout claim jumpin'. That leads to violent stuff. Less of it now, but keep your guards up. I talk more generalities than ask a man his personal business."

Lodie Glenn's arrival threw conversations into chaos. He rode to the edge of camp and dumped two large canvas bags hung over his saddle onto the ground.

"Supplies, mates! I've scouted out general stores for picks and pans and such. Ridiculous prices, all — you'd think the goods themselves were made of gold — but I struck a deal for bulk. I pick up more tomorrow — this was all I could carry. Anybody interested, see me and we'll settle up."

The crowd pounced on the bags. James wandered up rubbing a towel on the back of his neck. "Now here's a telling little scene . . . ye'd think there was a race amongst us."

"What makes you think there isn't?" chuckled Lodie. "From this point on we separate the sheer base characters of our neighbors from how they see themselves."

"Or want others ta see them," James interjected.

"All about who you can trust, my friend. I have a few thoughts concerning that. But let's not spoil the party yet," said Lodie then shouted, "All right — who's got the most outrageous story of the day?"

Tim Speeks, Ella Louise's father, called out, "Ah, that's gotta be me — I've got two for ya — but I've gotta have me a plate in my hand first; I'm starved!"

The children, now fed, gave chase with a rousing game of tag. The adults settled around the fire with a hot meal and warm fellowship.

"All right, Tim — did ya find out how to make us rich today?" laughed Lucille.

"Absolutely. Key to success is cleanliness!" he stated between mouthfuls.

"You going to get rich selling us soap, now, Tim?" yelled one man to laughter.

"There's so much gold here," began Tim, "you can't overlook anything. I heard tell one man in Nevada City washed eighteen dollars of gold outta his beard — his gamblin' money!" After the cackling died down, he continued. "But get this: another poor sot, sick as a dog, drags hisself into town and takes a soak in a Turkish bath to sweat out his miseries. Instead, he sweats out fifty dollars worth of dust! Musta felt better then."

"I think my Tim tells better stories than you, James," quipped Lucille.

"His have happier endings," winked James.

"Well, on a more serious note," continued Tim, "it seems what's to be had is further afield than before, unless we sign up with some of the underground works."

James listened quietly to opinions spilling forth.

"Aw, time for that later. I want at it myself first."

"Me, too."

Murmurs of assent resounded amongst them.

"Still gold in streams up around Grass Valley."

"A lot's already claimed."

"But some claims are deserted. People move on when pickings are slim. Sometimes they hear tell of another big strike and run to get closer."

"Yep, I heared after rains and the spring thaw, so much water floods down out of the

Sierras that it keeps washing down more gold."

"Can you pan what's already claimed if it's abandoned?"

"What if all the best *is* claimed?"

James cleared his throat to be heard above the ramblings. "Ye're only allowed ta claim a 'reasonable amount of land.' Meaning, what one man can work in a season — no more. Once ye leave it, it's up for grabs. Committees rule on miner's codes and such. Claims must be marked clearly and filed with the recorder."

"Might serve us to consider teaming up some," suggested Lodie. "Safety in numbers to control a bigger piece of property?"

Matthew Cleary looked uncomfortable. "No offense lads, but what *I* find, belongs to me."

Grumblings and mutterings made it clear others felt the same.

Lodie waved his hand signaling the remark of no great importance. "No offense taken; only an idea. We've all different goals in the end. No harm. But I'd hope," he eyed them all in paternal fashion, "we remember our trials together and trust each other as neighbors. I call every man here my friend. We arrived as strangers to everyone else, but we do know each other."

James noted the thoughtful nods moving on faces illuminated by fire glow as the sun began its descent.

Matilda broke their reverie. Rising, she slapped her hands upon her knees. "Well, these dishes won't wash themselves . . ."

The women began to clear. Tired children wandered in close to the campfire at the first dip in daylight. Dusk was setting as a great sleepy eyelid closing down before its night's rest.

The men continued to discuss findings of the day, drawing closer to the blaze. Max Cleary brought wood to feed the flames. Little Charlotte MacLaren crawled into her usual place in her father's lap.

"Hye now," said James looking down, "have ye finished helping yer mother with yer chores?"

"Yes." She nodded decisively. "I carried all the plates."

James intercepted a thumb on its way to her mouth and placed her hand in her lap. He kissed the top of her head, saying, "Good girl."

Justin scrambled in beside her. "I helped, too."

Entertainment began with short funny tales, sometimes jokes. James often spun wonderful long stories. He favored narratives of clan feuds in Scotland or legends of knights and fair maidens. He painted images with the intensity, pitch, and wave of his voice. His head tilted slightly back, his eyes focused on something in the distance as if reliving a deep memory told by an aged and wise ancestor.

Other nights they played music. Treasured fiddles, harmonicas, and guitars appeared. Everyone loved to contribute. Those that could not sing, tapped toes, clapped hands, and stomped feet. Occasionally, James joined with his fife, ignoring jibes about a man playing an instrument so small and delicate. But play he did, and soulfully.

Sometimes, Charlotte sang songs he taught her. Her childish voice, clear and pure, remained a group favorite. She could run a scale, her high notes trilling like a bell. She sang as naturally as if talking. Try as he might to hide it, James's expression would be bursting with pride. He'd watch her green eyes shine brightly and her head tilt back, mimicking the way he told stories. A time or two, Emma protested the adult lyrics taught to her by some unknown prankster. She disapproved of Charlotte performing in public.

This evening all were tired and more in the mood for one of James's adventures as they lingered by the fire.

James ruffled Justin's hair. Inclining his head to Charlotte, he pointed at his cheek. "Before I start give yer best beau a kiss."

She dutifully pecked his jaw and then swayed towards Justin, who lurched away from her.

"Best enjoy it now, James; one day it'll not be you!" called out Matthew.

They all laughed.

Beginning his tale, James lowered his voice to a husky whisper, leaning in as if to impart a secret. A heavy fog lay over the country now so far away. But as his tone warmed and his words drew them in, the veil that lay over the past began to lift until they imagined the depths of a distant land and the souls of its ancient people. He shared the misty edged realm he knew so well, and, in the telling, they came to know a clan history, detail by intimate detail. Why, if his grandfather, Duncan MacLaren, had approached any one of them, they would recognize him by the craggy, weathered features of his face. The rhythm of his voice lulled Charlotte to sleep; she and Justin slumped together with his blond head resting on her dark curls.

By now, a host of innumerable stars materialized overhead, so thickly gathered in places they appeared to form streaky rivers of light flowing into a faraway sea of darkness beyond the ridge. Crackling cedar fires conveyed a musky fragrance mixing with the heady scent of sage and honeysuckle. Families huddled together against the cool of evening, the flicker of flames reflected in their faces. Affection generated warmth amongst them — a hodgepodge clan bound by their past and future journey together.

Charlotte shivered in the chill of morning air. She awakened early to wash up for breakfast, the animated discussion of adults outside her wagon jarring her from sleep. Justin appeared, yawning. He followed her to the water bucket and, not yet alert, stepped on the back of her shoe, pulling it off her heel.

"Ow! Justin watch where you're going . . . ." She pushed him in front of her and, hopping on one foot, tugged the shoe back into place.

"Don't shove me!" he warned grumpily.

"Why do we have to wash up now, anyway?"

"Cos they always send us off when they don't want us to hear what they're saying."

Approaching the water bucket, he turned

61

as Charlotte examined her wrinkled thumb.

"You best not let James see that."

She tucked her hand behind her back. "Don't know what you're talking about."

He grinned with an air of superiority. "I see you sometimes when you're sleeping. Only babies suck their thumbs . . . and you're almost five!"

"I don't even know I'm doing it!" she wailed. "I stopped a long time ago, but I can't help it when I'm asleep!"

"I heard Mum say they're gonna put quinine on it if you keep it up. You should lay on top of your hand, or put on an old glove or something or you ain't never gonna quit."

"Don't say 'ain't.' It isn't proper."

"Everyone in America says it."

"Well, Mother says if we aren't careful to keep the Queen's English she's sending us both back East to finishing school for manners."

Justin shook his hands free of water, purposely sending a rain of droplets on her as she washed. He sneered. "Boys don't have to be proper *or* have manners!"

At that moment, a damp towel hit him smartly on the back of the head.

"Ow!" He turned to see the transgressor, only to be faced with James pointing a long

finger at him.

"Boys," he stated with emphasis, "have ta be twice as mannered because they are so lacking. Now, be off ta get yer breakfast, the both of ye. Be quick about it, because we're going inta town."

They raced back to the wagon, their quarrel quickly forgotten. Charlotte started to ask which town, but decided it did not matter.

The mothers, eager to return to Marysville and press their case for moving there, invited Lodie and Matilda to come along for support. Lodie convinced James to speak with Sean Miller, an experienced local miner with insight. With many plans in the offing, animated chatter abounded on the ride into town. Tim Speeks lent them his new spring wagon for their trip and Althea offered to pick up supplies for Lucille. As much as he hated parting with his savings, James realized the purchase of a team and buckboard was now essential. He had already acquired a dark bay gelding and negotiated a deal for a solid saddle horse for Lodie as well. He decided to hang on to the oxen until he purchased and cleared his homestead.

James and Lodie led the way on horseback, with Matilda guiding the spring wagon full of women and children. Lodie relied on James's knowledge of horseflesh, but was not impressed with the particulars other than transportation. James could not help himself. He was drawn to the big bay for the spark in his eye and the snap in his step. In his view, there was nothing wrong with enjoying the journey and he did so admire a fine horse.

Arriving in town, the only thing keeping Charlotte and Justin glued to their seats was a promise of penny candy. The women conversed excitedly as they passed enticing shop windows, pointing and exclaiming at each new venue.

James called over his shoulder, "Ye might well take yer time strolling in front of those windows and I'll look for ye at the general store. I cu be awhile."

Women and children piled out of the spring wagon, drawn to the storefronts.

"Not sure they even heard you," said Lodie, watching them hurry across the street.

"Given the hasty wave, I'd have ta say ye're right."

"Well," Lodie stretched his back from the long ride, "I've only a few errands. I'll mosey up to the tobacco shop and then off to find Sean Miller. There's a pub toward the general store; can't remember the name but that's where we'll be."

"Ye think a partnership is the way ta go, then? Why not with the lads at camp?"

"You heard them. Not interested. I put it out there though, so nobody feels excluded. It *is* a race, you know. We've shared our findings up to now, but I already hear men protecting turf they don't even have yet. Proceeding with someone with local bearings is an advantage. You come and meet Miller. I'd be interested to know what you think of him."

He nodded. "I'll give a listen."

They parted, and James set out for the livery stable in hopes of finding a used buckboard. If not, he would check with the blacksmith. He passed a saddle shop near the livery and noticed a Mexican sitting with his back against the barn, braiding a lariat. James tossed him a nod and the man smiled slightly in recognition. As he passed, he realized he had bought tamales from the man's wife on an earlier trip into town.

Not hearing a reasonable price from the liveryman, James headed for the blacksmith's. Here he spent considerable time bargaining and found a value more to his liking. The smithy agreed to replace two worn wheel rims and James found him honorable. They spoke at length concerning farms with horses to sell — which were honest and had the finest stock. He made arrangements to pick up the wagon the following week and set out to find Lodie.

As he left the blacksmith's, he became vaguely aware of the same Mexican man now standing across the street, leaning against a shop wall, still working on his lariat. He glanced about for the man's wife; her tamales had been excellent and much cheaper than lunch from one of the shops. James quickly forgot about the man when he spied Lodie ahead near the riverbank with a younger fellow.

Deep in conversation, the two absentmindedly watched the riverboats unloading cargo. As James neared, he heard Miller remark, "Now, that's a gold mine," nodding at the dock full of wares. "Danged shovel costs an arm and a leg."

"Hmm." Lodie seemed immersed in thought. "Yes, they forget we common farmers need shovels, too. It's harder to pay for tools with turnips than gold."

James studied the man as he approached. A full head shorter than Lodie, or himself for that matter, Sean was robustly lean and well muscled. His flannel work shirt rolled past the elbows revealed burly arms accustomed to heavy labor. He gave James a side-glance, allowing him to scrutinize Sean's hazel eyes, bright and engaging, set in a sun-browned face. He sported a thick, dark, horseshoe mustache, its vertical extensions dripping from the corners of his lips straight down to his jawline.

A dozen gruff-looking men disembarked noisily from another boat.

"And here come new customers, making a beeline for the stores to buy 'em up!" said Sean. He snapped his head to the side in a quick, practiced movement, slinging his long fringe of hair out of his eyes.

"Where are they coming from?" asked Lodie.

"Mostly San Francisco. Other countries . . . a lot of damn Chinese," he muttered. "Easterners who don't want to take time going overland. A lot of 'em are sailors jumping ship. Ain't as bad as 'twas in the beginning. Frisco's harbor was full of abandoned, rotting ships with no one to man 'em. Supplies got thin in a hurry. Still seems to be a shortage. You're lucky to score the picks and pans you did."

James listened with interest before introducing himself. Lodie grasped a hand on each man's shoulder and said, "Well, gents, I planned on having this conversation sitting down with a beer in my hand. What say you?"

"Good by me," said Sean amiably.

"A wee early in the day for me, Lodie."

"Oh, you need it, my friend, what with both of your wives nattering at you this morning."

"One wife," intoned James to the startled Sean. "Best friends. Does seem so when the arguing starts. They're a frightful team against one man. Are ye single, Sean? Perhaps ye can take one of them off my hands?"

As they settled in the bar, Sean began, "I hear you got experience mining, James?"

"Aye. Coal, tin, some silver. Underground stuff, na like here. I tell ye, it's tempting ta go straight for the steady salary at one of the companies."

Sean leaned in. "They pay pittance compared to what's still out there."

"For those lucky enough ta find it, I suppose. How long ye been at this if ye don't mind my asking? I'm na detecting ye're a rich man yet."

"Well," Sean looked away, scratching his head. "I struck my share. Twice, you'd a called me a wealthy man. Bein' a lot more foolhardy than I care to admit, couldn't seem to keep away from gambling tables.

Drank myself into oblivion celebrating. Ain't the best way to hang on to your judgment or a dollar. At the start, it seemed like gold was endless. Now it's tougher. I haven't touched a card or a pair of dice since last time I lost it all, and I won't. I know what to look for. I know a lot about *where* to look."

"Ye're a bit of a Merry Andrew, aren't ye? Ye're honest 'bout it, anyways." James nodded at Lodie. "We both know what we're aiming for at the end of it all. What is it that ye're after?"

"Choices. I stick with mining. I'm not a farmer. I got no inclination that way. Maybe I'll buy a business. Hell, maybe I'll buy the gambling tables to get even."

Lodie broke in. "You working anything in particular now?"

Sean looked around for eavesdroppers. "I got a place. Room either above or below me for claiming. Only a matter of time before somebody wanders in, and I'd as soon be surrounded by men I trust."

"How profitable?"

"Steady. I ain't gettin' rich, but I'm putting money away. It's a start. After that I'm open to suggestions."

Lodie looked to James. James shrugged. "As good a place ta start as any. I admit

I'm getting restless ta begin."

"I kin take you to have a look, or you kin file a claim and we start work. It ain't like I'm selling you the land."

Lodie looked to James again. James offered Sean an outstretched hand. "Let's go file some papers."

Sean agreed to lead them to the site, and Lodie, to bring the supplies. James sauntered towards the general store with a bounce in his step at the prospect of working. As they approached, he smiled at the sight of his lovely Emma sitting on the bench outside with a number of parcels at her feet. Althea and Matilda were still finishing up inside. The children remained exploring in the store, each with a licorice in hand.

"Work comes none too soon," said James eyeing the packages.

"Aye," sighed Lodie. "I'll be fetching the wagon."

Charlotte skipped out of the store with a small bag in her hand. "Da!" she cried.

"Halloo ta ye too, my lovely. What've ye got there — more sweets?"

She shook her head and motioned for him to bend down. He did so and she whispered in his ear. "Ah." He peeked in her bag at the small pair of gloves and nodded his approval. "I really only need the one," she

70

whispered.

Emma looked up at her husband. "It was her idea."

He sat beside her on the bench and took Emma's soft, delicate hand in his. "And a good one," he agreed.

"Oh, James, we've walked all over today. It's such a splendid town, and there's a school starting back up in a few weeks! The teacher is lovely — she thinks the children are a bit young, but they could start. Especially since I've worked with them using the slates and old primers Mistress Margaret gave us. Althea thinks she found work. James, we must live in town!"

He patted her hand patiently. "Slow down. I see there's a lot ta talk about. Lodie and I start a claim tomorrow. First things, first." He saw her mouth pop open to protest, but he winked and they shared a sweet smile instead.

The rest of their little group assembled outside, and Lodie appeared with the horses and wagon. The children piled in far less exuberantly than at the start of their day; their short legs had done a lot of walking. They proceeded with a slow, leisurely exit from town. James walked the big bay alongside as Althea and Emma chattered. He glanced up to see the Mexican once again on the edge of town. He nodded and the man bobbed his head in reply. It was curious.

CHAPTER 4

San Francisco — 1851

Though only twelve, Dutton knew the importance of the visitor. His father prepared him in advance and instructed him to pay close attention. At the moment, he immersed himself in his own world spread meticulously across the floor of Father's study. His miniature kingdom was a diverse grouping; the tin revolutionary soldiers sporting vivid blue uniforms stood at arms to protect various sections of Duttonville. Wooden block buildings painted in studious detail lined his imaginary street; large wooden spools enhanced with paper cone tops represented his storehouses of grain. His cast iron locomotive engine loomed taller than the buildings with a string of makeshift cars drawn and cut out of cardboard.

He worked on new additions: storefronts of a bank and a bakery placed near the sheriff's office. The courthouse dominated his town, for nothing else was more important. A few of the red-coated tin soldiers, as well as legless bust cutouts from a millinery catalogue, stood in for townspeople. He needed a depot, he considered thoughtfully. That would come next.

Dutton heard his mother's cheerful laughter in the hallway as she ushered their guest into the study, the swishing sound of her taffeta skirts entering the room before them. He disliked interruptions in his town planning. He stood in the midst of his creation as Garth Collier entered with his mother.

"The judge will be with you momentarily, Garth." She turned slightly as if to leave, all the while pausing to watch the well-taught display of manners. Dutton waited patiently for Mr. Collier to look in his direction, and, when he did so, he gave Dutton a friendly, paternal smile.

"Good afternoon, Mr. Collier. It is good to see you, sir." As Dutton reached confidently to shake the man's hand, his mother beamed, nodded approvingly, and took her leave.

"And you as well, young man." Dutton watched the man survey the town, noting amusement as his eye rested on the passengers of Noah's ark lined up to board the train. "That's an enterprising little city you have going there."

"Thank you, sir." In truth, the interruption annoyed him and he detested being spoken to as a child. *"Father would never be so indulgent,"* he mused to himself.

"What's this?" Collier asked, bending over for a better look at the locomotive. "Got a railroad, have you? Must be, oh, New York City then?"

"No, sir. It is here in San Francisco. Father says the railroad is coming soon enough. California needs great minds to build up its cities to compete with New York."

Garth pursed his lips. "Right on both counts, I'm sure." He nodded at Dutton's efforts. "Very ambitious."

Dutton returned to his seat on the floor and observed quietly as Mr. Collier strolled the perimeter of the stately office, stopping to admire his mother's rose garden through the large picture window behind his father's fine mahogany desk. From there, he made his way to the various plaques and awards on the oak paneled wall. Hands clasped behind his back, he leaned in to read the Harvard diploma hanging in the center of the judge's accolades.

"Impressive." He turned to meet the boy's

eye. "Impressive, indeed." He smiled. "I understand the judge expects your name to follow his in those hallowed halls. I have the same hopes for my oldest boy, Neil; he's top notch in his studies, but says he will have quite a chase on his hands to catch you, young man. He tells me you two have met on a number of occasions at chess tournaments."

Dutton received the compliment with good grace, though he did not relish it. Neil, though very bright, had yet to best him. Dutton was exceptional and he knew it. It irritated him when adults talked down to him, or, worse, underrated him. But he'd learned to bide his time. He realized the advantage of being underestimated: people always told you more than they intended to about themselves.

He allowed his attention to drift back to his town's construction as he answered politely, "Yes, sir. Neil is, without a doubt, stiff competition. It is probably good that he does not live here in San Francisco, or we would be rivals at everything."

Mr. Collier gave him a wink. "I suspect you are being generous in that summation."

Dutton met his gaze and smiled. *"Nobody's fool, and not prone to flattery,"* he thought. He decided he liked the man.

"Well, I consider Neil to be a friend, sir." Indeed, he did like Neil. Easygoing, intelligent, athletic with a competitive spirit. He fought Dutton as if under attack, in chess, debates, and sport, but took loss good-naturedly.

Their discourse was interrupted by his father's harried arrival, unbuttoning his long black robe as he burst into the room. "Garth, my deepest apologies for the delay," he began. "I thought I'd made my escape only to be cornered by an over-eager prosecutor. Had I stopped to remove the robe there at the courthouse, he would have had me another twenty minutes. Heavens, it's good to see you, man." He clasped Garth's hand vigorously.

"Dutton has been keeping me company, so not to worry."

"Very good," he said with a smile to his son. "Ah, one more moment." He grunted as he struggled out of the robe, his exit from the garment impeded by his portly physique. "There!" he exclaimed as he hung the object of his confinement on a coat rack near the door. "Much better. Let me pour us a drink."

As he turned towards the decanter on the small corner table, Garth's eyes widened at the sight of the .44 Colt Dragoon strapped

77

to the judge's bulging girth.

"Have they given up on the gavel in your courtroom?"

The judge raised his bushy eyebrows in question as he handed Garth a whiskey.

"I mean, are you keeping order with that thing now?" He pointed at the hefty gun.

"Oh," chuckled Judge Dandridge, "that. Ever since English Jim killed Marysville's Sheriff Moore . . . well, let's say I'm reminded that we are not yet a fully civilized state. Sit, sit." The judge nodded towards a pair of overstuffed green velvet chairs facing the picture window.

"I suppose one can't be too careful, especially with the gangs you've dealt with. California appreciates your iron hand in the courtroom." Garth lifted his glass to his friend.

The judge took a generous swig of his drink. "Yes, first the 'Hounds'; now this recurring business with the Sydney Ducks. Seems like everyone has someone to avenge these days. Bolsters my confidence to have something more imposing than a pepperbox under the robe. Partly what I wanted to talk to you about today. Goodness, it's been awhile since I've seen you. You need to make the trek from Sacramento more often! How's the family?"

"Growing like weeds, all four of them. Eugenia's got her hands full to be certain."

Dutton noticed Mr. Collier's look of admiration as he said with all seriousness, "I have to hand it to you, Walter. It's an important stand you're taking with these vigilance groups. The Hounds were the scourge of this city until you put them in their place; the Ducks are nearly defeated with the number you've put behind bars. If we could tie down that rambling rogue Sam Brannan and his so called 'Vigilance Committee'. . . ."

Dutton glanced up from his place on the floor. Listening, he looked fixedly back at his town, aimlessly moving soldiers in front of the sheriff's office. He knew for a fact that in the beginning his father favored the Hounds. "The only way to control a runaway society," is how he put it. And the powerful Sam Brannan . . .

"Now, now . . ." smiled the judge. "Not that I agree with his tactics, but you'd be surprised how many hooligans he's flushed out where local law can snatch them."

"Man has more money than sense. He'll soon be bored and on to some new endeavor." Garth swirled the dark liquid in his glass and continued. "It's his type of support that allowed the Hounds a foothold —

nothing but a desperate move by merchants to hire hoodlums while we were left with stinking rotting food and supplies in the harbors because sailors jumped ship to look for gold. Then our apathetic legislature moved too slowly to make necessary changes from existing Mexican sovereignty to American law. No order from chaos." He shook his head. "I hate to say it, but the ranchers and mining communities deal more decisively with violent crime than our seasoned representatives. Out there with no courts and no law, vigilance works in its purest form."

"Seasoned!" spat the judge. "Try marinated! With our 'Legislature of 1000 Drinks,' as they dubbed us in the beginning, California is widely ridiculed. Is it any wonder we attract the least serviceable of public servants? When the public won't pay attention, these miscreants attract more thugs like themselves, like fleas on a dog." He shook his head in disgust. "Honestly, Garth, I'm a judicial representative in a government I'm embarrassed to say I'm a part of."

"Governor Burnett was an admirable man, a stern conservative. He led us to statehood. Had he remained in office, perhaps this atmosphere of self-indulgence

80

wouldn't have happened. McDougal was hardly the man to take his place, but, as Lieutenant Governor, what choice did the people have?"

"Burnett wearied of fighting the tide alone, McDougal undermining him at every turn." The judge shrugged. "McDougal, 'the gentleman drunk.' Now there's a title that invites confidence. Why would the federal government give us the time of day with that reputation? It's best they ignore us until we can make a reasonably good show. Why would New York, Boston, or even Charleston open markets to us? We can't expect to be taken seriously. Ill-repute is contagious," he warned. "It breeds incompetence on every level."

Garth sighed. "Admittedly, those of us on our isolated farms and ranches haven't been much help. If those around me prosper, so likely am I to prosper. People don't understand that. It rankles my soul."

His father grew too agitated to sit. He rose to retrieve the whiskey decanter, stepping carefully around Dutton's town. "No . . . You were one of the few that saw beyond self to stand for statehood. Why, the beginning of the boom caused overwhelming scarcity of everything — even food was imported. Filthy tent cities sprouted every-

81

where. If it weren't for developers with vision like yourself . . . Garth, you've pushed boundaries and survived — survived and thrived."

Garth smiled. "I didn't come to see the elephant — I came to capture the beast!" He shook his head modestly. "Not that I blame my neighbors; remaining a territory allowed us to avoid being assailed with excessive property taxes. None of us wanted to support a government of irresponsible spendthrifts. We learned to be self-sufficient. That's the narrow-minded approach. But you give me too much credit, Walter. Not hard to convince anyone we needed help after that last flood. State backing's essential to help control the American and Sacramento Rivers. In good years, we see no need for government 'interference.' In bad years? Well, we best all teach our livestock to swim. The massive crop damage suffered was the end of the road for some."

The judge refilled their drinks, nodding. "Not to mention a crucial food supply for the rest of the state. Until we build the railroad, we are severely isolated from the rest of the country."

"And they from us."

The judge stood quietly, sipping his drink for a few moments. He pushed his thumb into a vest pocket so tightly stretched across his middle the fit seemed a physical impossibility.

"I'm tired, Garth — tired of watching the short termers breeze in and out of the state. Here to make their fortune and then run back to wherever the hell they came from. No better than marauders here to rape and pillage California. They see no reason to put money into opportunities for growth here, nor, as I see every day in my courtroom, do they think our laws apply to them. Outcome is not important to them; fast fortunes are. We need a leader with roots, one with ties to our communities. Hell, we can't get a decent turnout at the polls for these no-name shysters. I cannot abide total disregard of community values." He looked hard at Garth. "People need a name they know will be here tomorrow; someone who has a stake in California — whose family carries on the legacy of what he has built. That's a man they can believe. That's a man they can support. That man, Garth, is you."

Dutton looked up to see the stunned look on the man's face. His father continued. "I'm involved through the law. I've taken the role where I can best serve. You fit the profile in every way."

"Except that I am no politician," Garth replied.

"That may be the best and most potent reason for running — people can identify with you. What do people demand of their government? To be effective, facilitate and regulate economic growth. You answered the pioneer call; this office is no different."

Garth frowned, shaking his head. "Walter . . . I agree with all you have said. I'm not a man that can tolerate public life. Other than running for governor, how can I lend my support? I can rally those in power in Sacramento and rattle their chains. We can come up with a candidate. We'll find ways to influence locals to take responsibility at the polls, and give a damn. I don't want the mantle. But, I pledge to you, I'll do everything in my power to get behind the man we see fit to wear it. I, like you, can be of more use behind the scenes. Folks aren't much harder to move than a bunch of mindless cattle — that I know how to do. I'm also known to be pretty mean with the prod."

At this, his father smiled.

"You keep stirring the pot here in San Francisco, and let me go to work on Sacramento. Let's see where that takes us. You have the right idea. But let's double our efforts — from both industrious and presti-gious cities. There are men with foresight out there — we'll gather them and build the state one man at a time, no differently than Dutton's empire over there, layer by layer. You identified the need; now we'll bring it to the public."

The judge began to nod slowly, his satis-faction growing with each of Garth's sug-gestions. "You know, you're only proving my point that you *are* the man for the job."

"Not entirely altruistic motives I have. It is my family's future," Garth stated.

"Granted. But you never turn down an opportunity to help those in need. Besides, who would believe you if you said you did not stand to gain?"

Garth gave a hearty laugh. "There's noth-ing wrong with that as long as you bring your neighbors along with you." He stood to leave. "Walter, I have thoroughly enjoyed the conversation. You've given me a lot to think about. Perhaps our next meeting should be in Sacramento — and bring Dut-ton along."

Dutton stood. "Thank you, sir. I would enjoy that."

"I'll tell Neil to expect you."

"I'll walk you out, Garth."

Dutton sat back down amidst his town . . .

just another day of schooling at his father's feet.

CHAPTER 5

James returned to camp to find seven of their wagons broken from the encircled formation and gone. Many single men struck out for the mining camps dotting the countryside in Coloma near Sutter's mill, but the majority gravitated to Grass Valley. As their community dwindled, the remaining families became eager to regroup and re-settle with the comfort of their collective divided.

James knew Grass Valley, like Nevada City, was not yet fit for women and children. The Clearys, the Speekses, and three other families opted to relocate wagons fifteen miles from Grass Valley, essentially splitting the difference between mining towns and civilized Marysville.

While tempted to fall in with this group, James found himself pummeled by objections put forth by Emma and Althea. In his opinion, their anxieties took over all sense of reason. For two days he endured Emma's icy silences expressing lack of patience for yet another campsite. He and Lodie continued formulating plans and, scarcely as he decided her reticence was to his advantage, she ambushed him.

Deep in thought, he rounded the back of their wagon to ladle a drink from the water barrel secured there. The canopy from a cluster of oaks shaded the wagon pleasantly and a gentle breeze tousled his reddish-brown locks. As he raised the ladle to his mouth, his eyes suddenly met Emma's glacial stare. Startled, he froze. Then, annoyed, he dashed the ladle back into the barrel and growled, "Confound it, woman, how long have ye been standing there?"

The soft wind blew her dark curls lightly across her face. Emma stood rigidly before him, arms crossed and right foot tapping. Ignoring his question, her pent up accusations spilled forth. "James MacLaren! It has been nearly a year since we've had a proper roof over our heads! And the only person you have time or conversation for is Lodie Glenn! Is it too much to ask what and where our future is to be?"

Bewildered, he sputtered, "Ye have na uttered a word ta me in days!"

"I *hoped,* if I waited *patiently* for you to

work out details, you would come to *me*."

"Och. This is *patience,* is it?"

"How long does it take to find a bit of land?"

"Patience is what it takes ta find the right land. I'll na rush inta a foolhardy decision, nor wager every cent we have on it. Lodie and I need ta make our stake in the gold-fields before we settle on a permanent home. Matilda understands this; why is it so difficult for ye?"

He heard a soft voice behind him. "Matilda's child is yet born. Children need a proper home. After you find land, it takes time to build." James pivoted to face Althea.

"Children are resilient — as long as there's food, shelter, and plenty of space ta run and play, they'll get along," James insisted.

Emma countered, "What about school?"

He turned back to Emma. "A wee bit young, aren't they?"

"They're smart. Even if they are young, they learn by listening to the older children's lessons," stated his wife.

"James, they need friends. Be amongst other children," said Althea.

He twisted around again to listen to Althea. In frustration, he whirled about, grasped Emma by the arms, picked her up, and placed her beside Althea.

"I'll na have one of ye yipping at my head, and ta other at my heels."

James noted Althea hiding an amused smile. Irritated, his eyes narrowed. "So what is it the two of ye have cooked up here?"

Althea grew solemn. "I, too, must plan for my family."

He glanced from her face to Emma's. "Ye're a part of our family, you and Justin."

"Yes. And no," she said plainly. "As long as we contribute — yes. But I need to make my own way. I've taken space at the general store in Marysville. I'm employed as a seamstress until I can build a business of my own. I insist upon it."

Emma burst in, "We've found a suitable boarding house. The rooms are small, so we'll require two. We have to stay *somewhere* safe while you and Lodie are gallivanting around the countryside. Matilda took a room there already; Lodie agrees town is best since she is expecting. The children can walk to school. James, we need the protection and support of a town. Surely, it'll bring peace of mind to you while you are away? We'll have lovely reunions when you and Lodie come to town. Which you will have to anyway — for supplies. This way, you can take your time looking for the land

90

and Althea and I can plan what we'll need for the house. Furthermore . . ."

James held up his hand. "I see ye have a great deal more arguments for the ready. I can na fight ye both."

The two women grasped hands excitedly.

"It's a solution for now, but I'll na watch my savings dwindle in rents!" he declared.

"Oh, James!" Emma stood on tiptoe and kissed him on the cheek. "Thank you, dearest!"

"I think I've been had. I mean ta talk ta Lodie about how long he's been in on this!" he muttered.

"We'll talk later." Emma gave him a sweet, dimpled smile, somehow making the aggravation worthwhile. "The women are planning a little celebration for our last campfire together on Saturday!"

He sighed with relief. At best, breaking work at midday Saturday and back late Sundays met the expectations of the partnership. Settling in Marysville meant fewer worries and, in truth, he hated to deny anything to his darling Emma. Despite the hardships of the past year, she always greeted him with an enchanting smile and embrace. The extra ten miles to reach them would pass quickly on the big bay he called Rusty — additional time in the saddle he

intended to use exploring the countryside
for land.

CHAPTER 6

Along the South Yuba River

James and Lodie met Sean at the pre-
arranged spot two miles off the road to
Grass Valley. The three partners picked their
way up the spare and winding trail into the
foothills on horseback. At times, the path
disappeared altogether under forested cover.
James surveyed the grandeur of the terrain
as they rose, certain that its appeal belied
the harsh and strenuous labor awaiting
them. Each new plateau with an unob-
structed view lured James's attention away
from thoughts of gold as he gazed out on a
vista where, somewhere, there was land
destined to be his.

Here along the western slopes of the
Sierras, minerals settled over time into
milky-white veins that he could at this very
moment be standing upon. Veins exposed to
erosion were crumbled and carried. Frag-
ments scattered like hidden leprechaun's

pots. As their threesome ascended, he noted evergreens grew taller and the hills were dense with pine, spruce, and cedar, a distinct contrast with the long yellow grasses and sparsely populated ribbons of deciduous trees he glimpsed below.

By now, James heard the showering rush from the Yuba River. Sean led them to a tributary on a path tucked sharply behind an enormous stand of hemlocks. They traveled up along the ridge of exposed rock bordered by trees and then down to the banks of a wide, fast-flowing stream.

"We're a mile or so from where she joins the Yuba," said Sean, nodding towards the stream. He pointed left. "Past that boulder, you kin see bottom markings of my stakes. See how she snakes her way uphill? This area was prob'ly worked at first holler. I found spots along banks already dug away, but it don't matter . . . when that snow melts come spring, everything below us is under water. That river bleeds out like nothin' you ever did see, carryin' more gold out of the mountains and the process begins again. Like I say, my prospects been steady. No promises for how much more we'll find."

"It's a place to start," said Lodie. "We filed above and below you, guessing that we'll pick up some of what was missed in either direction."

James pondered aloud. "The land below? Could give a man a devil of a time trying ta get close enough ta water ta survive without being carried away by it in spring?"

Sean nodded, "That's the hitch. But I ain't a farmer. For panning . . . mining, it suits me fine. As for that, I've been thinking. It's up to you fellas, but maybe we work all three claims together. If we run one spot dry, we move to one of the others for a while to get at something more productive, then split the findings. What do you say?"

James caught Lodie's nod and stated, "We would na be here if there wasn't a level of trust."

"Good. No quarrelsome personalities. As long as we're all hard at it, we'll get rich all the quicker. Let's pace off and stake them other claims and then I've got some things to show you."

James found the day largely instructional, but promising. And then came the soaring feeling of finding his first shiny pebble in the stream.

Sean stroked his mustache and chuckled. "Some days, that's a bonanza. But you know to keep lookin'. Here . . ." He picked up a rock and struck the pebble. "See how it changes shape, but don't break? That's gold. Now, your sulphuret of iron looks like gold, but it's brittle. Those little flakes of mica are like that, too. Check the crevices — you kin pull ore outta there with your knife. Then you go after what's underneath by breaking it up with the pick. Now grab those pans and we'll poke around to see what this section is hiding."

They waded knee-deep into the stream, still cool at the end of summer. A gentle spray of water spilled over outcroppings of rock and misted their pant legs. James decided panning required little finesse. He and Lodie watched Sean scoop some of the muddy bottom into his pan and dip it back into the water. He lifted the pan out slowly and patiently, swirling it around, hoping to find the heavier gold settled at the bottom as sand and soil washed over the sloping sides. James watched him smile as the slight contents of the pan were revealed. "It's here, but it's going to take a lotta work to get it out. Times a'wastin'."

By sundown, in spite of chilled feet and sore backs, their spirits were buoyed. Skies were clear, so they did not bother to set up tarps, but pulled their bedrolls close to the fire. Evenings cooled quickly at this altitude. James settled the horses for the night, giving Rusty an extra handful of grain and an affectionate pat. He pulled Matilda's carefully wrapped parcels of food from Lodie's saddlebag and carried them to the fireside.

"I'm glad you fellas got need to visit families." Sean eyed the slab of leftover meat sizzling as Lodie tossed it in the hot skillet, its beefy scent wafting on air almost immediately. "That means supplies stocked and fresh food to boot."

Under starry skies with a bare whisper of clouds, they dined on the remains of pot roast, cornbread, and cold boiled potatoes. With crumbs dotting his chin, Sean reminded them, "As the week goes on, we rely more on bacon and beans."

James sat holding a tin mug close to his face, letting the warmth and aroma of the coffee tantalize his senses. "I saw a few fish in the stream today. I'm a right fair fisherman," he boasted.

"You wanna spend your time fishing for food or money?" challenged Sean.

James shrugged. "There are ways ta set some lines and check them from time ta time. It would na hurt ta set a few snares as well."

"Well, aren't you the woodsman." quipped Lodie.

"I am when I have ta be. I had a lot of practice having ta be."

"As long as you don't attract bears, wolves, or mountain lions," cautioned Sean. "So far, dirt and rocks fail to draw them in."

"Hmm. Stored meat is best sacked and hung from a tree. We won't be surprised by animals rummaging 'round camp."

Lodie and Sean looked at each other. "Are you any good at biscuits?" Lodie asked him.

"Sorry, that's where my expertise ends."

"Ah, that's a shame," sighed Sean. "But today was a gainful day. Steady, with a promise of more tomorrow. Come morning, I'll take you downstream to my site and show you somethin' while the sun warms the water up. We should walk the claims with a careful eye from one end to the other. We'll walk back on the opposite bank . . . to size things up."

The next day exhibited the same even-tempered weather as most until rainy season. Hidden behind a stand of river birch in Sean's section, James watched him pull out his version of the latest mining innovation. Sean pointed at it with pride. "This, friends, is a cradle. Some folks call it a rocker. It's a two-man proposition and keeps you from squatting in icy water *all* day. After yesterday, I think you kin appreciate what this means come winter."

The wooden box was two feet wide and four feet long, mounted on rockers.

"One of us shovels dirt in here — top of the sieve." Sean traced the route of the gold on the outside of the box with his fingers. "Then you dump water on top to wash it through while you rock this baby back and forth. The dirt goes down here . . ." Bending over, he pointed to the lower extension protruding from the box. ". . . and over the riffles at an incline. Water and dirt go out; gold sticks in the riffles." He smiled up at them.

Lodie grinned. "What happens when too much gold goes through that contraption? Don't want to clue anyone in to jump high or low on us until we *want* that news to get out."

"Now who's protecting turf?" James observed.

"Then we build a long tom," explained Sean. "But we'd need a couple more men to run it. It's only a longer version of the cradle, anywheres from ten to thirty feet."

Lodie jumped in. "Like those trough-lookin' contraptions you see scattered on the hillsides?"

"Yep; you let gravity do the work for you. The ends have this perforated metal sheet they call a riddle: gold passes through the riddle and down to the riffled box. When you kin get enough troughs linked together, then you got a sluice system. Need a team of blokes to run that. But we're getting ahead of ourselves and behind on work."

"Agreed." James reached for a shovel.

"Let's rock the cradle then!" cried Lodie as he trudged into the stream.

The partners worked until no light remained in the day. They began again at the first glimpse of dawn and packed up when dusk threatened to fall over the edge into the abyss of night. Day after day, without deviation, James, Sean, and Lodie toiled together. The week's end found them content with their spoils. They split their findings, each carrying a pouch until their share amassed into an amount worthy to be converted and banked.

As they tidied their camp to leave for town, James heard men's voices and the sounds of iron picks hitting rock on the ridges below. Often, when the wind shifted, sounds from scores of large and bustling camps sprinkled along the Yuba reverberated upward. He decided to investigate. He walked upstream about a hundred yards and crossed at a point where boulders caused the stream to shallow. He heard Lodie shouting from behind him, "James! We're ready to roll out; where're you off to?"

"Checking on the neighbors," he called without turning. He picked his way judiciously over the flat tablets of algae-covered stone, taking care not to slip. Reaching the other side, he climbed an embankment so steep he grabbed handfuls of the long, yellowing grasses or the odd shrub to pull him up. As he crested the hill, the ridge leveled out for a few feet before it broke off into fragmented levels of rock and dirt scattered with offshoots of lonely plants.

James stood topside with the breeze in his face and gazed out on groupings of independent little civilizations below. He surveyed miles of clustered tarps and tents dotting the banks of the Yuba — horses, wagons, and men in motion going about the business of collecting gold. Hammers and picks clinked steadily as the men below worked. He looked down upon the closest village, counting a dozen large canvas domes below. He smelled stew simmering on their fire. He cupped his hands on either side of his mouth and shouted, "Halloo the camp!"

A barely discernible figure in a red wool shirt and suspenders poked his head out of a tent. He shaded his eyes as he peered back up the hill and shouted, "Hello, your own self!" Two more men wandered into view, looking up the side of the ridge for the source of the shouting. James saw both had long, dark beards. "Can't see ya, friend," called one.

"If I was ta get any closer ta this edge, ye'd be seein' me roll on top o' yer tent, there," returned James.

One bearded man began backing up. He held onto his wide-brimmed hat as he craned his head backward. James stood waving both arms in the air.

"Ha, ha! There he be!" The man pointed as his two comrades joined him. They waved back at James.

James called down loudly, "I heard voices. Thought I would see how many folks were in the neighborhood. I could stop in on my way down if that's all right? Like ta ask about land in the area?"

"We hear things, too!" shouted the first man with a black beard. "Which one of ya's sings with the pleasing baritone?"

"Aye, that would be myself. It passes the time."

"Then which one of ya's sings like a wounded crow?" All three men broke into raucous laughter.

James smiled. "That would be my partner, Lodie. My apologies."

"Well, have ya got any whiskey to trade

for information, singing man?" Yelled the fellow in the red shirt and suspenders.

"Aye, that I do!"

"Then you're as welcome as rain in the desert."

James opted for a quick return, sliding down the steep slope on his rump and sending a grinding spray of pebbles when his boots hit bottom. Again he negotiated the slimy rocks in the stream and waded through the ankle-deep shallows to reach the campsite. He laughed as he looked up at Lodie standing with his hands on his hips, waiting.

"Ye look like my woman, ye do! Is it a fierce tongue-lashing I'm due for?"

Lodie cocked his head. "Sean cautioned wariness. Here we're getting ready to leave and you want to alert half the camps in the area about it."

"Develop a wary trust, I believe his words were." James's long strides quickly closed the gap between them. He clapped Lodie on the shoulder and spun him towards the camp. "There's little for them ta observe as we've hardly struck it rich. They might as well see we have nuthin' ta hide, and they'll stick ta their own."

"And you want to stop for tea with 'em? I've got an anxious wife, heavy with child, to get home to," he grumbled.

"So ye should. Did na invite ye anyways; ye've already offended them with yer singing."

Lodie gave him a warning frown. Sean wandered towards them.

"Go on with ye. I aim ta have a look at the countryside anyways. It stands ta reason that misunderstandings are less likely if we're readily recognized. I'll stop for a friendly chat."

Sean chimed in, "He's right. We'll ride down with you, James, say a quick howdy, and be off. I know a few of them fellers anyways." He looked at Lodie's irritable expression. "It might keep ya from gettin' that ugly mug shot off, ya know?"

"Hello. That's it; I'm on to town." Lodie stalked off to his horse.

James looked at Sean, "Ye want ta stay awhile? Have a look around?"

"Naw. It's Saturday. I like to pay my respects to as many saloons as possible; don't like to play favorites." He paused. "I know what you're thinkin'." He held up his left hand as if giving a solemn oath. "I hadn't been near the tables in months. Few hands of poker, maybe, and as much beer as a man can float in," he grinned.

"Let's go!" came the shout from Lodie,

who was mounted and holding the reins to their horses. "James, I got a mind to tell Emma that you're off exploring!"

"Och, she'll know that the minute you get ta the boarding house! *Tell* her I'll be home for supper."

CHAPTER 7

Marysville

James tugged the collar of his old corduroy coat up as a shield from the windy blasts assaulting his neck and ears. His big bay, Rusty, shifted his weight impatiently back and forth as James surveyed a long view of valley land from the edge of the bluff. He departed camp before dawn to explore this area of the Bear River before his family expected him in Marysville. Satisfied with findings of good water, trees, and grass, he determined to investigate from the basin floor when time allowed. He glanced at the gray clouds breaking apart to release a glimmer of sun. He suspected, even with a stiff breeze, the sun would win out and make it a fine day. He turned Rusty's head for home.

The long rides to Marysville he did not mind. He spent this time alone planning, but today's thoughts drifted longingly to his family. He pictured Emma anxiously waiting while managing expectations of excited children. He knew she found the weeks lonely, even surrounded by friends and children. And he sorely missed her tinkling laugh and gentle companionship during his long week away. He gratefully acknowledged Marysville as a favorable location, admitting his wife's wisdom was as keen as her beauty.

Months of solid laboring gave James a sense of security as his savings increased, especially now as the entire family committed to work. Althea's mastery with a needle brought in more clients than she could handle at the general store. Charlotte and Justin earned a few pennies performing odd jobs around the boarding house. Charlotte cleaned lamp chimneys and swept porches. Justin stacked firewood, hauled water, and carried heavy stacks of clean linens upstairs.

James was particularly proud of Emma, who took over for the expectant Mrs. Timmons at the school. Currently, she worked alongside the young teacher, getting to know her future students, who ranged in age from six to sixteen. He knew the challenges required to stay ahead of the students helped to fill her lonely time, and it set a strong example to the children as part of a happy, working household.

As a reward, James promised the family a day of shopping and arrived on this unprecedented Friday morning. He neglected to mention the prior two days he spent roving the countryside. By his calculations, he could spend down time in December researching in the land office. This thought outweighed his disappointment of not working their claim.

October and the first of November treated them unusually well — temperatures pleasant by day, nights significantly colder. They raised tents to keep out wind and rain, but the last two weeks of showers put a significant damper on their spirits. Sean warned it was nothing compared to the coming months — soon they would all spend more time around town.

The continual rain while working along the streams chilled his bones to the marrow. James looked forward to a shave, a steaming bath, and a hot meal as he pictured his evening at the boarding house. Dinners were frequently as lively as church socials depending on the transient guests. Permanent boarders roomed upstairs and were well acquainted with their immediate neighbors. Travelers lodged downstairs. All met in the front parlor and James looked forward to a glass of sherry to aid in warming up new friendships.

After settling Rusty at the livery stable, James braced himself for the celebration of his homecoming. He walked stealthily up the wide veranda steps of the boarding house and peeked through the lace curtains into the parlor.

Emma sat the children clean, groomed, and waiting in the front room on the large, black, horsehair divan. Charlotte wore a new green ribbon in her hair to match the embroidery on her pinafore. Justin's hair was parted and slicked back, instead of the usual way of falling in front of his eyes. James pulled back against the wall abruptly as Justin got up and ran to the window where he stood watching. The boy pressed his face against the glass and then wheeled to run back and give his report. James smirked as he saw Justin turn and jump with his bottom landing first into the cushion, bouncing Charlotte. She, in turn, jumped up and bounced him back. They giggled at their sport whilst Emma raised her eyebrows at their fun. James chuckled and threw open the door. Charlotte and Justin leaped up and ran into his outstretched arms.

"Ah, now that's what I've been sorely missing all week!" he exclaimed.

"Really, Da? You missed us? Are you glad to be home?"

"This isn't really home," insisted Justin.

"Well, it's better than the wagon, isn't it Mother?"

"Yes, it most definitely is." Emma rose and greeted her husband with an affectionate embrace. "Not a moment too soon," she smiled, glancing pointedly at the children.

James laughed. "So I see. It's a fine day! Who wants ta take a stroll? A long ride, it was, and I could stand ta stretch these legs."

"Me!"

"Me!"

Justin and Charlotte jumped up and down like opposing springs.

"It seems you aren't the only one. I'll get my hat," said Emma gratefully.

"All right now; one hand for each of ye."

James held his head high as the family strolled the boardwalks of town. He allowed the laughing tow-headed boy and curly-headed girl to pull him along. He leaned away from the tugging children towards Emma.

"With all this commotion, I can na fully admire my wife." He eyed her proudly. He carried the picture of her delicate features in his mind all week. Her mass of glossy, dark hair was pulled back, the curls cascading down her back the way he liked it. The inky tendrils that escaped and framed her face sharply contrasted with the pale creaminess of her skin. She peeped up at him with a slight smile; he felt her deep-blue eyes cast their magic in his soul. Over the tops of the children's heads, his all-consuming glance embraced her, and she returned his gaze with a look as amorous as the blowing of a kiss. He shook himself from their reverie and turned his attention back to the children.

"I think ye've both grown again; can it be possible?"

Justin immediately stood taller, and walked straighter. "I have. I'm much taller than Charlotte now."

Emma groaned. "Yes, and his feet! He's already blistering his toes in shoes only a few months old. I promised Thea we'd get him some new ones today; he's very hard on them."

James laughed. "That's boys for ye. My mam used to wail over the cost of outfitting us passel of boys. She used ta say she'd trade any three of us for just one girl."

Justin tugged on James's coat. "Can I get a new marble? Maybe two? We play at recess. They have new ones in, a red and yellow cats-eye that I really like."

"The storekeeper says you smudge up his glass and you should buy something or don't bother him," said Charlotte.

"That would be another blessing for your mother," stated Emma. "He takes Althea's buttons to practice with and manages to lose the ones she needs the most."

"We can have a look at that." James leaned down as if imparting a secret. "Ye know I'm quite the marbles master. Maybe we'll have a game later?"

"Yes!"

"And is there anything that my lovely has been eyeing?"

Charlotte cocked her head as she decided. "Colored chalks."

Emma nodded approvingly. "She draws while the older students do their lessons. She finishes her work quickly, and asks questions later about what the older ones studied that day."

"Good ta know I'm na raising a simpering flirt."

"Oh, no. She's more interested in competing with Justin. Running races and jumping off of things. She's exceedingly bright; they both are."

Customers crowded the boardwalk as they drew near the general store. James noted the clear day enticed many into town. Two

Chinese men in coolie hats conversing animatedly with one another hurried past them. Emma drew back sharply, pulling her skirts close to her as they went by.

James gave her a questioning look.

She whispered, "They steal your souls."

"Oh, rubbish!" he bellowed. "We came here for work and opportunity; why do ye assume they are na here for the same?"

"But so many of them! They way they talk . . . I heard it was incantations."

"They're entitled ta their gibberish. I've met men that cu na oonderstand a word I uttered either and were na likely ta have the patience ta try," he said emphasizing his brogue. "Don't be repeating that silliness ta the children."

As they approached the store, James noticed a young Maidu Indian boy as he squatted by a wagon tied near the entrance. A tall Franciscan priest with thinning hair exited with his arms loaded full of packages and the boy sprang to his feet to help. Noting the authoritative simplicity of his dark-brown robe, James stepped forward respectfully. "Is there anymore there we can assist ye with, Father?"

"Oh, thanks very much," said the priest, mopping his brow and balding pate. "I believe the proprietor is loading the larger barrels. There's a counter full of smaller packages, and they don't allow the boy inside, of course. I'm Father Stephen."

"Justin, hop in there and help the good Father. James MacLaren," he reached to shake the priest's hand. "My family," he gestured towards Emma and Charlotte.

Justin ran into the store, came back with an armload, and passed them off to the waiting Maidu boy. "One more," he said as he dashed back inside.

"Is there a mission nearby?" asked James.

"The beginning of one," the priest said. "At the moment, we're little more than a chapel near Sutter Buttes. We offer assistance to the indigenous tribes there."

James nodded. "Yes, I've seen the Buttes from a distance. Never got close enough ta explore it." Amused, he watched the Maidu boy and Justin, standing toe-to-toe, each equally curious about the other. The Maidu boy was smaller, with coppery skin and very thin. He began to circle around Justin, staring at the top of his head with wide, coffee-colored eyes. Justin turned as he turned as if wary of the boy.

Father Stephen laughed. "It's your yellow hair, son. It fascinates him. We call him JoJo."

Justin grinned and lowered his head. The

boy reached out to touch it, and gently patted Justin's soft, blond hair. He then rubbed his own stick-straight, shoulder-length dark hair.

"Nice to meet you, JoJo. I'm Justin, and that's Charlotte and my Auntie Emma."

The boy backed away, his expression somber. He glanced at Father Stephen, who made a hasty hand gesture and said, "Friends."

The priest turned to James. "We're all loaded up and I thank you for your help." He bowed to Emma. "Nice to meet you, ladies." As he climbed into the wagon, he called to James, "Stop in and say hello if you're traveling in our direction. I can at least offer you some meager hospitality."

"Will do, Father."

They watched the wagon pull away. Charlotte and Justin both waved good-bye to the solemn little boy. Emma stood close to James, and whispered in a sharp tone, "Really, James." She raised her eyebrows and inclined her head towards the retreating wagon.

He folded his arms on his chest and looked sternly down at her. "Oh, so its devils ta yer left and savages ta yer right, is it? And all God's children walk the middle ground."

115

"Well he *is* a savage, is he not?"

"I suppose it depends on yer definition. I take umbrage ta the term — considering the fine English referred ta our clans as such. I might point out ye're the one that wanted ta live here in 'civilization.'"

Emma looked hurt. "I suppose I'm not accustomed to all these foreigners living so close together."

"Well, this is America; ye best get used ta it. More ta the point, that little boy is the only one who's na foreign. Imagine his thinking." James realized his preaching had ended their jovial mood. "Och. We're here ta do some shopping, eh?"

Justin bolted through the door in the direction of his favorite counter. James reached out hastily, barely hooking a finger in his shirt collar, and redirected him.

"Shoes first!"

Laden with packages, their good humor returned. They met Althea for lunch and made a party of it by ordering a round of lemonades. Althea had spent an industrious morning sewing at the boarding house and intended to meet clients that afternoon. Justin scraped his new shoes against the timber floor as he swung his feet to and fro under the table. His mother laughed and shook her head.

"Gracious, Justin! Have pity on your poor mother. I'll be spending our hard earned money on another pair before the end of the week!" Althea tousled his fair head affectionately. She turned to Charlotte. "Did you tell your da what you've been working on this week?"

Charlotte's face brightened. "Mrs. Glenn is teaching me to bake!"

"Really? Now that's a handy skill. Will ye be taking over while she tends baby Robert?"

"Not unless the guests are willing to eat bread shaped like flowers and animals," laughed Emma.

"Now, I think that would be marvelous. Did ye happen ta make any horses?"

"Of course! They're your favorite!"

"Well, then I can hardly wait."

"Charlotte, perhaps you should make more for the church picnic on Sunday," suggested Emma. "I need to fill our basket, and those would be divine with the elderberry jam."

Charlotte beamed.

"I hate to break up the party," said Althea, dabbing her mouth with her checkered napkin, "but I must get back to work." She rose to leave, but paused as James announced nonchalantly, "I've invited Sean ta

117

join us on Sunday."

"Well that's . . . that's fine," she stammered. She glanced at Emma, blushed, and hurried on her way.

Emma stood. "Let's go, children. We need to take these packages home." As Charlotte and Justin gathered parcels, she leaned in to whisper, "He *does* fancy her, doesn't he?"

"Merely a neighborly invitation."

As they made their way up the street, James spotted Sean going into a saloon. He needed to discuss supplies with him, but did not want Emma to know how many days since he had last seen him. Then he heard Emma squeal with delight, "Lucille! Oh, look, James! It's Lucille Speeks and Ella Louise."

Ella Louise skipped up to Charlotte. The girls embraced and immediately began chattering and, likewise, their mothers. Justin shot James a hangdog look.

"Eh, Justin," he began, "why don't ye help the ladies take the packages back to the boarding house . . ."

Justin's soft-blue eyes widened with pleading.

"And we'll have a game of catch when I arrive."

Emma looked up with surprise, and James quickly continued. "You should have a nice visit . . . give the girls a chance to play. I have errands ta tend to and I'll be there directly. No sense in all of ye waiting."

"Land sakes," began Lucille, "it's been a moon and a half since I seen you. I'd be plum tickled to sit anywheres as nice as that parlor. Tim's workin' as fast as he kin on our house, but it ain't near ready. 'Bout as dusty inside with his buildin' as it was out on the prairie. And I'd like to talk a spell about school, Emma. It's high time I send Ella Louise."

"I suppose it's decided then. Are you certain you don't mind, James?"

He reached out to squeeze her hand. "I won't be long."

"Justin, you can play with us!" called Ella Louise.

Justin pulled a sour face, to which James sternly admonished, "Hye, hye — none of that nonsense. Ye mind yer manners, and we'll have a catch as promised, hmm?"

"Yes, sir," he sighed as he picked up packages.

James gave Emma a quick wink, and turned to find Sean. He was certain he had disappeared into Murphy's Tavern.

Adapting from sunshine to the dingy light inside the tavern left James blinking Sean into focus. Murphy's was heavy with the smell of stale tobacco, spilled beer, and the faint odor of kerosene burning in the lanterns. When his eyes adjusted, he found Sean at the long oak plank of a bar clustered with Alton Quigby, the blacksmith, Tom Price from the saddle shop, and Hammond Creed, the mayor.

"Hey, partner!" called Sean. "Am I still blurry?"

"That all depends. How many have ye had?"

"Aw, now. You know I don't start serious drinking 'til dark. I'm sharing a beer with the fellas to find out what's goin' on around here while we're off earning a living."

Tom Price, normally a quiet fellow, patted James's shoulder. "I got to get on back, but let me buy you a beer before I go, James."

"That's right fine of ye."

Tom was slight in build and would have been taller if it were not for his stoop-shouldered stance. He held up a finger to the bartender. "Well, I surely do appreciate your help patchin' the schoolhouse roof. Don't like to see my young'uns getting colds from a drippin' ceiling."

"Not at all." James glanced at Sean. "I believe I'll have a bit of time on my hands come winter. In fact, I'm sure Sean'll be happy ta help me caulk the windows."

"Hey, I've been talking business with Hammond. We got town meetings coming up."

Hammond straightened from his leisurely lean on the bar and stretched. "Wait up, Tom; I'll walk out with you. Sorry to run, but my staff at the hotel can't manage but so long unsupervised. If I don't get back, I'll find them all napping. Sean can fill you in," he said to James. "River traffic stuff — the Feather and the Yuba are both looking bloated for this early in the year. Say, you'll be at the church picnic, won't you?"

James nodded as he sipped his beer.

"We'll talk then." Hammond picked up his new bowler hat from the corner of the bar and polished its domed top with his elbow. He ran his fingers through his wavy, dark hair before setting the hat carefully on his head and securing it with a pat. He smiled and touched its brim as a good-bye gesture.

Alton Quigby gave a quick wave. Sean gawked at his display, but James hid a smile behind his mug and said simply, "Mr. Mayor."

As the pair exited into the burst of daylight from the opening door, Alton shook his head and remarked, "He shore is proud of that billycock."

"Hammond likes to make an impression. Guess that's his mayor hat," said Sean.

The bartender slid a plate of cold mutton and beans towards the blacksmith. Alton's complexion was sooty and dark, and no amount of face washing would erase the hours spent over his forge. He kept his bristly hair short. The droopy mustache he favored was recently singed and cut back drastically. "Thanky," he acknowledged before addressing James. "How's that wagon workin' out?"

"Could na be better. The new wheel is solid."

"Got a nice little sorrel mare over at my place. Thought you might wanna check her out."

"I might at that. All right if I stop in the first of tomorrow?"

"That suits."

"We'll leave ye ta yer lunch. Sean and I have supplies ta gather and the family is waiting back at Flanagan's boarding house."

Sean and James moseyed out, content to enjoy a slower pace, knowing vigorous labor awaited them Monday morning. They stood leaning against the hitching post in front of Murphy's Tavern. The sun had clearly won its battle over the early morning clouds and warmed their faces as they discussed replenishing provisions. Sean looked past James to see a Mexican man standing a few yards away, waiting patiently to be noticed.

Sean pointed at the man. "You know him?"

James turned. "Aye. Vicente. I bought a lariat from him a few weeks ago. Does good work. His wife makes a pretty good tamale, she does."

"I think he wants to sell you somethin' else," said Sean as Vicente beckoned to James. "Maybe you ought to run him off."

"No harm in seeing what the man has ta barter. As I say, he does good work."

Sean followed closely as James approached him. "Good day ta ye, Vicente."

The man smiled, humbly nodding. "*Buenos dias, señor.* Come, please . . ." He backed up slowly until James followed him. He looked over James's shoulder at Sean and frowned. "Please, only the *señor.*" Vicente bobbed his head.

Sean shrugged. "No skin off my nose."

James followed the Mexican down the street where the man's donkey stood tethered to the railing. Vicente motioned again. "Come close . . . please." James watched him put his hand hesitantly on the saddlebag. Sean observed from a distance.

Vicente looked at James as if summoning

his courage. "I watch." He pointed at James. "You, good man. I want to trust."

James shrugged. "We've been fair — each ta the other."

"*Sí*. I want partner."

"A partner?"

"I need partner."

James smiled kindly. "What are ye needing a partner for, Vicente?"

Vicente leaned on the donkey's side, blocking the view from passersby. James inclined his head as the man pulled something out of the saddlebag. His smile vanished. He glanced up the street at Sean with an expression of shock.

Sean wore an anxious frown.

James caught his breath and covered the Mexican's hand with his own larger one. "I see yer concern." He rubbed his jaw as he tried to think. "Vicente," he indicated Sean with his head, "Sean is my partner. He, also, is an honest man. I think we may need him."

Vicente looked uncertain. He studied James's face, and nodded reluctantly.

James called, trying to keep his voice even. "Sean, could ye come down for a minute."

Sean walked towards them grumbling. "What's he got in there, a severed head or something?"

James stared at him. "Try not ta react," he

said and lifted his hand for Sean to see.

"*Holy* Mother of God!" he cried.

There, shielded by two hands, was the biggest lump of gold Sean had seen in a year.

"Good job not reacting, that. Would ye keep it down?"

Sean glanced around quickly. He smacked his head in disbelief.

"Remind me never ta count on ye if I decide ta rob a bank," muttered James. "Vicente, this is Sean. He'll be fine once he's located his wits."

"I think we need to move off the street to discuss this," said Sean.

"Ah, there, he's found them," said James. "I agree. Where can we go?"

"How 'bout we walk slowly out of town?"

"Is this all right with ye, Vicente? Say, have ye got another lariat?"

Vicente nodded, nervously.

"Perhaps ye should give it ta me as if I'm buying it, then, if anyone is watching, they'll see that we're conducting other business."

Vicente nodded, slipped the gold back in the bag, and pulled out a lariat. He unlashed the tether, and they led the donkey down the street.

James spoke in a low voice. "Do ye need help cashing something that size in? Is that it?"

"No, *señor,* there is more."

"Sean, stop lookin' wildly round like a gunfighter has got ye in his sights! Keep yer head about ye, man." He turned back to Vicente. "More? More like that?"

"*Sí.* I can do nothing with it. The tax . . ."

"Tax? What's he talking about?"

Recognition sprang into Sean's face. "Oh, the Foreign Miner's Tax."

"*Sí, sí, sí!*" Vicente nodded quickly.

"Folks got afraid they'd lose out on the best claims with so many Chinese and Mexicans filing. So, they started the Foreign Miners Tax to drive 'em out. It's steep — twenty dollars a month. Most of 'em couldn't afford to pay and survive, so they left. The ones that stay get harassed from the other miners to prove they've paid."

"*Mí familia* . . . I send them back home. Too hard. It is not safe for them."

"That's why I have na seen yer wife around?"

He nodded. "I want to make my money. I need to make lots of money, then I send for them. There are many bad men, *señor.* They would take what I have found."

"You got a claim, then?" asked Sean.

Vicente shook his head. "The bad men, they would kill me and take it from me. And if I pay the tax, they know I have claim and

126

they kill and take." He pointed to the two of them. "We be partners. I can show you."

James looked to Sean, dumbfounded.

"Vicente. We have one more partner . . ."

He shrugged. "I see him, too, the smiling one. You trust, I trust."

Sean blew out a big breath of air. "I gotta hand it to you, Vicente. You got *huevos.*"

"We have a lotta work out here. Ye need ta meet Lodie, and we don't want ta call too much attention ta ourselves meeting in the open." James's face lit up. "What if ye come with us ta our claim? We'll make it look as if yer working with us, like we've hired ye on as a laborer. No one'll be suspicious of our spending time together."

Vicente grinned. "I like this idea. It is safe for me."

"It's good," Sean agreed.

"Meet us Sunday evening at the boarding house and we'll all ride out together. Is this good?"

Vicente grabbed his hand and pumped it vigorously, "*Muchas gracias. Sí,* is good."

The quick rap on her door startled Althea.

"Almost ready," she called.

"I have Justin, and James has the picnic basket. We'll wait on the porch," replied Emma from the hallway.

Althea listened to the sound of her brisk, light steps down the stairs. Always *the organizer,* she thought. Annoyed with the amount of time spent fussing in front of the bureau mirror, she turned her head for what seemed like the tenth time and adjusted the tortoiseshell combs pulling her honey-colored locks up and away from her face. "That will have to do," she sighed as she reached for her pale-peach colored hat and secured it defiantly with the hatpin.

Holding her hands in front of her, she shook them as though the motion would shoo away the nerves. Still feeling jittery, Althea looked down at the brooch lying on the lace doily — taunting her. She had worn it to church many times and today should be no different. She fingered the coral-hued cameo possessively, then raised her chin and quickly pinned it to her lace collar. She glanced at the small silver-framed daguerreotype displayed on the bureau. Now that Emma had seen it, there was no reason to hide it. She stroked the ornament at her throat lightly. The only gift Edward ever gave her.

A pleasing reflection from her last passing glimpse into the mirror assured her it was time to go. *Try to appear cheerful,* she told herself. Althea grabbed her reticule, locked the door to her room, and scampered swiftly down the stairs to join the family.

Emma waited in the front of the buckboard and the children on the back row while James packed the baskets and blankets behind them. When he looked up at Althea as she alighted on the porch stairs in her soft-peach colored dress, he grinned, bowed low, and said, "Well, now . . . M'lady." He offered her his hand to help her up to the seat beside her son.

"Oh, do hush." She smacked his shoulder lightly with her embroidered handbag.

"You look pretty, Mum," said Justin.

"Thank you, dear," she said stiffly. She adjusted her skirts around her and then noticed both Emma and James turned about watching her.

"What?"

Emma was smiling. "You look lovely."

James nodded. "*Someone* is in for a treat."

Althea pursed her lips, then stood abruptly. "This is a terrible idea. I'm going back upstairs."

"No!" Emma and James cried in unison.

"Stop teasing her, James!" admonished Emma.

"Me?"

"What's wrong, Mum? Aren't we going to the picnic?"

"We aren't going? I made special animal biscuits!" wailed Charlotte.

Emma commanded, "Thea, sit. You're being silly." She placed her hand lightly on Althea's arm. "Of course we're going, Justin . . . right after services. Your mother's had a long workweek and is understandably tired. Let's all be quiet on the ride to church and think about what to thank God for today, hmm?" Althea watched Emma turn forward to look pointedly at her husband and place her finger against her lips. James, with raised eyebrows, made a huffing sound, slapped the reins, and addressed the horses. "Gee-up!"

Althea found repose from her family's questioning eyes during Reverend Blanchard's sermon. Even Justin's usual fidgeting in the pew did not bother her. After the resounding final hymn, *Rejoice, Ye Pure in Heart,* the steeple bell chimed and the front doors of the church burst open as children spilled excitedly into the churchyard for games. Prattling women searched for the right spot on the lawn to set up picnics as their men headed for buggies and wagons to retrieve baskets of food. Out came the packed hoops, balls, jump ropes, and marbles as children scattered into groups to meet friends.

Althea brushed aside her earlier flutter of feelings even as she looked up to see Sean watching her struggle with the placement of the quilt on the ground. Having regained her poised demeanor, her pale-blue eyes displayed all the serenity of the clear, cloudless sky above them as she watched him place the parcel he was carrying under the nearest tree and step forward to grab one end of the patchwork blanket.

"Let me give you a hand with that. What do you think?" he asked, craning his head around to look at the river. "Should we turn it so the long side views the water?"

The river was some distance away, but here under the scattered elms made a tranquil setting. Sean had put some strenuous effort into dressing himself up, she noticed. His coffee-brown hair parted down the middle and slicked back neatly brought to fore his large, hazel eyes. His long, horseshoe mustache was trimmed close and combed. The tan pants he wore looked new, and, though his sleeves were rolled up to his elbows, the striped shirt was starched and pressed under his dark-blue waistcoat; even his shoes were polished. She rewarded him with a smile.

"Delightful," she said lightly. Each walked an end of the heavy coverlet about, glancing up more at the other than where the blanket landed. As the quilt settled, their gaze locked hesitantly and for a dash of a moment, Althea felt a flush of inquisitive attraction between them, a moment that vanished as soon as she saw James and Emma standing a few yards away, frozen in place and gawking.

Startled by discovery, Althea watched James and Emma simultaneously turn and bump headlong into each other. James pushed Emma forward holding a platter of sliced ham. He fumbled his large hand about in the picnic basket as if he had forgotten something. He resumed an awkward stroll towards the pair, pretending to see them for the first time. Sean turned away to grab the parcel he left under the tree.

"Looks like a marvelous spot," called James. "Glad ye could join us, Sean."

Emma added, "Well done, Thea — plenty of shade, lovely view, easy to watch the children running about." As she placed the platter in the center of the blanket, Sean cleared his throat and handed her the gift.

"James kin tell you I'm a campfire cook . . . so I took the liberty of bringing a little something from the general store."

Unwrapping the package, Emma exclaimed, "How thoughtful! A tin of oysters and saltines; this certainly is a treat! Thank you, Sean."

Justin sprinted across the lawn towards them trailed by three boys from school. "Mum! How soon 'til we eat?"

"Manners, Justin! Give us a few minutes to unpack the food and spread it out," replied Althea.

"Can Harry, Jim, Bob, and me go down to the river? Please? Bob's dad brought some boats and we want to race them." He turned and pointed to the tiny toy fleet lined up along the riverbank. "Is it all right? Is it? For a while?" he pleaded.

Althea smirked. "Oh, very well. Come back when you're hungry."

The boys bolted. The wind carried Justin's hurried yell of "Thanks, Mum!" over his head back to her.

"Honestly!" she laughed.

"Typical boy." Sean was smiling. "Kinda want to go with 'em. Been a long time since I've sailed a boat."

"I think we should take advantage of a moment's peace and break out the food," suggested James. "I think ye'll find the ladies put together a spectacular spread, Sean."

As Althea and Emma reached into the huge basket, tin plates filled with corncakes, sliced meatloaf, deviled eggs, sausages, Charlotte's animal biscuits, and apple pie emerged along with jars of pickled cucumber and jellies. Throughout lunch children, like birds, swooped down for a few morsels and quickly took flight to rejoin their games, leaving the meal oddly tranquil without childish chatter.

Lodie, holding baby Robert, and Matilda, bearing a partially eaten custard pie, arrived to visit. "Pie swap!" he called gleefully. "I hear you have Emma's apple over here. There's no resisting Matilda's custard, I'm telling you!"

The women groaned they were too full, but James and Sean eagerly tucked into the new delicacy.

"What I'd like is that sweet thing," stated Emma, reaching for Robert. "Hand him over!"

"Wonderful. Now I have two hands for eating. Ooh, I can smell the cinnamon!"

"Don't hurt yourself," warned Matilda.

"I remind you it's back to camp cooking for us tomorrow. I'm here to eat for my week," declared Lodie with a forkful of streusel-topped apple hovering in front of his mouth. "Mm. Don't care if I pop, the memories will carry me until Friday next."

"Terrific stuff, Matilda," said Sean after a

few bites. "I best stop now. I've promised to partner up with a friend in the three-legged race."

"Looks like pleasure is about ta turn ta business," said James. He nodded towards Hammond Creed strolling the perimeter of scattered blankets and picnicking families.

Sean stroked his mustache free of crumbs. "He's got his mayor hat on, too."

Hammond gathered a number of men who excused themselves from their families and gravitated towards the impromptu horseshoe pit. He gave a jolly wave as he approached.

"Everyone looks well-fed and happy, I must say," he began.

"Would you care for a slice of pie, Hammond?" offered Althea.

"Thank you, no. I believe I've eaten my way across the meadow. I'm beginning to feel like a real scavenger. I came to see if the gents would like to join us for a game."

James smirked. "A game only?"

"Your mayor never fully takes a day off. You're all busy fellows. I need to nail down a few committee details on river traffic. We could be in for a rough year depending on the rains, and, as you know, that season is well upon us. Don't want to get caught unprepared like last year. I don't fancy taking a rowboat down Main Street again."

"Duty calls, ladies . . ." Lodie stood and stretched. "Don't suppose there's any hard cider over there, hmm?"

Hammond winked as his followers reluctantly rose. Sean turned and bobbed his head to Althea. "Back soon. I'm going to swipe that mayor's hat," he grinned.

Emma bounced baby Robert and cooed. "We won't miss them a bit, will we darling?"

Matilda looked up and exclaimed, "Oh, there's Ginny Taylor! I haven't seen her in ages!"

"Well, go say hello. We'll be fine here with Robert," Althea said.

"Oh, are you sure you don't mind?"

"Heavens, Matilda. Emma and I both remember what it's like to be tied down with a new baby! You see us all the time at the boarding house. Go on. Besides, we might not give him back."

Matilda giggled like a child set free from chores. "Oh, thanks! I will!"

Althea smiled as her friend darted off to catch Ginny. She turned to Emma. "I'm going to demand a turn with that baby soon."

Emma rubbed noses with Robert. "Ah, it seems so long ago that Charlotte was this size." She glanced up to watch her daughter running a peg-legged canter, tossing her long, dark hair and whinnying like a pony along with Ella Louise and a herd of girls from school. She sighed, and Althea noticed a sad shadow of a look cross her face. "I suppose there won't be any more babies for us."

Althea shook her head. "Now, Emma, you're still young."

"But I've lost three, now. I cannot bear to lose another."

"Give yourself time." Althea lifted her chin to feel the sun on her face. "It's such a beautiful day. There are happier thoughts to think about."

Emma smiled gently at Robert. "Yes. I agree." Althea looked to see her friend studying her face.

"Well?" demanded Emma.

"Oh, don't turn this on me."

"You can't hide a thing from me, Althea Albright. I've known you nearly all your life. I'm not blind, you know. The two of you have been giving each other looks for weeks, and earlier today . . . why if James and I hadn't wandered up . . ."

"You have a vivid imagination," she retorted. "The whole town is within view."

"I'm simply saying. You look . . . happy."

"I'm . . . well, it has been a very long time. And I am only half the equation." She tilted

137

her head thoughtfully. "How does he look?" Althea surveyed the group of men at the horseshoe pit.

Emma chuckled. "Besotted."

Althea's cheeks colored brightly. "That's ridiculous." She frowned slightly as she saw Justin running towards the assembly of men. He stood before Sean, talking with great animation, she noticed. Then the two of them ran across the field.

"What on earth?" Althea stood and shaded her eyes. She watched as Sean and Justin hurried to the starting line of a group of men gathered in pairs, arm in arm. Sean bent quickly, picked up the piece of rope on the ground, and lashed his right leg to Justin's left. Her mouth fell open. "Emma, you have to see this!"

Emma rose with the baby and began to laugh. "Justin is his partner?"

Justin was clearly the shortest participant. Sean bent over with some difficulty to put his arm about Justin's shoulder. They stood ready. Tom Price officiated. Faintly they heard the call . . . "Ready! Set!"

At the bang of the starter's pistol shouts soared from the crowd gathered along the sidelines. Sean and Justin suffered a clumsy start and their uneven, clod-hopping gait put them behind. Althea caught the squint of determination in Sean's face as he reached under Justin's arm, and lifted him. He ran, half carrying a giggling Justin, who had by now fallen forward, with his head bobbing pitifully with Sean's every step.

"Oh, my!" Althea clenched her fists as she watched them pull ahead of the other competitors to cross the line first. Even as Tom Price disqualified them, Justin was hugging Sean and laughing. In that instant Althea Albright decided she would risk her heart to such a man. They both grinned ear-to-ear when they reached the women.

"You certainly made that exciting!" exclaimed Emma. "Well done, Justin."

"That was fun! I was flying! We shoulda won."

"No points for ingenuity," shrugged Sean.

Althea beamed at them. "I was very proud of you . . . both."

Sean gave her a sideways glance. "Would you like to take a walk along the river?"

Althea looked back at the men in the horseshoe pit. "Don't you need to finish the discussion there?"

"Hammond bent my ear for long enough two days ago. I'm all caught up."

"Then, I would be pleased to accompany you."

"Mum, is there pie left? I'm hungry."

Emma shifted the baby to her hip and reached for his hand. "You come with me, and I'll get the pie."

Sean offered Althea his arm as they strolled towards the grassy banks of the Yuba.

CHAPTER 8

Bear River Country

He needed time alone with his thoughts. After waiting as long as he could without drawing attention to himself, James told his partners he wanted to stretch his legs and stalked up into the moonless hills out of earshot. He leaned against a gnarled pine on a rocky ledge. The light from their campfire was in view as he looked below. He watched its glow upon their faces as they huddled close to the fire, talking, laughing, taking their coffee. His breath appeared in ragged puffs against the cold night air. He was glad they could be at ease. He could not.

James slid down the rough bark of the tree, his coat catching as he descended into a slumped sit on damp ground. He stared out into the quiet of darkness and, somewhere close, a night owl complained of his presence. His mind retraced the steps of a

141

tumultuous week, one of wondrous discovery and hard facts.

Monday began a particularly unforgiving week of continual rain. He, Lodie, Sean, and Vicente put up a convincing show working their claim by the river. They rode in close proximity past the other camps, making sure Vicente fetched and carried when anyone was of a mind to notice. A few miners catcalled to Sean about striking big enough to require the little Mexican. His easy reply had been, "Damn straight! Struck it rich at Faro on Saturday. I figure my feet can take a break from the cold water for a while. There's help for hire, boys; you might want to think about doin' the same!"

A plausible tale, as many were familiar with Sean's affinity for gaming tables. The four men conducted business as usual, and impatiently waited for Friday when they would follow Vicente further into the mountains to investigate his find.

In the evenings, Vicente pieced together his story, despite his broken English. Lodie filled in details from newspaper accounts about upheaval in Mexico. Even in the face of good fortune, James felt a familiar gnawing in his gut as Vicente spoke and was unable to quell his anger. The details of the injustice buzzed in his head like a hornet

142

threatening to strike.

Vicente, his brother, and several men from their village near Oaxaca had come to California to make their fortunes. The Mexican-American War capped years of poverty and loss in a battle-ravaged Mexico. In an era of coups, the antics of Santa Anna's on-again off-again reign of power led to nothing but upheaval and unrest for the Mexican people. Since 1833, Santa Anna occupied the office of *presidente* intermittently with nine other Mexican presidents, many of whom also served more than once during the years leading up to the war. Returning from exile, Santa Anna promised a despairing President Farias use of his military prowess to fend off invasion of Mexico. He also pledged to the United States that, in return for allowing him past naval blockades back into his country, he would sell the contested territory to the Americans at an agreeable rate. He reneged on both. Declaring himself president once again, he took his people into a fruitless fight with the United States. At the inevitable changeover of Mexico's highest office, the treaty of Guadalupe Hidalgo was signed by President Manuel de la Pena y Pena, and Santa Anna returned to exile.

Throughout the political angst, the poor

and starving Mexican people looked to California for a better life. Vicente's group arrived during a difficult influx of peoples from Australia, the Hawaiian Islands, Chile, and Peru as well as Mexico. The men from the village of Oaxaca moved to Dry Diggings, near the sawmill in Coloma.

The converted sawmill became an overcrowded miners' lodge. Dry Diggings' shaky boundary of peace amongst cultures was broken by the murder of two Americans. The shock of the stabbing awoke a latent need to arm and protect. Suspicion permeated their midst, aggravated by language barriers and unfamiliar customs.

Dry Diggings' escalating population brought the usual vices to ease boredom. One night, five men attacked and robbed a gambler named Lopez. An impromptu vigilance committee formed and the robbers were captured, tried, convicted, and publicly flogged. Then a shout arose from the crowd accusing three of the men, all foreigners, of a robbery and murder on the Stanislaus River. By now, the miners were drunk and their judgment warped to a frenzied mode. Again, vigilantes held court, and the sentence of hanging quickly was carried out. Whether as warning or testament, Dry Diggings was from that point dubbed as Hangtown.

In this growing atmosphere of distrust, a more dangerous evil grew. "Misunderstanding" in the case of language barriers worked to the advantage of unscrupulous minds. Finding a voice to vouch for foreigners when the majority wanted them to leave proved difficult. Fear loomed large on both sides.

The men from Oaxaca worked their claims on the northern side of the American River. Vicente had gone to Auburn for supplies when bandits confronted his brother Luis. He gave up the gold he had on hand, but they shot Luis anyway. Hearing the noise, men from several neighboring claims came to investigate. First to arrive, Vicente's friends were promptly and loudly accused of claim jumping by the killers. The bandits staged a compelling show, and anyone uninvolved in the dispute proved unwilling to take a stand for the Mexicans. The argument escalated until someone accused Vicente's countrymen of various unsolved crimes.

The villagers from Oaxaca had seen enough violence in the preceding months to know the grave danger they faced. They fled. The bandits treated their flight as a blood sport and gave chase. Two of the men were caught and immediately hanged. Luis, though already dead, was hanged alongside them. Three others escaped into the hills; one intercepted Vicente on his way back from town, and they found a well-concealed cave to hide in.

The bandits took their claims. There would be no justice. The defrauded group sneaked out at night to retrieve the bodies of their friends and bury them. They decided to return to their village — all but Vicente. He grieved deeply. Vicente refused to let failure return him to poverty and could not face his family. He remained in the cave for many weeks and watched the bandits become bored with manual labor and move on.

Reclaiming his diggings carried too high a risk. His cave provided a safe haven, and was deceptive in size. The entrance, well hidden by the abundant trees, only allowed a large man to squeeze through sideways. In fact, at first glance it appeared as a cleft in the rock. The narrow passageway snaked around walls of rock until it opened into the first of several taller portals. After his friends left, Vicente explored the corridors, marking the maze of detours with charcoal from his fire. Growing desperation caused him to reconsider working his abandoned claim and hiding his proceeds here. Then he reached the seventh and largest opening.

Cold, lonely, and succumbing to despair, the broken man sat against the cave wall, head in his hands, and gave in to pent-up tears. He shouted angrily at his plight and in frustration scooped up a handful of pebbles and flung them. In the dim light from his lantern, something glittered. He stared, as if uncertain whether he could trust his vision. He picked up more pebbles and sorted through them, selecting one or two, and held them close to the light. He bit one. The malleable metal gave way in his teeth, but remained an indented whole. Vicente jumped to his feet, holding the lantern low as he walked around the large room, kicking rocks aside, picking up some. He raised the lantern up to examine the ceiling and froze. Veins in the rock shimmered enticingly.

In his reconnaissance of the old claim, he had sneaked out nightly to retrieve what tools he could and take them back to his lair. Now, he had a purpose.

Vicente gathered all the loose rocks and pebbles he could find. He decided to avoid Coloma and Auburn and go into Grass Valley for supplies. He didn't take enough gold to raise interest in his comings and goings.

As he accumulated more, he decided on a larger town to bank his money, a little at a time. After awhile, he returned to Mexico for his family.

He found it easier to be inconspicuous in Marysville. He settled his family in a small shack outside of town and his wife sold food on the streets and took in laundry. He cleaned stables and did odd jobs when he could find the work. He continued to work patiently in the caves until he could figure out how to hide his riches. He worked much of what was within reach, or could be pried loose with a pick. He needed help.

And now, after biding his time and waiting for opportunity, he brought his new partners up the narrow trail. Before dawn, they slipped away unobserved from their camp and traveled south towards the Bear River and back up into the Sierras. A murky sunrise greeted them as the rain continued. Silver mists hung on the hills as they rose on their furtive trek, light appearing in muted gray-gold slivers through the pines.

They tied up their horses in a dense cluster of trees several hundred yards away from the cave opening and Vicente led them in.

When they came to the seventh open space, they stood in the center and marveled. James walked the entire perimeter, running his hands over the rock walls and then standing back for a more detailed look. He ran calculations in his head.

"Glory be . . ." said Sean. "There's enough here to keep us busy for months . . ."

"And, out of the foul weather . . ." smiled Lodie. "Do you know something about this type of work now, James?"

With his head tilted way back, attempting to see in the feeble light, he acknowledged, "I do."

Sean said, "I guess we'll be needing some timber in here . . ."

"Aye. For support and for laddering up ta reach the stuff."

"Much is deep in the rock, is difficult," added Vicente.

"Not a problem," smiled James. "I worked with the powder man. There's a bit of an art in controlling the stuff. I can teach ye double-jacking."

"Vicente, you checked any other caves coming in, or past this?" asked Sean.

"Only a little. Could be gold there, maybe cannot see it so good. I work here, where I know what I see."

Lodie continued to walk around, looking up. "We must be in the middle of the mountain. I doubt anyone would even hear much of us working in here."

Sean muttered, "This range is pretty big for this to be the middle. I want to be cautious. We still need to be seen fair regular down on our own claims."

"Agreed." James nodded.

"But with weather this foul, nobody goes at it every day," contested Lodie.

"Maybe we only come on the worst of days," answered James.

"And how do we explain the timber?"

Sean suggested, "Perhaps we can say it's for a sluice system."

Lodie frowned. "That'll work for some of it, but we're going to need some pretty large beams."

James looked away from the walls. "I've got an idea there. We don't need the beams yet, just more ladders and scaffolds for now. Vicente, ye've got a pile that should be in a bank over there."

He shrugged. "I can only take a little at a time."

Lodie looked thoughtful. "Well, what's already dug is yours alone. But it does present a problem for all of us." He hesitated. "Why don't we just claim this?"

Sean shook his head. "Lots of reasons. We don't want folks crawling all over us. We don't want to have to guard it all the time. We don't want one of the big companies buying all the land around us and swallowing it up. If this thing don't play out and gets really big, I'm sure the government is going to demand the mineral rights. I say we work it as fast and long as we can before we say anything."

"I've been at the land office a fair bit lately looking for a place ta homestead. I'll poke around and see what the status of the land is here."

"I like Vicente's banking idea," began Lodie. "What if we banked the bulk of it in San Francisco?"

"You're thinking big!" Sean scoffed.

"Sacramento's closer," added James.

They all looked at one another and grew quiet.

Sean shrugged. "Sacramento it is."

And that had been the gist of it, James thought as he shivered in the damp darkness. He peered over the edge and watched Lodie add a shot of whiskey to their tin mugs. It *was* cause for rejoicing. But at what cost to Vicente? His heart felt like a leaden orb in his chest and he grieved deeply for loss of family all around, Vicente's and his own. He wrestled with feelings of estrangement, shame, regret.

He attempted to push the pieces of his past aside, but, here in the quiet, the ghosts surrounded him, tapped him on the shoulder, and laid at his feet images he renounced. Suddenly they became present and living and real again. The sight of brother Lachlan, the youngest and kindest of them all, his leg mangled beyond repair. Mam's eyes pleading with James not to leave as she clung to him, her short self not nearly reaching his shoulder. His four brothers huddled in conspiracy to hide him on a colliery train leading far away from Greenock. Pap's staunch Presbyterian beliefs set aside to mislead the authorities.

He remembered brother Tom gave him his new shoes, brother Dooley his coat, and Gerald three pair of wool socks as they stole away that night. He recalled clinging to each article until it fell apart, as if each one represented the last thread to his family. His final memory of Mam was of him holding her face in his large hands, crooning to her that he would be all right, wiping her tears with his thumbs. And Pap . . . whose last words to him had been a mournful, "This, should na ha been yer battle. I . . . should ha fought sooner . . . harder." He wondered if his parents still lived. To contact them put them all at risk.

Beloved unreachable faces haunted his dreams. His demons. Vicente's story churned them up. He blamed his own temper as the demon catalyst. But he would do it all again. Never stomach tyranny in any form. The wealthy MacFie's arbitrary despotism strangled Greenock for generations. Oppression never died out on its own; this he knew. He felt the familiar fire burning in his chest as he promised himself aloud, "*My* children will na face this, ever. No rich, overstuffed lords will they bow ta. No threats ta life or livelihood will they suffer nor allow others ta suffer. And they will stand on their own strength."

His plan demanded this land, this time and place for him to build a life of self-sufficient stability. Charlotte, and Justin, too, would be secure once his sweat and ingenuity produced the farm to allow him to answer to no man but himself and God above. But in order to realize that plan, he must go below and begin the building with these good men. Vicente, he vowed, would have his steadfast loyalty and protection.

He felt a chill on his face. Spilt tears absorbed the cold wind.

CHAPTER 9

San Francisco — 1853

Sunday afternoons meant leisurely activity, pleasant diversions from the rigors of big business, toiling on farms or in factories, even schoolwork. The salt air, warmed by the sun and cooled by a breeze, wafted pleasantly through the open carriage as twin black horses clopped their way down the weathered wood-plank road leading away from the old Mission Delores.

Dutton imagined this as just such a jaunt. Father intended it to appear that way. Mother stayed for afternoon tea at the secularized Mission, now a popular resort. Dutton glanced back at the gleaming two-story adobe structure crowned with clay tiles. Its open balcony settled high above the huge cathedral doors flanked by enormous columns. Families strolled in the covered walkways of the adjoining buildings, once home to novices and padres. He searched distant faces, seeking familiar ones, his view interrupted by the blur of buggies rolling towards the former sanctuary. He turned away and listened to the horses' hooves noisily hammering the creaky timbers.

Carriage rides sufficed as the fashionable pastime. Other than the Mission, driving about town, or gawking at magnificent homes such as theirs, Point Lobos drew crowds to the shore to view the sea lions lazing about the rocks. Dutton liked riding horseback across the sand dunes but he couldn't fathom the point of admiring such noxiously foul smelling beasts.

The judge seemed in a pensive mood, he noted. Sitting quietly, Dutton enjoyed his position in Father's confidence. He felt important, even worldly, at his young age secluded in the carriage, bound for seedy parts of the waterfront. They chose a convoluted route, to be seen in areas appropriate for a Sunday drive — trotting by Happy Valley, the home of breweries and boat builders, sawmills, flour mills, and foundries. His father invested in legitimate business interests here.

Dutton frowned. He decided to break the silence. "Father? I know you said the best place to hide is in the open . . . but why must we hide? You've met with Mr. Brannan many times before."

His father gave him a wry smile. "Largely because Mr. Brannan apologizes to no one for his actions. Not even to God. Do you remember the newspaper articles about him?"

Dutton did remember. It was reported that Sam Brannan sailed to the Mexican territory of Alta California aboard the *Brooklyn* in hopes of claiming land for the Mormon Church and relocating 240 of its settlers in a place where the United States held no jurisdiction. He carried with him the antiquated printing press of his profession and a complete flour mill. Upon arrival, Brannan discovered his destination of Yerba Buena occupied, the Mexican War over, and the American flag flying high at the Presidio. Eyewitnesses claimed an irate Brannan cried out, "There's that damned rag again!"

Allegations of financial improprieties arose and Brannan's leadership was called into question by his Mormon brethren, who demanded court action. California's first impaneled jury trial issued a verdict of not guilty. His relationship with Brigham Young faltered when he failed to persuade him of California's superior climate, land, and water. Young preferred the seclusion of Salt Lake City. The two leaders exchanged heated words and, upon Brannan's return to San Francisco, he soured his congregants' vision of their alternative in Utah.

He went on to publish the newspaper *The California Star* as well as establishing two flour mills and a hotel, and building a fine house. He opened a general store in Sutter's Fort. Despite the efforts of Sutter to stifle news of the discovery on his New Helvetia, Brannan was credited for releasing this kraken to bolster business. Running through the streets of San Francisco with a jar filled with gold flakes bellowing, "Gold from the American River!" enticed a flood of customers, enabling him to open more stores. He began buying land in San Francisco. Sutter eventually plunged into debt to Brannan, amongst many others.

Sacramento's development also fell under Brannan's influence when he advised John Sutter's son that the town would never prosper on his father's original land grant. He convinced him to move the new city three miles north beginning at the embarcadero, and to sell city lots to retire the debts. They hired lawyer Peter H. Burnett, the future first governor, for a large percentage of the gross proceeds of lot sales. The junior

Sutter commissioned army engineer Captain William H. Warner and his assistants, Lieutenants William Tecumseh Sherman and Edward O. C. Ord, to survey and plat. Sacramento's growth began, Brannan's association with Sutter, Sr. ended, and he collected influential partners on his path to prosperity. Brannan proceeded with plans to establish Yuba City.

Though he no longer recognized Brigham Young's authority, he continued to collect "the Lord's tithes" of ten percent from his prosperous flock. Eventually, Young sent an apostle of the church to make a formal demand for "the Lord's share." Brannan agreed it was indeed the Lord's money, and, as soon as he received a receipt signed by the Lord, he would pay it. Brannan resigned from the church.

Dutton's father told him, though not detailed in any newspaper, Brigham Young dispatched his glorified gunmen, the "Destroying Angels," to collect the debt by force. Brannan's bodyguards arrested their flight in the desert.

Escalating San Francisco crime and a particularly vicious attack in the Chilean quarter brought Judge Dandridge and Sam Brannan into the same arena. Brannan raised his voice to denounce the Hounds and organized the outraged citizenry against them, forming the Committee of Vigilance.

The Hounds originated as part of a regiment of New York volunteers sent to fight in the Mexican War. Arriving at war's end, they were recruited by merchants as bounty hunters to return runaway sailors to abandoned ships at the break of the gold rush. They began as a self-appointed military presence, called themselves the San Francisco Society of Regulators, and acted as a deterrent to the most violent crimes. Some deserted in favor of the minefields, others fell under the influence of the Know-Nothing party, whose strong platform in Boston and New York waged a campaign against Catholics and foreigners. Many owed allegiance to the gangs of New York's Bowery and Five Points, members well trained in the fighting, stealing, and terror to which the group evolved.

All this, Dutton knew. At the time, shopkeepers and businessmen beseeched his father for legal advice. The Hounds extorted "protection" money: those choosing not to pay were beaten, robbed, or burned out. They wandered into taverns demanding the best food and beverage and told merchants to bill the city. Attacks on foreigners were largely overlooked and encouraged by Know

Nothing politicians. They became a savage mob and, until the brutal attack at Clarke's Point, remained unrestrained.

Sam Brannon, Captain Beezer Simmons, and Alcalde Dr. T. M. Leavenworth called for an assembly of citizens at Portsmouth Square. A large sum of money was raised for the destitute Chileans, and over two hundred and thirty men volunteered as armed deputies. They began immediate pursuit. Most of the gang fled the city, though twenty members, including their leader, Sam Roberts, were captured. Judge Dandridge sentenced Roberts and another leading gang member to ten years imprisonment, lesser terms for the rest. To Dutton's father's fury, the Know Nothing politicians overturned the convictions.

Brannan developed a kinship of justice with the judge. The Committee of Vigilance wielded heavy influence and Judge Dandridge became a trusted supporter and advisor. Dutton struggled to unravel the complicated relationship between the two.

"Samuel Brannan is not always judicious in his boldness. The Vigilance Committee, at times, must take unpopular action to remain effective. I must maintain a certain public impartiality," said the judge, breaking Dutton's reverie of the past.

"But, Father, if we have the law, why do we need the Vigilance Committee?"

"A delicate balance to be sure. I say this to you only, in confidence," intoned the judge. "When innocents are attacked, justice must be swift to show our intolerance of such behavior. An immediate sentence and execution succeeds at thwarting future crimes of the same nature. Many believe the first law is that of self-preservation and most citizens are not bothered if a gunman kills another gunman. But a bystander?

"Our institution's ability to convict and punish the guilty is inadequate. Convictions by jury are difficult to obtain. Prosecutors must convince all twelve jurors, witnesses often move on by trial time, and cash buys a convincing defense."

"Aren't you the law?"

"In many ways . . . on the bench and off. Cases such as a land dispute, a cheated business, disagreements in dissolving partnerships — even vice crimes — present more details, evidence, technical issues. Sentences are more easily rendered. The law prevents chaos and maintains a consistent standard. Violent uprisings should be put down, which makes my committee work necessary. Decent people needn't walk in fear on the streets. As you shall see, I often aid law enforcement in making certain perpetrators end up in jail, and thus my courtroom."

Dutton frowned. "Is Mr. Brannan as powerful as you?"

His father laughed. "A great deal more so, I dare say! And I begrudge him not one bit. Dutton, it's advantageous supporting a man with means and vision, one who doesn't lose sight of goals. Equally important, be aware of your own goals and know when to cut ties. Understand to whom you attach yourself at all times — be ready to advance or retreat at a given moment. Mr. Brannan is a strong ally. Difficult situations demand blocked paths be cleared; as long as you don't lose sight of the purpose and act in a moral manner, it is right." The judge gave a tiny smile. "Look carefully at any tycoon, man of power, builder . . . His greatest creation is always . . . himself."

Dutton nodded slowly. He looked up, noticing their surroundings change as they neared the waterfront. Taverns and gambling houses wedged tightly together lined the downhill street. He saw a disheveled figure with lank, shoulder length hair waiting under a saloon sign labeled *Shades*. The man carried a polished wooden box under one arm and began moving towards them as his father curbed the carriage. Dutton slid to the center of the seat as the man ducked his head and boarded.

"Y'Honor," the man growled lowly. "If'n you likes, 'round the corner is quieter."

The judge snapped his whip in the air and turned his team onto the next street. A warehouse loomed large, locked up on Sunday. They stopped there.

"I trust you made the connection, Tolliver?" asked his father.

"As always, sir. Our friend says to give ya this first." Tolliver handed over the box. "A gift, he says."

The case was weighty, finely honed mahogany with brass corners and latch. On its cover, a shiny brass plate displayed engraved initials *W.D.* Dutton craned his neck and peered as his father lifted the lid. Nestled in a bed of red velvet was a .36 caliber Colt Navy handgun.

The judge breathed in deeply, picking it up and brandishing it in the light. "My! Now that's a fine piece. Dutton, have a look — I'll have to retire my old dragoon. Marvelous! Lighter, more balanced, more accurate," he said, admiring it.

"There's a card, Father."

"So there is." The judge held up the small card, squinting and read aloud. "In appreciation of service. S.B." He nodded, obviously pleased, returned the pistol to its resting place and handed the box to Dutton. He looked up at Tolliver expectantly.

Tolliver reached inside his coat and pulled out an envelope sealed with wax. Judge Dandridge took it and tore it open, immediately immersed in its contents.

Dutton discreetly studied Tolliver's appearance. He wondered that his father didn't object to this unwashed specimen. His shirt appeared to display part of today's lunch, his stringy hair was unkempt, and he sported several days' growth of beard. Dutton tried not to stare at the man's badly mangled earlobes. He thought perhaps the injury was due to a fight of some kind, but, as both ears were affected, the affliction seemed deliberate.

Tolliver turned suddenly, his catlike yellow-brown eyes fixed on Dutton, startling him.

"I hear you're off to a big fancy school soon, boy."

His composure resettled, Dutton answered, "Yes. Harvard. Next year when I'm fifteen."

Tolliver shrugged. "Long ways to go by yourself."

"I have a friend from Sacramento whom I

shall room with."

The judge shuffled the pages. He studied the last, folded the lot, and placed them in a valise on the carriage floor beside Dutton. He withdrew a piece of paper and a sharpened graphite implement, and dashed off a few quick lines. Without looking up, he enquired, "Do you have contact with Charles DeMone?"

"Dutch Charley?" Tolliver scratched the patchy whiskers on his chin. "Yeah, I kin find him, I suppose."

"I'd like a word with him. Ask him to meet me Tuesday morning at my office. He's to tell my secretary it concerns the Firehouse Committee." He folded his response and handed it to Tolliver. "This goes back to our friend."

Judge Dandridge sat back and folded his hands over his large midsection. "Have you anything else for me?"

The man jolted forward in his excitement. He grinned. "Thought you'd never ask. Sydney Duck, name of Billy Wharton — 'twas him and his what broke into the Foundry owner's house and robbed it. Saw him trying to fence the wife's jewelry. They meet at the *Magpie*. His two thugs, Donavan and Spears, is the ones that beat that stable boy last month and grabbed two horses."

Dutton watched his father purse his lips and nod with satisfaction. Then he reached inside a vest pocket and produced two small pouches of gold dust. He hesitated, then tossed the larger one to Tolliver, who eagerly snatched it from the air.

"I'll inform Sheriff Hayes immediately. That's all for now."

Tolliver tapped his brow with two fingers in salute, and hastily departed. Dutton watched him disappear around the corner.

"That should make a nice headline. I'll be seeing those thieves in court by the end of the week." He turned and patted Dutton's knee. "A fine day's work."

"Isn't Mr. Tolliver a Hound, Father? Is he dangerous?"

"Former Hound. He received leniency from the court for his crimes by cooperating in efforts to bring the other gang members to justice. Since then, I have found he has certain useful skills. And, like a good dog, he sees the value of loyalty to one master."

"What happened to his ears?"

"Hmm. Sign of his time prospecting, I expect. Miner's law deals with thieves decisively. First offense, the perpetrator is flogged. Second offense, they cut the ear lobes as a warning — much like marking a bad horse. Third offense is hanging. I

166

suspect Tolliver reformed somewhat after the second offense."

The judge released the carriage brake and snapped the reins. The coach lurched forward.

"Time to pick up your mother. Furthering your education, young man, as far as other business is concerned, it appears Mr. Brannan will be running for state senate and would like my support. He also has a buyer interested in my lots in Yuba City. Do you think we should sell?"

Dutton squinted his dark eyes as he considered. "Well . . . we haven't owned them very long. Has there been any change in the market there?"

"Good question. No. Not recently."

"Then, I would say not yet. Not until demand increases. Can we lease the land?"

"Yes! Capital idea. One fellow wishes to open a feed store. I'm sure once settled and profitable he will see the wisdom of a higher price."

Dutton looked squarely at his father. "How will you support Mr. Brannan if you are being discreet?"

"By using my contacts and influence to round up sufficient votes. I needn't bang the drum myself." His father gave him a stern look. "Always be aware of a man's weaknesses, Dutton, whether he's a subordinate or a colleague, and don't expect that you can change them. Remember, you can only expect to pull from a man that part of him that already exists."

"Are you speaking of Mr. Tolliver or Mr. Brannan?"

"Both," the judge stated firmly. "Both."

CHAPTER 10

Marysville

The most awful day in the history of days happened with everyone in the entire world mad at her. Worse yet, she waited alone on her cot in the bedroom for Mother to tell Da. Charlotte sat on her hands, her feet swinging rapidly back and forth above the floor as she contemplated her side of events.

Charlotte loved school, loved everything about it. Arithmetic was easy. She scratched her chalk rapidly on her slate to finish problems fastest and shot her hand eagerly in the air when done. Real books, not primers, fueled her imagination. History, Justin's favorite subject, brought true stories to life. Da said to learn it all well because opportunity came from learning.

When Mrs. Timmons delivered her baby, Mother substituted for two months. Charlotte's new friends advanced her education. Watching older girls with their coquettish ways fascinated her, but older boys teased younger students when not attempting to impress one another. She considered them a nuisance. Even so, she found their antics amusing. Mrs. Timmons returned to the classroom and now Mother assisted only a few days a week.

Most exciting of all, she and Justin walked to school by themselves. No longer the new kids or the youngest, she felt a growing kinship with town children and friends riding in from nearby farms. One day soon, she and Justin would be farm kids; they told the most interesting stories.

This morning Charlotte listened to Ella Louise talk about a new baby goat. The girls huddled together in groups chatting and waiting for Mrs. Timmons to ring the bell. The schoolyard was littered with books held together with straps, lunch buckets, discarded caps and jackets. Boys of all sizes chased, kicked, or threw balls in any available space. Some raced around a well-worn dirt path encircling the schoolhouse. Charlotte found it difficult to hear conversation over noisy shouting, or even the tittering gossip of the older girls nearby.

"Well, Trinka — that's our goat — had twins, but one died. It was really tiny."

A sympathetic chorus of "Aww's" arose

from the girls. Charlotte had already cuddled the kid, seeing as she *was* Ella Louise's best friend. She wanted to chime in, saying how darling it was, but it was Ella Louise's story and her goat so she politely kept mum.

As she listened, she glanced around, studying the clusters of calico and the array of ribbons of every color donned by the other girls. Most dresses were store bought — some faded by the sun and harsh lye soap washings, but a few of the more stylish ones Charlotte recognized as Althea's work. Sally Morton wore the bright pink gingham she had admired as Althea added a fine crocheted collar to it. She scrutinized how beautifully the fabric draped, nearly to the ground, since Sally was sixteen. Charlotte deliberated whether the sophistication of longer skirts when she reached twelve would be worth the restricted movement. As it was, she excelled as one of the fastest runners in school, and, with her dress reaching just below the knees, it left her high-buttoned shoes unhindered. She envied the boys' uncomplicated clothes — simple cotton shirts and wool trousers with suspenders — far more practical for moving about.

"Twin goats ain't common, and the one that's left is really cute," Ella Louise said.

"She's got a big brown splotch on her side, 'bout the color of sand. Pa said I could name her Sandy. She still runs kinda funny, all stiff legged."

"Oooh, can we come see it?" asked a small town girl named Mary Alice.

"Sure. She's real sweet, too. She'll sit right in your lap."

Charlotte ducked as a ball whizzed past her head.

"Sorry!" yelled a classmate as he scooped up the errant ball and chucked it across the lawn to a friend. Sally Morton's group of older girls squealed in protest. Charlotte kept looking up, waiting for the teacher to call them in. It did not appear as though Mrs. Timmons had arrived yet.

At first, she didn't notice that the shouting boys seemed louder than usual, or that they massed into a tight circle. Only when she heard cries of, "Fight . . . fight . . . fight!" and saw girls abandon their cliques did Charlotte follow the curious spectators. She pushed her way through the crowd, poked her head under the arms of taller onlookers, and peered into the ring. She felt her face flush hotly as she saw Justin at the worst end of a brawl with the much larger Lyle Hibbitt.

A cloud of dust powdered the air as the

combatants' feet scuffled the dirt. A hard thud resounded as Justin hit the ground. He leapt up and lunged at the older boy's middle, attempting to knock down superior size with momentum. The boys slid around loose soil in an awkward dance. Lyle tried to sling Justin away, but he held on fiercely. Justin buried his head against his opponent's shoulder and managed a couple quick jabs to the ribcage. Enraged, Lyle pulled back and swung hard — landing a solid punch to Justin's cheek and sending him sprawling. Lyle stood above him now, his chest puffed out, waiting for Justin's answer.

Charlotte was livid. The stern, tight set of her small jaw so mimicked her father it was almost comical. Her heart burned within her chest and she squeezed her fists tightly by her sides. She steeled herself and went in.

Charlotte weaved her way in quickly from amongst the other children, ran straight to Lyle and gave him an outraged kick in the shins. First one pointed shoe, then the other, punished him at a fast and furious pace, giving her the look of a mad hen scratching the dirt. As he hopped on one leg to escape her sharp blows, she changed feet and pummeled him all the more. She said not a word, but continued a determined onslaught of strikes moving forward. Lyle tried to catch her head with his palm and keep her at arms' length, but quick she was at darting under his defensive moves and going in to wallop his shins further. Her comparatively small size allowed her to fight like a yellow jacket.

Lyle's face showed the wear of rage and confusion.

"C'mon, Charlotte, you know I can't hit a girl!" he protested.

She continued fighting forward as he backed up, removing himself from the assault of her flying feet. He looked up at the sound of the crowd snickering. A few of his friends catcalled to their comrade, teasing him, and some even cheered Charlotte on. Lyle hesitated . . . and she landed a particularly painful blow to his kneecap.

"Ow!" he bellowed and grabbed his knee with both hands. She then stormed up to the beleaguered bully and stomped on his other foot with all her might. He lost his balance and fell over. The ring of children erupted in laughter at the sight of the schoolyard champion lying on the ground in disbelief and the small girl with her hands planted on her hips puffing and panting like an over-boiling teakettle.

Charlotte glared at him, daring him to get

back up. Lyle was a slow thinker at best and couldn't decide what to do in his humiliation. Even his best friend ran forward and threw her little arm triumphantly in the air as she scowled at him.

He was visibly shaken by the laughter. Until today, Lyle reigned as the strongest and most feared. Charlotte sorely bruised his ego far more than his smarting shins and ankles. He leapt up. And ran. Ran as far away from the sound of his shame as possible.

Mrs. Timmons realized she had arrived at the end of some childish scuffle and moved to reassemble her wayward pupils. Her bell pealed its brassy complaint at an urgent pace. Students disbanded and moved away before they forfeited precious recess time.

Charlotte stood her ground, huffing with exertion and cooling rage. As the crowd dispersed, she looked up and saw Justin — his hair disheveled, dirt smeared across his bruised cheek, and a trickle of blood at his nose. And he glowered at her with a white-hot temper that burned through her like lightning bolts. She gazed at him, trying to make sense of his demeanor as the others filed into the classroom. She moved towards him, her hand outstretched. He stared her down as she reached for the hand at his side. He abruptly turned and stalked away.

"Justin?" she called after him. He did not speak. Her heart nearly burst at his rebuff. She would not cry, not now. Later, alone, she could allow herself that weakness. She straightened her dress, clenched her jaw, held her head erect, and walked to class.

Justin refused to acknowledge her for the rest of the day, and did not wait for her after school. Both were remanded to stand in the corner for fighting. She felt the irritation from classmates losing outdoor privileges before school for the rest of the week. And she had disappointed Mrs. Timmons.

She possessed no allies. Da was home mid-week preparing for his upcoming trip to Sacramento and now she awaited his judgment. Her mother expressed horror at her less-than-ladylike demeanor. Althea attempted to soothe Justin's wounded pride, but he continued to avoid her. Charlotte's agony grew with waiting. Agitated, she hopped off the cot and tiptoed into the hallway. She crouched at the railing of the stair and peeked down into the foyer of the boarding house, where she heard her mother angrily informing Da of her exploits.

She saw Da's back, but not the telltale signs of a smile on his face as he listened to Emma chastising her behavior. He promised to have a word with her. She turned and darted back into the bedroom, quietly closing the door. James climbed the stairs to their room to find her sitting on the edge of the bed staring out the window.

"Where's me mighty mite?" he teased. James walked over, threw up her arm as if declaring her champion, and grinned. Her eyes filled with tears.

"Hye, now, what's this?" he said gently as he sat on the bed and pulled her into his lap.

She said sullenly, "Justin is mad at me."

"Ah . . ." he inclined his head as if he understood. "Unfortunately, friends aren't always as grateful as we'd like." He kissed the top of her head. "But, that's not why we act — not for gratitude, but because ye're friends."

"But *why* is he mad at me? Lyle's the one that hurt him!"

"Well, darlin', we men like ta think we can take care of ourselves. And that it's our job ta protect women folk. I think Justin wanted ta prove he could take care of Lyle himself. He's probably afraid of looking silly in front of the other blokes. But it sounds ta me as though Lyle is the one who looked silly."

So far, his words did little to comfort her misery.

"Child, ye did right. The times ta fight are few, yet a battle that shoulda been fought can never be revisited. The opportunity ta say something important by taking a stand, defending one ye love, is gone and ye can never get it back. Especially in their eyes.

"Understand though, that when it's done, leave it on the battlefield. If ye carry the hurt with you, ye carry the wound, and if ye don't lay it down along the way, it may never heal. But if ye walk away at the wrong time, think about this: who was it did ye leave stranded ta fight on alone? Winning is standing up ta wrong, even if the world tells ye that ye lost. Now . . . Justin will come round in time. I, myself, think ye were very brave. *I* am very proud of ye." He dabbed at the tears on her face with his sleeve.

"Really?"

"Aye, very much. It is good ta know I have one so brave ta watch *my* back."

"And I will, too."

"I'm sure of it. Now come on down ta supper and if Justin happens ta be sulking, ye let him be with it."

She hugged him and they walked downstairs to dinner, hand in hand.

Emma raised her eyebrows when she saw them. "Did you have a chat?"

"Of course. She understands perfectly."

CHAPTER 11

Sacramento — Late 1854

Nearly forty miles separated Sacramento from Marysville as the four partners began their eighth deposit trip. They left before dawn, armed in case of trouble, but James felt generally more relaxed this time. Each man continued making small deposits at the bank in Marysville to keep up the pretense of their river claim, but the bulk of their efforts lay under a carefully concealed tarp in the wagon. Bales of hay were stacked on top with a few farm tools tossed in convincingly to the side to avoid the interest of thieves. Sean and Lodie rode up front. James and Vicente followed on horseback to keep watch from the rear of the wagon.

James's research in the land office revealed little information about their cave. A corporation out of San Francisco owned an option on the surrounding land, but it remained unclear if they or the government possessed mineral rights. Unable to ascertain if the option had expired, the group voted to keep mum for now.

The foursome built an expansive framework hidden inside the mountain. Rain fell hard enough throughout the winter to discourage activity in the area. The partners made impromptu showings at their claims and then commiserated about the weather with miners in the dwindling camps. Otherwise, they spent every waking minute in the cavern.

During the quiet ride to the city, James mulled over options. Looking at his companions he realized each possessed a far-off look of his own.

He knew the group's secret endeavors made them secure, if not comparatively wealthy men. After months of hard labor, tough decisions loomed large. Close to extracting all within reach, he cautiously resorted to blasting powder, but only during thunderstorms so as not to call attention to their activity.

A great shuffle of ownership arose with miners who teamed up to form small operations, dotting the countryside for a whisper in time. Huge outfits claimed enormous granite yields requiring massive equipment and backing. Veins pursued often petered out, forcing a search for more profitable areas. James and his partners explored surrounding chambers in their hidden mountain cell and found little gold. Certain more existed, they knew removing it required more men. Could they trust additional partners? Should they attempt to claim the cave and sell it? Or did they simply walk away? Unanswered questions of ownership suggested problems.

James glanced ahead at Lodie, the ideologue. Once Lodie liked a plan, no amount of argument shook it loose. In fact, James mused, he remained stuck on *this* particular idea ever since the day he initiated the partnership by the banks of the Feather River. Months of digging allowed Lodie to work out details of a scheme spinning in his mind, occasionally throwing out tidbits for James's review.

James nudged his horse to a trot and came alongside the front of the buckboard.

"Sean, how about spelling me a bit at the rear? My back is nagging at me."

Lodie pulled the team to a halt.

"Yep. If Rusty don't mind."

"He'll be relieved ta have less weight on him."

"Ah, if we weren't about serious business, I'd be makin' this big fellow dance," said

Sean, admiring James's bay. Even powdered with road dust, the horse's deep reddish coat gleamed with a groomer's practiced perfection, showing off a well-muscled physique.

James dismounted and handed him the reins. "Say the word and I'll find ye a mount nearly as handsome." He pulled himself up to the seat beside Lodie as Sean turned Rusty to take his place at the rear with Vicente.

Lodie grinned at him and clucked the team to a start. "Hope you're expecting Emma's matchmaking to take — I've spent the last hour quizzed on what kind of notions ladies like. He's determined to do some shopping in Sacramento."

James smiled. "It'd be good for the both of them." His focus zeroed in on Lodie. "I wanted ta finish our conversation from yesterday. I cu hear the wheels whirling in yer mind from back there."

"My goals have changed, my friend."

"So ye said. Are ye sure ye want ta give up the idea of farming? It is what ye know."

"That's the trouble with it. Probably why I got restless on the farm in Pennsylvania — too isolated and every season more of the same. Matilda's attached to town life now, and, I've got to say, I like the activity. I want to be a part of something bigger."

"I fancied us as neighbors, ye know."

"Plenty of opportunity in town, James. We could still be partners."

"Och. The heart wants what the heart wants. I suppose ye know yer own."

"Robert's toddling around; Matilda's expecting another child. I want to leave them a different sort of legacy. People *like* me, and trust me — there's value in that. The store is merely a beginning. It keeps me in touch with everyone in the know. I want to plan town growth — to leave my mark."

"Sounds like politics."

Lodie shrugged. "Maybe."

"So, how far up yer sleeve do I need ta be looking?"

Lodie laughed. "I'll always watch out for friends. But . . ." He paused. "I do need you to cover for me. The assay office won't open for at least an hour after we arrive. I need to go down to the docks and make inquiries of the shipping clerk on duty . . . and run a few personal errands."

"The docks? What's that about?"

"Perhaps nothing. But if I'm right, could be the start of something big. You'll be the first to know."

James nodded. "What about Sean and Vicente?"

"I'd rather wait until I have something solid. No sense in stirring things up unnecessarily. Tell them I'm off on banking business — which is true enough."

The remainder of the journey passed quietly. James felt moisture in the breeze. The day was cool, clear, and inviting. A few small clouds, rounded and fluffy as sleeping lambs, spotted the sky and drifted towards the expanse of the Sacramento River. The road arched to a familiar bend and Sacramento stretched out before them. The means to their ends lay covered by the tarp in the wagon behind them. The future lay ahead.

Lodie pulled the team to a stop in front of the assay office, passed the reins to James, and hopped down, taking off at full stride in a way that suggested he intended to avoid conversation. He mumbled a hasty "Meet you back here shortly" in James's general direction.

Sean shoved his hat to the back of his head as if to get a better look at his retreating partner.

"Now where's he off to?" he demanded. "We got a fair bit of unloading to do here. Ain't exactly light work, neither."

"He'll be back before heavy lifting begins." James looked unconcerned.

"Yeah, well . . . sometimes I get the feelin' he thinks he's the brains of the outfit. Runs off; don't tell nobody nothin'."

Vicente shrugged. "He restless. Like he worry he miss out on something."

"Psshh. Leastways he could bring back some coffee or somethin'."

Smiling, Vicente caught James's eye and gave Sean a reassuring pat. "I have five children. Each one think he work harder than the other four."

James laughed. Sean looked irritable.

"Each one think he smarter than the other four, too," he continued. "But they know, *I* am the smartest." He thumped his chest. "Lodie no bother me. Cos *I* am the smartest here, too."

Sean whipped around to stare at the grinning Vicente. James burst out laughing.

"Oh," Sean relaxed. "Okay, I get it." He nudged Vicente in the ribs. "You might *be* the smartest."

Vicente turned to hide his smile. "*Sí,* is all I am saying."

The window shade of the assay office rolled up suddenly.

"Ah, we could be in luck," said James moving towards the door. "Looks like he's opening early."

Sean began tossing bales aside and turning back the tarp. "Might as well start pullin' bags down. Lodie'll pay me in whiskey for doin' his share."

As the day progressed, James noted luck prevailed all around. Scoring their largest deposits, their payout on the ore would be complete in two days time. Shopping for items hard to come by in Marysville filled his time, and James dutifully checked off Emma's requests. He assessed Lodie was in a particularly jovial mood during dinner at the hotel and he observed him happily making up his disappearance to Sean in shot-glass form. It did not escape James's notice or concern to see Sean's high spirits lead to a bender at the bars. He waited up until midnight worried that, cash on hand and carousing in his soul, Sean might succumb to the gaming tables. Finally deciding Sean capable of dealing with his own conscience, James turned in.

The next morning, James and Vicente settled in to a late breakfast at the hotel when Sean arrived, bleary eyed. James glanced up from sopping the runny yellow yolks on his plate with a crust of bread.

"Coffee," Sean muttered as he slumped into the nearest chair.

"Eggs are good," said Vicente, lifting his cup in a mock toast.

"Ugh . . . not yet." Sean rubbed his temples. "I swear . . . I gotta learn to take it easier first night out."

Vicente shrugged. "This you say every time."

"One of these days I'm gonna mean it."

"Lodie still sleeping it off?" James inquired.

"Nah, he turned in early. Where is he, anyway?"

"He's not in the room?"

"I thought he was with you."

Vicente looked at James, puzzled. "We no see him."

Sean let the steam from his coffee tantalize his nose. "Maybe he went back to wherever he slipped off to yesterday. What was that about?"

"A man's business is his own. We'll run inta him 'round town eventually." James's tone remained calm even as his mind raced with questions — queries to remain unanswered until their rogue partner was found.

Late in the day, Lodie pulled up to the hotel in James's buckboard, grinning like a Cheshire cat. The tarp used over their ore now covered an even higher pile. He yanked the brake, hopped down, and joined them on the porch, ignoring the small bags signifying check-out resting at their feet. He clapped James on the shoulder and stated, "First, I need a drink. Then, I'm going to need a favor, lads."

"Back inside then." James tossed the bags in the wagon. "Make it quick; I want ta get on the road."

Sean hustled to the bar for four beers and, even as he plopped mugs on the table, he blurted out, "What's in the buckboard?"

"An investment," Lodie announced. "One I need to move on quick." He winked. "I got to thinking . . . we're doing very well, but we're reaching a crossroads. We're all itchy to begin new ventures, but the work's so steady it's hard to think about stopping until we've tapped it out."

"Getting close . . ." offered Sean.

"Exactly. And, I'll tell you . . . I, for one, will miss how lucrative this job's been. If not for Vicente here, none of us mighta stumbled into this kind of luck on our own."

Vicente nodded slightly.

"So, I'm wondering . . . what else can I do to pull down this kind of money?"

Sean cut in eagerly, "You thinking more partners and expansion, or moving to another site? 'Cos I'm hearing about big doings in French Corral."

188

"I'm ready to quit digging."

Sean looked astonished. "Meaning?"

"What makes more money than gold?" Silence and blank expressions caused Lodie to continue. "The supplies to get the gold, that's what! How many times have we said this ourselves? So, I acted on it."

Lodie took a quick swig of beer and wiped his mouth on his sleeve. "Yesterday, I checked the day and time of the next supply ship in." He tapped a pointed finger on the table. "It was *this* morning! So, I took almost everything I had in the bank in gold coin, put it in bags, tied them to my belt, and got a rowboat. I rowed out the Sacramento River to meet the steamers coming in before dawn. I bought up every pick, pan, shovel, axe, or any other tool they had. For cash they *happily* discounted things, turned around, and left." He laughed heartily. "I can hardly move my arms. I was rowing back and forth past full light."

James smirked, realizing Lodie's original plan took a wild turn. Vicente shook his head, and Sean cried, "But what now? What'll you do with it all?"

"First off, I'm getting the heck out of town before the merchants realize the goods they're waiting on are gone. I rented a second buckboard from the livery — gonna take it to Nevada City. Of all places, they're always shortest on supplies. It's a baby of a town and after November's fire burned a huge portion of it, I figure it's a bargain time to put my stake in. I'll sell out this batch before I can get it unloaded. I'll double, even triple, what I had in the bank."

"But then . . . you come back to the cave?" Vicente asked.

Lodie shook his head. "Nope. I'm a merchant now, fellas."

"Like a whole store? If you sell out that quick, what are ya gonna stock it with?" Sean persisted.

"This is my stake to get me a reputation. I see a repeat performance coming on in the near future, maybe San Francisco for a really big score."

James chuckled. "Seems yer scheme took on a life of its own. Lucky ye were na shot nor drowned."

"Oh, that dang rowboat was rocking. Crossed my mind more'n once — with all that gold tied to me, I sure as hell'd sink straight to the bottom if I capsized. I felt Neptune's pitchfork poised right under me," he laughed.

Sean gawked at James. "You knew about this?"

"Only that Lodie was closer ta the changes

we all know ta be comin'. He's the first ta begin, is all." He looked back to Lodie. "What would ye be needing of us?"

"One of you to drive the other wagon back. And we leave now. I don't want a riot or anyone to figure out who's responsible for the shortage. It'll make it easier for me to come back and do this again."

James glanced at the others around the table.

Vicente shrugged. "I will drive a wagon."

Lodie slapped his knee. "Good! Sean, you riding with me or Vicente?"

Sean glowered at him.

Lodie motioned. "You come ride with me. We'll talk."

"Guess that's right. Looks like you and James got things straight at any rate." He grumbled, "I don't like bein' kept in the dark. I thought we're equal partners." He moved towards the door.

James shook his head. "He'll be fine," he said lowly. "But while yer at yer explanations ye might remind him gently . . . Vicente and I have plans, too."

Lodie sighed. "I'll remind him — so does he. And he ought to start thinkin' on it."

CHAPTER 12

Near the Bear River

He brushed the hanging twig out of his line of sight. From where James squatted beneath the willow oak, the valley rolled down and unfolded before him, the vista open for miles around. For over a year he studied it, walked it, and observed all creatures inhabiting it — in all seasons, in all weather. Whenever he managed to steal away to think and plan, he came here.

He shared thoughts with no one, but made subtle inquiries. He checked county records, cut into trees, studied roots, soil, growth patterns, bird migrations, and, most importantly, native migrations.

A gentle breeze ruffled the auburn hair now touched with early gray in spits and spurts. His pale-green eyes surveyed his purchase with pride. He bought the best sections, though not consecutive, planning to tie the rest up later. His savings he poured into the land like the wooing of a woman and the dreams that went along with winning her.

He pried secrets from the soil, the culmination of thousands of years of the ebb and flow of nature. James headed into the dense line of trees, exploring the southernmost border of his property where the elevation began a significant drop. He frowned as he studied a watermark — mud and brush appeared along the trunks at heights over twice his own. He reached for the highest twigs, broke them, and examined them with great scrutiny. He gave a short, sharp nod — he had suspected these findings. As improbable as it seemed from the miles he stood from the American River, he knew the area up to this point flooded — an event oft repeated.

As he followed the trail of water-smudged trees, it astounded him to see where the river course ran. The experts he consulted about this phenomenon possessed a standing history on the land. The Nissenen told him an inland sea annually covered nearly a hundred miles of valley. Others scoffed at the warnings of the natives, calling them ignorant beasts disguised as men.

But James listened and observed firsthand the results of rainfall and melting snow combining forces each spring to rush down the mountains overwhelming the American, Feather, Yuba, and Sacramento Rivers and their smaller tributaries. Icy streams high in the Sierra Nevada ravaged the rock, breached it, and swept away metallic particles embedded there, sifting and floating them away to new locations.

Until natural forces temporarily reclaimed it, this was an enticing valley — a deceptively green desert coerced into producing some of the finest farmlands by the manipulations of men. His research found the navy's twenty-five-year-old pronouncement of the navigable ease of the Sacramento River by large vessels — guaranteeing prosperity for the area in shipping, making surrounding land even more appealing to farmers.

Crops played into James's plan only to the point of his own self-sufficiency. He needed grazing land and enough acreage to produce fodder, and so wagered on a few cheaper land parcels to supplement feed for livestock. He intended to breed, train, and sell horses, mostly working stock broken to carriage, freight wagons, even stagecoach. He dreamed of raising fine saddlebreds such as the ones he had handled on the Vernon estate, but, being a practical man, he focused on demand.

The stingy Scot lived no better than his neighbors, but smarter. He squirreled away every penny, calculated every risk, took patiently measured steps towards his goal, and never took a second drink — a trait attributed as much to self-discipline as his frugal nature.

Reaching a point of higher ground, he turned and gazed northward to the spot he selected for the house. He visualized the proximity of the first barn, the corral, and the smaller cabin for Althea and Justin. He pictured surrounding fields of alfalfa and hay, training rings, and a tack shed. Satisfied with the mental view of his little realm, he began to calculate a work schedule to bring it into being. He sighed and dusted his hands off on his pants. A troublesome thought crossed his mind. Emma was disappointed.

The location was the ideal bridge between mines and mining towns, farms and river traffic — though not nearly close enough to Marysville for Emma. He suspected she felt her modern comforts stripped from her with each step forward. For Charlotte and Justin the allure of independence balanced a change in schools, so he was relieved not to throw the entire family out of balance.

Glancing skyward, he realized the day grew late and returned to the grove of trees where he left Rusty tied. Emma did not expect him for supper, but he thought it best to arrive early.

The ride home afforded him time to think. His master plan called for practicality. With such a substantial investment in the land, and more needed for livestock, James hired out his blasting skills to independent mines. Emma fretted about the dangers of explosives, but he scoffed at her fears, reminding her that his experience with double jacking came long before he stumbled on to the Vernon estate, and he was nothing if not cautious. His well-known circumspection led growing corporate mines such as Empire and the North Star to call on his expertise when questions arose in their operations. He pointed out safety issues and noted problems with efficiency he recognized from his years spent in Northumberland coal mines, and his later travels leading him to silver mining. With each job grew his reputation as an authority and the work was a welcome supplement to his income.

James slowed Rusty from his easy canter to a trot as he left the Browns Valley Road and approached D Street. As he rode for the boardinghouse, his eye was drawn to a familiar figure slumped against a post on the steps of Murphy's Tavern.

"Whoa." James halted in front of Sean's sleeping form — his hat pushed cockeyed on his head where his face pressed awkwardly against the pole, his jaw slack, and his mouth open in a drunken snore. James dismounted and looped Rusty's reins over the hitching post. He squatted in front of Sean and involuntarily turned his head from the reek of whiskey.

James patted his friend's cheek and called firmly, "Sean! Sean!"

Sean's eyes popped open, though James saw nothing there but the dullness of alcohol. He waved a hand in front of him, and Sean frowned, swatting at his hand.

"Leave me 'lone," he grumbled, closing his eyes.

"Sean! It's James. What are ye doing here, man?"

"Waitin'."

"For what? It's nearly dark and getting cold. Sean!" James jostled his shoulder and Sean's head rolled back and then snapped forward, his eyes searching James's face.

Murphy pushed open the door of his bar, clutching a piping hot mug of coffee.

"Try this," the man sighed, handing it to James. "I cut him off over an hour ago."

197

"Thanks," James waved the cup under Sean's nose. "Easy," he said as Sean lurched to grasp the cup.

Murphy hesitated. "You know, it ain't my call to monitor how many times a fella wants to get pie-faced, but this here," he nodded at Sean, "is gettin' to be a regular thing."

"I appreciate it. I'll take him from here. There now, sip at it, Sean. It's hot." James looked up at Murphy. "Did anything set this off?"

"Nope. No more'n usual. Been around town a lot more lately. Not that I'm tryin' to listen in, but he's takin' on some work up near French Corral. Maybe, sooner the better. Idle hands and all . . . Uh oh."

James followed Murphy's gaze and turned to see Althea standing at a short distance behind him.

"Yep. I'll be leavin' you folks. Need to get back inside." Murphy retreated.

"Thea?" began James.

Sean sat up at the mention of Althea's name.

Althea stood stiffly, her hands clasped in front of her. She looked down at Sean as he leaned against James's shoulder.

"I've been waiting for some time, Sean," she said quietly. "We were to have supper together; had you forgotten? I worried something had happened to you."

Sean dropped the mug as he struggled to stand. "I . . . no. I didn' forget. The time . . ." He trailed off, looking at the sky as if startled at its darkness. "Wha' time is it?"

"Too late for supper, I think." She said firmly, "Good night, Sean."

James ducked his head under one of Sean's arms, grasped him around the back, and stood, nearly lifting him.

"Thea, let me take him across the street ta the hotel. I'll walk ye back."

Althea nodded. She went to where Rusty was tethered and pulled the reins loose. "I'll lead the horse."

In a matter of minutes James joined her on the street in front of Hammond's hotel. He reached for the reins and they turned silently towards Flanagan's boardinghouse.

Looking straight ahead, she asked, "Is he all right?"

"Dead asleep."

She nodded. "I've been wondering whether or not I should speak with you. It's difficult because we're both friends."

James studied her stalwart expression. "He's a friend. Ye're family."

She smiled wanly. "It is not my place to

199

ask him not to drink, but I am concerned."

"It does seem ta be more of late."

"If only that were all of it."

James cringed inwardly, hoping he did not know what she was going to say next.

"I hear . . ." Althea hesitated. "I hear that he is gambling. Quite a lot."

"Och, the man has na been himself lately. He seemed a wee lost when Lodie quit and moved ta Nevada City."

"You left as well."

James stopped. "The cave played out. There was na a choice but ta move on ta other work. I have. Vicente also. I thought the two of 'em were on ta French Corral together."

She turned to face him. "They are. But Lodie has the store. You're moving to the farm soon. Vicente is planning to open a saddlery as soon as he can manage it." She sighed. "Even my business has expanded. I'm taking a corner in Lodie's Emporium as well as the general store in Marysville until I can start my own shop. Don't you see how this makes him feel? It's all of us, James."

James saw the pleading look in her soft, blue eyes. "He's spoken of it, then?"

Althea nodded.

"How . . . how serious is it, between ye?

Sorry ta be blunt."

She blinked hard, and looked away. "Fairly so, I thought. He's very kind and caring. Justin adores him." She took a deep breath and straightened. "But I have to be concerned about stability. Especially where my son is concerned."

"Of course." He understood her stance. She had grown up from the flighty girl he once knew. "I should talk ta him."

Althea started to protest but James held up his hand, "For his own sake — or his and mine anyway. He gave us all our start; it is na right to leave a friend floundering on his own."

"Thank you." She looked up at the boardinghouse ahead. "Mercy, I'm keeping you from the family. Emma will skin one of us."

James laughed. " 'Tis true. Run and tell them I'm here while I bed Rusty down. And Thea . . . don't worry." He winked.

CHAPTER 13

Nevada City, April 1855

A turgid transformation seized the Sierras and its valleys. Every town, mining expedition, farm, and family roiled in a state of construction and change. The rise of new prosperity grew from those with vision, ingenuity, and determination. Althea resolved to cut herself a piece of that pie.

While riches in individual gold endeavors waned, bounty in land and business opportunity abounded. Thousands of transient placer miners abandoned played out pursuits and moved on, chasing new strikes and rumors of strikes. Others sought a more settled life by securing steady work in growing corporate mines backed by capitalists or formed their own smaller outfits. Towns bustled with optimism for the future, capturing the spirit of new Californians. Professionals and families drawn to the area pushed out seedier elements. Althea rode the swell of occupations desperately needed for a culture eager to grow in sophistication.

Enticing Emma with shopping for the nearly completed farmhouse, Althea pried her from an ensconced position in Flanagan's boardinghouse in Marysville to an excursion at the Hotel de Paris in Nevada City. Eager for Emma to adjust to the move, Althea was pleased to see that James wisely left the convincing up to her. As she engaged Emma in the details of decorating the first home to call her own, James fielded questions from Justin and Charlotte sitting beside him on the front seat of the spring wagon. An overnight stay in Rough & Ready gave respite from a tedious journey with two rambunctious children. James promised to take them to the farm for a few days while Althea introduced Emma to the splendors of town.

Upon approach, they carefully navigated the rising twists and turns of terrain leading to what appeared to be a haphazard planning of a town. Nevada City was built on seven hills, its population spread over Piety, Prospect, Boulder, Aristocracy, Buckeye, Nabob, and Lost Hill. Crowned by Sugar Loaf Mountain and adorned with tall rows of pines behind the queue of businesses lining each ascending street, a certain regal beauty emanated from the town setting. James stopped the wagon before the twin wooden bridges crossing Deer Creek, the left bridge leading to a more elevated Broad Street, as opposed to the primary thorough-fare of Main Street on the right. Silence prevailed in the wagon as the family took in the sprawling vista, the gurgling rush of the creek, and the heady scent of pine — much of it freshly cut on the edges of the little civilization.

Emma broke the reverie. "How lovely," she breathed. She leaned forward from the back bench and gently touched her husband's shoulder. "James, what an enormous change!"

Althea smiled at James's understated, "It's growing in the right direction." He slapped the reins and pointed his team towards the Broad Street bridge. "Let's get ye ladies checked inta the hotel and I'll take these two hooligans out ta the homestead."

A duet of cheers arose from the children as the horses clopped over the timber structure. Althea gave a panicky squeak as she watched her son lurch over his seat rail-ing to peer into the water. James reached deftly behind Charlotte, grabbed Justin's coat, and yanked him down.

"There will be none of that," he growled.

Althea sighed with relief. "It seems some vigorous outdoor time is in order."

"I can find plenty of tasks for them, rest assured," James intoned. "Perhaps we shall start with painting the house?"

Justin turned to look back at the creek. "But why is the water so dark and cloudy?" he asked.

"Because a lot of men are doing a great deal of work in the rivers. It's from the sluices; it will clear in time."

Althea pointed out several fine houses along the route to a delighted Emma, telling her what she knew of the residents. As they reached the corner of Broad and Bridge Streets, they faced the less than imposing front of the small Hotel de Paris with its simple whitewashed plank façade — a meager single-storied structure.

"The name is a bit pretentious, I must say!" retorted Emma.

Althea laughed. "Silly, it is named so because Madame Falcot hails from Paris. It's a sentimental gesture. You'll see the Virginia House, the Galena and Dubuque House, Buckeye Lunch and Bakery, the Iowa Store, the New York Hotel, and so forth."

James gathered the luggage after helping

the ladies down from the wagon. Althea tugged on Emma's arm and pointed at the front door.

"Look! Read the sign — *'Hotel De Paris, by M'me Falcot & Co. Wishing to keep this establishment in the same manner as those of San Francisco, we will endeavor to deserve the patronage of persons visiting the house, which will be as comfortable as possible. Travelers will meet with a good welcome at all times, with good, neat rooms and CLEAN BEDS. Furnished rooms by the Month, Week, or Single Night. Wines and Liquors, the best French brands.'* Charmingly put at any rate." Althea nudged Emma. "And, from what I hear, the food is the best in town."

The simple furnishings of the small rooms radiated cheeriness with colorful coverlets and floral hooked rugs. The headboards and wardrobes in each room were painted with soft gold and green hues. After a perfunctory look around, and admiring the matching hand-decorated blue scroll designs on the basin and large porcelain pitcher of the washstand, Emma declared the room, "Quite satisfactory." The two women happily sent James and the children on their way.

Embracing the brisk April air, Althea guided Emma down Broad Street's moderately steep descent. Scaffolding adorned most storefronts in various stages of brickwork and painting. Crews of workmen bustled about freshly constructed wooden sidewalks. A wagon full of large pipes intended to supply water to homes and businesses strained under its load as it advanced uphill and turned on Pine Street. Stepping around several large covered pallets recently delivered from the Nevada Brickyard, Althea and Emma faced the loud clanging of sledgehammers in front of Lodie Glenn's Emporium. The man himself stood barking orders to men perched in front of his second-story windows, banging away on iron shutters. Lodie had turned to pick up a bucket of bolts to send up to the men when he noticed his expected guests.

With a grand sweeping gesture he bellowed, "Welcome to Nevada City, Queen of the Northern Mines!"

Emma received the first embrace and exclaimed, "Why, everything is so fresh and new looking."

"Yes. Well, fire tends to have that effect on a town. An unfortunate way to initiate change, but then again I wouldn't be the beneficiary of such a bargain on my Emporium. Truth be told, I think old Jenkins got the itch to move further north and begin a new store — Nevada City's getting too tame for some tastes. Fire damage made him a much more reasonable negotiator. What do you think of it, ladies?" Lodie stood beaming at his creation.

"Magnificent, Lodie!" Althea answered, looking over his progress. "It's much larger than I remembered."

"Good eye. Since the gambling house next door burned to the ground, I offered the new owner, a tobacconist, a fair price for part of his lot and expanded fifteen feet before I bricked the outside."

Emma turned to see the small, nearly completed shop next door as two men labored to put in a plateglass window. "A far better neighbor than a gambling den," she remarked. "Did your store suffer much damage?"

Lodie nodded. "Lost the storeroom completely, some of the roof, and most of the wall I expanded; a lot of smoke damage inside. The whole thing might have come down if not for the proximity of Deer Creek. It's a comforting location at the bottom of the block, but I'm not taking any chances. I'm here for the long haul. What you see now is a fireproof building," he stated proudly.

"Truly?" asked Althea.

"Absolutely. This town's seen four major fires in four years. I'm organizing a fire brigade — we shop owners don't like rebuilding. We're all turning to brick to keep the fire from spreading down the street out of control. And see here?" He pointed to the crew working on the second-story shutters. "Iron; same as the front door — all imported from Pacific Iron Works in San Francisco. Seals all the apertures and keeps the fire out." He winked at Emma. "There's progress for you."

"I must say I'm impressed. And eager for the inside tour so I can officially become a customer," said Emma, smiling.

"Music to my ears. Watch your step here; still a lot of construction going on."

Lodie guided them around a scaffold where a man stood painting trim on the doorframe. Inside, they admired the gleaming counters polished to perfection, each row its own little avenue of merchandise. Shelves stacked to the ceiling were tracked with a brass railing for sliding ladders.

"Matilda's marked some catalogues that might interest you, Emma. She'll show you what we have on hand. And, before I forget, tell James the stove he ordered has arrived. Althea, I imagine you'd like to see your workspace? You're such a draw in Marys-

209

ville I've decided to put you at the front of the store."

"Lovely. The light will be much better there."

"Oh, no you don't. No shop talk!" called Lodie's wife from behind a far counter. "They're mine first!" She eased down from her stool with some difficulty. A grinning Matilda approached with open arms. "It's been far too long since our last visit!" she cried, hugging them both.

"Matilda, you look positively ready to pop," laughed Althea.

She rubbed her protruding belly and rolled her eyes. "Robert never weighed on me like this one. I seem to be carrying higher this time."

"Must be a girl," offered Emma. "Either way, it appears your joy is not far off."

"Let us hope," said Lodie. "I'm not a patient man waiting for babies. Well, my dear, I see you have our customers well in hand, so I'll leave you and attend to those men in the hardware section."

Matilda lowered her voice. "From the looks they're sending our way, I'd say they're more interested in the girls here. You might mention only one of them is available."

Althea's face flushed.

Emma exclaimed, "Mattie!"

Lodie shook his head. "Forgive her, Althea. She bores easily in her confinement."

Matilda cocked her head. "Well?"

"Let's look at rugs," Althea stated firmly.

"All right. But don't think this conversation is over. We have much catching up to do," Matilda warned.

Emma relaxed her refined, straitlaced position and settled back into the dining chair with the air of a contented cat. Althea swirled the last bit of sherry left in her glass and smiled at her friend.

"Feeling as decadent as I am?"

"Oh, Thea! The squab was delicious, the pear tart — divine. I'm feeling a bit guilty. Here we sit in candlelight at this charming little hotel and James and the children are no doubt cooking by a campfire. I do hope they'll be warm enough."

"To them it's adventure. They'll be so exhausted from chores and exploring they'll sleep like bears in winter. And don't forget, we did our part today. We accomplished a great deal outfitting the house and the cabin."

Emma winced, then giggled. "I hope James thinks so when he sees the bulk of our packages."

"Oh, it's not so bad. The rugs are large, yes, and the kitchen crockery is heavy, so it looks like more than it is. Besides, nearly half of it is mine. We've made all the curtains, linens, quilts, and pillows ourselves. We should be comfy upon the move," Althea reasoned.

"You're forgetting the rocking chairs we ordered."

"You said James would enjoy those most of all."

"Well, he can't very well sit in four of them at once, now can he?"

They looked at each other and burst into laughter.

"He'll be relieved that I'm feeling better about leaving Marysville," admitted Emma.

"As am I. And grateful — this is a grand opportunity for Justin and me. I can't thank you and James enough for making room for us."

"Don't be silly. We've been a family for a long time now. I couldn't bear the isolation of the farm without you," Emma scoffed.

"This move comes none too soon — as Justin grows, so does his energy and propensity for mischief. A boy his age needs space to run and hard work to wear him out. The Speekses and the Clearys are settled and not too far; it'll be nice to have good neighbors."

Althea glanced around the cozy room at the other diners; dim lighting allowed for a certain amount of privacy. A soft flicker radiated from the fireplace centered on the wall behind her and small brass sconces shaped like twisted vines provided delicate illumination above each of eight tables. White and black pastoral toile curtains draped elegantly back from the windows on the opposite side offered bright notes against peacock-blue walls. Two groups of four businessmen occupied the larger tables, a man supped alone at the table in front of them, and a married couple sat near the door. She looked up to see Emma watching her.

"I would needle you by asking if you note any prospects, but Matilda did a thorough enough job of that this afternoon," quipped Emma.

Althea sighed. "She certainly did her best. I'm sorry to appear aloof, but it's not an easy time. I'm not searching for a husband. Sean . . ." She stopped abruptly.

Emma reached across the table and gave Althea's hand a gentle squeeze. "You did the right thing. Sean . . . well . . . you can't save a man from himself. Matilda wants to be helpful."

"It would not be seemly to add to the gossip. Sean is kind and good. I'll not add to his burdens."

"Of course, you're right! He's still our friend. I know you aren't seeking a suitor, but it can't hurt to be . . . open to one, perhaps?"

"It is far too soon to think of such things and utterly unfair to Justin."

"Understood. However, your ignoring a town full of single men won't stop them from approaching *you*."

"Then I'm grateful for all I have to do to get my business off the ground. Lodie is giving me a great deal of leeway in purchasing fabrics, trims, and notions and *that* will establish me with suppliers and creditors before I open my own shop. For now I can hide in my work."

Emma gave her a level gaze. "You mean hide right there in the front window of Lodie Glenn's Emporium where countless men pass each day. Lodie is no fool, Thea."

"Oh, good Lord! I had not even thought . . ."

Emma sat back with a look of satisfaction. "I'll wager Lodie did. He somehow finds a way to profit on his kindnesses."

Althea started to protest when she noticed

214

the couple at the front of the room rise to leave. As the woman stood, she turned and smiled in their direction and Althea realized she seemed vaguely familiar.

"That hat . . ." she began, as the couple approached.

"What?" asked Emma.

"It's Emily Rolfe," Althea whispered. "We met her this afternoon at Lodie's — you admired her hat."

"Oh!"

Stopping beside their table the woman began, "I'm terribly sorry to intrude, ladies, but I wanted to take the opportunity to introduce my husband."

"Not at all, Mrs. Rolfe. How very kind of you since we are so new to town," answered Emma.

The dark-haired woman smiled prettily. "Call me Emily. This is my husband, Tallman." She nodded to each of the seated women in turn, "And this is Emma MacLaren and Althea Albright, dearest."

"How do you do," said Mr. Rolfe, giving a curt nod.

"I believe your wife said you run the newspaper, *Young America*?" asked Althea. "How exciting."

"Right. I was the former printer for Sam Brannan's *California Star*. Nevada City's charm and progressive nature convinced me to choose it for my new endeavor," said Rolfe. "This town attracts so many professionals, I'm sure you'll like it. And you, Mrs. Albright, word of your talents precede you. Emily's eager to become one of your first customers. You've saved me a pretty penny on trips to Marysville. I'll be certain to give you a mention in the paper once you've begun."

"That's very generous. Thank you."

"Not at all. We support one another here. I understand from Mr. Glenn you have expansion goals in the future. Perhaps you will place some advertising at that time."

Althea laughed. "I look forward to that!"

Tallman Rolfe gave a quick sharp bow. "It's been a pleasure. I hope to meet your families soon."

As the Rolfes turned to leave, Emily called over her shoulder, "I'll look for you at the Emporium, Althea."

Althea and Emma waved good-bye.

"They seem like lovely people," said Emma. "I dare say you'll get some business from her."

"Hopefully her friends as well."

"I knew Lodie set his sites on an upscale town when he chose Nevada City. Grass Valley is so overrun by miners. I'm glad the children can attend school here instead, but it's so far from the farm to travel every day." Emma sighed.

"They'll be fine. Speaking of the children, what shall we do with our child-free day tomorrow? I suppose there's a bit more shopping to do."

"Hmm. Yes. I think perhaps the milliner. I'd like to find that hat!"

CHAPTER 14

The Farm, May 1855

Three days until moving day. James bowed his head under the faucet, pushed down the pump handle, and gratefully let cool water splash over the back of his neck. As the stream slowed to a trickle, he shoved it again. Standing upright, he tossed his head, slinging wet hair away from his face. He mopped his ruddy brow with a handkerchief, then jammed it in his back pocket as he sat on the adjacent trough to rest. The towering woodpile beside the house bespoke his morning labors. He looked around the courtyard, pleased with his surroundings. The farm was ready for the family.

James took great satisfaction knowing his vision was a lifelong work in progress. The Speekses, the Clearys, Vicente, Lodie, and especially Sean became part of his home in shared toil by pitching in to frame the major buildings. He created a large quadrangle, loosely closed in by the house, the cabin, a large barn, and tack shed next to the corral. He would erect the first training ring next.

Althea and Justin's clapboard cabin contained two small rooms and a loft, a smaller version of the farmhouse with its large front porch — both with sturdy front doors on leather hinges. James built the farmhouse for growth, intending to spend all available time procuring, training, and someday breeding stock. Painted a cheery pale yellow with stark white trim, the farmhouse's large main room housed the kitchen, the dining table, and a sitting area by the fireplace. Doors placed on either side of the chimney led to each of two small bedrooms. James knew where to expand in the event of the arrival of another child, though he resigned himself to remaining largely in a household of women.

Inhabiting the farm to James's north was an irascible character possessing few friends and disliking most neighbors by the name of Bracuus Donovan. Donovan kept to himself and preferred others do the same. The man stopped in to see about the ruckus during James's barn raising, declining the invitation to stay for lunch despite Lodie's most charming entreaties. James chuckled to himself as he remembered Sean's remark:

219

"Must need to get home to take a pull on his jug of bile."

Rusty nickered from inside the barn. James turned to see an older black man sitting quietly on a swayback mule.

"How do," said the man, tugging on his tattered hat. His face displayed deep creases from age and sun. A hand carved pipe hung from his mouth, producing a thin line of wispy smoke with a sweet aroma of cured tobacco.

"Hallo," James responded, "Caught me dreamin'. I did na hear ye ride up."

"Dint wanta interrupt your work. Benjamin Jones. I got a farm northeast of you, next to the Donovan place." He pointed with the pipe, then returned it to his mouth with a clacking sound as his teeth clamped it.

James extended his hand, "James MacLaren."

"Looked like you be fixin' to move in soon. Brung you some supplies." He untied the sacks hanging from his saddle and handed them to James. "Some cornmeal, sugar, coffee, a ham."

"Well now, that's very kind. Won't ye come inside and we'll see if my work on the stove'll do something with that coffee?"

Benjamin nodded and dismounted. A

slight man, he moved slowly but deliberately. "I'd save the coffee; got my pipe for now."

"I'm sorry I canna offer ye a seat yet . . ."

"Porch be fine."

James placed the bags by the door and they sat looking out on James's handiwork.

"You done good, s'far." Benjamin nodded slightly. "What you aim to raise?"

James ran his hand through his damp locks. "Stock, horses. Mostly working brutes, trained ta wagon and such. Ye're my neighbor, then? I've seen corn fields as I pass; is that what ye grow?"

"Hogs. Corn is to feed 'em mostly. Chickens, too, if you interested. Good laying hens."

"My wife will be very interested, thank you."

"Children?"

"A daughter. My wife's kin live here as well. She has a son. Yerself?"

"Mine done growed and gone. Wife's gone home to Jesus. You'll like the ham. You need bacon, side meat — I sell that, too." Benjamin stood and stretched. "Won't keep you from work. Wanted to say welcome."

James rose, "I thank ye. I hope ye'll come back when I've some chairs and perhaps ye can tell me more about the land around here. I'd be interested ta hear how the weather has treated ye the last few years."

Benjamin pointed his pipe at James and nodded. "You do same. Quiet at my place. Would like the company." He mounted the swayback mule and tugged his hat good-bye.

CHAPTER 15

French Corral

"Magnificent!"

James shouted over the thunderous hiss of water hitting rock. Standing next to Sean at the edge of the precipice, he witnessed the power to simultaneously destroy, create, and discover. Exhilarated, he watched as the four enormous hoses trained on the mountainside generated great clouds of red foam that all but concealed the cliffs. Whoops and cheers resounded from the men controlling the forceful hydraulic arcs blasting away earthen hills and sending rock hurtling down steep slopes. James gazed out on miles of ditches and the network of flumes trailing down the natural contours of the terrain, laden with alluvial treasure. Swarms of miners hustled along, checking sluices, clearing the corridors of larger debris, and collecting gold-veined granite chunks. Far below on the canyon floor, men veiled by the mist descending like rainfall loaded wagons to haul to stamp mills. The air was heavy with the scent of wet minerals and red clay.

"Ta move a mountain of rock, change the flow of a stream — bend a force of nature to yer will. That's power," James yelled above the roar of the water.

Sean grinned and jerked his thumbs in an upward motion, signifying the need to move higher and away from the rumbling cascade. James nodded and followed him to a more elevated landing, further back from the brink. Sean wiggled a finger in his ear as if to clear the noise.

"That's a bit better. Told ya this was a sight to see."

"I had no idea. The magnitude of this is . . ." James shook his head, looking out on the crumbling landscape and the flurry of activity on the valley floor. "I remember that fella Chabot a few years back, took ta ground sluicing over on his claim on Buckeye Hill. He had thirty, maybe forty feet of hose washing from the bank ta the bottom of his diggings in a wooden box . . ."

Sean walked closer to the edge and stood with his armed crossed. "Ya know, before your time a bunch of boys dug a ditch from Mosquito Creek to Coyote Hill — at least a mile long. Later, they took water from Little Deer Creek and channeled it to Phelps Hill. They had rightful claim to the ditches. Owners took what they needed to uncover their claims, and then sold water rights to other long-tom owners below that had claims there. First in line folks paid top dollar — four bucks a day for the water. Down below them, next set of claims paid a little less. Fellers at the top made money coming and going — that being the beginning of the big idea *here*. Direct the stream against the bank, water carries through deep cuts to a flume; then a system of flumes with sluices, the riffles catching gold; then the water gets discharged into some ravine.

"Chabot never thought to pressurize it though — or direct the stream. Edward Matteson, there . . ." Sean pointed down to a man in a broad-brimmed hat barking orders to the hose operatives, "He put a nozzle on it — first one he made outta canvas about half an inch around. Didn't take him and his partners over on American Hill long to figure a small stream under pressure did the work of several men. They went to a two-inch canvas nozzle . . . then he got with the tinsmith. Each contraption I see come up here gets bigger and bigger. There's talk of switchin' out the canvas hose with iron pipe."

Sean waved above and behind them. "We're in the process of constructing three dams at higher altitudes using stone blocks, faced with wood. Vicente is up there with a crew workin' on it. The idea is to form and feed a reservoir before the next snow's melt. The water'll hold there to keep the work going in the summers. Without water, we're nothin' up here. You can only imagine the volume used. Then we'll work on adding more flumes. North San Juan Ridge is showing a lot of promise, too."

"Ingenious ta divert that kind of force away from flooding the farms and towns. Ye say there's blasting work ta be done?" asked James.

"There's a few prickly places along the bluff. I told 'em you were their man."

Sean squinted, watching the men working far below. "You know, moving all this rock there's hope that one of the main rumors is true — that all this gold came from one big vein, one mother lode. Blasting at these mountains every day, you stand here waiting, watching, wondering if you're gonna see it appear right before your eyes."

"What about the theory some ancient volcano blew the bits all over?"

"All guesses. Only fact I know is gold is

still heavier than anything else whether you're swishing it around in a pan, rocking the cradle, or rushing it down a flume."

Sean gave James a sideways glance and continued. "Back off these rivers where you find a spot the watercourse *used* to run . . . there's pockets. I've learned to dig deep, my friend. On my time, in places companies got no interest. I dragged the old rocker up here. No reason to give up the search or the promise. There's still a world to find here. I know it. Can feel it. That's my future."

James looked surprised. "Are ye talking about a new claim, or just odd bits?"

"Oh, I stumble on a chunk or two every now and again. Sometimes some 'corn gold.' That's my savings plan."

"Isn't it all supposed ta go ta the outfit?"

Sean stroked his moustache while contemplating his answer. "Depends if I stumble on my time or their time."

"Ah." James smiled. "Splitting hairs."

"If I have to fight for it while keeping the hairs from being split from my skull, then yeah, it's mine, brother. They sometimes send me wildcattin'. Sometimes what I find is useful to them; other times it's small enough to be useful to me. I'm talkin' stray bits, not 'tin cup diggings' where you can fill up once a day." Sean sighed. "I'm trying to recoup what I lost."

"From the cave?"

"Mhmm."

James sensed there was more to this conversation than money. "How much did you lose?"

Sean stood with his hands jammed in his pockets and stared fixedly at a point somewhere in the mists. "All of it. Leastways, pretty much all of it."

James saw Sean cut his eyes over as if to gauge his expression before blurting, "Hey, I don't need nothin' from nobody."

Silence hung above the rolling hydraulic rumble.

"She ever ask about me?"

So that's what he's on about, James thought. He sucked in a big breath, weighing his answer.

"Look. I know. I know I threw everything away with both hands." Sean gave an odd grunt and looked down at his feet. James felt sad for him, for them both, really.

"She told me she didn't want to raise *two* kids. I can't blame her. But I do miss her. Justin, too," he continued in a rush.

James placed a hand on Sean's shoulder. "I wish I knew how ta answer ye. She's plunging inta her work . . . living in it. Not so different than you. She and Justin have settled inta the farm; he likes the school in Nevada City."

"Sometimes I find reason to be 'round town — when school lets out. I want to still be friends with Justin. I need him to know it wasn't all because of his mother, y'know? Treat him like a man. I hope Althea doesn't mind."

Sean held his hands up defensively. "I'm not trying to worm my way back into her good graces; it ain't about that. I dunno. I can't get the feel of tying myself down. Same time, I think I want that."

"I don't think she minds," James offered. "It means a lot ta Justin. He talks about seeing ye."

Sean sighed. "Damn. I always got to be fightin' something. Conquerin' it, pushin' ahead . . . I got too much warrior spirit . . ."

He looked at James as if his explanation made sense and rambled on, "Had to fight my way out here on the trail. Battled my way through the worst of the scum in '49. People'd kill you for looking at 'em wrong. A lotta cheats, a lotta thieves, and a lotta murders. Had to keep your wits about you all the time. Then our partnership . . . What the hell is wrong with me? I can't stay in one place — something out there is always calling. My old man used to preach on a thing not being worth having if it didn't take hard work — so, that I don't mind. Guess I ain't figured out what to do once the work is done. Gotta have some purpose, or I gotta move on."

James attempted to bring him up short. "Was there purpose at the tables, Sean?"

"Hell, no. Just a place to hide."

"Good ye know that. Now what are ye going ta do about it?"

Sean wagged a finger at him. "You got it — that warrior thing. You get a glint in your eye when somebody pisses you off, when something ain't fair — or you sense a liar. Hell, shoulda had you beside me at the gaming tables — lookin' at your face I'd *know when* to fold."

James cocked his head. "I see ye're dodging my question."

Sean laughed, picking up steam. "Okay. My deflated financial status has got me up here . . ."

"I thought twas yer sense of adventure."

"You ain't exactly moved on. What makes you cart yourself up here to blow up stuff? How come you ain't done with it all?"

"I'll admit ta a certain fascination with the process. Good golly, man! Look at the sheer power of this!" James spread his arms wide. "I'm invested in land, the homestead, and barns. I still have stock ta procure and more to build. I'm splitting my time."

"Ain't you got enough tucked away to cover that?"

"For now perhaps. Times are good — a man needs ta hold a fair bit back for the bad. What if something happens ta me — one of my brutes kicks me in the head? Where would Emma and Charlotte be then?"

Sean squinted at him. "I bet you still got the first gold pebble we ever found."

James smiled. "That I do. Still has yer tooth mark in it."

"Psh. Figures. Hey, you got a name for your place yet?"

"Aye. 'Thistle Dew,' " he stated proudly.

Sean laughed. "This'll Do? What kinda name is that?"

"Thistle D-e-w, ye pisser." James pointed a finger in his face. "And don't be mocking it; Emma named it. She thought it should remind me of Scotland. Labor of love, it tis, too!"

"And yet, you're still playing with the mines." Sean shook his head.

"I have friends up here, ye know. I love the building. Discovering. Creating. Ta see a man come up with a new idea like this. It's ideas — and the freedom ta execute them.

231

This is a thinking man's game. Look at ground sluicing." He shrugged. "Showed me how ta get water ta one area of the farm where I want it and can't get it, taking it from a marshy place. Making something from nothing. Making it better, without breaking yer back."

"Well, you and Lodie got that in common, both full of ideas. Lucky his didn't get him strung up. He took runs at those ships to stake his store — just short of being threatened by merchants in both Sacramento and San Francisco. He alternated his strikes, but they discovered who was responsible for their lack of merchandise and they weren't amused."

James nodded. "It hardly mattered. He was well staked and made his overtures ta the wounded shopkeepers. They couldna help but be friends with him in the end."

"See, now — that's where I say he ain't a fighter. Once they figured it was him, he sure as hell cut and run."

"He made his amends."

"That's what I'm saying. He's good at pulling everybody together to make 'em think they're all on the same side. Ehhh, Lodie. Always knew what he wanted from the start. Worked it and got it. Won't root him outta Nevada City for nothin'. He's a stroller."

James laughed. "A what?"

"A stroller. He'd like Hammond's mayor hat is what I think. Nothing wrong with that. He cares . . . wants everybody to prosper; he really does. Thinks he knows the best way to go about it and likes to be in charge. Kinda like a papa bear. Don't see him in a fight. He'd try to break it up, reason with everybody."

Sean nudged James in the ribs with his elbow. "He ain't got warrior blood like you and me."

James chuckled. "I'm glad ye've got us all pegged in our proper holes."

Sean scratched the back of his head. "Yeah. Guess I oughtta work at figuring myself out."

"Ye're doing fine." James winked at him. "Let's start making our way down. I hoped I'd see Vicente today. I could use some things for the tack room."

"Vicente's a loyal friend. Smart. Hard worker." Sean frowned. "He's gotta deal with folks that don't like Mexicans. Or lump him in with the damn Chinese. I guarantee you he knows how to sleep with one eye open. But don't you worry, I got his back."

James gave him a look of concern. "So I hear. He told me about a skirmish?"

Sean shook his head as they plodded their way down. "Idiots wandered into our camp, tried to rob him. Didn't count on me being close by. I watched them skim the outskirts of camp for an hour and then decided to make scarce enough to see if they'd make a move. Didn't wait long, either."

"Vicente says ye pulled a knife on 'em."

"Well, I got a bead on 'em with my rifle first; made 'em toss their weapons. Vicente tell you he keeps a bowie knife in his boot?" Sean laughed. "He pulled that thing out slow and deliberate. Gave 'em the meanest look you ever saw, mumbling in Spanish. Those boys thought he'd carve their livers. While they watched him, I pulled out that pig sticker I carry and planted it right between the younger one's feet. Pissed himself right there."

James chuckled. "Vicente's learned a few things. I suspect no one'll give him much trouble. Good for ye both ye stayed partnered up."

Sean grinned. "Feels good to see him walk a little taller, you know?"

CHAPTER 16

Sacramento Valley — Spring 1856

If James followed as the crow flew, the imperceptible rise in elevation from the bay through towns in the enormous floodplain was a mere sixty feet above sea level through the whole of the Sacramento Valley.

Officially, the flatlands situated downstream from Red Bluff equated to 247 river miles, if one counted the winding switchbacks from the Sacramento River's mouth. At midpoint he would find Sutter Buttes, a small, steep island of volcanic mountains providing a singular interruption in the plains as seen from Yuba City and Marysville.

The Feather River's meandering streams grew and forked into three distinct river paths and converged directly north of Marysville. Similarly, the Yuba River's northern and southern sections rambled into the stronger middle Yuba. Both rivers, at full strength, split around the town of Marysville and met below it, picking up the Bear River further downstream and eventually pouring into the Sacramento River.

In each tributary, naturally deposited silt built up over time and elevated the beds. As waters overflowed the stream's borders during floods, natural levees formed. In the rush of spring's melting snows, the waters overflowed barriers and water ponded between rivers, creating an expanse of water that appeared as an immense inland sea going on for hundreds of miles. Brimming with tule rushes and water plants, it hardly seemed temporary. Birds and wildlife grew accustomed to this ebb and flow of life. Humans moved to change the course and force of nature for underlying soil rich in mineral deposits.

Skirting the water's dry edges, James waded thru parched rushes like an original explorer, cutting a path with his scythe. As far as he could tell, the Sacramento was in normal times a beastly powerful river. He heard rumors that floods expanded it 120 times its size before converging with the American River above Sacramento. Well-watered farmlands became too lush when tributaries grew full, leading to engorged rivers with no hope of containing waters within their own banks.

He watched the wind play with the wild oats, tossing their fronds in a ripple effect in the warm breeze. Oak, sycamore, cottonwood, willow, and ash trees scattered the valley. James rode past waters full of fish, and often saw wandering herds of antelope, deer, and even elk grazing. Indian villages huddled by the water, years of observance teaching them to move on in migratory fashion. From a distance he rode along their camps; the village appeared smudged by a reddish hue from salmon strung up to dry near tule huts, creating an earthy crimson tone. There existed a rhythm of life here as natural as breathing, taking and giving back to the land in a respectful manner.

Only the peculiarity of the white man attempted to bend nature to his own will. James believed ingenuity did not conquer all: something or someone — bigger, stronger, and not controllable — always came along. Inexperience fooled a man into a false confidence where he no longer heeded signs of disaster.

As he often did, James stopped to visit Benjamin Jones on his way home from Nicolas, an important town for him. South of Marysville, Nicolas established itself as a ferry crossing as far back as 1843 and grew prosperous with river transportation for passengers and freight. The new American Hotel built there brought transients and traders. The busy mail station at Nicolas, as well as Wells Fargo, relied on the location for its relay of horses. A smile crossed James's face the first time he watched the march of horses to the low-roofed shed for rest. Filled with envy, he observed their replacements escorted to the front of the stagecoach. He planned to provide their future stock and word of James's growing horse farm, Thistle Dew, spread.

He reflected on their earlier conversation. James found Benjamin oddly soothing to talk to. Steady, wise, and even-tempered in all things, his qualities amazed James, knowing the difficulties he had faced in his lifetime.

Born into slavery, Benjamin's wife and children were auctioned away from him as it suited his master. When the master died, he found himself bequeathed as property to the man's son. It galled the son to the core of his soul to own another human being, but he could not afford to free Benjamin. The small plantation fell to disrepair and most of the other slaves were sold to keep the owner solvent. The son entered into a contract with Benjamin: for $3,000 worth of labor, he allowed him to buy his freedom.

At the end of the term, they parted with a handshake. After an exhaustive search for his family, Benjamin suffered beatings and accusations of being a runaway — and never located his children. He learned his wife had died. At fifty-eight years of age he traveled to the West to find a quieter, more isolated way of living.

Benjamin's journey presented a new perspective for James, whose own past left him feeling trod upon by wealthy employers. Seamus, the stable master at Lord Vernon's estate, chastised James's lack of gratitude for a job, hot food, and a kind master. His life in California brought work he loved, beautiful land, and opportunities unavailable in Greenock. There, countrymen were riddled with rich aristocracy. Seamus often chided, "You're a lot more cocky now that your belly's full. Don't forget who's filling it." James obeyed, followed rules, but the taste of being owned lingered.

Comparing his life to Benjamin's, he felt ashamed. Yet, he harbored deep anger for those who forced him from his home. Benjamin counseled gently, "There be a time for anger. Time for fighting if you got strength and power; if'n you don't, got to know when to stop."

James joked. "Talking philosophy now, are we?"

He had let the subject drop, but his nightmares returned. Injustice stirred a part of him he thought buried only to resurface in the darkness of night terrors. To rid himself of this curse, he reasoned he must follow Benjamin's example of a tranquil life. This he set out to do, but just the same he tutored Charlotte and Justin, "Never let another own ye in any way. Be ready and able ta leave on yer own steam. Raise yer voice and stand up."

James recalled discussion on the current drought. Benjamin had sat on the porch with his pipe and James with a tall glass of cool water as he continued his quest for understanding where he stood with nature.

"It's hesitant I am, ta take on any more stock at the moment. I've a buying trip ta San Francisco upcoming for a quality group of broodmares." He shrugged. "Fine ta buy and sell stock, but it's truly my aim ta breed and raise them myself. The alfalfa's suffering terribly under these conditions and I'll barely squeak out my needs for the string I have."

Benjamin took a long draw on his pipe and held it. Slowly he released the smoke and bobbed his head in agreement. "My crops doin' right poorly as well. Been drivin' my shoats into the forest to let 'em eat acorns. It be a long, hot one, but we'll get by."

"It sounds ungrateful ta wish for our usual flooding, but we cu surely use the water now."

Benjamin squinted, looking at the sky. "We'll get by. But a big un's comin'."

"A big flood?"

"Uh huh. Always gets a big flood after drought. If'n we don't get it this year, it'll be even worse the next. Worst one I recall, we had rowboats down mainstreet Sacramento. Drove more'n a few folks out of business."

"What about around here?"

"We all had corners of property got right soggy. Donovan's furthest north; he got hit worst. Imagine that marshy stuff you got planted wouldn't make it."

"I'm hoping ta get enough good years out of it ta outweigh the bad."

"I reckon you get by. Say, you goin' *back* by Nicolas any time soon?"

"I'm taking a stunning pair of Belgians down there ta sell on my way ta San Francisco. Why?"

"Like that brand of pipe tobacco they sell by the freight station. Mind picking up some

241

for me?"

"Not at all."

"When you aim to stop dickerin' at them mines and stick to horses?"

James laughed. "Soon. I've only stayed this long ta repay some old debts. That and ta make sure Justin gets a start there if he wants it. My preference is he stick ta horses, too. But he likes being around the men."

"Most boys do."

"True enough." James stood and stretched. "I'm sure my supper'll be waiting on me soon, so I best not be too late. I'll come by with yer tobacco when I return."

" 'Preciate that."

He had left Benjamin's farm thinking of the future — droughts and floods, horses to acquire, jobs with the mines — for himself and for Justin. With Sean somewhat out of the picture as a role model for the boy, he felt the need to be a strong presence in Justin's life.

James was the man to call in when there was blasting to be done, and he consulted with the Cornish engineers from Grass Valley about structural issues with old tunnels and creating new ones. Some older passages concerned him. Moisture built up, weakening structures and leading to dangerous gases. He walked miles of tunnel each week, inspecting and making recommendations. He enjoyed this role, and it allowed him to keep up with old friends and colleagues.

Often he brought Justin along for odd jobs, mostly as a mucker. Justin was the closest thing he would have to a son, and, living with a household full of women, they both appreciated the spirit of fraternity amongst the men.

The Cornish miners took the boy under their wing. He worked with mules pulling the carts of rock and ore. They showed him how to give the stubborn beasts the knee, forcing them to blow out air they bloated themselves with, making passage through the tunnels difficult.

They introduced him to the pasty, a meat and vegetable pie carried in their tin lunch pails and heated with a candle. Sometimes the miners gave him a pick to test his strength against the granite. He tired quickly, but each time Justin determined to last longer than the previous encounter. On trips home to the farm, he recounted excitedly for James everything he did that day.

James noticed Justin teased Charlotte about singing, but loved when the men belted out in convivial song. An eerie reverberation in the tunnels magnified the power of bass voices. A deep resonance could be felt as it bounced off rock walls and rumbled in their chests. Justin's favorite was James's beautiful baritone leading the men in the *Collier's Rant.* In full voice and brogue, they crooned about dangers in the mines. Superstition said catastrophes were the devil at work.

As me an' me marra were ganna' te' wark,
We met wi' the De'il it was l' the dark,
Aw up wi' me pick it being l' the neet,'
Aw chopped off his horns, likewise his
    clubfeet.

Foller the horses, Johnny me laddie,
Foller them through, me canny lad, oh!
Foller the horses, Johnny me laddie,
Oh, lad, lye away, me canny lad, oh!

As me an' me marra were puttin' the tram,
The light it went oot, an' me marra went
    wrang,
Ye wad ha'e laughed had ye seen the gam,
The Dei'l tyeuk me marran an' aw gat the
    tram.

Foller the horses, Johnny me laddie,
Foller them through, me canny lad, oh!
Foller the horses, Johnny me laddie,
Oh, lad, lye away, me canny lad, oh!

James smiled, hearing the chorus of men in his head and remembering bonding with Justin.

As he topped a hill near home, a harrowing sight below jolted him. There, streaking across the field, he saw a runaway team. The driver of the wagon, bouncing all over the seat, was none other than his daughter. He charged down the hill after her with scattered recollections of an argument concerning her ability to take on this challenge. It was not a skill he allowed the much stronger Justin to attempt yet, which was, of course, the appeal. Convinced she was the better rider, Charlotte obviously set out to prove her point.

She clung desperately to the reins, now realizing the difference in controlling a team versus her pony. Hairpins jutted out of her hair, which tumbled to her shoulders. As James gained ground he saw her ashen face and her jaw set tight. White-knuckled, Charlotte aimed the team at a clump of trees to slow them down, a gamble at best. Out of sheer will she managed to pull them to halt.

When James rode up to her, she sat waiting stonily in the wagon. He did not chastise her as he reached to unbend her fingers from their locked position before taking the reins.

"You're not yelling," she said in a small voice, without looking at him.

"I'm saving that for yer mother if she hears of it. We'll leave it as a lesson learned. Although I could probably recommend a few things ta ye ta keep it from happening the next time."

CHAPTER 17

The Collier Ranch — West of Sacramento
*   1856*

"Neil, Stop!"

Dutton's head rested against the horse and he laughed until his sides hurt.

"I'll never get this poor beast cooled down."

"Okay, okay."

Neil swung his saddle onto the fence railing, smirked, and added, "Bet old Luke is nice and cool, though."

Dutton yanked his cinch upward until the buckle released, then doubled over as the saddle slid off and fell at his feet. He remained crouched in the grips of this new wave of hysteria, his hands propped on his knees as he struggled to catch his breath.

Neil laughed, and Dutton straightened as he heard the sound of jingling spurs approaching. He turned to see Royce stomping up behind him, rounding the corner of the barn.

Royce batted the dust on his clothes with his large-brimmed hat and gave them a steely glance. "What's with the two of you?"

"Ah, you should've come with us. We took a formidable run." Neil sauntered over with the look of a story to tell. He threw his arm around Royce's shoulder, his sandy colored hair contrasting sharply with the dark brown of his younger brother. Only fourteen, Royce stood as tall as Neil, though in Dutton's opinion the boy walked like he thought he was well over six feet.

Royce eyed them both, one then the other. "Wouldn't have been much of a race."

Neil ignored the remark. "But you'd have enjoyed the outcome."

Still chuckling, he said, "We met up with Luke Jenkins on the road. We agreed to run through the south quarter past the Halford place. So, we're racing through the pasture, right where you get to that clump of trees, and we see Halford's put up a fence line down the side . . ."

Royce cut in sharply. "He didn't cut off the waterhole did he? That's a community pond."

"No, no, nothing like that. Anyway, Dutton and I see we can't cross through that way, and there's this huge mud hole right before you get to the pond, so the only way left is to pick your way through the trees. Dutton here manages to duck every branch — I knew the way, but it does slow you down. So Luke . . ." Neil started snickering at the thought. "Luke decided to jump the mud hole."

At this, Royce began to grin.

"He takes off too soon, his horse slides clear down to his haunches and Luke spills off the back, getting completely dunked. So there's his horse, sitting in the mud like a dog and Luke sputtering oaths and spitting out mouthfuls of muck."

Royce threw his head back, chuckling deeply. "Luke Jenkins is a bonehead. I'd have paid to see that."

"Knew you'd appreciate the humor. Say, we're going to town tomorrow; you should join us," said Neil.

"Not all of us are on holiday," Royce retorted. He squinted up at the sky. "They'll be expecting us in for dinner soon. Don't forget to rub those horses down good," he commanded and then stalked towards the house.

Dutton shot Neil an incredulous look.

Neil shrugged, his jovial demeanor intact. "Royce works a tough schedule — largely one of his own making."

"I think I'd have to cuff him."

Neil laughed. "You could try. He'd have jumped Halford's fence or busted through it. That's Royce. He'd go head first into a hurricane if he's riled."

"I take it he's not much on diplomacy?"

"Can't run a ranch *and* rule the world, I suppose."

Dutton smiled, feeling smug. "Best leave that to us, eh?" He hoisted his saddle on the fence beside Neil's and leaned down to soak a sponge from the water bucket. He let the cool water drizzle down the horse's back; its shoulders quivered as he stroked. "You think he'll follow you to Harvard next year?"

Neil sucked in a deep breath. "Not if he can help it. Pap wants it, but Royce'd rather be closer and focus on agriculture. He's Pap's shadow; knows every inch of the place already. Knows with every fiber of his being, this is the life he wants."

Dutton shrugged. "Something to be said for that." He glanced up across the back of his sweaty stead and found the vision he'd searched for all day. Adele Collier alighted the back porch steps of the house with a flower basket on her arm. Even in the distance he saw she had dressed for dinner, her periwinkle-blue frock outlining a pleasingly slim and graceful form. He found her mesmerizing.

Neil droned on about next year's workload at Harvard. Dutton preferred to study Adele's face. Her dark tresses, pulled elegantly up, displayed a hint of auburn. She was genteel, sophisticated, and two years older than Neil, though it hardly mattered to Dutton. He thought of her soft voice, her gracious and kind manner, and through their conversations he knew her to have a superior intellect.

". . . Yes, you agree?" Neil stared at him expectantly.

Startled, he answered quickly, "Of, course . . . yes."

Neil scoffed good naturedly. "Precisely what I thought." He put his fists on his hips. "I asked if you'd like to eat with the pigs tonight."

"Sorry . . ." Dutton chuckled sheepishly.

Neil punched his arm. "Your secret is safe. Though I have to tell you, old chum, the family's expecting an announcement of sorts from a young doctor in town."

"With a scarcity of proper women, it was unlikely one as beautiful and charming as your sister would be overlooked. A man can dream." He sighed. "She deserves to be the wife of a powerful and successful man —

though it *ought* to be me." he grinned.

"Ah, I'm certain she'll rue the day she missed out. C'mon, let's put these beasts in the barn and get cleaned up. Father will expect us in the library . . . he tends to pour the bourbon generously before dinner with guests!"

As they approached the house, Dutton observed Adele's slim form arch like a lithe willow branch as she cut a bunch of pink peonies. He nodded in greeting. She smiled and called out to them, "I'm afraid the fathers are in there plotting both your futures. You best get in there to defend yourselves." She dropped the posies into her basket.

"Thanks for the warning," Neil yelled back.

Dutton heard Adele call, "Celeste, darling! It's time to go in for dinner."

He hadn't noticed the littlest Collier playing in the garden. A pretty child, he watched her trounce around her tea party table in circles, swinging her doll in the air as if dancing with it. Her strawberry-blonde curls bounced as she took great, wide swooping steps and giggled. She placed her dolly back in the small chair and bowed to it. He was watching her in a detached manner when suddenly she looked up and saw him. She stared at him momentarily, then lowered her blue eyes demurely and curtsied.

Neil guffawed. "Celeste is very dramatic. Women learn these wiles very young, eh?"

Refreshed, Dutton followed the path of the rich Aubusson carpet down the grand curved staircase into the foyer. He glanced up at the magnificent crystal chandelier and wondered if Neil waited for him in the library. Hearing the titter of women's laughter he hesitated, slightly annoyed that he still wished to see Adele round the corner. Instead, his mother appeared in tow with Eugenia Collier.

"Yes! Thirty clerks! Huntington, Hopkins & Company, right over on K Street in Sacramento. Mary, we must go while you're here. Oh, good afternoon, Dutton — I didn't see you there."

Dutton smiled and gave a short, sharp bow. "Good afternoon, Mrs. Collier. I hope you've had a pleasant day. You both look lovely." He turned and gave his mother a grazing kiss on the cheek. "Mother."

A petite and prim woman, Eugenia patted her strawberry-blonde hair and answered, "Thank you, dear; always a pleasure when your family visits. Where on earth is Neil?"

"Coming, coming." Neil's tall, linear form took the stairs quickly, his square shoulders held erect even at his current speed of descent.

"You know your father's waiting?"

"Of course, Mother." Neil gave her a quick peck as he latched onto Dutton's arm to propel him towards the library. "Mrs. Dandridge, good afternoon." He flashed a charming smile. "Dutton and I are going to Sacramento tomorrow. We'll drive you there if you like."

"Oh, splendid. How very kind." Mary Dandridge beamed at both boys.

Eugenia nodded her approval. "We'll discuss plans over dinner. We won't keep you."

Neil nodded as he nudged Dutton down the short hallway. Massive oak doors hung open, beckoning their entry. As they crossed the threshold, Dutton heard lively discussion well underway. He glimpsed Royce seated in the corner where two towering walls of books met, and noted two glasses of bourbon set on the edge of the round table in the center of the room. He eyed the new billiard table in front of the back windows with envy.

". . . felonious parasites. I do wish our esteemed Senator Brannan would concen-

254

trate on the issues before him instead of chasing trade with China." Dutton listened to his father admonish from his perch on the chesterfield sofa near the round table. Always a delicate balance — to glean information without giving too much away, he thought.

"He's built an enormous house on J Street, so I assume he means to be a permanent thorn in our side," said Garth Collier, a stately figure, hefty and strong, sporting a well-groomed beard. Dutton saw him standing by the window, drink in hand as he declared, "Well, we got what we wanted — Sacramento is finally the official state capitol. Politics is simply liar's dice — everyone with an eye on his own hand."

He turned as Neil and Dutton entered the room. "Ah, here's our true future! Grab a drink, men." Garth peered at them with kind blue eyes. "What's the talk at Harvard?"

Neil passed a drink to Dutton as he breathed deeply and answered, "Far too much talk on slave states versus free. One has to take care giving opinions. Conversations heat quickly and there never seems to be resolution."

"Good California got in front of that issue from the start, at the territorial level," said

Garth. "Have a seat." He gestured to the opposing chesterfield beside him.

"Had to. Part of why we were granted statehood. I ought to know; I helped draft that part of the constitution," stated the judge, sipping his bourbon. He smirked. "So much for all of Mr. Calhoun's noise about us being too eager to govern ourselves."

"I find Mr. Calhoun very loud and very angry. He can call us impatient if he likes but Utah and New Mexico both submitted for statehood the same time we did and they're *still* waiting," stated Garth. "Reason enough for taking control of our own destiny."

"I wonder how he likes the symbolism of Minerva on our state seal. Sprung from the brain of Jupiter; no infancy for California — she was born ready!" Neil added.

The judge chuckled. "Very good, Neil."

Dutton jumped in the fray. "Did I hear that Broderick is president of the senate now?"

His father shifted his bulky weight. "You did, indeed. Bears watching, that one — too much Tammany Hall talking."

"Yes, if we ask them to empty their pockets before a session, I'm not sure *who* would spill out," agreed Garth.

"He does seem to sway his fellow senators

to accomplishment," said Dutton.

"But how . . . that's what worries me. Tammany Hall tactics could make the One Thousand Drinks legislature look tame." The judge shook his head. "Still can't live that down in the press. If only Governor Burnett hadn't left office — some say he lacked confidence in himself. Governor McDougal gambled and drank with all the legislators, then quarreled with them over minutiae." His father frowned. "He made an enemy of me when he tried to reprieve criminals put away through the Vigilance Committee, the whiskey bum. The democrats refused to nominate him in '51."

Neil prodded. "I believe you led that charge, did you not?"

Judge Dandridge smiled with satisfaction. "Governor Bigler put us back on track, settled us down. He's getting back to business as it ought to be. You can thank your father for that. His support prodded folks to action."

Garth pointed at the judge. "We did that together; it was the right call. Sometimes people don't look up from their work to see what can be done when we put our minds together, bringing the right people to the table."

"Champion of the small farmer, advocates

restricting Chinese . . . ," recited Neil, "which puts him at odds with Senator Brannan. Devoted to reducing state debt, revising tax laws, cutting government expenses. He's steering things in the right direction, so it seems."

Dutton noticed his father give Neil an appraising look. Neil was engrossed in the conversation — excited, vibrant. He possessed this same sort of enthusiasm at school, whenever a crowd gathered, always digging for the thoughts and opinions of others and well versed enough to give his own. People naturally gravitated towards his genuine countenance.

"As long as our senators continue to be elected by our legislators, we can put forth strong men that are a known entity in the political arena to support him," interjected Dutton.

Neil laughed. "Oh, not this again! There's something incestuous about that arrangement. Shouldn't the people decide?"

Dutton grinned. "You know I must be contrary to keep you on your toes. Answer me this: what good is the public when they can barely be bothered to vote at all?"

"Usher them to the polls in good faith with debates and information to make up their own minds," Neil challenged.

"And I'm uneasy about the tainted information and persuasive tactics that may be stuffing our ballot boxes," he answered.

Garth gave the judge an amused look. "I say, very impressive, you two! Looks like we're getting our money's worth, Walter. Dutton . . . what is it you're studying?"

"Finance. I hope to manage Father's investments; grow it into big business."

"Something for us to do together when I retire the bench. Neil? How about you?"

"I'm straddling law and business. I don't see myself as a lawyer, but I'd like a strong understanding of it as it relates to our interests."

The judge nodded thoughtfully. He turned to Royce, seated slightly behind him and nearly forgotten. While lively debate enraptured Neil, Royce sat like a stone. To his credit, Dutton noticed, he remained attentive.

"No politics for you?" asked the judge.

Royce smiled politely. "Father says I hold to a Jacksonian goal of minimal government."

Judge Dandridge chuckled. "A man that knows his own mind."

Dutton eyed him curiously. Politics might not be Royce's forte, but it didn't mean he didn't understand them.

Adele swept gracefully into the room, holding Celeste's hand, and beckoned, "Come, you men! That's enough debate. Mother says after your bellies are full, you'll be a lot more placid and a great deal more pleasant for the rest of us. Dinner is served."

CHAPTER 18

Early May 1856

For Charlotte the Boston days were largely forgotten, lapsing into a distant place her parents spoke of from time to time. Her prairie memories remained soft and fuzzy around the edges, though, in her mind, life began in the covered wagon. She remembered an endless carpet of wildflowers spread before them and the thick bluestem grass. When Justin spoke of it, she recalled picking wild strawberries and chasing prairie dogs into their holes. In her most vivid recollection, she played with the extraordinarily fine child's tea set emblazoned with the Vernon family crest as she set the table on a sea of grasses. Given to her by Mistress Doyle, and still a prized possession, it remained a visual reminder of life before California.

New memories pushed the old aside while exploring the woodlands, creeks, and rivers

surrounding the farm. Chores in the countryside multiplied from town living. She and
Justin shared garden duties — weeding and
gathering vegetables. Charlotte fed chickens
and learned the fine art of coaxing eggs
from reluctant hens without getting pecked.
Justin carried buckets of water from the rain
barrels and troughs to the barn stalls and
chopped smaller pieces of firewood. He
worked alongside Da mucking stalls and
caring for the growing number of work-
horses.

Charlotte helped in the kitchen as she had
with Matilda at the boardinghouse. She
learned to can, preserve, and dry most
anything, and scoured the forest around the
farm for wild berries, apples, nuts, and even
honey. She collected mullein plant to make
into candy for warding off colds in winter.
She discovered the ingenuity of making the
best of everything and something from nothing.

Their supply shelf held quinine for fevers
and shakes in case of the ague; whiskey,
kerosene, and turpentine as antiseptics; a
steel pair of pincers; and a knitting needle
that sufficed as a probe. Well stocked for
emergencies, Da did not take their distance
from town lightly. The proximity of Auburn
to the south and Grass Valley to the north

meant provisions reasonably close by. Mother, accustomed to life in the Doyle's grand house, had grown partial to many of her employer's fineries — her fondest indulgences being sweet smelling soap and, of course, English tea. Evenings proved productive as well as Mother taught Charlotte tatting and making lace.

Their first trips to school in Nevada City by themselves transpired on Betsy, the most ploddingly reliable of nags. It irritated Charlotte that Justin considered the old mare his horse, enjoying his place at the front and the sense of leadership it brought. Charlotte locked her arms around Justin's waist from behind and obliged him by complaining about her back seat.

As their experience grew, Da produced two ponies and gave strict instructions of "no racing on the way to school." Increasingly, the rule deteriorated into a suggestion. Enticing spring days tempted them beyond all resistance. Soft breezes playfully blew wisps of hair into Charlotte's face. She longed to feel the fullness of the wind lift her locks to form a banner flying behind her as she picked up momentum, bringing all her senses vibrantly to life. A mere glance from Justin, a glimmer in the eye of one to the other, and a race was on.

Finding new deviations in their path to gain advantage became challenging as the rolling hills of their wide-open route offered little change or place to hide. Experts in the fastest way to navigate a slope by judging its steepness and descent, they learned to be light handed with their reins and to secure the quickest response from their mounts. To vary their game, they set a course including designated clumps of trees off the path — requiring leaping ditches, toad hopping over roots, and increased speed to reach school on time.

On this day an early summer sun presided over the skies, and Mother instructed Charlotte and Justin to go together and help at the Speekses' farm. With her husband away and too ill to get out of bed, Mrs. Speeks found chores mounting up. Ella Louise was Charlotte's very best friend and a hard working girl. She fed the chickens, but was hopelessly terrified of pecking when it came to collecting eggs. Charlotte would tend the birds and help watch Ella Louise's younger sister. Justin was directed to chop wood and do some heavy lifting.

Charlotte looked forward to completed tasks to earn a free afternoon. Discussing plans as their ponies walked the wooded path to the Speekses' farm, she found Justin less than enthusiastic.

"Hope you don't expect me to play with dolls," he grumbled.

"*I* am too old for dolls. Ella Louise likes them though. I play to be polite."

"No tea parties, either."

"What if there's real cookies or cake?"

"I wouldn't count on it with her ma being sick. They've got some real good woods to hide in. There's all kinds of games we could make up there."

"That'd be okay. But Ella Louise can't run fast. Maybe we can sing part of the time."

"You sing enough for both of us."

"Folks like my singing." She noted the crankiness in his voice and tried to encourage him. "You sing well, too, you know. Don't you want to be in the church choir one day?"

"Not if I have to stand next to you. Just because you can sing loud doesn't mean you always should."

"I don't sing loud!" she protested. "Sometimes when the music is especially pretty, I feel strong about it. I get carried away, that's all. Besides, Mrs. Timmons said I have a strong voice. That's why she always asked me to lead in school."

"Maybe that's why I don't want to sing,"

he reasoned. "Always makes me think of church or school. I'd rather be outside."

"Well *you* pick the first game then."

"Okay. How about right now? Let's race!" He bolted ahead out of the woods and into the full warm light of the field ahead of them.

"Hey!"

Not to be beaten, Charlotte kicked her fat pony into a run and leaned over his neck to urge him on. She spoke his name in encouraging tones and watched him flick one ear back listening to her as he ran. She pumped her fists full of reins at the base of his neck as if to push power from his shoulders down to his hooves. She closed the gap between them and yelled triumphantly, "Ah, ha!"

As she guessed, Justin turned to see what she was aha-ing about. She bumped his pony, throwing off its stride, and surged ahead. Justin's pony recovered and he gave chase, nearly catching her at the farmhouse.

Mr. Speeks left for Sacramento to buy farm equipment knowing Lucille suffered from morning sickness. As with her previous three pregnancies, she toughed it out, though each case seemed increasingly acute. The children tended her and the chores and then Ella Louise put her two-year-old sister down for a nap.

Justin peered over the side of the crib as the girls crooned to the toddler.

"What's that?" He pointed at a small leather bound book on the pillow.

"That's my ma's prayer book. She always puts it in there."

Charlotte and Justin gave each other puzzled looks.

"The baby can't read!" declared Justin.

Charlotte giggled.

"No, silly," said Ella Louise. "That's to keep the devil from getting her while Ma's not watching her."

Justin nearly broke into mocking laughter but Ella Louise continued, "It's protection. We didn't know about such things when Timmy got taken."

The mood grew somber. Charlotte remembered the terrible day Timmy fell off the box seat of the wagon and was crushed by the wheel. Ella Louise kissed the book, put it back beside her sister, and they tiptoed from the room.

Once outside, their spirits lifted. Charlotte suggested hide and seek and they played until boredom set in. For awhile, the threesome lay in the grass and stared into a soft blue sky looking for animal shaped clouds, calling out loudly when spotting one. Justin pointed at one resembling a cow's head, causing Ella Louise to sit up with a start.

"Hey, I know what! Let's go look at my pa's bull! He's pretty scary."

"Where?" demanded Justin.

"Come on, in the barn." Ella Louise jumped up, skipping the way.

Charlotte knew the Speekses earned good money putting their bull out to stud. Big, black, and ornery, he was pampered and protected. When not grazing in a fenced area, he occupied the largest corner stall of the barn. The children approached him carefully.

"He's huge, but he looks kind of sleepy," said Charlotte. She noted his great, red, drooping eyes and wet, running nose.

"He's not scary. He looks like a big ugly cow," agreed Justin, climbing the side of the stall for a better look.

"You best get down from there. My pa says he's dangerous."

Justin rolled his eyes. Keeping a careful watch on the bull, Charlotte observed as Justin raised himself to a standing position on top of the stall, waving his arms outright for balance. The bull showed no interest in the boy.

"See, he's nothing to be afraid of. I bet I could ride him."

"No, Justin!" cried Charlotte. "Maybe you

should get down."

"Well . . . I guess horses that aren't used to being ridden buck, so it's probably not a good idea." He glanced up.

The ceiling above the stall was low to allow room on a floor above for hay storage. Charlotte watched Justin work his hands along the rafter above the bull and put his foot out tentatively to touch the bull's back. The girls gasped, but the bull merely shifted his feet. Justin grasped the beam above him with both hands, and stepped onto the bull's back. He walked along the grand animal's spine, carefully holding the timber above his head. Charlotte stared, silent and wide-eyed.

The beast uttered a sudden groaning noise and Justin quickly bailed out by swinging himself into the next stall and landing in straw. He laughed. "See, not so tough, is he?"

Charlotte exhaled loudly. "Oh, Justin, that was scary!"

"It was easy. You try."

"I don't know . . ."

"You can do it. What if I do it with you?"

"Well, I'm not doing it," declared Ella Louise. "And you shouldn't either, Charlotte. We're girls."

Charlotte hated being told girls had limitations. She looked hesitantly at Justin. He held out his hand. "Come on," he urged.

"Maybe I'll get a better look."

He grinned. They climbed up and looked over the stall. He stood in his former position, grabbing the rafter in one hand, and pulled Charlotte up with the other. She reached out cautiously and touched the beam, balancing in indecision.

"Here, I'll get in front," he said boldly. "Latch on up there, and step out on his back after I do."

He repeated his performance and glanced back at Charlotte barely dangling her toes above the animal's back.

"You gotta step down or your arms'll get too tired."

She touched down as if walking in a high wire act, holding tightly to the rafter. "He doesn't seem to mind much."

"Now, walk!"

She took a few mincing steps behind Justin, when the creature snorted.

"Oh!" she pulled her feet up and clung to the beam. The bull became agitated. He shifted in his stall and threw his large head about trying to reach the giggling gadflies above. He bellowed loudly. Ella Louise screamed, prompting both Charlotte and Justin to swing out into the safety of the next stall. They landed laughing in the pile of sweet smelling hay.

"Ella Louise, for heavens sake, don't holler! You scared me to death!" exclaimed Charlotte.

"I scared *you*! We need to get out of this barn right now. I'm sorry I even showed you that old bull." Her eyes welled up with nervous tears.

"Hey, it's okay," said Justin in soothing tones. "Let's find something else to do."

Mollified, Ella Louise led the way out of the barn. "I get to pick the game now," she announced.

Thistle Dew
The frequency of the discussion continued to increase and James was no more fond of the topic on this day than any other. With the children at the Speekses' farm, he found himself without diversion or defense in facing Emma's insistent argument.

"Out of the question, Emmaline. There's no money for 'finishing school', even if I did na believe it ta be a ridiculous notion."

"It is *not* ridiculous. You, yourself know the importance of proper speech for Althea and me. Growing up in Lord Vernon's household guaranteed us to find work in higher stations. Here, it's crucial she lose

271

that guttural, uneducated sound."

"Ye mean *my* uneducated sound."

Emma dodged his gaze sheepishly.

"I did not mean it disrespectfully. Her tone is so growling at times."

"Ye've corrected her from the day she said her first words. Enough with the Queen's English! She's only a flare of it here and there, maybe more if angry. I'm sure given time ye'll drive all the objectionable Scot right out of her."

"It isn't simply her speech, James. She runs about this farm like a field hand. She needs to behave like a lady, more genteel."

"I think ye can handle that. Isn't it enough she plays that cultured thing in the corner?" He pointed accusingly at the spinet.

"Young ladies must be accomplished. This campfire singing you do together for the amusement of the miners is not helping."

"Helping what? I'll na have a hand in teaching her ta be hoighty-toighty. She's a well-grounded girl. There are no stations here, Em."

"There are when it comes time to marry."

"Och, and there it is!" He threw his hands up in disgust. "She's a wee bit young ta be worrying about matching her up with the peerage."

"Don't be condescending. There's no

shame wanting her to have the best life possible."

"We've very different ideas of what that would be then," he fumed. "I don't want her ta have a life tied ta someone else's ideals. She needs ta make informed decisions, live her life according ta her principles, not bound ta some ridiculous rules of superiority or *society,*" he sneered. "I'll na raise an unfeeling elitist."

Emma's dark-blue eyes grew stormy. Seeing her ready her retort, James tried to defuse her anger. "Have ye done so badly with me, Em?" he said softly.

She halted, mouth open. He gave her a wounded look. She sighed and looked at her feet. "Of course not. No one has worked harder than you to give us a comfortable life."

"And we have it, don't we?"

He held out his hand to her.

"Yes. I . . . oh, dear. Hush now."

James heard the youthful laughter on the front porch.

"The children are home. I don't want them to hear us argue . . . ," she began.

The door swung open and two disheveled and muddy youngsters stood before them. James winced.

Emma's hands flew to her hips. "There!

You see? It is precisely this I'm speaking of."

"They're kids, Emma. When ye play — ye get dirty. When ye work — ye get dirty. Such is life."

Emma turned to the offenders. "I certainly hope Ella Louise does not appear in your same dreadful state. Her mother needs no extra work now! What on earth happened to the two of you?"

Justin glanced at Charlotte, choosing his words carefully.

"We were playing leap frog at the base of a hill. The grass was long, so we didn't see that a slough cut through there."

"I jumped and got a boot full of water . . . ," offered Charlotte.

"Then I jumped and slipped. I slid on my back. We were already dirty, so . . ."

Emma waved her hand for him to stop. She collected herself and stated firmly, "Please go wash up for supper. Put those muddy shoes outside."

Charlotte, the least dirty, returned first to set the table.

She gave her parents a curious look. "Were you two quarreling?"

James and Emma looked at each other.

"But . . . you still love each other?"

"Always, darling." Emma smiled. "Love is

a delicate balance of what disappoints us with one another, and what disappoints us with ourselves." She gave a wistful smile. "Somehow the arrow of blame never seems to point at ourselves."

Emma glanced at James. "No one person can be the all and all of another. We're lucky for laughter, shared joys, and strength to bear pain. Peace, caring, kindness — all these things mean love."

James interrupted. "It never hurts ta be unspeakably drawn ta a person — almost against yer will." He swept Emma into his arms, then noted her frown.

"For beauty of their character, of course. Other kinds are considered a bonus," he amended, addressing Charlotte. He grinned, turning back to Emma. "Oh, come now, ye know my rugged handsomeness had ye shivering in yer shoes from first we met."

Emma pushed him away, annoyed. "It certainly was not modesty. Honestly, James."

He winked at Charlotte. "Canna help it. While true, I did na overwhelm her from the start — she bewitched me the moment I set eyes on her." James stood facing his daughter. "Honestly, we men are weak creatures when it comes ta a pretty face. Her pretty face drew me in, but her pretty heart made me never want ta leave." He tapped Charlotte's nose with his finger. "Remember that."

Charlotte smiled up at him.

The door opened and Althea entered with Justin, his hair slicked down and combed.

"Ah, to come home to such a dirty child. I hope he hasn't been a nuisance, Emma."

"No, not to me. A great improvement, Justin," she said, nodding at him. "Now that we're all here, shall we sit and eat? By the way, Althea, I hear a cotillion class begins after school on Fridays. I think they could both benefit from a little instruction on social graces . . . what say you?"

James was surprised. His wife had saved this little ace up her sleeve. Althea nodded in agreement; Justin groaned. Emma smiled graciously. "Would you bless us, dear?"

CHAPTER 19

The successful trip to San Francisco brought James confidence in his growing farm. It helped take the sting out of the cross words with friends that were weighing heavily on his mind.

He secured a fine price on his pair of Belgians in Nicolas, and a chance meeting with a stagecoach company official proved fruitful. Word had spread that he provided good quality, well-trained animals and Wells Fargo expressed interest in procuring teams from him. Freight companies began to seek him out.

He called on a number of sources to put together an outstanding string of brood mares. For pulling freight wagons, he looked for lines reminiscent of English war horses: solid, large boned, heavily muscled beasts — sturdy enough to pull the weight required of them. For stagecoach teams he looked for speed as well as brute strength. Finally,

277

he indulged himself with a cream colored two-year-old filly he christened Glory. She was a fine saddle horse, the first of what he hoped to be many, with nearly perfect lines. Her stride was fluid and sure; her temperament easy, yet spirited. He took great pleasure in herding his bevy of beauties home.

Though well pleased with business, James felt disgust thinking of his last visit to Marysville. He attended their town meeting along with friends, neighbors, farmers, and miners — all with a common, growing concern over changes to the Yuba and Feather Rivers.

Riverboats struggled to make their way to port, passage became bogged down, and the suspected cause was the accumulation of tailings and sediment coming downstream from the mines. Livelihoods from river traffic feeding the northern mining towns choked. Raised riverbeds brought mass flooding during the spring thaw, washing out stores in town and cutting off passage to major roads. The course of the river mutated into a spreading wetland where none existed before. Waters encroached on business, then thinned out and became shallow — further impeding river travel.

Mayor Hammond Creed formed investigative committees and hired engineers to suggest corrections. In the meantime, attendees agreed to stem the leaky overflow by walling off errant bends in the river with sandbags to fortify the Yuba's course. All had a stake in the survival of river traffic.

The meeting itself showed monumental community support. The discussion afterward took a downward spiral. James heard disturbing reports on the progression of vigilance committees, once a necessary entity in the mines. Rumor said vigilance had evolved into a principal agency of violence against Indians, Latinos, and particularly the Chinese. Sean Miller was a leading member on the committee.

Not their usual cheery reunion, James sought out Sean looking for answers and found he bristled easily. Lodie stood by listening, the Brown's Valley Road being an all-important route to move his merchandise from the port in Marysville to his emporium in Nevada City.

"Jobs are hard to come by these days, James. Livelihoods are being stole out from under us by godless souls. It ain't right." Sean stood facing James with his back rigid, his tone laced with testiness.

"Seems ta me they take on the worst jobs . . . the most dangerous ones no one else will touch."

"And that gives them coolies an edge over our boys."

"Sean, didn't ye learn anything from what happened ta Vicente?"

"He's okay; everybody likes Vicente."

"Wasn't always that way. He can na be comfortable with this . . ."

"Vicente's not a decision maker. He knows when to keep quiet and tend to his business. Besides, I remember you being in favor of the committee back in the day."

"And I remember ye did na favor Vicente until ye discovered he was a person, same as you. How can ye treat his countrymen with such contempt? Or the Chinese? Sean, back in the day it was 'common sense for the common good.' As with all things that begin nobly, growth and greed deteriorate them. Is it true . . . there have been lynchings?"

Sean looked away. "I don't know much about that. In some cases . . . maybe. Only in serious cases."

"Lynching makes any case serious. No man deserves ta die over a job!"

"That's fine for you, James. You ain't there. You got it easy."

"Ye had the same luck as me. The difference is what each of us did with it."

Sean lunged forward, gritting his teeth, and James stood to his full height and squared his shoulders. Lodie stepped between them. "Okay now. Let's back up a bit before things get too personal."

James shot him a look. "Ye've been mighty quiet, Lodie. Where do ye stand in all this?"

Lodie sighed. "I don't like it. But they got pressures outside and inside. Mine owners are demanding more. Backers are demanding more. It isn't our business anymore, James."

"I hear a lotta words, Lodie. But I did na hear ye pick a side. A thing is right or it's wrong. Well, I've kept a hand in, so I believe that entitles me ta an opinion."

"Yeah, I seen you strolling through the tunnels like you're somebody important," Sean said hotly. "I can do that job, same as you, and I wouldn't be doin' it in my spare time."

James glared at him. "Then do it. But don't go blamin' yer woes on the Chinese; they got nothing ta do with yer decision ta live inside a bottle." He turned an angry eye towards Lodie. "If yer meetings are tied ta the committee, I'm out — before I find I can no longer tolerate my friends and neighbors for the stand they take." He stalked away in disgust.

That night, he had woken Emma as he bolted upright in bed, shivering and dripping with sweat.

CHAPTER 20

Nevada City — July 19, 1856

"Really?" Althea brightened. She rolled and bundled the gown draped across her lap and laid it on her worktable. "You found something?"

Lodie's eyes twinkled as if holding the answer to a riddle. "I told you, you wouldn't be here much longer. How's the upper end of East Broad Street for a location?"

"What?! You're joking! Where?"

"A small place, one of Oscar Thornton's buildings. He intended to use it for the telegraph office, being so high on the hill, but when the council voted for a different locale he used it for storage. I heard him say he was looking for a tenant. It's ideal for your shop."

"I know exactly the one. When can I get a look at it? What if I can't afford it?" Althea peppered him with questions as she rose from her seat.

"I've spoken with him, negotiated a modest rent . . . well within the budget you gave me. It does need freshening up."

Tittering laughter echoed from the back hallway of the emporium, interrupting Lodie, as Emma and Matilda came down from the upstairs living quarters. Emma held little Robert's hand and Matilda cradled a squirming Albert.

"Ah, naptime is over I see," said Lodie, giving Robert a wink.

"Indeed." Matilda shifted the toddler to the other hip. "Althea, I'm sorry you couldn't join us after lunch; it was ever so quiet with the boys asleep. We actually *had* a conversation."

"Well, tell her your news," demanded Emma. "Oh, wait, perhaps Lodie already has."

"No, I was telling her . . ."

"We've bought a house!" blurted Matilda. "Isn't that grand? The Dietrichs moved back to Sacramento. You know the house with the lovely veranda on Nevada Street? It has a well-kept little garden in the back, spacious and rambling enough for the boys."

Althea turned to Lodie. "Aristocracy Hill? Well, well . . . you're certainly full of surprises today."

"Purely an economic decision . . ."

Emma raised her eyebrows and chortled. "Oh?"

"As I was about to say, I'm growing a business here. I have no time for building a house. Mattie and the boys need more space and frankly I need the upstairs as an office and for storage."

"Let's take the boys and go have a look," suggested Matilda.

"We'll all go when James finishes up at the Empire offices," Lodie answered, visibly irritated by the interruption of his news. "I'm about to take Althea to look at her new shop. Would you mind the store while we're gone?"

"Of course, dear; I'd forgotten."

Emma looked questioningly at Althea.

"I'm as shocked as you," she replied, smiling. "Upper East Broad Street, no less. Want to come with?"

"My, my. Aren't we all moving up in the world! I'll walk halfway with you. Mattie tells me Hamlet Davis finally received a shipment of goodies from San Francisco. I'll take a peek before my husband arrives to take us home."

Lodie jammed his fists on his hips, staring at Emma in mock disgust. "Shopping at the competition?"

Emma gave him a dismissive flip of her

wrist and disappeared into the hallway to fetch her shawl. She returned with a purposeful air. "Don't give me grief, Lodie Glenn. James does nothing but complain about our bills from your establishment." She whipped the rose colored shawl over her shoulders and nodded to Mattie as they departed. "I'll be back shortly. Perhaps I'll see some items for your new house."

"Oh, that's cheeky, Emma," laughed Althea.

Lodie rolled his eyes as they departed for their uphill stroll.

"Whatever is the holdup with new merchandise? I noticed your shelves are rather depleted, with nothing new to be found since my last visit." Emma let the shawl slide to the crook of her arms. "Oh," she said, squinting in the summer sun, "I didn't realize how warm it is."

Lodie's long, leisurely stride measured one footfall to every four quick steps of the women as they wove their way through the lazy afternoon crowd. He smiled and nodded as they passed friends and customers.

"I can't blame you for looking around," he admitted. "I'm hoping for a freight wagon delivery from Nicolas tomorrow. Shipping is backed up with river traffic bogged down."

Althea agreed. "I'm overdue for supplies myself. I'll be making buttons out of silk covered pebbles if a shipment doesn't arrive soon. The drought really set us back."

Lodie shook his head. "That was last year. Granted, this year's moderate wet season should be enough to raise the levels of Feather, the Yuba, *and* the Sacramento. Channels have narrowed and riverboats get mired in the muck trying to get to Marysville. She's still our hub — when she suffers, we suffer."

"What's to be done about it?" asked Althea.

"I'm not sure. Pray for floods this winter, I suppose. Perhaps the rush of water will blast its way through, reopen the channels."

"A rather dire solution. I don't think the farmers will hope for that at all," remarked Emma. "I know James won't."

"He will if he runs short on feed — though he benefits from the increased need for overland freight. The demand for horses must be steep."

Emma nodded and stopped in front of Hamlet Davis's smart brick building. "It is. He's training new animals sunup to sundown. With school out for summer, he's got the children helping him. I was surprised he took the day to meet with the Empire supervisor. But it allowed me this visit . . ." She smiled mischievously. ". . . and opportunity for shopping."

"Don't rub it in," chuckled Lodie.

"I'll stop in on our way down," said Althea.

"Psshhh. I'll be having tea with Mattie by the time *you* two are finished. Detail people, both of you!"

Althea smiled. "She's right, you know."

"Hmmm. Probably best she doesn't have to wait on us. We'll take our time. Glorious day."

Althea continued to climb, breathing deeply, glancing about as they crested Nabob Hill. She admired the graceful beauty of this town, feeling grateful for it. They rounded the curve on Upper East Broad and she turned to walk backwards for a few steps looking off towards the craggy Sierra Buttes, purple in the summer haze. A hot, dry, westerly wind gained momentum, creating a dance of tiny dust devils on the dirt street. She brushed back her blonde locks as the heavy breeze conspired to cover her eyes, robbing her of the view.

Lodie stopped in front of the small Thornton building, a simple wooden structure with an adequate front window, Althea considered. A short distance from the street, sloping gently downward and with only one step before the landing, it provided easy customer access. She noted the plum and cherry trees planted on either side, conscious of the birds diving into the branches seeking fruit. Beautiful blooms in spring, she thought, and turned to survey the maple, locust, and elms lining the streets, as well as rows of stately pines behind the buildings.

"It *is* lovely here."

"That it is," he agreed. "Exactly why your affluent neighbors chose to build homes up this way. Beautiful and conveniently located for the patrons you most want to attract."

"Do you always look at everything from a business angle?"

"Of course. All else is bonus. Shall we go in?"

Althea frowned and stepped back, scrutinizing the exterior. It would need a more cheerful coat of paint, she decided. Lodie worked the lock and pushed at the resistant door.

"Sticks a little. Ah, here we are."

The door groaned with disuse as they entered. A potbellied stove sat next to the left-hand wall almost ten feet from the front window, leaving another six feet to a counter running perpendicularly across and cutting the one-room building in half. A flipboard for admittance to the back extended from the counter and rested on its ledge on the right wall. Stacked against the back wall Althea saw large crates and abandoned pieces of furniture.

She walked slowly around the space, tapping her finger against her lips as she thought. Visually she measured the walls for shelving, turned, and imagined placement of seating and a small table for showing wares close to the stove. Lifting the flipboard, she wandered about the back estimating workspace available. After several minutes Lodie broke her reverie.

"Well?"

Althea cocked her head as she considered. "It needs some freshening. The location is wonderful. I think . . . oh, I have a million questions! But I think this could work."

Lodie grinned. "I'd love to welcome you to the merchants board . . ."

"Oh, gracious! You aren't serious?"

"Why not? Having you at the emporium, you've developed clientele and increased trade in women's clothing, as well as accessories that you sell more than I. You've been invaluable to me ordering fabric, notions, laces . . . all things I'm hopeless in selecting. You've delivered quality product, and you're well respected and liked. All I've done is given you a corner."

"You've done a great deal more than that. I couldn't have leveraged the materials. Without them, there's no business. And therein lie my questions. How long do you need me to stay at the emporium? My new orders haven't come yet . . . if the riverboats ever fight their way upstream to Marysville. How much stock do you need me to leave with you?"

"Details, Althea, only details. We'll work all this out. Our businesses work in harmony; all you need do is say 'yes.' And I'm serious about the merchants board."

Althea threw him a suspicious frown.

"Listen. You're a great sounding board — fair, logical, practical. We've spent many hours discussing town issues during lulls in business, you and I. Matilda tells me repeatedly how respected you are in this community. And liked. Women will strike a common chord with you, seek your counsel — and be overjoyed to have their viewpoint represented. A seat on the merchants board leads to the town board. Growth and expansion affect families and children. Strong families are what we want in Nevada City. Wives voice opinions; husbands listen and are greatly influenced by those opinions."

She squinted, and looked at him with the utmost scrutiny. "Yes. Influence on husbands. Husbands who vote . . ." She began to smile. ". . . vote for public officials who are suddenly very popular for promoting family interests with a woman on the board."

He grinned big and bold. "See what I mean? You don't miss anything."

"Are you sure you aren't opening the can of worms?"

"I'll ask you the same when every woman in town wants to bend your ear with complaints. Think of it, Althea. You could be a deciding factor in town development. It's important. I didn't bring you here merely to look at your shop. I brought you to look at your future, yours and Justin's. This is more than business. It's creating a way of life, watering it, feeding it, and pulling more people into the circle. I like the buzz of activity, the excitement as people succeed and I like being part of solutions."

She stood smirking at him, not responding.

"Ha! I knew it. You're not hating the idea."

"It's a bit overwhelming. Perhaps I should start with step one. 'Yes' to the shop," she stated with confidence. "And I warn you, I proceed cautiously from there."

Lodie held up a hand in submission. "I hear you. And I'm delighted. I'll let Oscar know he has a tenant. Are you ready to head back?"

"Yes. I'm eager for Matilda's tour of your new house."

Althea gazed at the front of the building as Lodie locked up. If anything, the gusts of wind had increased in power. Her eyes stung, watering from airborne dust. She turned her head to avoid the onslaught, and brushed tears away. Lodie walked towards her with his head bent into the blustering breeze. Blinking, she turned her back to him trying to regain clear vision. An acrid odor invaded her nostrils, its bitterness attacking the back of her throat. Suddenly, she realized it wasn't dust. It was smoke.

"Oh, God!"

Althea clutched Lodie's arm. A dervish of thick black clouds spiraled from the west, the currents of air pushing them forward, dissipating at unimaginable heights. A wall of flame engulfed both sides of the road and raced unfettered in the distance.

"Pine Street! It reached Spring Street, and it's lighting up both directions!"

"Lodie, I can see it moving!"

The bell on the top of the Methodist

church began to ring wildly. Two more churches picked up the cry.

"Althea, go up! Run up to Medicine Rock and wait there."

"No! I have to find Emma!"

A man darted past them, jostling her. Lodie reached to steady her as more townspeople poured into the streets, grasping hastily snatched belongings, running past them, scurrying up, bolting down in bewilderment, calling out the names of loved ones. The conflagration ran parallel with Gold Run Creek until it jumped the upper part of Deer Creek and hurtled, careening in both directions of Spring Street up to Bridge Street, working towards Broad.

Lodie shouted, "She'll be with Matilda. Mattie knows to cross the bridge at the bottom of Deer Creek and head for Prospect Hill. I've got to get down there and start a bucket line."

She pushed him. "I'm following you then. Go! Don't wait on me."

"Don't take chances; if it comes too rapidly, cut over to Commercial . . . to Main if you have to. Keep moving down and away!" He began running.

Althea grabbed her skirts and fled. Panicked screams now assaulted her from every direction. She lost sight of Lodie as she dodged her way through the crowd, working her way down the hill. She was shoved from all directions, the horde jamming in its confusion and fright. She glanced up momentarily to look for an opening and saw the smoke advancing quickly, obscuring her line of sight, burning at her throat.

Tall pines ignited, pitch feeding the demon devouring city blocks in both directions as the towering spires formed the gates of hell. Fiendish tongues of fire lapped up wooden structures hungrily in rapid succession. The mind-numbing roar of the firestorm was punctuated only by booming snaps and thunderous cracks as it consumed the chain of timber buildings, and vaulted to the rooftops of the unassailable brick edifices.

In the thick of things now, Althea realized if she stumbled she would be trampled. The unbearable heat smothered her and she alternated holding her breath and coughing. She reached the first cutover to Commercial Street and hesitated, knowing she should take it, but unable to shake the need to find Emma. Faces smudged with oily grime, the refuse of destruction, concealed identities. She heard men crying out in frustration at the standpipe at Pine and Broad, shouting and milling about uselessly. Others sprinted past with wet blankets, buckets from the troughs, and one man shrieked as he bounded by with his back ablaze.

Yelling from above caused Althea to look up. A figure in a second-story window of the Kid & Knox Building frantically waved and shouted at someone inside. He screamed for "Fletcher" to follow him. She stared as he scrambled out, gripping the iron shutter for support, flattening himself against the brick. Fiery fingers reached to claim a victim and Althea watched his hazardous flight from the roof. His comrade flew to the window, slamming the iron shutters closed. To her horror, Althea saw the inferno greedily blitz the buildings on either side, igniting Broad Street. Her path now blocked, she broke for the cutaway street, turning by the New York Hotel on the corner, and ran with all her strength.

The ground trembled as a loud explosion rocketed behind her. Terror clawed at her; a burning in her chest felt like a gaping wound. Overwhelmed by smoke, she pushed her face into her shoulder and breathed against the cloth as she stumbled along, bypassing Commercial, fleeing towards Main. From the corner of her eye she glimpsed the monstrous beast in pursuit, springing from rooftop to rooftop, ravenously engulfing all of Nevada City.

"Down and away, down and away," she kept telling herself. Shouting voices grew more distant, though she could not escape the suffocating fumes. Fearing to again run up against Perdition's wall, she veered off Main Street away from town, turning on Coyote, following Manzanita Ravine, away again to Nevada Street. Althea trudged on until she crossed the bottom of Deer Creek, dragging herself towards the gathering of women and children at the base of Prospect Hill.

Too tired to speak or advance another step, she stopped short of the crowd and turned to gaze back at town. Thick, smoggy blackness gave the appearance of dusk, though it was several hours away. Smoldering ruin, char and ashes; utter annihilation met her view. Nevada City lay scorched nearly beyond recognition . . . devoured in barely thirty minutes.

She blinked stupidly as she looked at the bottom of the hill. The Nevada City Hotel had been spared. Next to it, The Silver Moon remained intact, and then Lodie Glenn's emporium stood with roof damage, but it stood. A few surviving structures remained on the opposite side of the street, but not far beyond. Exhausted individuals hauling buckets and wet blankets persisted through the wreckage.

"Althea?"

She turned wearily towards the anxious voice. Matilda stepped out from the crowd and ran to her, simultaneously laughing and crying.

"Praise God, praise God!" Matilda flung her arms around her, hugging her fiercely. "Lodie was beside himself with worry."

"The emporium is still there. A few . . . a few places made it."

"Yes. The Silver Moon was full of miners. They worked the pump and hoses until the pipes gave out, then they emptied the store of pails and linens." Matilda glanced quickly around. "Where's Emma, dear?"

Althea stiffened with a jolt. Her mouth fell open, gaping for air, and she stared at Matilda as if uncomprehending. She looked over Matilda's shoulder, her eyes scanning the group clustered there, shaking her head. Althea dropped to her knees. Her wailing sob seared the silence.

Thistle Dew

"Lo, how a Rose e'er blooming from tender stem hath sprung
Of Jesse's lineage coming, as men of old have sung.

298

It came, a floweret bright, amid the cold of
   winter
When half spent was the night."

Her pure, sweet voice pierced the stillness.
The clear, lilting melody wafted on air,
reaching for the trees, soaring above them.
James focused on the wisp of a girl standing
graveside, holding a single red rose. A sea of
mournful faces surrounded her, blurring
into a wave of sorrow he couldn't cope with.

He searched Charlotte's face as she sang.
How like Emma she was, in grace and
stature. She sang unwaveringly, her lip never
trembling. Only the deep sadness in her eyes
betrayed her.

His mind drifted to his discussion of the
service held at the kitchen table.

The pastor had begun gently, "It really is
more of a carol . . ."

"Does it matter? It was her favorite."

"The choir is . . . well, dismantled at the
moment. There are ten more funerals in
these few days. Possibly Mrs. Simpkins
could . . ."

James shook his head, "No, she can na
carry it alone. It has ta be right."

"Mr. MacLaren, believe me, I understand.
There is no way to express what we carry

for a loved one with finality. Perhaps a poem?"

Anger had swelled within him, a sharp retort ready on his lips when he heard a small voice from the corner of the room say softly, "I can do it, Da."

He had turned to see her pale, earnest face watching him. He had grappled with her words.

"Sweetheart. I think . . . I think it would be very difficult for ye."

"I want to. I want to do something for Mother," she had insisted quietly.

Her resolute plea had caused him to pinch the bridge of his nose. "Are ye . . ." His voice broke. "Are ye sure?"

Charlotte nodded solemnly.

The pastor had cautioned, "Mr. Mac-Laren, she's just a girl."

James had stood. "No. This one has never been *just* a girl." He held out his bandaged hand and she came and slipped her smaller hand in his.

"Isaiah 'twas foretold it, the Rose I have in
    mind;
Mary we behold it, the Virgin Mother kind.
To show God's love aright, she bore to us a
    Savior,
When half spent was the night."

Her mellifluous sound haunted and soothed at the same time. He had slept little. Odd flashes of memory came at him like a maddened dog he tried to strike away. On a day he thought like any other he had witnessed the blackened clouds soaring like ill tidings of a raven — and he panicked as he approached the last glowing embers of devastation.

Snatches of visions raced in his head — the streets a gruesome combination of mud and ash, Lodie's grim face, a crowd gathered in front of the scorched remains of Hamlet Davis's fireproof store, men at the door with sledge hammers beating heat-swollen hinges, flesh burning on his hands as he wrested open the hot steel door, throwing aside smoky fallen timbers, calling to a voice that could not answer, discovering the last refuge of desperation under the basement stairwell, Emma's pink shawl.

He shut his eyes tightly. Charlotte's voice broke through his trance, calling him back to the present.

"The shepherds heard the story proclaimed
    by angels bright,
How Christ, the Lord of glory, was born on
    earth this night.
To Bethlehem they sped and in the manger

> they found Him
> As Angel heralds said."

She sought his face as she sang, her noble tones taking an ethereal quality, floating ever higher, ever stronger. Her mouth quivered as their eyes met. Charlotte's eyes flashed the same pale green as his, but their shape, their expression, belonged to Emma. He held her gaze, letting his thoughts retreat to a different day with joyful pink roses surrounding Emma, encircling her hair, covering the arbor where they took their vows. He pictured the depths of her deep-blue eyes, her dark curls, her laughter, and her loving smile. He saw her at the estate in England where she first took his breath away, nuzzling their baby daughter, walking with him along the River Charles in Boston, soldiering across the country in the covered wagon, working alongside him to build their home. Home. Now he brought her home. Here, on the hillock where she would face the sunrise each day, overlooking her garden.

> "This Flower, whose fragrance tender with sweetness fills the air,
> Dispels with glorious splendor the darkness everywhere;

True man, yet very God, from sin and
   death He saves us,
And lightens every load."

Charlotte's last note resonated in the silence. She stepped forward and placed the rose on Emma's grave. James closed the gap between them, placing his red rose gently beside hers. He put his arm around Charlotte, staring at the roses, and said hoarsely, " 'We are but a mist that appears for a little time and then vanishes . . . though we die, yet shall we live.' "

The pastor gave final benediction. James and Charlotte led the wordless march down the hill back to the house, followed closely by Althea, Justin, and Sean. Melancholy supporters trailed behind. The house was laden with food prepared by Matilda, Ruth Cleary, and Lucille Speeks — friends feeding a hungerless horde to fill the futility of the moment.

A large contingent from Marysville came to console and comfort. Alton Quigby, Hammond Creed, Tom Price, John Murphy, friends from church and schools both there and in Grass Valley attended. Benjamin Jones, Peter and Rob Stuben and their families, even Bracuus Donovan gave solace. James wondered if the fierce suddenness of the event might remind them of their own sense of impermanence — an uncomfortable realization that mortality merely tiptoed behind looking for opportunity. The day was long. James and the family worked through it numbly, accepting heartfelt condolences and offers of help, but in the end they felt grateful when all went home.

Ready to give in to exhaustion, James left his bedroom door cracked for two reasons. First, in case Charlotte needed him — though he suspected she would soon give in to fatigue as well. Second — he fought the odd sensation that to close the door somehow sealed him in without Emma, or sealed him in with her non-presence, or gave him the feeling he was closing her out. He lay quietly pondering these peculiarities, hoping for the mercy of sleep to overtake him, when he heard the creak of Charlotte's door. Almost soundlessly she padded barefoot into the main room and sat on the floor close to the hearth. From where he lay on his bed he could only see her left side through the narrow opening. She hugged her shins close to her body, her chin resting on her knees, and rocked slowly back and forth, staring into the fire. Understandably, sleep eluded her. He debated whether to check on her, but remained watching.

Perhaps she needed time alone to think. The last few days had been as a swirling eddy, spinning madly out of control.

James heard a barely discernable knock at the front door. He raised himself up on his elbows and saw Justin open the heavy door and poke his head inside. Charlotte lifted her chin as if aware, though her gaze remained fixed on the fire and she continued moving to and fro. Justin observed her for a few seconds and then walked over to her quietly and sat down beside her. He draped his arm around her. She peered sightlessly into the fire, her eyes brimming with tears at his touch. He hugged her gently to him and she let her head rest against him. Her shoulders began to shake uncontrollably.

From his hindered viewpoint, James sighed with a heavy heart. He lay back down and turned away, leaving them to their silent vigil.

CHAPTER 21

Nevada City, 1860

Althea tapped the pencil against the table lightly, intermittently, as she listened to the discussion. The slow, monotonous rhythm brought order to her frustrated thoughts. Decisions came slowly to the Nevada City Town Council and, as the only woman serving on the Merchants' Board, she learned to make her views known last, if at all.

In truth, only one issue before the closed council session today mattered to her — the vote to begin construction of the fire station. Incredibly, nearly four years past the tragedy and destruction of the town, and no established fire department existed. Bickering between the merchants of Main and Broad Streets slowed the progress by escalating competition, each group demanding the firehouse for their own street. Men and their egos, she marveled. Humility slapped them in the form of yet another fire two years later, jarring a complacent citizenry to demand more of its leaders. She would insist they be heard.

She glanced around the vast assembly room. The smell of fresh paint and recently polished flooring of the new Nevada County courthouse reminded her of all things redeemed by the men seated down the table in front of her. Unraveling the mysteries of the fire took time, though rebuilding had commenced at once. To be fair, the city raised itself from a charred square mile of scorched earth. In only one month, nearly half of the four hundred demolished buildings were rebuilt. The courthouse, completed days before it burned completely to the ground, now stood reborn.

Althea grasped the pencil, rolling it between her fingers as she recalled harrowing events, allowing herself only the barest of detail. Embers from a forge in the blacksmith shop had burst the bellows into flames, engulfing the adjacent wall of a brewery, and then leapt across the road igniting the United States Hotel and the stables of Kidd & Knox. From there, high winds fanned the flames, consuming homes, frame businesses, and supposedly fireproof brick buildings. The well, pump, and standpipes — properly laid out sources of running water to homes and businesses — was the only defense. This last hope vaporized as lead pipes melted in the heat, and the precious water disappeared into the ground.

She studied the councilmen. Sunshine streamed in from tall courthouse windows and fell down the queue of distinguished faces at the table. Mr. Thatcher, the assessor, sat on the end, shielding the side of his face from the light with his hand. Mr. Stapp, the treasurer, moved his lips as he studied his ledger. Mr. Marsh, whose water company supplied gold mines, sat with them to discuss supplying the city's water needs. Missing was Hamlet Davis. Bankrupt and burdened over those who had perished in his building, including his nephew, he sold out and moved to Dutch Flat. The remaining members — a physician, a pharmacist, a newspaperman, a lumberman, two lawyers, a stamp mill operator, and Mayor Lodie Glenn — all jockeyed for position on topics of concern.

Lodie quickly rose to leadership after the fire. Possessing one of the few surviving businesses, he worked tirelessly to organize Nevada City's recovery. He tapped everyone he knew to volunteer skills and materials; mobilized social, church, and women's groups; kept a mental roster of the willing and able; and filled his own home with displaced citizens.

The cost of raising buildings left the town few funds for a firehouse. Not giving up, Lodie instigated fire patrols — eight-man teams walking every street, twenty-four hours a day, seven days a week. He took many a night shift himself to fill the gaps. His presence was so entrenched in the minds of the townspeople they became accustomed to his voice in all city matters and easily elected him mayor.

Althea felt her face grow hot. She scanned the long table where she sat. An array of bearded fellow merchants sat on both sides of her chewing on topics they had no hope of resolving this day. The looming possibility of war, the imminent flood problems, rumors of a new silver strike, and Crazy Judah's railroad had the men so abuzz they batted one subject after another across the room to the opposing table of the town council members, equally absorbed in loudly fielding each of these themes.

She shuffled the papers before her, unable to contain her restlessness at the meandering of subjects. Too many lives lost and ruined came to the forefront of her mind. She felt time and decorum slipping away. She wished silently they would all adjourn and "Go to *Blazes*" — the inside joke of Jim Blaze's bar, where men went to discuss the politics of the day.

The overbearing volley of men's voices increased in volume. The rumbling sound of so many gnats had escalated to banter and shouting. She could bear it no more. Althea smacked the table in front of her loudly and bolted to her feet. A stunned silence resulted and austere stares protested her interruption. A clean-shaven face in the row of beards leaned forward from his end of the table. Lodie's clear, blue eyes sparkled.

"Gentlemen — pardon my intrusion . . . but I fear I must interject," she stated firmly. "I believe we have lost sight of the main purpose of these proceedings."

Althea cleared her throat and continued. "We simply *must* pass today, without delay, the motion to begin construction of Nevada City Hose Company No. 1, as well as appointments of fire chief and training schedules for the volunteer fire brigade. We have covered the details of the past in all profundity. Indeed, I cannot help but recount the painful losses we have all suffered in my head and have no desire to engage them further. The only logical course is to embark on the details of the building process."

Althea turned to the merchants sitting on either side of her. "These good men have come to offer their time and talents to that end. Our citizens demand the security of our action today. We have overcome tremendous catastrophe with brilliant effort from everyone in this room." She sighed, acknowledging the weight of the other concerns. "I understand that we have *many* unprecedented challenges ahead that will demand our complete attention . . . in their own time. But our fire brigade . . . is a problem we can solve today. The discussions we hold now should concern its implementation to ensure the continued growth and success we have all worked so hard to procure."

She spoke so quickly and assertively that the end of her oration caught her by surprise. With a slight inclination of her head she added, "That is all I have to say." She folded her hands in front of her and waited.

The merchants and tradesmen at her table began murmuring their assent. Lodie rose from his seat and stated, "The lady is entirely correct. Gentlemen. You have in front of you the budget and proposal for Nevada City Hose Company No. 1, as well as a secondary proposal for the Eureka Hose Company No. 2." He stopped and aimed a stern look at both directions of his table. "These are not *competing* projects. We will pass them both. Before we delve into the details we will vote. All in favor?"

A round of deep toned "ayes" resounded.

"Opposed?"

Silence.

"Very well, then. Thank you, Althea."

As she quietly sat back in her seat, she heard him add drily, "Apparently, our English Rose is prickly enough to keep us on point. Let's get to work, people."

CHAPTER 22

Spring 1860

The beauty of the day discouraged lingering in Nevada City. Lush trees appeared full and green, poppies and lavender covered hillsides in brilliant reds and purples.

Charlotte and Justin completed their errands as quickly as possible. They invited Lodie, Matilda, and their three growing boys to picnic after church on Sunday, and Justin picked out a tie to wear to an upcoming birthday party. Charlotte noted his glance as he made his selection. Though technically he had not asked her opinion, she nodded her approval. After brisk hellos, good-byes, and thank-yous, they bolted for the freedom and sunshine. A horserace was in the offing.

Cutting through forest paths led to jumping courses over fallen logs. Their horses took the mountain switchbacks with ease, prancing in a serpentine trek as they ducked low-lying branches. Their unabashed independence sparked a brief chase of a fox, which took them off their homeward trail and to the discovery of wild berries. Time belonged to the moment.

Completing their descent out of the hills, the egress of the shady path hinted brightness at its end, and they burst forth into the light of the open field building to full speed. Foliage brushed Charlotte's side as she emerged from the cover of underbrush into the dazzling meadow, the tall grasses slapping their feathery tops against her boots. The smoothness of her mare's flight was a sensory delight after days of working the bumpy gate of freight-wagon steeds.

Justin tucked tightly against his mount and surged past her in a determined bid to victory in an undefined race. She reined in her sorrel mare and trotted up to where he crossed the imaginary finish line to let his black gelding take a rest.

"More fun than working the teams?" he grinned.

"Da says teams are our bread and butter. Though I see him sneaking in saddle worthy animals," she answered. "Besides, I'd rather be outdoors breaking the stock to carriage than stuck inside the shop helping Althea sew. Apparently, I need a 'worthy skill.' "

Justin's horse stretched out his stout neck to snatch the clusters of grass within reach, tearing the spring shoots from their roots. Charlotte dropped her reins and the sorrel mare shifted to a relaxed grazing stance, joining in the endless grinding as searching lips moved from one mound to the next, methodically pulling and cropping the grass close. Charlotte swung a leg over her saddle horn, the breeze lightly sweeping escaped tendrils of her hair.

Justin held a finger in the air, giving his best James imitation. "Freight animals are proven moneymakers, the mainstay of our trade."

Charlotte giggled. "True enough, but I know Da. He longs to raise a gentleman's horse, but says that's a luxury. The only thing he misses about Boston is the quality of the stock he trained for the Doyles. He loves speed and agility."

"Hmm. Well he didn't much care for the 'Lord-let' being in charge of him."

"Lord-let? The Doyles weren't titled. Perhaps he was a third or fourth son with no inheritance. They came to America for Mr. Doyle to go into business with an uncle. Mrs. Doyle was one of the Vernon daughters on the estate where Mother and Althea grew up together."

315

"Still, James was indentured to Lord Vernon to pay for their passages. They all were. Mum was ready to bolt the second her time was done. And you know how James hates grand manners and superior airs."

Charlotte raised her eyebrows. "Nothing makes him so cross as arrogance. But if he wants to raise fine horses, then he'd better adjust or he'll have no one to sell to!"

Justin dropped his stirrups and leaned his elbows back to rest on the gelding's rump. Each step his mount took foraging rocked his position in a gentle sway.

"One more day of chores, then Sunday," he sighed. "What'll you and Mum fix for the picnic?"

Charlotte dismounted and sat on a boulder, loosely hanging on to her reins as the mare grazed. "These berries are bound to make their way into a pie. We've got one of Mr. Benjamin's good hams, biscuits, jam, some deviled eggs, and corn pudding. I suspect Mrs. Glenn will bring her fried chicken; maybe some pickles."

Justin hopped down and stood beside his horse, fussing with his saddle cinch. "You suppose anybody else will picnic after church?"

She glanced up at him suspiciously. "Who

316

are you looking for?"

"Nobody," he answered quickly. "Besides, it's you who should look out. I hear Hoyt and Frank are kinda sweet on you."

"Och." She uttered an annoyed tone. "I wish you would tell me what's wrong with the both of them."

Romantic notions were of no consequence to Charlotte, considering herself too young and too smart for such ideas. As she saw it, her childhood chums had hardly materialized into masculine stature; they were simply boys. She looked at her father's example of steely confidence and knew the boys were ridiculously silly. Hoyt and Frank came around a lot lately, finding reasons to ask her opinions. Unbeknownst to her, they struggled to speak up at this awkward age and she gave the decided appearance of being aloof.

"Have they both gone goofy or something?" she demanded. "You know, a year ago, either one of them would argue me up a wall on any topic, right or wrong. Now they stand there and gawk like they've forgotten how to talk. If they do ask something, they don't even listen to what I say. Sometimes I change answers to see if they notice, but they don't. They agree with anything."

Justin pondered this while trying not to implicate himself in similar behavior, but she knew him too well.

"And don't think I haven't seen you looking at Sarah Midland the same darn way! Bunch of scatterbrained, moony-eyed, addled boys, all of you!" she muttered.

"Well, Ella Louise follows me around like a puppy."

Charlotte grinned. "Not for her own sake."

He looked surprised. "Who, then?"

"Guess you'll find out at the birthday party."

"Oh, come on; I'd tell you."

She rolled her eyes. "Well, who's been glued to her side lately?"

"Not Nancy!" He groaned. "I *have* to be nice because it's her birthday."

"What's wrong with Nancy?"

"You like her?"

"Sure, why not?"

"See, now that's half your problem. You tend to like people first and figure out why later."

"So? It's not a bad way to be; I give everybody a chance."

"And then some. You make too many allowances. You don't think she's trying to cut you out with Ella Louise?" Justin scowled. "I notice Ella Louise's been kinda cool towards you this week. The two of them off whispering together all the time."

"Oh, Ella Louise got upset last Saturday. I had to gather eggs before I helped her pick out ribbons for the party. She's scared of most things, you know. She followed me to see the chickens and that fox was lurking around. I took the shotgun Da keeps behind the henhouse and let him have it. Unnerved her, it did. She started crying and carrying on about the poor fox. I told her it served him right for stealing Da's breakfast. What about the poor hens? They're defenseless, I said. She thought I was mean."

"She's a big baby. Her Ma does everything for her. Nancy's a mean one though. I don't like the way she looks at you."

Charlotte thought about his observation. She took Nancy's demeanor as blunt, but harbored a nagging doubt. She had caught the peculiar intensity of gaze that could not be mistaken as directness. Her fixed look scrutinized for confirmation of Charlotte's trust, a quest for signs of uncertainty. Even when Nancy lied, her fierce countenance dared Charlotte to question.

"She doesn't have many friends."

"Small wonder. Charlotte, she's jealous of you."

"Then why would she invite me to her party?"

"Beats me why she invited either one of us."

"I guess you know now why she invited you."

He blew out an exasperated breath. "You have to stick close to me at that party."

"There'll be plenty of people to talk to. I'll keep an eye out. But you do the same for me. I can't abide another speechless staring contest with Frank or Hoyt."

"Agreed. Geez, who'd have thought a party would be something to dread?"

"It won't be that bad. Half the school will be there." She glanced skyward at the sun's position. "Say, we better move towards home. I don't want Da to worry."

"Right." He tugged his reins, pulling the stocky gelding reluctantly away from the grass. "If we leave now we should make it right on time."

CHAPTER 23

Marysville

The massive flock burst from the tule rushes as if a stone had been thrown into their midst. The teals, mallards, pintails, and geese, startling in their numbers, bespoke the magnitude of the reservoir from whence they arose. The vast lake lay hidden and quiet for miles until the cacophony of thousands of wings beating the air reverberated over the water and their honking cries sounded retreat.

James watched in wonder, as the colossal covey took flight. Only months ago the towering tules swayed and rustled drily in the cold wind. Spring rains and melting snows from the nearby Sierra Nevada hurtled violent quantities of water down the mountainside, saturating the valley below. Once the valley floor consumed its fill, ponding and spreading, it began its advance on farms and towns unprepared to deal with the excess. James rode into town on his favorite blood bay, Rusty, instead of taking the wagon. He minced his way through the forest since the usual path was swallowed up by a tide overdue to recede.

More mysterious than hundreds of miles of terrain encroached on by floodwaters was the time taken for the inland sea to withdraw. In Marysville, the Yuba rose three feet higher than the previous year. Water appeared in town during years of torrential storms and two weeks was insufficient for it to drain away. Boats became necessary to navigate the streets in Sacramento, where the Sacramento River merged with the American River.

Marysville's Mayor Creed called the meeting for the two towns most affected by flooding and the mining districts in all Nevada County. Directly across the Feather River from Marysville sat Yuba City. Both towns colonized at relatively the same time. As settlers steamed up the Feather and advanced to where it branched with the Yuba, some chose the left bank, while others went right; a simple choice as they scouted for farm and ranch lands. Once gold was discovered, those on the right bank became inundated with miners. Marysville's businesses thrived by virtue of convenience to the mines and her population surged ahead of Yuba City. Like jealous siblings, an unspoken resentment began.

Of the hordes of pioneers lured into brief romance with found riches, some sensibly abandoned pursuits in favor of fertile soil. In the goldfields they labored day after long day, barely filling their stomachs, much less their pockets. When the delirium of gold fever passed, they recognized the glittering promise as a cruel mistress. Prosperity in the form of black soil lay inches beneath their feet, enhanced by a wealth of minerals carried to the valley floor by spring thaws and nurtured under a blanket of inland sea. Their mode of digging changed — no longer roughly taking from the land, they coaxed in a more respectful manner. Farmers from states of scarce and coveted rain could not believe their luck, and also their curse. Untouched lands made an enticing gift for those bold enough to grab them.

Miners and farmers lived in symbiotic harmony up to this point and James successfully made a living in both vocations. Then an intruder was discovered building in the riverbeds. Tailings from the mines choked river traffic and exacerbated the seasonal flooding.

Rusty's hooves squelched the mud as

James guided him down C Street to the Gold Feather Hotel. In advance of the meeting, the bars were staggeringly full. Dismounting, James loosened his horse's cinch and noted the disposition of the crowd. Men hurried through the streets, heads down and stony faced. The damp air felt even heavier with concerns over clashing livelihoods and frustrations at the hand of nature. Rumors escalated of secession and war, and he knew California's physical distance from the emotionally charged debate was aggravated by the slow arrival of information. People based point of view on ways of life engrained since birth. Opinions over slave state or free and state's rights were all theories except when one still had family half a continent away.

James sidled through men tightly jammed in the doorway of the Gold Feather Bar. The noise level escalated to shouting in order to be heard. From the snippets of arguments he caught as he passed, James detected suspicions of ambiguous origin circling the room like a tantalizing wisp of smoke. An insidious, poisonous mood caused neighbors to look upon one another with distrust.

The threat of war hung suspended above them, along with uncertainty of when it might drop suddenly in their midst. James knew fear made men jumpy and stupid; made them react instead of act; made them leap to conclusions. He had seen men find blame as an excuse to fight. He knew frustrations often boiled down to the need to fight something: the need to prevail, win, beat back a foe. But, so far, no tangible foe presented itself.

And then ugliness broke out. At the back of the crowded saloon, he saw Bracuus Donovan acting upon his inclination to lash out. Living in close proximity to the man, he knew a quarter of Bracuus's land was under enough water to render it useless for planting this season. James heard enough of his grumbling to know he did not particularly care about solutions for the future, nor did ethical, honorable, or honest thought enter his equation. The man hinted he had a remedy to square things for this year. James watched Bracuus as he inched his way through the closely bunched throng.

"You'll never pass muster," Bracuus growled.

James saw an attack well underway. A few men with hostile feelings of their own clustered around. Then he caught a glimpse of the man's target.

"I fit the rules. I be of correct age . . ."

began Benjamin Jones. He stood grasping his hat in front of him tightly.

Bracuus cut Benjamin off, threatening more loudly. "Seeing how things are, I ain't sure legally you got the *right* to own land. Somebody might still own *you* for all we know."

Angry mumblings of agreement echoed around the elderly black man.

"I've been to the land office. As a legal . . . voting . . . citizen . . ." sneered his tormentor.

"Then you know I got clear title to my land."

"No one'll vouch for you," Bracuus scoffed. "Takes witnesses to say improvements have been made to give title. It'll take years to straighten out and you'll starve before that ever happens. Best to cut your losses and cut out. That land don't belong to the likes of you. I'll file a complaint. I say it's all a lie —"

Benjamin watched Bracuus steadily. His lips moved ever so slightly as if saying an inward prayer. The crowd stirred and he flinched, then took a deep breath and calmly held his ground. Nervous bystanders shuffled out of the way and the gathering slowly parted as James stepped into its inner circle.

"Donovan. I won't take kindly ta ye calling me a liar."

James's tone quieted the room. His eyes flickered with anger and his stance dared Bracuus to make a move.

Bracuus chuckled uneasily, and glanced around for support. "Come now, Mac-Laren. I've your interest at heart as much as any others here. You're downstream of him; surely you don't want the water fouled from above?"

James's jaw tightened. "A man works for what he claims. That makes him worthy of respect. It also makes him worthy of protection from thieves. Benjamin here has put half a lifetime inta buying his freedom and his land. I hate ta think anyone I knew was willing ta steal from another man's sweat — ta take his livelihood. Isn't that what ye all fear from a company mine?" He glanced around the bar. "And yet, look at ye — ready ta take what isn't yers, what ye have na earned. Why? Are ye jealous he's been smarter?"

James continued to seek the eyes of individuals with his steely glare. Each in turn looked down. "We're neighbors. We stand together as men," he urged.

Bracuus looked down. "There's still a legal question here . . ."

"I see none. In fact, for you, Donovan, I

327

intend ta send an inquiry ta the federal land commissioner in Washington. I hope ye have yer own paperwork in order."

James extended his arm towards his friend. "Benjamin Jones, would ye care ta join me for a drink before the meeting?"

"Believe I will."

As they walked to the bar, the mutterers dispersed back to their own worries. Bracuus was left standing alone to mull over his options, of which he chose wisely to leave.

After ordering drinks, James asked lowly, "Aye, in case of trouble, ye do have those freedom papers on hand?"

Benjamin Jones nodded. "Lock box in my house. Been duly recorded in the county where I was set free."

"Good. But I think I'd bury that box or put it in the bank." James tipped his glass. "To yer health."

Known in San Francisco as the distinguished Judge Dandridge, he banked on anonymity here in Marysville. He switched his feet on the brass foot rail, shifting his considerable weight to a more comfortable lean. Standing at the bar for awhile, he nursed a bottle of fine brandy while listening in on conversations around him. In the shouts and swells of opposing opinions, he surveyed and scrutinized the crowd. A fascinating scene had played out before him and he was instantly drawn to the magnetism of the tall Scot. He watched heads turn when the man spoke and shouters hush their clamor to hear his words. Intriguing. He made a mental note to inquire about this MacLaren chap.

As a speculator, Walter Dandridge's interests at the meeting varied. He owned property in Yuba City and he considered the floods to be a damned expensive nuisance. He held stakes in mining — mostly hydraulic — but he recently began backing quartz and hard-rock operations, and therefore his investments seemed to war with one another. To diversify, he dabbled with Chinese imports and he fostered a growing involvement with railroad interests.

He studied Theodore Judah, and saw nothing crazy about the man but his tireless drive. Judah's passion for bridging the gap between oceans promised to open markets for California. He proselytized in the streets of Sacramento, extolling the virtues of the Pacific railroad and looking for backing. He explored the towering Sierras for a pathway through, lobbied Washington for survey funding, and published his plan to build the transcontinental effort. In the end, a discouraging President Buchanan suggested he forget the railroad until the bickering nation settled its differences. Begrudgingly, Judge Dandridge admitted fighting over a northern versus a southern route could keep Congress tied up for years.

Lately, he found the only endeavor no longer of interest to him was the bench. His years as adjudicator of the law garnered significant clout in political circles and his range of influence rose. The recent duel killing Senator Broderick at the hand of a chief justice of the Supreme Court took the sand right out of him. He liked Broderick. Most people did, though his own interests grew complicated by the fact that Broderick and Brannan despised one another.

Judge Terry was a Texan with a hair-trigger temper and, even though Broderick once defended him during difficulties with the Vigilance Committee, back room deals caused Terry to lose re-election. Along with the senselessness of Broderick's death, soaring altercations with battling north-south allegiances tainted everything — business, politics, and the law. Disheartened, Judge Dandridge decided to retire and he wrote to Dutton at Harvard to tell him so.

The judge glanced at his near empty brandy glass and wondered that his mood had not improved. He tossed back the rest of his drink, paid his tab, and left unnoticed as he made his way over to the meeting.

The Presbyterian Church filled quickly. Judge Dandridge noted the contingent from Yuba City took a large portion of pews on the front left, merchants from Marysville on the right. A long plank table sat in the front of the church as a podium for selected speakers. Mayor Creed took the center chair to officiate over the proceedings.

Representatives from developing Empire and North Star mines filed in as well as the far away Bloomfield. They came largely to listen and report back to their superiors about concerns of the towns and any legal action of note.

Farmers and businessmen from both sides of the Feather River crowded into center aisle seats, their towns competing for river control. With plenty of blame to spread around, Bracuus Donovan sat near the front. The judge observed wryly that he also sat as far from MacLaren as possible. He saw MacLaren wave to a man named Sean Miller, who banded with a party of hydraulic miners. Mayor Lodie Glenn arrived with a delegation from Nevada City — Steven Swift and Peter Stuben from the Silver Moon and Tobias Clark from the Nevada

City Hotel. The northern mining towns' supplies dropped dangerously low when steamers bogged down before reaching port. Floodwaters covering the Brown's Valley Road out of Marysville had stopped freight wagon deliveries.

Once the church filled to capacity, Mayor Creed stood and pounded his gavel. Conversations closed and all focused on the front of the room.

"All right," he began sternly, "I want order. Everyone will get a turn. But first I insist on patience since the spokesmen need to lay the facts before us. Once they finish, I'll open the floor."

"Now," he continued, "let's begin by reviewing the problem at hand — the history of floods in these parts. Many of us survived the big one in '50. In Sacramento, that January brought a flood that dislodged homes and carried essentials from stores into the streets — floating away at the whim of an angry river. Everything within a mile of the Sacramento River was ruined. Most homes and businesses saw water invade up to their first floors. During this crisis, we sent a small steamboat chugging through streets to make deliveries of food and supplies. The troubles in *our* area follow this pattern — if Sacramento is hit hard, so shall we be. We'd be wise to look at how they fight this problem.

"Marysville built levees in response to flooding. Yuba City did likewise. For some time it appeared we made progress stemming this tide. Now we've got the additional burden of our rivers — our lifelines, the Feather and the Yuba — being choked out. Furthermore, this state of affairs suffocates our commerce and increases flooding yet again. Farmlands are suffering and not necessarily the same areas as before."

A ripple of murmurs broke out as groups acknowledged their individual hardships.

Hammond Creed banged the gavel on the table. "So we agree thus far. I'd like to introduce the editor and publisher of the *Colusa Sun,* Will Green. Colusa's tremendous flooding stretches as far away as Sutter Buttes and all farmland in between. Mr. Green has spent considerable time studying the situation. Mr. Green."

A thin, bearded man with spectacles rose from his seat at the table.

"Thank you, Mayor Creed. It's no secret there's a considerable fight with the ebb and flow of nature. As a new territory here — there were no rules — there was no precedent to follow and different conditions to this land. Trial and error was our way, often begetting a devastating cost when wrong. Unfortunately, we ignored the warnings of the Indians and the Spanish concerning the flood plain of the Valley. They knew Sacramento was built in the middle of a seasonal ocean. The rich soil proved too tempting to ignore, and we willingly put ourselves in the face of a force we couldn't hope to conquer. In quieter years we believed we made progress, and indeed levees seemed to alleviate the problem. But we must face the fact the levees we built are inadequate."

Shouts flew from the townspeople.

"Inadequate? We paid bloody fortunes in taxes for those levees!"

"Where is our money now, then?"

"I suppose you're here to suggest more taxes?"

Mayor Creed pounded his gavel again. "Let the man finish!" he bellowed. The crowd quieted to a low grumble.

Will Green waited for them to settle. "Cost."

He waited again. "The estimates on the original levees were overwhelming. What we wanted to build was many feet longer along the course of the river *and* higher. Our current levee is approximately three feet high and twelve feet at the base. Its construction is built from earth scraped into a mound.

For us on the Yuba City side, we found most of Sutter County lies below the height of the Feather River at flood stage. At its worst, water backs up all the way to the Buttes. Folks, we've seen cattle drowning in the lowlands caught with no outlet. And, while our levee holds for now, we're dangerously close to the river topping over due to our current problem — and that is the mines. It's no secret our river problems are caused by hydraulic mining. *Look* at the Yuba. It's permanently yellow from mud and deposits. Silt and slickens pile up and raise the riverbeds. Every spring operations start up and every creek that feeds our rivers is overwhelmed with tailings. Navigation is impeded on the Feather and the Yuba. How long before the Sacramento is permanently clogged and we're cut off from *all* river transportation? Before our farms are *all* under water? The damage is too great. We need to put a stop to hydraulic mining."

Sean Miller stood angrily. "There's a long history of floods in this valley and that ain't the fault of the mines. We got as much right to earn a living as the farmers *and* the merchants, who, by the way, make most their money off'n us!"

"No doubt," conceded Will Green, "flooding is not the fault of the mines. But the rivers are directly affected by the mass of soil the mines dump there with such force."

"Maybe towns and farms shouldn't a built so close to the river."

"No one could have known . . ."

"The Indians did! Some of us noticed right off they knew *exactly* what months to pack up and move. Shoulda told you something."

"Nature *will not* tolerate anything we choose to do to it without devastating results!" huffed Will Green.

Bracuus Donovan stood. "I didn't have none of the trouble I got now until the country went gold crazy, and I been here long as anybody. The way I see it, the mines are stealing my land by putting it under water!"

Shouts broke out in all parts of the room. Hammond Creed stood and thumped his gavel for a full minute before the noise died down. "All right! No more interruptions or I'll disband these proceedings." He waited silently, staring down the gathering. "We can work through this. We're not here to shut anyone down. It's good to have our miners at work. They bring prosperity and growth to our towns. In California a man's got the right to do what he sees fit with his own property whether it's a mine, a farm, a store, or a bar. I remind you all, we have a free enterprise system here."

"Mayor Creed?" James MacLaren rose from his seat. "I am in agreement with ye, sir; might I have a word?"

Hammond Creed hesitated. "I've two more speakers up here MacLaren. Make it brief."

"Of course." He turned and looked at those seated behind him, rotating as he spoke, seeking their faces. "What we don't want is relentless warfare amongst neighbors. Too easy ta start and too hard ta stop. Therefore — we decide here and now there is no enemy *here*. Let all speak ta the details they know so we find a solution. Nothing'll stop rainy season or snow melting. The reason yer land is fertile is because of the minerals the floods bring out of the mountains. I got my start in the mines — many of us did — and now I have a farm. We're going ta have ta make adjustments. All of us."

Will Green interjected, "And have you, Mr. MacLaren, encountered an increase in flooding on your land?"

Sean Miller sang out from his seat, "No, 'cos the stingy bastard talked to everyone in three counties before he spent a red cent. Indians included."

There was a ripple of laughter.

MacLaren glanced over at Miller, grinning. He shrugged. "True enough."

At this, the laughter grew louder and people relaxed. Miller winked at his friend, who continued, "Look, I'm no engineer. But many of us came from places affected by floods or rivers. There's got ta be a wealth of experience amongst us. For example, I spent a few years in Boston, a city built right on the River Charles. Over a great many years, the city tripled in size by land reclamation. They filled in marshes and mud flats, even gaps between wharves and such. They called it 'cutting down the hills to fill in the coves.' They brought in gravel ta build on."

"And how does that help the farms?"

"I don't have the answer, but there *is* one in this somewhere. A pity we can'na harness the silt clogging up the rivers the same way excess water was used ta create the hydraulic mining. The point is — we have ta be open about the challenges without attaching blame."

Will Green irritably quipped, "What we have is a self inflicted problem!"

"Perhaps so, Mr. Green. But what we have are different ways of life here — all dependent on each other. You don't cut off your nose ta cure hay fever. What we're looking for is the way for *all* of us ta survive and prosper."

The crowd murmured in agreement. The judge considered all points of view.

Mayor Creed took control. "Thank you, James, for that perspective. We're here to pull together in crisis, not pull each other apart. Now . . . I'd like to introduce Sidney Raymond, a surveyor working closely with Mr. Green on gathering facts concerning outputs of mining debris and its effect on our rivers. I caution you," he pointed the gavel at the group, "this information is to help us find an answer, so let the man get through his findings without interruption. Mr. Raymond."

Sidney Raymond appeared nervous. He stood tightly grasping a sheaf of papers.

"Thank you." He glanced at the crowd. "Please remember these numbers are estimates for discussion purposes. I will, at various points, mention suggestions if that meets with approval?" He looked back at Mayor Creed, who nodded.

"First, there's a legacy of potent forces here — water and gravity. On that we all agree. It's how our gold came to be in stratified beds to begin with. We resorted to doing whatever necessary to get the profit out in direct defiance of the natural course of our rivers. Hydraulic systems put out a pressurized column of water, 120 feet per second, and literally dissolve a mountainside.

"French Corral, for example, is one of many sites and is less than thirty miles from Marysville. Ten thousand tons of dirt a day run through their long sluices. Now consider nearly a hundred different mining operations, of all types, making similar assaults on our landscape daily. The very mechanics of this has brutal results. Rivers adjust to the amount of debris dumped by jumping their banks or changing course — and, in rainy season, carry their load all the way to the Sacramento River through the Yuba and the Feather.

"We believed a network of ditches and flumes would contain this. The mines own close to fifty-six hundred miles of flumes and aqueducts combined. It hasn't been contained despite our best efforts. Debris and sediment impact gradually. We don't know *which* mines originate the problem. But we've determined where the problems accumulate, so this is what we must address. All that said — where are our problems located?"

At this point, Mr. Raymond put down his

stack of papers and held up a large map of the valley's river system. Creaks and groans emanated from chairs as people strained to see.

"Our riverbeds are rising; our banks are not. Drainage channels can't carry floodwater without overflow. As previously noted, the Yuba is yellow from heavy mud, sand, and gravel it takes on from the mines. Sands and silts now reach the mouth of the Yuba, here . . ." He traced the path of debris along the map with his finger. ". . . moving into the channel of the Feather, here. A large sandbar has built up in the shape of an arc in the Feather at its eastern bank. This leaves only a curved, narrow passageway for vessels. This means severe limitations to size and draft of such vessels, *and* restrictions to the amount of its cargo. Blocked rivers are choking our livelihoods. The points below Marysville and Yuba City have debris pushing into the channel, causing the river to breach its banks and invade farms. This build-up is the reason the Browns Valley Road from Marysville to Grass Valley and Nevada City has been under water the past two seasons.

"Suggestions? We can look for dam locations to hold part of it back. We can expand, reinforce, and heighten our existing levee systems. We can make true channels of the existing sloughs to relieve stress points in controlled flooding and let them act as rivers. Some sloughs, such as the Gilsizer, already require a ferry to cross them. Or, if we built a levee across the head of the slough, closing the mouth where it joins the river, it may keep the river from over running the farms. These are suggestions. Any option carries significant costs, and for that you must be prepared. It will be minor in comparison to damages. Engineers must be hired for the success of any of these undertakings. Thank you for your patience."

Judge Dandridge felt his head pounding as he processed the information. Low conversations erupted in small groups as Hammond Creed rose from his seat. "Thank you, Mr. Raymond, for that overview. I want to introduce now the mayor of Yuba City, Leonard Caisman, who'll speak to the need of a unified plan to solve our common dilemma on our shared riverfronts. Mr. Caisman?"

At this time a man from Bloomfield looked behind, searching the crowd. He caught the eye of Judge Dandridge, who nodded almost imperceptibly. Taking his cue, he turned back to the speaker.

Mayor Caisman stood abruptly, his hands

in his pockets.

"I'll make this brief; I don't have a speech. However, it's come to the attention of both Mayor Creed and myself, the need for a combined effort in addressing our levee systems. I also appreciate the need for engineering advice. Currently, we're doing little more than putting our fingers in a leaky dike. We're responding in haste to emergencies instead of planning how to prevent them. Independently, we're only pushing the flood from one side of the river to the other, or further downstream.

"Hammond and I will work together to hire advisors, present a plan to both cities, and share costs and benefits. In the meantime, we've called a halt to *any* additions of the levee system on both sides so we don't aggravate the situation. We invite members of both towns with ideas and suggestions to bring them to our attention prior to our posted meeting times. Thank you. That is all."

"Well said, Leonard. At this time I will take comments from the floor."

Bracuus Donovan jumped to his feet before Hammond could strike his gavel. Mayor Creed sighed. "Mr. Donovan?"

"I've got a problem with Mr. Raymond's suggestion of making channels out of our sloughs — I point out a lot of those sloughs cut right through the middle of farms. Placer Slough cuts my land nearly in half. If you make it a channel, it'd separate one side completely from the other, making it near impossible to work it."

"Does the slough itself not cause this problem?" asked Mayor Creed.

"In high water times, yeah. But not year round. If something permanent's done to my land, reparations should be made." He nodded indignantly.

"It's something to consider, yes, thank you, Mr. Donovan. Multiple suggestions will be fielded before we settle on a solution. Next, Mayor Lodie Glenn?"

Lodie rose. "We in Nevada City, Grass Valley, all the mining towns, are dependent on both river transportation out of Marysville and freight carriers on Browns Valley Road. Spring and winter the last two years, we've lost our freight traffic to flooding. In hot weather, the rivers run low and shipments run aground before they make it to the docks. We bring a great deal of business into Marysville, and I ask if there'd be room for a representative from our area — we'd like to help."

"Thank you, Lodie, excellent idea. See me before you leave. Next . . . I'm sorry, sir, I don't know your name?"

The man from Bloomfield spoke. "Some of you miners know me; I'm Judd Olmstead. I work outta French Corral. Me and the other managers along the ridge want to reassure folks we're looking for ways to help the situation. Floods and rain been particular bad this year and we don't want to add to the problem — we need supplies, too. So, the next coupla months, we're gonna do more blasting than using the hoses. Maybe the roads'll dry out faster." He gave a quick nod and sat down.

A few men answered with cheers and whoops.

"Well, now," began Hammond Creed, "that's the kind of spirit needed. Cooperation! As I said earlier, we'll be posting meeting times and dates. We welcome ideas before the first meeting — which will be in two weeks. Thank you all for coming." He banged the gavel hard for dismissal.

The attendees broke into groups exiting the church, each rehashing their own problems and any ideas they favored. Judge Dandridge watched MacLaren make his way over to Mayor Glenn. The two men grasped hands warmly. Curious, he turned his back as he listened in.

"Good to see you, James. Saw your young-

sters up at the store recently. How is everything?"

"Busy, as I'm sure ye are as well. I've been
meaning ta get up there — one thing's for
certain — it's easier ta get ta Nevada City
from Thistle Dew than ta Marysville with
the roads in the shape they are."

"Must be tough for a man with children
to be away."

"They're good kids. They bicker, as kids
do, but they're a big help."

Lodie sighed. "Matilda misses Emma
something fierce. We both do."

James paused. "We manage. Say," he
lowered his voice, "I'd probably be shot for
saying this, but you ought ta look into
Nicolas for back-up supplies. They don't
get large steamers ta dock, but it's steady.
Whichever way the river bends, they don't
seem ta have the same problems getting
stuck."

"Appreciate the tip. I've one for you as
well. Keep an eye on Caisman."

MacLaren sounded surprised. "Meaning?"

"I had dealings with the man early on.
Not the most upstanding of sorts. I'll say
this — he'll push those meetings, making
sure changes are to their advantage. He's
got a real grudge when it comes to Marys-

ville. He lost a business he blames on the gold rush and unfair advantage on the river. He means to recoup his losses."

"Hammond's a shrewd business man; he'll catch on."

"Sure, sure. But he'll still need help. A lot's at stake here and I don't see a solution to split things fifty-fifty. Marysville could end up paying for projects that only benefit Yuba City. Caisman says they stopped adding to their levees, but he's lying. I intend to tell Hammond so."

"I thought we'd moved beyond feudal battles. Bears watching I suppose."

"I intend to," answered Lodie. "Care to meet me in town for the first meeting?"

The judge reached to gather his things, intending to slip quietly away.

James smiled and clapped his friend on the back. "There's better reasons ta get together, but if this is what it takes to pull us away from work, so be it."

"Good. Drink?"

"Had mine for the day, thanks, but I'll walk over with ye."

Leaving the church, Judge Dandridge passed by Judd Olmstead, who waited for him. He gave the man a firm nod as if to say, "That's all." He turned on his heel, walking quickly away.

347

As an investor at North San Juan Ridge and North Bloomfield, he had asked Olmstead to deliver that speech. In truth, a real slump existed in hydraulic mining on the ridge. They had reached harder gravels, requiring more force to break them apart than the current equipment could handle. Blasting was the *only* way for progress, but the judge felt it couldn't hurt to present facts in the best possible light. It might keep folks like that crusading newspaperman from Colusa off their backs. Overall, it proved to be an enlightening day.

CHAPTER 24

The Games of Dueling Cities

Floodwaters had receded from the roads, but deep mud ruts appeared with enough frequency to make travel onerous. Althea decided to take James up on his offer to drive them all to town in the spring wagon. The day of the birthday party finally arrived, coinciding with the first Feather River Flood Committee meeting.

"You know the road to Nevada City hasn't been too bad," she said peering ahead. "Bumpy, maybe. We could have made it all right, and you wouldn't have to go so far out of your way."

"No sense in chancing it," answered James. "Besides, one good bump and ye cu lose a wheel. Look at all of ye, scrubbed and pressed in new clothes. Would na do ta arrive covered in mud at the Potters'. Anyways, I'll catch up with Lodie on the way ta Marysville, so it works out fine."

349

"You'll get an earful. I expect to hear the latest details after dinner tonight. He certainly chats up his customers for all the local tidbits."

"Is that opposed ta all the chinwagging ye ladies do?" He laughed. "What makes ye think ye haven't heard it all already?"

"Oh, hush. I, like Lodie, am obligated to listen when customers are in the shop. Our roles in town management make us both targets when issues weigh on someone's mind. Engaging them only makes good business sense."

"Of course. Ye're both gracious that way." James clucked to the horses as their hooves pounded a hollow rhythm over the Deer Creek Bridge. He guided them up Broad Street.

"Growing up a lady's maid was excellent training. No matter what's said, you mind your tongue and your opinions." She sighed. "For the most part, I love working in town. Every customer arrives with different expectations. Friends visit; some want a confidant; others want to play grand dame and treat me like a servant. I'm certainly trained for it all." She looked at James earnestly. "It's rather personal when fitting someone for clothes!"

"I can imagine." He glanced in the backseat of the wagon at Charlotte and Justin talking about their school chums. "But I dare not."

She shot him a disapproving look.

"What? Ye brought it up. Speaking of grand dames . . . how did ye rate an invite ta the festivities?"

"It's a chaperone role, I think." She lowered her voice. "To hear Claudine talk, I don't think she really likes children."

"She's got three bairns! Spoiled rotten, all of 'em." He nodded, talking to himself. "Well, there ye go. Perhaps it's why she doesn't like them. Ye ha ta discipline or they become miserable creatures."

As James pulled the wagon in front of Althea's shop, he noted, "Ah, there's the wee littlest one now."

"Hi, Nancy!" Charlotte scrambled down to meet the girl waiting by the shop door.

"Oh, dear, she's early." She reached inside her reticule for the key. "Justin, let her in, please."

Althea watched the girls giggle together as Justin dutifully unlocked the door. James secured the reins and walked around to help her down. She shook her head as the children rushed inside. "Three pampered Potter girls. I do believe sense of entitlement trickles down. That one's grown into a manipulative bully with perfectly coiffed hair!"

James burst out laughing. "Why, Thea!" He lifted her down.

"I'm sorry. That was uncalled for." Althea shook out the front of her dress, smoothing it from the long ride. "The family brings me a *lot* of business. But the child is quite calculating with other girls. She's not always kind to Charlotte."

James smiled at her fondly. "I appreciate ye wanting ta protect her. Ye know I feel the same for Justin. Aye, we're a patched together crew."

As he took her arm, he patted her hand as they entered the shop. "Charlotte's got a big heart. She'll learn ta protect it. She knows how ta fight when she's had enough."

"I suppose. Still doesn't make it easy to watch." She looked curiously at Justin hovering by the front door.

James chuckled, and nodded towards the girls.

"Ah, yes." Althea smiled. "I'll only be a minute. I need to run to the back and get Nancy's gloves."

"Sure." James nudged Justin. "We men will wait for Lodie, eh?"

"Oohh, Nancy!" Charlotte cried. "What a beautiful dress!"

Nancy beamed and turned for the full effect. She wore a pale-pink, silk dress with a lace sash that encircled her waist and ended with a dramatically large bow in back. As she spun around she showed off her new white-kid boots. Althea returned from the back and handed her a small tissue wrapped package.

"Mummy bought it in San Francisco. It's from London. I'm here to pick up these lace gloves I ordered to go with it."

"You look lovely. Happy Birthday," said Althea.

"Thank you." She tugged on the heel of the gloves as she put them on. "I must get back to the house now. Thank you for ordering them, Mrs. Albright, they're perfect."

She stopped in front of Justin and batted her lashes at him, "Hello, Justin. I'm glad you're coming to my party. It's going to be grand!"

"Yes. Thank you." He coughed, trying to break her steadfast gaze. "We'll see you soon."

Nancy smiled and flounced out of the shop. James rolled his eyes at Althea, who was stifling a laugh.

"How beautiful she looked. Don't you think so, Da?"

"Hmph. Seemed like a lot of fuss and

feathers ta me. And even more preening. Personally, I like yer dress very much. Pink and purple and blue. Much more interesting."

Charlotte smiled. "Oh, Da. It's ordinary calico. But I liked the colors. And Althea showed me how to give it wonderful pintucking details. Men don't know anything about these things, do they, Althea?"

"Not much."

Lodie entered the shop and slapped James on the shoulder. "Ready for battle?"

"Och, I'm hoping not. Thea, I'll be back late afternoon. I'm off ta talk about things I do know about. And, Justin, good luck ta ye."

Althea occupied Charlotte and Justin with sorting thread and buttons for her until time for the party. They worked quickly as if completion of the tasks would move the hands of the clock. Minutes mercifully ticked away until the hour arrived and they began walking up West Broad.

The small, but stately, home peered down from Nabob Hill. Mr. Potter held an executive position at the bank, and Mrs. Potter volunteered on every beautification, arts, or events committee in Nevada City. Althea knew social standing to be extremely important to Claudine, which made her a valuable client, as she dressed elaborately for every occasion.

Justin charged ahead. He stuffed both birthday presents under one arm as he held the white garden gate open for the ladies. An immaculately manicured lawn lined both sides of the walk, and rows of perky, red tulips stood at attention in front of the lower lattice of the veranda.

As Althea ushered her charges inside, she saw fine furnishings meant for display. The imported wallpaper in the drawing room was hand-painted from London. The heavily carved hall table boasted a small, but exquisite, Italian crystal chandelier hanging over it. Oh, so delicate was Claudine's most treasured piece. The fixture's center gave the impression of a bubble floating above the table, and its six wispy, twisted arms gracefully curved up. The heavy, velvet drapes in a shade of rich Dutch blue swept dramatically back from tall windows. The carpet displayed an intricately woven floral pattern. Nancy's mother stood in front of the drawing room with a small cluster of women, discussing the finer points of her collection.

". . . and so I, of course, want Nancy's friends to have a marvelous time, but we must be diligent ladies to watch for sticky, dirty fingers. Oh, Altheeeaa!" cooed Claudine. "So lovely that you're here."

Claudine breezed forward to greet her, yet managed to hold her shoulders back in a way meant to show off her dress. Althea wisely accommodated her by responding, "Claudine, that gown is superb. Is it French?"

"Now, I *knew* you would appreciate it. Your discriminating eye is correct. Isn't it luscious?"

Althea walked around her slowly, noting the details. "It certainly is." She sighed in admiration. "You have a wonderful sense of style. I do so admire French fashion," she stated truthfully.

"Oh, you're sweet." Claudine's smile stiffened as she looked down her nose at Justin, waiting patiently with gift in hand. She possessed a presence that could unsettle the soul of a child in one icy glance.

Charlotte lightened the mood with a quick, but charming, curtsy in her ever-cheerful manner and offered up the gift in her hand. "Thank you for having us, Mrs. Potter. This is for you, from Althea. Justin has our gift for Nancy."

"How delightful," she answered, taking the gift from Charlotte. "You may place Nancy's gift on the divan in the drawing room where the other guests are gathered."

Nancy appeared with Ella Louise glued to her side and called, "Come in to where the party is, sillies!"

Althea noticed Hoyt hovering in a corner of the next room waving Justin over to a group of boys. "Manners," she reminded them as they hurried off.

Merriment bloomed amongst the guests. One of Claudine's closest friends, Martha Simpson, arrived with her gift for the hostess. She and Claudine kissed cheeks and exclaimed who should and who shouldn't have. The gaggle of girls giggled and squealed over one another's hair and dresses. The boys chose a different corner, mostly standing with hands in pockets, waiting for games to begin. Mothers hovered around Claudine, awaiting praise as she opened hostess gifts.

Martha Simpson's gift came last. Claudine peeked in the box containing four etched wine goblets.

"Lovely, Martha, thank you," she said, almost immediately putting the box down.

Althea saw that Martha hoped for a bigger reaction. "They're Irish crystal," Martha stated.

Claudine snatched one from the box and held it to the light.

"Really?" she sniffed. She set down the glass and clapped her hands. "All right, boys and girls, everyone gather for musical chairs. Nancy's very accomplished sister, Suzanne, will play the violin for the game. There will be prizes for the winners!"

"Those'll be for me!" bragged Howard Simpson.

The remark caused an eruption of crowing and boasting amongst the boys. Their noise stopped suddenly, evolving to crooning admiration as they watched servants carry a large punch bowl to the round foyer table, followed by an impressive triple-layer cake generously adorned with pink sugar flowers.

"It's raspberry butter-cream on the inside *and* coconut," announced Nancy.

This disclosure brought exclamations all around. Suzanne played "Pop Goes the Weasel" on her violin as the games began.

Marysville entertained its own games as the flood control meeting started late. Gathering at Murphy's Tavern, Tim Speeks, Bracuus Donovan, and James MacLaren represented the farms. Lodie Glenn stood for Nevada City's interests. Alton Quigby, the blacksmith, and Preston Price from the general store in Marysville were present for local business owners.

Hammond Creed was due to arrive with a small contingent from Yuba City over an hour ago. He ferried across early that morning to look around their waterfront and to meet Mayor Caisman.

The assembled men passed time talking over how river problems affected them personally, but each began to glance frequently at the door. James and Bracuus carried on as if no argument existed between them. Alton grew concerned over leaving his business unmanned for so long a period.

Lodie rose from the table and stretched. He blew an exasperated breath. "I'm reluctant to have a third beer at this point. I'm starting to think I may need my wits about me."

Suddenly, the swinging door flung open with such force that it banged the wall of the tavern. Hammond strode in and, without looking around, made straight for the bar.

"Hey!" shouted Bracuus. "Did you forget we was here?"

Hammond did not turn around. He waved his arm behind him, pointed at their table, and shook his finger three times. He glared at the bartender, saying through gritted teeth, "Whiskey!"

The group at the table looked at one another.

"Hey!" shouted Bracuus again.

Hammond downed his shot and banged the glass on the bar. "Again!"

The bartender poured. Hammond turned to lean on the bar with the glass in his hand.

"Well," he said facing them, "you were right, Lodie. That son of a . . ." He bit off the last word and walked to the table.

"Where's Mayor Caisman?" asked Alton.

"I un-invited him. Him and the lot of them, the lying bunch of hyenas."

Lodie grimaced. "What happened?"

"First off . . ." Hammond rolled his neck from side to side, relieving tension. ". . . I went early to get a handle on the flooding and look at the levees. You were right, Lodie. They're still building up the levees over there. Not by bits, either. You can see from their side how the water is rising up over on our side. They've carried it well beyond the bend! I thought the river hadn't calmed yet, but it's actually pushing the flooding over to our side. If they keep it up, next rain'll bring the river right over the edge and creeping back into town."

"Ohh," moaned Preston. "I don't have time or resources to clean up a floor full of muck again. I've still got merchandise up on crates as it is."

"Ah, but you haven't heard the kicker. They say now that the river is 'stable' we can move forward 'together.' I didn't tell 'em yet I looked around. Pretty obvious to me they only came here to the big meeting to find out our position. From what I saw . . . the flooding we endured wouldn't have happened if their levee didn't shove the overflow in our direction. *And* they knew it."

Hammond let them grumble while he downed his second shot.

"Mayor Caisman . . ." he sneered. ". . . suggested we both start a tax campaign to 'build for the future.' "

"What's he want to do with the money?" asked Tim.

"Why, build a dam. On their side, of course — sort of a levee-dam project. They propose starting from the highlands of Sutter Buttes right across the channel way of Butte Slough to tie into their 'previously existing' levee system."

"That won't help us!" Preston declared. "It'll put even more pressure on the Yuba."

"Yes, well . . . They don't consider the Yuba their problem. Only the Feather. And where the Yuba merges with the Feather? That's our problem. That's why they think

361

we should chip in for their dam. He says our town's built closer to the river than they are, so he suggested we move our establishments back."

"What!" Bracuus pounded the table with his fist. "Are we supposed to rebuild the whole riverfront?"

"That's what he suggests."

"It's not just the riverfront," said Alton. "We had water all the way down Main Street and for city blocks in every direction."

James had remained quiet up to now. "This is only the 'town versus town' part of it. What about the mines? What about the tailings?" he asked.

"Caisman's backing Green on the campaign to shut down hydraulics. Says they don't get benefits from the mines. Another reason we should put up money for a joint project."

"It's ridiculous. They still need to get steamers in for their supplies," said Lodie. "Did you call him on those levees?"

"Oh, yes. Told him I took a lengthy stroll down there and what I found. The man looked me right in the eye and claimed that's what's always been there and said the current building I saw was purely repairs. Even had the gall to ask us to take down part of our levee wall near the bend."

"Did he now?" exclaimed Preston.

"I called them all liars and extortionists and said we'd be finding the need to make our own 'repairs.' Then all hell broke loose."

"We've been caught napping, men!" declared Bracuus.

"We've been slow to act until prodded by crisis, that's for certain," added Preston. "We didn't fully understand how these levees work for us because we reacted to emergency. For myself, I've worried the town and merchants carry the brunt of the cost."

"As you should! *You have* built close to the river," grumbled Bracuus

"Let's na let them divide us against ourselves. Then they win," began James calmly. "The truth is, we've all seen benefits and setbacks. The mines brought prosperity and now the tailings. We have ta deal with it. Increasingly, farms feel the pinch. We have ta move our produce. We *need* the mines; we *need* the merchants; we *need* the farms. End of story."

Tim agreed. "James is right. Come on, Bracuus, it'll cost us in taxes, but where on earth you seen results from land like this? In the Midwest, I averaged fifteen bushels an acre. After a heavy flood year, I get sixty to eighty bushels. After a couple of dry years, I need the floods to drive out rodents moving in on my crops. We got to protect what's ours in an organized way."

Alton nodded. "Easy to see we're on our own to fix it."

"Frankly, I'm happy to deal with solely our problems," interjected Hammond. "I've no guilt about Yuba City's issues now. After years of these shenanigans I'm not sure anyone remembers how the ebb and flow of the river's pattern should be. Both sides have been altered, each according to what seemed most beneficial to their own holdings. But we *will* have to raise taxes to build up our own levees."

"We're not through this rainy season yet," Lodie reminded them. "We'll never get money raised *or* build in time to avoid getting hit again. Nevada City's poorly equipped to be cut off again."

James was oddly quiet. Almost musing to himself he said, "Perhaps we should look ta take *down* some levees."

The group looked at him blankly.

"Not ours. *Theirs.*"

As the thought sank in, smiles appeared on the faces around the table.

"Ah, see now!" Bracuus slapped him on the back. "When you get off that high horse

364

of yours, you're damned useful! What did you have in mind?"

The parlor games successfully removed the fidgets from the children and they now sat eating birthday cake. Althea looked around at the contented faces, pleased to see Charlotte sitting with Ella Louise. Claudine Potter finally relaxed. Her grand finale, a magician, readied his staging area for a show.

The ladies chatted amongst themselves in the dining room with tea and petit fours. Althea marveled at the detail on the tiny glacé confections. The gifts for Nancy heaped on the divan across the hall waited for the conclusion of the magician's act. She smiled, thinking of merry children singing "Happy Birthday" around the magnificent cake glowing with candles on the center hall table. The candlelight had danced enchantingly off the chandelier and created a warm glow against the punch bowl. Nancy was delighted with the adoring attention.

Hoyt's mother, Miriam, exclaimed, "Claudine, this party won't soon be rivaled! Everything is amazing. Suzanne is a very accomplished violinist; you should be very proud."

"Truly," added another friend, "this afternoon has been a treat. And, my, that Mac-Laren girl can sing! It couldn't have been nicer if you'd hired a choir."

Claudine beamed. "Thank you, all. It was wonderful to have such good friends here to celebrate with Nancy." She looked across the hall and frowned. "You know, that magician is very slow in preparing." She stood and asked, "Would anyone like more cake?"

A stampede of boys stormed the center hall table. Althea rose and walked back to the table with her hostess saying, "Oh, do sit, Claudine; I'll serve them. You've done so much already."

"The cake was exquisite, Claudine. You are to be commended," said yet another guest.

Claudine smiled and nodded. The children huddled at the table again. The girls came and stacked their plates neatly on a tray, as it would be unladylike to indulge in seconds. Claudine tugged and twisted her necklace restlessly as she monitored the magician. "Oh, I do hate delays," she muttered.

Althea looked up from slicing cake to reassure her and saw her staring at the wine glasses Martha had brought. Claudine picked one up absent-mindedly and examined it. Martha immediately appeared by her side.

"I do hope you like them."

"Yes, lovely. Crystal you said?" She held the glass up to the light. "Hmm. You know, I was thinking. I've heard it said that opera singers, or fine singers anyway, can shatter a crystal glass with the purity of their voice." Inspired, she spun around, scanning the faces of the children until she found the one she was looking for.

"Charlotte, dear," she purred. "Could you come over here for a moment?"

Charlotte excused herself from her conversation with Ella Louise and went to Mrs. Potter as summoned.

"Charlotte, I would consider it a favor if you might help us with a little experiment," she smiled enthusiastically. "You can sing scales, can you not?"

"Well, yes, ma'am."

"Very good. I am going to hold this glass, like so. I would like you to run your scales until you reach the very highest note you can. Then I want you to hold that note as loudly, and as long, as you can."

Althea knew quite well that Martha had ordered the glasses from Lodie's emporium. She grew uncomfortable by this sort of intended humiliation and attempted to intervene, saying, "Oh, Claudine, I hardly think Charlotte can . . ."

367

"Oh, pish posh. It will be fun!"

The other children and their mothers circled close around the table out of curiosity.

Justin could not help himself and asked, "Why?"

Obviously enjoying herself, she gushed, "I'm glad you asked! It's been said that a singer's highest, purest note can shatter crystal. Do you suppose Charlotte's voice is strong enough to do that?"

Justin considered this. "If anybody could, it would be her."

"Wait, Claudine. You want her to break one of the glasses? But then they will not be a set," said Martha nervously.

Claudine bestowed her with a warm smile and a very direct look. "I'm not too terribly worried." She turned to Charlotte "Will you try it?"

Charlotte looked doubtful. "I'll do my best."

"Wonderful."

"Come on, Charlotte, bust it!" cried Hoyt. The boys chanted, "Bust it! Bust it!"

Claudine clapped her hands to quiet them. "Now let's not interfere with other noise. Let Charlotte concentrate. You may begin, dear." She held the goblet high in front of her by its base.

Charlotte looked at the glass as she sang her scales. She held her last note until she ran entirely out of breath. A collective "Aww" arose from the group.

"That's all right," said Claudine gleefully. "Try again."

Several shouted, "You can do it, Charlotte!"

Charlotte stood tall, cleared her throat, and shook her shoulders. She held the last note even longer this time. Nothing happened.

"And again!" instructed Claudine.

Charlotte complied.

"Louder," she called.

Althea stifled annoyance as she saw Charlotte's cheeks flush red from exertion. She determined this would be the last attempt as she watched her take a deep breath and blow it out slowly. Charlotte stared hard at the glass and began to sing with all her might. She put so much power into the highest note that she creeped up on her tiptoes without even noticing. Suddenly, there was an odd sound. A *chink*. Everything happened at once. Charlotte stopped singing. Claudine, startled, looked closely at the glass. And one of the beautiful twisted arms from the crystal chandelier broke away from its delicate bubble and splashed into the punchbowl.

A chorus of girlish screams resounded from around the table. Loudest of all was Nancy, whose pale-pink, silk dress showed the splattering of dark punch stains.

"Look what you've done!" she shrieked at Charlotte. "It's ruined!"

Horrified, Charlotte backed away from the table. Althea struggled to push her way through the other guests. Claudine stood gaping at the severed crystal arm in the punch bowl . . . then looked up at Martha and scowled.

"I . . . I . . . I don't understand," Martha stammered.

"*I* understand perfectly!"

Nancy began to cry as she continued to scream at Charlotte. "Get out! Leave my party! You've ruined everything!"

Charlotte stood glued to her spot, unable to find words as everyone stared at her. Justin appeared at her side and took her arm.

"It wasn't her fault, Nancy. She did what she was asked to do. I'm sorry your dress has punch on it, but it can be cleaned," he stated solemnly.

"What do you know? You're a nobody! Both of you!"

"Nancy, that will be enough," said her mother.

"Nobodies, get out of my house! You're such a nobody, you don't even have a father!"

The room went silent. Althea's face drained of color and she found she could not breathe. She saw Justin grasp Charlotte's hand in his and turn to Mrs. Potter.

"Thank you for having us," he said stiffly. "Good day." He turned before Claudine could respond and marched Charlotte quickly from the house.

Claudine looked at Althea, who stood poised and stately.

Althea held her head erect and allowed the silence to weigh heavily. Then she said with all dignity, "I believe my son has spoken for us all." She turned to retrieve her bag and left without a backward glance.

Charlotte and Justin waited several yards up the street from the house. As she approached, Althea heard Charlotte talking.

"Thanks for getting me out of there, Justin. I'm sorry you'll miss the magician. That was a terrible thing for her to say."

"To both of us." He shrugged. "It's not like I cared, anyway. Maybe she won't act so goofy around me now. And her ma . . ." he laughed. "Did you see the look on her face when the chandelier broke?"

"No," Charlotte said. "I was too terrified."

They looked at one another and burst into hysterical laughter.

Althea walked up and hugged them both, relieved.

"I'm sorry, Mum," Justin said, but then laughter got the best of him.

"You have nothing at all to be sorry for; you behaved impeccably — both of you. I'm very proud."

"Serves them right." He chuckled. "Nancy putting on airs, and her ma barking orders at Charlotte like she was a trained dog." He started laughing anew. "I can't believe you did that with your voice — it was fantastic! That's a better trick than any magician could come up with!"

Charlotte giggled. "It's not one I'll be trying again, I can tell you. But I wonder why the glass didn't break?"

CHAPTER 25

Marysville — Winter 1860

Citizens of Marysville and Yuba City acknowledged floodwaters, whether by slow melting drizzle or a deluge, to be an annual event. Entrepreneurial impatience ruled their thinking — hubris outweighed control. Added mining debris increased the burden of destructive power. Costly and frustrating projects caused each town to dig in for position.

Following the abandoned joint river project, each town fell into a pattern of adding levees as fast as one appeared on the other side, as though engaging in a colossal pie-eating contest. The course of the bloated Feather and Yuba Rivers remained in flux by their antics.

Marysville endured a state of alert. Hammond and Lodie joined forces to form squads of volunteers. Miners, merchants, and farmers worked side by side, piling mounds of earth along the riverbank to upstage the berm already confronting them from the Yuba City banks. Horses, oxen, and mules pulling wagons and plows worked a steady schedule throughout summer. As fall arrived, Lodie's lookouts from east of the Yuba River kept watch for overcast skies. At the first threat of storms, emergency volunteers from the countryside reaching to Nevada City readied to ride for the riverfront.

And now James peered down the river, standing low on the bank at a bend, squinting to see in the gloaming. With the day's meager light nearly elapsed, he knew all of their plans came down to this. Months of work exchanged floods back and forth with no apparent winner — a grand show of one-upmanship, with high stakes and an unscrupulous adversary.

James played his trump card on this moonless night. He smelled the rain coming. A bitter chill and murky skies foretold the storm's imminent arrival. James looked northward far up the river. He held up a thumb. He looked southward and did the same. He pulled the crude hood over his head and climbed into a rowboat with veiled accomplices.

Winds whipped choppy, white peaks on

the river's surface. Five rowboats manned with masked marauders silently battled their way to pre-arranged points. Working in teams, they pulled their maritime assault ashore. With axes and shovels they cut open embankments in each spot, allowing the river to rush forth and reclaim marshland in the Sutter Basin. Spreading out the breached positions, James hoped to avoid causing an overwhelming flood, but to alleviate pressure on Marysville.

Within hours of their return, black, billowing clouds tore open in a relentless siege. The surging downpour dumped unabated torrents. As the church bell clanged its frantic appeal for help, merchants and farmers alike flocked to the riverfront. James, Lodie, Bracuus, Tim Speeks, and Matthew Cleary so happened to be in town and immediately took charge of a brigade armed with shovels and sandbags. Merchants rushed to the scene with tools and manpower. Ruth Cleary, Althea, and Matilda manned the stove at Murphy's Tavern, churning out food and hot coffee. Glancing skyward, James urged his comrades on as Marysville set in for a long skirmish.

He was grateful to see Hammond Creed charge in on horseback and rally his town, riding the riverfronts, directing them to plug every seeping low point. Not stopping for food or rest, battling elements and mud, the Marysville mayor pushed them to the limit. For two days they built up the levee to its highest point. Just as the fight seemed hopeless, the rivers stayed the course within reinforced boundaries and the rain abated.

Exhausted, jubilant, mud-covered men dragged themselves to food and hot beverage lavished on them by grateful shop owners' wives. Hammond had lost his voice shouting orders during the melee and merely nodded thanks.

Althea was standing by a pile of blankets pouring coffee for a clay-covered figure when James approached for some soul-warming brew.

"I'll be a happy man ta see high ground again. Hope the young ones managed with the animals."

"You left plenty of instruction," she said, handing him a steaming cup. "The horses were all under shelter, the cow and chickens all tucked in. Justin and Charlotte could nearly run the place without us, you know."

"Ah, that's good." He closed his eyes, feeling the comforting liquid ease down his throat.

"Blanket?" asked the clay-covered man standing there.

James's eyes popped open with surprise.

"Sean! I thought ye were still in the Comstock! Whenever did ye get here, man!" He shook his hand warmly. "Bit hard ta recognize anyone at this point."

Sean chuckled. "I'll say. I was on the north end. I got to town when the weather broke, so I jumped in."

"That was good of ye." Though exhausted, James felt giddy. "Och, it's been months! Ye took off without a word. I would na ha known where ye went if I had na seen Vicente!"

"When big strike news breaks, you go a runnin'. I was lucky to be in Nevada City precisely when Ott did the assay." He rubbed the back of his head. "I'm doing well up there . . ." he said a bit sheepishly. "Really well."

Sean looked pointedly at Althea. "I've been writin' . . . didn't Althea tell you?"

James glanced at Althea, who blushed. Seconds ticked by before he answered. "I see. No. I . . . I did na know."

Althea turned away quickly. "I'll get sandwiches."

They both watched her hurry away and disappear into a bustling group of women.

Sean looked at James. "Look, it ain't no big thing. Not sure why I thought she'd tell

377

you. I'm puttin' some money away, buildin' for a future. I wanted to hear from her. See if there might be some chance . . . later . . . maybe. We're talkin's all."

"Sean, neither of ye owe me any explanation. It's between the two of ye."

Sean smiled. "I forgot how fond of town life I was."

"Aye. The town."

"Where's the other, Mr. Mayor? — I haven't seen him yet." He squinted at James. "And I'm thinkin' there's a story here . . ."

James cleared his throat. "Mm. Best save it for the Silver Moon." He nodded towards the other end of the bar. "Let's see if we can find him amongst the mud people."

Thistle Dew

"Justin, dry the bottoms of those plates before ye put them in the cupboard, lad," James admonished.

"Sorry." Justin took the next plate from Charlotte after she rinsed it of soapy water.

"Ye can't be in such a hurry. Och. I'm taking a cup of tea over ta yer mother."

James grumbled to himself as he walked out of the house holding two mugs of hot tea. He hesitated on the porch. He looked across the courtyard at Althea's cottage, but he saw no one stirring. He wondered if he should sit in one of the rockers to wait her out.

"Well, she did na come last night," he thought. "And now I'm holding this bloody tea." He decided he best go before the tea grew cold, leaving him no reason at all.

He stalked across the yard and took a deep breath upon reaching her door. He rapped lightly with the knuckle of his middle finger, trying not to spill the cup.

She opened the door. "Oh. James. My goodness, what are you carrying?"

"Well, ye din na come out after supper, so . . ."

She stood aside. "Come in, come in. I'm sorry — I guess I'm tired. You know, catching up in the shop after staying through the Marysville crisis."

She spoke very quickly, nervously he thought.

She gestured to the small kitchen table. "Please, sit. How thoughtful of you."

James set down the mugs and walked around to pull out her chair.

"Oh. Thanks very much. Have you spoken to Lodie? I haven't seen him and I'm curious as to what happened in Yuba City."

James sat, grateful for a topic.

"We did na see that bad a storm coming

so early." He winced. "Yuba City suffered some major drawbacks. Lodie rode in ta see Hammond. He says the Sutter County courthouse stood like an island in a pond — it'll take weeks ta withdraw. Damaged crops around Sutter Basin. The embankments gave way at critical points, crumbling against the river's rise." He held up a finger. "But . . . far worse for us ta let their shenanigans stand. Nothing would get ta port in Marysville, the shops ruined again, and the Browns Valley Road, totally impassible."

Althea looked grave. "How awful. Has Hammond spoken to Mayor Caisman?"

"The man's furious. And suspicious . . . but he hasn't a clue how we escaped and they didn't."

"It's certainly been the other way around often enough."

James looked absentmindedly around the room. He rarely came inside unless he needed to fix something. Althea's soft, feminine touches were visible everywhere — cut flowers on the table and the sink, neatly tailored curtains in a cheery sunburst gold at the windows, the French rugs and quilts she and Emma had bought together giving the cottage a welcoming feel. Her worktable piled with dress patterns, lace trims, and odd pieces of fabric sat well organized in the corner of the room. His eye fell on a silver picture frame on the mantle. He frowned.

"At any rate," he continued, "the main priority now is the Browns Valley Road leading this way ta the mountains. By coincidence the alignment of the road is essentially along the same path as the new levee, thereby making it an extension of their road-building project."

"That's convenient."

"Hammond's beginning the work with existing tax funds."

James took a gulp of his tea. Althea sipped hers. A long, awkward pause seemed to scream silently in his head. "I . . ." he began. He stopped.

She gave him a puzzled look. "If you have something to say to me, James, . . . well, we've known each other far too long to mince words now."

He gave her a long look and sighed. "We have na had time ta talk since Sean came back."

She set down her cup. "You're concerned."

"Hard not ta be. You two have been down this road before and it did na end well."

"He's not *back*. He'll be returning to the Comstock by midweek." She frowned. "Don't you feel a bit disloyal?"

"Ta him, or ta you? It's one or the other." He glanced at the mantle. He felt irritated. "I don't want ta see ye pinning hopes on . . ."

"On what?"

"On a man that's never taken care of anyone but himself. And not done a stellar job of that."

"You don't believe Sean can change?"

"I believe he means ta. I believe he can for a while. Thea, ye *know* better than this. Ye must, or ye would ha told me ye'd heard from him."

She stood up. "Can't you allow me a little hope? Something to dream on while he's gone?"

"What worries me is yer best times together might be when he's gone. Look, I love Sean like a brother. All I'm saying is ta go slowly . . . and keep yer eyes open."

"How much more slowly can I go than with a man that's off in another territory?"

He saw she was upset and rose to go to her. "Be careful . . . I . . ." He inadvertently looked at the mantle again. "I . . ."

He stalked towards the hearth. "I can na talk ta ye any longer while I have ta look at this!" He grabbed the daguerreotype in its silver picture frame and slapped it facedown on the mantle.

Althea stared wide-eyed. She took on a curious look.

"What?" he demanded. "I din na like looking at his mug when this thing sat in the Doyles' mansion, and I don't like looking at him now!"

"Did you . . . ?"

"Did I what? Turn his pompous face down every time I walked in that room? Ye bet I did!"

"But . . . Lady Doyle thought the frame was broken. She gave it to me to get it repaired. I . . . picked it up before we took the wagon train."

"Och, that's rich! So I'm the reason the bugger made the trip?"

She looked at him sheepishly. "I shouldn't have taken it; I know. But it gives Justin comfort to see what his father looked like."

"A risky thing, I'd say."

She replied stiffly, "It hardly matters now."

James leveled his gaze to meet her cool, blue eyes. He sucked in a deep breath. "I'm sorry. Old habits die hard. I'm used ta keeping one eye on ye and the lad."

She softened slightly and moved forward to take his hands. "I do appreciate it. Your friendship means everything to both of us. But I'm not the silly girl I was. I've worked hard to make a life for Justin and myself.

I'm willing to let Sean try to do the same. Are you?"

He squeezed her hands and bobbed his head. "Of course. But ye can talk ta me, ye know."

"I will." She looked deep into his eyes. "When I feel the need."

He chuckled. "Fair enough."

"How about we enjoy the evening in the rockers? Just two old friends?"

"I'm for that. It'll be good ta get life back ta normal." He took her arm and escorted her back across the courtyard. Inexplicably, he felt the weight of a heavy heart.

CHAPTER 26

Sacramento, 1861

Reports of the fall of Ft. Sumter arrived by pony express. Newspaper offices chalked headlines on slates placed on outside sidewalks. Editors worked furiously at the presses. Beginning with a grave and silent crowd of readers, the news spread like a quick moving storm front to outlying towns and farms. Uncertainty and apprehension descended like a debilitating fog on Sacramento.

A strong core of Southerners in California spoke of secession. Impromptu and impassioned speeches broke out in favor of both sides, but physical distance from decisions and the war itself created a disconnection. Many wondered what new events had occurred in the nine days since the initial message left St. Joseph. Distant families and beliefs coaxed men to return and fight for lands they had left for their new life in the

West. A disconcerting tone set in amongst neighbors wondering where California stood.

Bulletins rolled out like a line of lit gunpowder with equally explosive consequences. A call for troops in California came in July, three days after Bull Run. General George Wright, a Northwest Indian fighter, was announced to be commanding officer for the District of California. His duties included protecting the frontier, safeguarding the coast, moving troops eastward, and, of course, keeping watch on secessionists.

Obliged to complete many tasks before he departed for Washington, Dutton felt as though his leap into the bureaucratic portal began here in the lounge of Sacramento's Union Hotel. A popular gathering place for political meetings and lobbyists, he felt fortune's pulse on the city as he met with the hands grasping the tiller of destiny for his state. The Dandridges' rapidly growing business investments required office space both here and San Francisco at his father's insistence.

Dutton had matured into a young man of swarthy good looks — of average height, but svelte and well proportioned. He possessed devilishly dark eyes and the look of a man with studious intelligence. Sharp and shrewd, his demeanor did not disappoint from that perception. He rose from the club chair to shake hands with the brawny, bearded gentleman seated across from him. Dutton admired him as the unrivaled combination of sagacious businessman and politician. Poised and dignified, Leland Stanford stood and grasped his hand warmly at the conclusion of their meeting.

"I can't thank you enough for this opportunity, Mr. Stanford. This war is an unfortunate blight on our country, and you've given me a purpose to serve as well as help complete a dream for the nation."

Stanford gave him an appraising look. The man was impeccably dressed, a trait they shared. Dutton knew appearances were important to him for Stanford certainly never went anywhere that he wasn't dressed the part and constantly aware of what part he played.

"You sold yourself, young man," he said, nodding approvingly. "You keep your eye on our project in Washington, and I trust this will become a long term business association. Give my best to your father. I appreciate his hosting my campaign rally in San Francisco."

"Father knows California's development

is at a crossroads, and staunch leadership is crucial. He's a scrupulous judge of character." Dutton gave him a charming smile. "A carryover from the bench, I suppose."

Stanford laughed, and Dutton took his leave with a sincere, "I look forward to your inauguration, sir."

He stood in the doorway of the hotel for several minutes, looking to swim against the tide of foot traffic. Worse than a Sacramento winter packed with people waiting out rains and floods, he thought, annoyed. Dutton launched himself into a crowd where the war effort created a buzz in the already busy city.

He had shared his steamship in from San Francisco with a passel of young men from outlying farms and towns, ready for assignment in the Sacramento Sutter Rifles, the City Guard, or the California Volunteers. Because troop transport to the eastern warfront carried prohibitive cost, conscription did not extend to the Pacific states. He watched the pumped-up volunteer patriots with interest, not at all sure if he felt them worthy of respect or indifference. Neil and Royce Collier both signed up with the Washington Rifles, Sacramento City and County. The last thing Dutton wanted was to fight, but he was concerned about appearances. Garth Collier had certainly pulled his iron out of the fire by bringing them this key investment to their growing empire.

He passed by the B. F. Hastings Building on J Street, where only this morning he had picked up the key for their offices. Coincidentally, Theodore Judah rented space on the second floor. He chuckled to himself at fate's turn of events. His father had shunned Judah's presentation in San Francisco, prospective investors there panning and mocking his efforts.

Judah took his campaign on the road to the St. Charles Hotel in Sacramento, where Collis Huntington and Mark Hopkins attended his presentation, as well as Garth Collier. Garth was drawn to the dream of a linked nation and tired of Washington looking at California as stagnant and isolated. The overwhelming scope and cost of the project sent potential investors scoffing and scurrying. Garth Collier left disappointed, seeing no relevant interest expressed. Huntington and Hopkins decided to dig a little deeper and, when satisfied, called for another meeting with interested parties of their choosing.

Judah refined his pitch to selective capitalist hearing. He tallied assets he offered: he had completed the survey work himself, navigating the offset twin ranges of the Sierras on foot over twenty times, proving the Donner Pass route viable. He spent years in Washington helping draw up bills and cultivating connections, including the newly elected, pro-railroad President Lincoln. Lincoln was pressing hard, especially now with a Congress empty of Southern representation. The transcontinental route debate ceased to be stalled by North-South argument.

This, the assembly of investors had heard before. The pièce de résistance came when Judah tempted their entrepreneurial spirits with a more immediate, and certain, return on investments — a chance to corner the market in the Nevada silver boom. The Comstock Lode ran at its peak. To construct the railroad, a wagon road must precede it. Even if the railroad never materialized, he promised, possession of the wagon road meant ownership of a toll road to a most lucrative destination.

This motivator propelled Huntington and Hopkins to take the lead, agreeing to the down payment on stock necessary to incorporate, and to recruit investors. They assembled a group of self-made overachieving men: Charles Crocker, James Bailey, and

Cornelius Cole, among the Sacramento elite. But Leland Stanford, prominent in California politics and finishing third in an attempt for the governor's mansion, already knew Lincoln as part of the emerging Republican party. Now engaged in a second run for governorship, Stanford was the key component Huntington needed to lend power and prestige to their enterprise.

Garth Collier jumped at the opportunity to invest and urged Judge Dandridge to join him. Immediately drawn to possibilities and influential company, Dutton pressed his father to action. Garth, impressed by Dutton's enthusiasm, proposed to Huntington that he join Judah in Washington as a liaison to the war department. Now viewed as critical to the war effort, the railroad tied the western states' gold and silver wealth to the union, as well as troop movement. Judah held positions as clerk of the House Main Committee on Railroads, clerk of the House Committee on Pacific Railroads, and secretary of the Senate Committee on Pacific Railroads. Huntington appreciated the benefit of Dutton's eye on the situation.

Dutton passed the new courthouse on 7th and I Streets, an impressive building in the Ionic style, showcasing ten massive pillars and currently housing the California Legislature until the completion of the new Capitol building. He turned down I street on his way back to his hotel, picking up his laundry near China Slough and contemplating Sacramento's constant state of change. Previous floods led to the raising of I, J, and K Streets to the same level as the city plaza and the installation of new sidewalks. It seemed to him the city constantly reinvented itself. He looked for the towering spire of St. Rose of Lima church in the distance and followed its dominating skyline presence to the nearby Golden Eagle Hotel.

He caught sight of his next appointment. Tolliver dodged and weaved his way through the crowd across the street, his shaggy hair bobbing against his shoulders. A distasteful man, yet Dutton came to appreciate the finer points of his usefulness, particularly his dogged loyalty. As he approached the corner, Dutton stopped and hesitated as if deciding on a direction. He sensed Tolliver falling in behind him. He feigned surprise as the disheveled man asked for a light.

Tolliver leaned in, pinching a cigarette between his fingers. As Dutton held up the match to the end, he felt something drop inside the pocket of his great coat. Tolliver took two quick puffs and muttered, "Thanks, much" and walked away.

Dutton entered the Golden Eagle and went straight upstairs to his room. He hung up his coat, kicked off his shoes, and poured himself a drink. He pulled the note out of his pocket and sat stretched out on the bed. He scanned the correspondence quickly. Father would be pleased. The judge had sent Tolliver to find Sam Brannan in Calistoga, where Brannan purchased two thousand acres to indulge his fascination with the natural hot springs there. The man intended to build a spa reminiscent of Saratoga Springs in New York. Through their long, but quiet, association, the Dandridges shared common investments in land, banks, and telegraph with this man said to own nearly a fifth of all San Francisco. Now that Judah had secured his backing in Sacramento, it caused a wave of anxiety amongst the Pacific Mail, Wells Fargo Company, and a multitude of other stage lines. Threatened by the impending railroad, they collaborated on their demand for banks not to invest. Dutton smiled — as he expected, Brannan would address the problem as a supporter of the railroad.

Feeling celebratory, he got up to take a cigar out of his valise. He dipped the end in his brandy. After lighting the cigar, he used the waning match flame to ignite the letter in his hand. Messages between the judge and Sam Brannan were always destroyed upon receipt.

No real conflict of interest existed now that the judge was retired, but it behooved them both to remain undisclosed allies. It allowed for a freedom of movement in dealings that might attract a higher level of scrutiny were the relationships known. This credo proved especially true in Garth's case. He despised Brannan and trusted nothing he touched. To present investments on their merits alone, untainted by Brannan's opinion, seemed to be the wiser course. Dutton smiled, recalling his father's favorite tenet, "Be wary when dealing with a rogue, although their deals are often the most lucrative. *Never* do business with a fool."

Dutton began to relax, knowing he would tie up the last of his loose ends on his visit to the Collier ranch in the morning. He owed a great show of gratitude to Garth Collier for this Washington position. He carried documents and business correspondence from his father to discuss with Garth, knowing he'd likely bring home more of the same. He toyed with the idea of sharing parts of his meeting from two days ago but decided to keep the information his own pet project — even from his father.

Operating on a hunch from the judge, Dutton approached a man who spent years in the mining business, kept his ear to the ground, and covered significant territory in the Sierras. The man's tip on the Comstock strike had secured their interests there far earlier than their competitors'; it helped to get news directly from the assay office. He proved a valuable inside man, one whose objectives they could satisfy and use to their own benefit. Many mining moguls nurtured political aspirations; after all, few came to California without the expectation of becoming, rich, famous, or influential. For Dutton and the judge, politicians were a favorite investment.

CHAPTER 27

"This is na my fight. Let another damn me for it if he will . . . but some things have ta keep moving — necessities must be provided; businesses have ta run. Let me be more useful than ta kill other men for an argument I've no part of. The latest skirmishes are but a scant glimpse of injustices brewing on both sides," he had ranted to Althea.

James refused to take a stand. He brooded — feeling like an outsider with limited knowledge rendering judgment on clan issues that had built for centuries. He took criticisms unflinchingly. He was determined not to leave Charlotte, already without her mother, nor let Justin fight. Inside, he ached for his new country. And his nightmares resumed.

He confided in Althea, who expressed relief that he remained to keep their family unit intact. He worried about her, too. Sean Miller heeded the call from distant relatives in Tennessee and bolted from the Comstock, leaving her a hastily worded telegraph wire.

"It's a stance on integrity most won't congratulate me for. Sometimes ye have ta decide for yerself if a thing is right or wrong. This American government — they're still babes with growing pains. They have na yet begun ta fight through what it means ta lead; this war amongst themselves is the very evidence of that," he told her.

"I don't believe I've ever heard you say 'they' instead of 'we,' " she had mused.

"Not a proud thing I say. I'll na let the passion of this fight get the better of my head. I've made that mistake before."

He meditated on these conversations often, finding no peace even in his resolve. He jabbed the pitchfork into the pile of sweet-smelling hay and tossed a load into the freshly mucked stall.

The war's distance made it difficult for James to feel its reality, excepting the arrival of random units of blue-uniformed guardians of the Union and the systematic disappearance of local men. Some Californians returned with missing limbs or weakened by disease. Others, though physically unscathed, shelved away memories of pain and death. Youths aged immeasurably — casualties of carefree souls and the ability to see only the best in their fellow man.

James sought active roles developing his community. He took over the building project of the Brown's Valley Road. He organized hired men, taking no salary, as well as providing horsepower needed to get the job done. His civic conscience and sense of duty to families of soldiers on either side kept him a very busy man. He determined that men at war should return home to a better town. No neighbor's fields went unattended for lack of manpower that he and Justin could provide.

He followed battle news with a fervent interest, yet never voiced opinions. His friends were divided, though California showed a decidedly Union presence. Lodie volunteered assisting the quartermaster of the Union army with supplies. James reluctantly sold horses to army officials Lodie sent his way. He wrestled with guilt, wondering if he had chosen a side by selling, but knowing the same to be true if he refused. And then he risked the army sequestering his stock if they suspected him a secessionist. No side soothed his conscience. He took a cold hard line — as a businessman with a product to sell and no more. He decided there would be no winners at war's end and peace, a long time coming.

His solace came from building his farm to tranquil maturity and becoming self-sufficient. He took pride as he watched Justin's growing skill breaking and training horses to wagon or saddle. Together they built barns and tack sheds. He spent long hours establishing a successful breeding program. And Charlotte, the joy of his heart, crossed the threshold from girl to young woman.

He stopped in the barn doorway, watching her dismount a gelding she worked in the corral. Her long, brown hair shone with glints of honey and auburn, and, though tied back, it fell across her shoulder as she reached for the bucket and sponge. The gelding's withers quivered as she squeezed cool water over his coat. She dipped the sponge and worked away sticky salt and sweat.

Charlotte was tall and lithe, with Emma's porcelain skin and delicate features. She had her mother's fine nose and soft mouth, as well as the dark, fringed lashes, but her eyes were a throwback to her father. Instead of the deep, rich blue that had graced Emma's face, she possessed the MacLaren color of a scintillating sea, which, depending on the light, could shine a lively, soft green or deep and stormy gray. Althea often said when Charlotte gave a sharp look, it flashed like lightning.

He observed her with pride. He called out, knowing she needed no instruction, "Comb him out good so no moisture's trapped. Don't want him getting chilled."

She answered without looking up, "Yes, Da."

He trained her well. She knew her way around a horse and loved them more than he. She took working stock as pure privilege, most of her time dedicated to home and Althea's business. She appreciated Althea's true genius for her work. She emulated her skill and became creatively deft with the needle in her own right. Pleased with her maturity on all levels, one thing was certain — James kept a wary eye on any male attention angled his daughter's way.

James knew every boy within possible range of age. He watched them. He anticipated the exact moment, even before they knew themselves, which ones were emboldened to act on an interest in Charlotte. He recalled Lodie's complaints from his last visit to Nevada City.

"You're killing business, man. Boys stop

hanging around the store for fear of running into *Mr. MacLaren*."

"Och, be grateful ye have sons."

"I'm *more* grateful my sons are too young for *your* daughter. They'd stand a better chance in the war."

"I don't bother the lads."

"James! Last time you came in with Charlotte, you scared Frank Sanders half to death."

"I did na say a word . . . must have been his conscience."

"The boy peacefully passed the time of day with a pretty girl. You walked up, rested your elbow on Charlotte's head, and stared while he tried to talk to her."

James had shrugged. "Can't hurt ta put the fear of James in all of 'em. One day they'll have ta answer ta God, but they'll answer ta me, *now*. And I'm not as forgivin' as the Almighty, I'll tell ye."

The sight of Justin riding in from planting alfalfa interrupted his thoughts, and he waved him over.

"How would ye like ta deliver a team for me in Nevada City tomorrow?"

Justin smiled in his easy way. "Sure beats digging in the dirt."

James squinted up at him. "I thought as much. I have ta go ta Sacramento for a few

401

days ta check out some new brood mares. There's an outfit there that raises Belgians, and I'd like ta steal a look at their operation. We might find some mutually beneficial endeavors."

"I'd like to see that myself."

James considered this. "I promised the team by tomorrow, and the account's been paid." He gave a quick nod. "Next time, though. It's time ye learn ta negotiate these things if ye have a mind ta." He glanced up at Charlotte, now walking towards the house, and taunted her. "I hope ye haven't forgotten there's two hungry men here!"

She called back, "Stew is on the stove. Althea isn't home yet, and she'll be hungry, too. Now, if I can be on with it, I might manage to get biscuits in the oven."

Justin opened his mouth to tease her and hesitated. "Probably should leave her be. I'm pretty hungry." He looked down from his perch in the saddle.

"James? You know anything about a family in Nevada City by the name of Hodges?"

James shrugged. "Ralph Hodges? Heard of him. Fairly well ta do — in management with one of the mines or something. Why?"

Justin looked irritable. "There's a son, about my age, I guess. Drew's his name. I've seen him hanging around Charlotte whenever she's in town. She thinks he's pretty nice."

"But you don't?"

"He seems all right when he's around her. But I came up on him talking with some other fellows. I think he said something about her, because the conversation stopped the minute he saw me."

"Ye don't say."

"I warned him there better be no loose talk about Charlotte, or he'd answer to me."

James said nothing for moment. "I think it best we keep this between the two of us for now. I appreciate ye keeping a watchful eye, and I'll do the same. No sense in getting anyone's feathers ruffled without cause."

Justin nodded. "Thought you should know." He clucked to his horse and turned him towards the barn.

"Good lad."

Althea's patience wore thin. She consulted the mirror and found what she expected. She looked tired. She turned her head to see fine crinkles in the corners of her eyes. Time taking its toll. She sighed and smoothed back her flaxen hair. Still an extraordinarily handsome woman, she encountered many interested and available parties. She was neither.

For a brief and happy time, she and Sean Miller rekindled an earlier romance until interrupted by the Comstock strike and then war. She wrote faithfully and often. His letters first came in snatches, often several together, other times stretching many months in between. A particularly long period passed with no word and much worry. She then learned he had been shot and seriously wounded. He wrote that he still possessed all his limbs, but he returned to Tennessee to recuperate and help his family put their shattered farm back to rights. It had been much abused by plundering Union soldiers on their way to other battles. His two sisters lost husbands; his brother, his resolve; and his father, his mind.

Sean expressed anger at many targets, governing bodies at the top of his list. His letters vacillated wildly from raging rants about all the wrong in the world to his deep desire to come home to California and begin a peaceful life with her. Then the letters stopped altogether. Months passed, and she grew tired of guessing. She decided to confide in James when he returned from the horse market in Sacramento.

But, James had been delayed for two days. When he finally came down the pathway home at dinnertime, he herded a bevy of fine mares and one surprise. The surprise had slowed his trek home.

Althea heard the sound of stamping and whinnies as he guided his lot into the corral. Charlotte rushed from the house, always excited to get the first peek at new stock.

Althea watched from the porch as Charlotte dashed to her father, gave him a quick peck on the cheek, and scolded, "You're late! We were getting worried." She then sprang up on the fence to look at the inhabitants circling the enclosure, trying to settle down from their journey.

"Aye. Couldn't be helped." He nodded proudly at his new brood. "You tell me if it was worth it."

"Da, they're beautiful! Look how muscled and well formed they . . ."

Suddenly, Charlotte caught sight of the colt. "What's this?" She reached out to catch his halter, and he darted away shyly.

Coming down the porch steps to greet James, Althea saw the silver-gray colt try to hide amongst the mares. Thin and gangly, she could count his ribs, and he had a terrible gash along his shoulder. Recognizing a father-daughter moment, she observed from a distance.

James leaned against the fence beside

Charlotte. "Yes, well." He gazed at the yearling. "He's responsible for holding me up. Slow going with that shoulder of his."

"What happened to him? He looks awful!"

"Two shifty fellows outside the horse market had him. I say 'had,' because I doubt he belonged ta them. They gave me a tale of traveling a great distance ta sell him, though it was more ragged than travel worn they looked. I watched them for a while, because they could na bring themselves ta put him in the lots for sale. Probably afraid of being caught — he's not exactly a color that blends in. He's in despicable shape, so they could na get much for him. I did na see them again until I was on my way home. They beat the poor beast with a stick. He broke away from them and injured his shoulder doing so. It's a deep wound — tore the muscle pretty badly — so they took out their frustration of a lost sale on him. Woulda killed him the way they flayed him."

"Oh, Da, what did you do?"

"I rode up and kicked the stick out of the first one's hands. As I jumped down, the second one ran at me, and I let him find my fist with his face. No excuse for that sort of thing," he muttered. "Then I said as long as we were beating on dumb animals I thought

I might have a go. I asked if they'd like ta go again, but they declined."

"And they let you take him?"

"We came ta an understanding. I gave them a few dollars and made them scratch out a bill of sale, for whatever that was worth."

Althea approached the corral quietly and rested her hand on James's arm. "Sounds like your trip was more exciting than you bargained for. Welcome home."

He sighed tiredly and patted her hand. "Glad ta be home."

Charlotte looked pityingly at the colt milling with the mares. "How bad is the damage?"

"Ah." James smiled. "Not as bad as I first feared. Granted, he'll always have a nasty scar, but he won't limp. We can nurse him back ta health." He gave his daughter a quick hug as they watched him. "He's going ta be our project, yers and mine. Take a gander at him. Once he fills out, he's going ta be a sizeable beast. Beautiful conformation. I'm betting he moves smooth as silk. He'll be nervous until we win his confidence, so he'll take a lot of patience. First, we'll take care his wound heals properly."

Charlotte could not take her eyes off him. "Then what?" she asked wistfully. "He might be difficult to sell with that scar."

"Sell? Never," retorted her father. "He's going ta be a first class stud, the beginning of a dynasty. Mark my words." James leaned in and pointed. "He's going ta be a gorgeous color — still got a lot of black hair mixed in. His coat will grow lighter with age. He'll look like a ghostly fog. What shall we call him, eh?"

Charlotte smiled. "Banshee."

After clearing dinner dishes, Charlotte dashed back out to the corral. Banshee did his best to stay in the middle of the pack, despite her entreaties. She talked and patted the faces of the other horses, and he watched her warily.

Justin came out to inspect the new stock. "I don't envy you the task ahead. He's going to take some babying," he said. "You won't get much chance to work any of the others."

"It's not his fault, and I don't mind."

"I'm heading back in. Are you going to sleep out here?"

She shot him an annoyed look. "I want him to get used to me."

Justin shook his head and waved good night. He passed James and Althea listening from the porch.

Althea nodded at Charlotte perched on the railing of the corral. "Ah, girls' hearts and helpless things . . ." She smiled.

"Well, hardly helpless," objected James. "He's going ta be magnificent."

"So you keep saying."

"Needy, maybe."

She sighed. "That will be enough to keep her glued to his side."

James gazed at her curiously. "Something else on yer mind?"

She gave him a direct look. "Alas, you know me too well. I wanted to talk about Sean. You haven't heard from him, have you?"

"And why would he waste time writing ta me, when he has you? I thought he was coming home after he was wounded."

"So did I. I'm not sure what to think."

"But he still writes?"

"Not for some time. Perhaps he's reluctant to come back."

"Thea . . . the man is besotted with ye. Always has been."

"It's been three years," she said softly.

James remained quiet for a time. "Maybe ye do sense something . . . violence changes a man. A war is a lot to put behind him."

"He has spoken of some of it . . ."

"And much he will never speak of," he

409

said grimly.

Althea looked out over the courtyard, not sure what to believe at this point.

"Time apart is wearing on ye, I can see that," he sympathized. "But patience, Thea. I'm certain he needs ta come ta terms with himself first. No doubt he remembers his recklessness drove ye apart before, and he wants ta prove himself a reformed man. Believe me," James stared into her sorrowful, pale-blue eyes, "he's doing it for you. Ye deserve the best. He wants ta give ye that."

She felt her eyes fill with tears and blinked them away. "It's hard for me, given the past, to believe in happy endings. Thank you, James. That is indeed what I needed to hear. I don't always trust my own judgment when it comes to men."

"You are a lifetime away from being that girl back on the Vernon estate, the one responsible for nudging Emma my way, I might add."

She met his eye, and they laughed together, each remembering how the other once was.

"Look at all ye've accomplished. Ye've raised a fine son, and I credit ye for much of Charlotte's upbringing. Ye're incredibly talented. An asset to the Nevada City board. Sharp businesswoman as well."

She reached out and squeezed his hand. She smiled, straightened her shoulders, and shook her head as if to push the past aside. She knew no words adequately summed up their journey, and they were both too pragmatic to dredge through it. Instead, she focused on the future.

"You're right. I've been patient thus far; no sense in losing sight of things at this point. You've soothed my spirits."

"Good. As for me, I'm dogged tired, and my bed is callin' ta me. Would ye mind prodding Charlotte in soon?"

"Of course. Good night."

Althea rested her head against the back of the rocker and watched Charlotte crooning to the colt. She felt peaceful. Yet she felt something coming to an end.

With the excitement of settling new stock, James forgot a particular conversation from last night's dinner. He glossed over it, hoping it might not materialize.

Althea desperately needed Charlotte's help for the next few weeks. Nevada City sponsored a fundraising ball for its new theatre, and orders for gowns increased daily. Charlotte readily pledged her time, assuring James it would in no way interfere with training the new colt. Then she dropped the first little hint.

"Althea, do you suppose you might help me with a gown for myself as well?"

James had stopped eating.

"Of course, dear. I'm working on one for myself. Did Mrs. Ferguson ask you to be on our committee, or might there be another reason?"

His eyes had darted suspiciously from one to the other. He wondered if this conversation had been rehearsed.

Charlotte cleared her throat. "Yes, now that you mention it. Da . . . Drew Hodges wants to know if he could stop by and have a word with you about the ball?"

Definitely rehearsed. He looked at Justin, who shook his head and shrugged.

Althea jumped in again. "Of course he would ask your father for permission to escort you. What a respectful boy. Don't you think so, James?"

He shot her a look that said *traitor.* He went back to his dinner. "No harm in that, I suppose."

Yes, he had conveniently forgotten about that conversation.

As promised, he saw that Charlotte got up with the chickens, tended her chores, and spent nearly an hour with Banshee. She spoke to him in soothing tones each time

412

she passed. She moved amongst the other horses and let him see no reason to fear her. She approached him slowly but firmly to clean his wound. She ignored the tension in his body and moved away as soon as she finished. As she left, Charlotte held out a small piece of carrot on her flat palm. Banshee shifted nervously. She placed it on the ground and walked away. He snatched it. It was a start. Then Charlotte left for town with Althea, calling out that she would work with the colt more this afternoon.

After a full day with the new mares, James decided to tidy up around the barns. Lost in his own thoughts and plans, he busied himself stacking firewood. He looked up to see that worrisome boy walking towards him with his daughter. He sighed inwardly. The lad certainly did not waste time.

James straightened to his full height, watching warily as they approached.

"Hi, Da!" Charlotte called cheerily. "I told Drew about the new colt, and he wanted to see him. Da, this is Drew Hodges."

Drew's arm shot up quickly as he reached to shake James's hand. "Pleased to meet you, Mr. MacLaren."

James mentally counted to three before extending his own. "And ye as well," he said coolly. "I understand yer father works in management for one of the mines?"

"Yes, sir. The North Star, sir."

"Good outfit, that."

"Yes, sir."

Charlotte excused herself. "I promised Drew some lemonade. You look like you could use some yourself, Da. I'll be a few minutes." She smiled at Drew and walked to the house. He gave her a small wave.

"So, Drew," James began nonchalantly as he walked a few feet towards the chopping block, "ye like horses?"

"Yes, sir." Drew watched James put his foot on the stump and pull out the axe. "Charlotte says you've built this place up all yourself."

"Mostly." He reached for a large log and placed it end up on the stump. "A lot of neighbor helping neighbor in the beginning. Since then, Justin's been there every step of the way. Ye know Justin, do ye?"

"We've met once or twice. We have mutual friends, I think."

"That so? And how do ye know my Charlotte?"

"Howard Simpson introduced us. I believe he went to school with Charlotte. He had nothing but nice things to say about her." Drew looked up at the house, cleared his throat, and hurried through. "Mr. Mac-

Laren, sir. I like Charlotte very much, and I would like your permission to call on her. That is, in particular, sir, there is the Nevada City ball in a few weeks, and I would like to take her. If that's okay with you, sir." He waited anxiously, looking as if he thought James grew larger by the minute.

James tightened his grip on the axe and squared his shoulders to the log.

"It's been my experience . . . being a young lad myself once," he began, "that sometimes lads don't always have a girl's best interests at heart . . . and seventeen's a tender age for a lass. Now, if he behaves like a gentleman and doesn't go trying ta take liberties . . . all is well."

He took an enormous swing and split the log in two with one blow. He looked up at Drew briefly. He had his attention. He reached out, picked up half the log, and set it up on the stump again.

"Now from yer part of town, sometimes boys get the idea that girls from humbler means are fair targets." Again, giving a mighty swing he cracked the log in two, emphasizing his point. "No one in yer parents' social circle may object with ye getting fresh with a farmer's daughter. Sometimes the well-ta-do think they've a different set of morals than the rest of us." He set up the other half of the log. "But I'm here ta tell ye, ye don't. It matters. And I will object."

James brandished the axe and splintered the log so hard that a quarter of it shot off the stump. Drew's eyes opened wide. James rested his axe on the stump and leaned on the handle. He towered over the boy with a glowering look. Drew's eyes locked on his, unable to look away.

"So we understand each other, if I hear even a whisper of rumor, I'll come straight for ye before ye even know I'm there. And after yer folks finish putting the pieces of ye back together, we'll have a long discussion on appropriate behavior. Do we have an understanding?"

"Yes, sir, yes, sir!" he nodded.

"The lemonade is ready!" Charlotte called from the porch.

"Ah, lovely darlin'. I think both Drew and I could use a cold drink."

Drew hurried to the porch. James followed closely behind, mopping his brow. He muttered to himself, "Though I cu use a shot of something in mine."

CHAPTER 28

War or no war, Sacramento experienced miraculous growth during Dutton's time in Washington. He marveled at the city's response to flooding. Sacramento raised her skirts to avoid the encroachment of the rivers. She lifted major streets downtown, reinforcing them with brick walls. Previous first floors of homes and businesses became basements. New wooden sidewalks enhanced the flow of city traffic. Engineers went so far as to redirect a troublesome curve in the American River at a point less than a mile north of its natural convergence with the Sacramento River.

During the worst flood of 1862, Leland Stanford traveled to his own inauguration by rowboat and was said to have entered his home through a second-story window on his return. The construction of the new state capitol building suffered stops and starts,

417

with the state legislature moving to San Francisco for the remainder of that year but returning to the Sacramento courthouse thereafter. Dutton saw the capitol structure nowhere near completion, but its bones looked spectacular — mimicking the United States capitol. The "E" shaped building was crowned by a 125-foot dome, making it a defining presence in the city.

Steamship, stage, and teamster companies flourished. Telegraph lines now traveled to Salt Lake City and on to the East Coast. The heralded wagon road to the Comstock opened and expected to earn over a million dollars a year. Sacramento's groundbreaking of the Central Pacific gave California the next determined step towards greatness. The pony express had come and gone, as had Stanford's term in office.

A feeling of prosperity permeated his state, far more than the war-torn East Coast. Granted an extended leave when the judge suffered a heart attack, Dutton felt grateful to be home. Though fully engaged with the war department and the railroad, Dutton's disposition of exploring and exploiting kept him searching for the next great deal. He never undertook anything with singular purpose.

He researched investment options striking

him as interesting, learning to recognize vulnerability during unfortunate circumstances. Wartime presented many. He preferred playing several hands at once so as to choose the best of options. And Huntington sent him home with confidential railroad business to deliver to his partners in California.

In truth, he knew he was merely the courier. The partnership of Huntington, Hopkins, Crocker, and Stanford put a shield up against the world, the tightest alliance Dutton ever witnessed. But he learned more from casual observation at their feet than all his years at Harvard. Dutton possessed keen powers of deduction. He pieced together railroad reports to the press and deduced the missing elements as events unfolded.

Dutton earned a certain level of trust with the cagey Huntington. Judah's increasingly frequent objections to the manner of the Central Pacific's operation began to taint its goodwill with the public as Judah felt himself losing control of *his* railroad. He protested when the Central Pacific hired Crocker as its contractor, seeing conflict of interest with Crocker a board member. Dutton thought it ironic that Judah saw no such problem with Governor Stanford's allocation of $15 million in state bonds as both governor of California and president of the Central Pacific. In a secret board meeting, Crocker resigned, was replaced by his brother and was appointed contractor.

Similarly, Judah condemned Stanford's reclassification of railroad mileage. Government bonds advanced $16,000 per mile on flat land, $32,000 in the foothills, and $48,000 across the Sierras. Using a geology manual Stanford questioned, where does a mountain begin? Twenty rather flat miles became designated as foothills, a brilliant move as far as Dutton could see.

Dutton's reports of Judah's continual opposition aided an already convinced Huntington's decision to move to Washington and take control. A showdown with Judah became inevitable, and Huntington gave Judah and his most fervent supporter, Bailey, two weeks to buy them out. Judah approached Commodore Cornelius Vanderbilt for a meeting in New York. Contracting yellow fever en route through Panama, Judah died before the meeting took place.

Having delivered Huntington's paperwork to Stanford at the Sacramento courthouse, Dutton took this opening to request a favor. His personal stock with the group was at an all time high. His keen eye detected the subterfuge on the part of the Union Pacific's

Thomas C. Durant. Political maneuverings being a constant state of affairs, Durant slipped in an amendment to a newly proposed bill ending the Central Pacific's line at the border of California. Huntington furiously confronted Durant, and they settled on the Central Pacific's territory extending to the halfway point through Nevada. Dutton smiled as he exited the courthouse into the crisp, cool air and sunshine. Missing the continuing battle between the wily Huntington and the calculating Durant was his only regret in leaving Washington.

Tending to more immediate matters, Dutton immersed himself into Dandridge business concerns. He succeeded in securing Stanford's political support for his mining industry *friend* — it only made sense to keep people supportive to the railroad in public office. His importance to the Dandridge cause in other matters was immaterial.

His morning mission completed, Dutton decided to return to his hotel. As he scanned the crowd from his viewpoint at the top of the courthouse steps, he caught sight of Neil Collier walking on 7th Street. Startled by the luck, Dutton shouted out his name. The sun at this hour caught his friend in the eye, making it difficult to locate the voice that summoned him. He watched Neil turn and shield his eyes with his hand. Neil squinted and chuckled in recognition as Dutton jogged quickly down the steps to meet him.

"Dutton Dandridge! My God, man, it's been nearly two years!" The two men embraced and clapped each other on the shoulders.

"No excuse for it either. I was planning to look you up on this trip, and here I nearly stumble over you. I wanted to make certain you weren't letting your Harvard brain turn soft in these backwaters!"

"Hardly!"

"Well, that is indeed what I wanted to hear. So few classmates on this coast, who else can I swap old times and old stories with?"

"When did you return from Washington? And what brings you here?"

"Ah, well. You know Father. He has his finger in a thousand pies, and he sent me to do legwork."

Neil smiled. "How is the judge? I heard he suffered a stroke."

"Gave me a scare, but it turned out to be minor. He's rich, fat, and sassy. Not necessarily in that order. You think our professors were tough . . . I'm grateful for them now that I'm working for him." Dutton paused, growing serious. "Listen, Neil . . . I couldn't believe the news. I was in New York when Father sent a telegram about the boiler explosion on the *Washoe*. I was sorry to hear about your parents."

Neil sighed resignedly. "Thank you. I did receive your wire. Eighty people went down on that steamer. Who would ever have thought that such a short journey so close to home would have ended like that? Father always believed in healthy rivalry, thought it was good for the economy to give California Steam and Navigation some competition. They determined Captain Kidd engaged in a race with the *Chrysopolis* and caused the accident."

"I'm sorry that I wasn't in touch sooner. The judge held Garth Collier in high esteem . . . he's an enormous loss. Father admired anyone who could build an empire like yours from scratch. How's the rest of the family?"

"We're moving on as best we can, taking different roles to keep things going. Adele has Mother's charity work. Royce and I are trying to divide up supervision of everything else. He's a tough nut . . . he has to be to lead seasoned ranch hands. And it's hard on Celeste, being so young. Especially having to answer to her two big brothers."

Dutton nodded thoughtfully. "I imagine

it's an enormous duty for all of you to handle. How is the lovely Adele?"

"Married now. Has a little one and expecting another any minute." Neil nudged him. "You really missed out there."

"Don't I know it!" He chuckled. "Although, I suspect she doesn't feel the loss. Listen, despite the fact you know me as well as you do, I've some business ideas to kick around with you. Father's eager to spread our interests outside of San Francisco, and Sacramento is brimming with possibilities. Besides, the dominant, if not overbearing, Dandridge personality is equally expressed in father and son. I need my own turf, so to speak."

Neil laughed. "Understood. I'm up for listening to a promising joint venture. The fathers did rather well together, and I'm looking for ways to grow the estate. Given that you're somewhat of a known entity — good and bad . . ." Neil nudged him playfully, "we could have a great deal to talk about. Do you have dinner plans?"

"I'm available."

"Wonderful. I have to run to a meeting at the attorney's office now, but perhaps I could meet you at your hotel later, and we'll figure it out from there."

"Splendid. I'm staying at the Golden

Eagle. Come by when you're finished." Dutton clapped his friend on the shoulder. "I'm looking forward to it."

CHAPTER 29

Thistle Dew — March 1865

Charlotte seemed unusually quiet at dinner. The silence was magnified by the fact that Justin drove the buggy into Nevada City to have supper with Althea. James glanced at her while he took a big swig of cold milk. She pushed her food around on her plate. He put down his glass and probed, "So. It appears Banshee is becoming doggedly attached ta ye. Looks for ye whenever anyone goes inta the barn."

She sighed. "I suppose."

"What's this? Come now. That's a comment that usually spawns at least ten minutes of details about how he's doing." He leaned in to look at her pouting face. He brightened. "Ye know, I'm thinking it's time we started him ta saddle. What do ye think?"

She looked up, interested, but hardly with enthusiasm.

"I'm also thinking," he enticed, "it should

be you ta ride him first."

She smiled a bit. "Really?"

"Well, sure. We've worked on a slow break for him. He trusts ye . . . nearly follows ye like a puppy, he does. He's filling out, but he's still a bit on the slight side. I'd rather not put too much weight on him at first. We can start tomorrow."

"Okay."

"That's it? Ye've been begging for me ta start breaking him for weeks!"

She sighed again. "I'm sorry, Da. It's just . . . well . . . the ball is in a few days. My dress is all finished, and I don't think I'm going."

"What do ye mean, not going?"

"I think Drew is breaking things off."

James stiffened a bit. "Why is that, love?"

"I don't know. Things are okay when I see him at church, I guess, but as the ball gets closer, I get the feeling he's avoiding me. Then Sara Jane told me he asked her if Amy Clodfelter was going to the ball. Yesterday I saw him in town, and he started coughing funny and told me he's not feeling well."

"Oh." James put down his fork and looked her in the eye. "I'm afraid it might be my fault," he said grimacing.

"Your fault?"

"I had a little talk with the lad . . ."

427

"Da!"

"Well, sweetheart . . ." he began apologetically.

"What on earth did you say?"

James took on a very matter of fact air. "I told him I expected him ta behave himself or answer ta me."

"You threatened him?" she looked at him incredulously. "Da, how could you do that?"

"I didn't threaten him; I only made certain we understood each other."

"You threatened him. At least you made him feel threatened." She crossed her arms and stared at the table.

"Now look here, girl." He pointed his fork at her. "That boy's reaction can only mean two things. One, he thought his position high enough that he fully intended ta try his way with ye, or . . ."

"I guess I'll never know, will I?" she interrupted loudly, her eyes blazing at him, her chin jutted out.

"Is that something ye really want ta find out? Is it? Do ye think ye could ha fought him off if I'm right?"

"I'd have fought."

"And most likely he'd still win. Even if there's no struggle, with him telling stories about what a hellcat ye are, I'd still be in jail for killin' the boy."

She sat sullenly, staring at her plate. "What's two?"

"Two what?"

"The other thing his breaking things off could mean."

"Oh. That he's a coward. Either way, ye're better off." With that simple explanation, James went back to his dinner.

She sat quietly fuming. He looked up at the stony silence and saw disappointment in her face. He sighed and put down his utensils again.

"Darlin'. I know it's na easy ta have a big brute of a father lookin' over yer shoulder. It'd be better if ye had your mother here ta talk ta, but it's solely me ta look after ye. I know a lot more about boys at this age than girls. It seems easier ta address their nature than yers."

Without looking up, she said softly, "I'm old enough to judge for myself. You're embarrassing me, Da."

"Maybe so, but I prefer this kind of embarrassment ta any other. Besides, there's something else ye need ta remember. The rich ones can afford ta change their minds about love as often as they like, and they will. Humbler men — provided they're smart and hard workers — can be a more solid foundation ta build a life on." He gave a quick nod, agreeing with his own statement.

Frowning, she asked, "You don't like rich people, do you?"

"It's na like that," he shook his head. "They deal with the added temptation of buying themselves out of responsibility. Easy lives don't sharpen wits or morals, and they fall easily compared ta those that treat their neighbor's survival as important as their own."

He reached across the table and chucked her chin. "Come, now. Cheer on. Ye know I want the best for ye." He smiled tenderly at her.

She gave him a begrudging look. "I know. I wish you'd let me find my own way. I'll have to fall down every now and then to learn how to pick myself up."

He shook his head and chuckled. "I want ye ta learn ta *step over* the obstacles."

"Okay, Da." She gave him an exasperated smile and stood to clear their plates.

Nevada City
A discreet word from Justin encouraged Drew Hodges that he could take the prettiest girl in town to the ball and live to tell about it. He also warned him that James's message was not to be taken lightly.

The nearly completed Nevada City theatre hosted the ball. The imposing brick building, unique in design, was a lofty, two-story affair. Its façade mimicked six pillars with capstones in brick extending to create four arched recesses. The two taller niches in the center sported curved windows with a double soldier row of brick, and beneath them were two sets of tall, deep-set, arched theatre doors flanked with steel shutters.

Inside, the newly assembled orchestra performed from the stage, as the unfinished orchestra pit needed funding from the ball. Risers and theatre seating also awaited money, so the town installed a temporary floor for dancing. The low level of the dance area with the elevated ceiling of the theatre made the balcony seem to tower above gaily twirling couples. The enormous balcony's elaborately carved oak front stretched the width of the room, and red velvet curtains trimmed in gold bullion fringe hung at either side, mimicking the same red velvet curtain adorning the stage. Gaslights fixed on the walls shimmered a soft glow on the large crowd watching and chatting from the perimeters of the room.

James approached the refreshment tables manned by women from the fundraising committee, mopped his brow, and reached for a cup of punch.

Lodie slipped up beside him and nudged him in the ribs. "Dancing works up a powerful sweat . . . which lovely lady was the benefactress of all that effort?"

"Och. Not a one. Running about setting up chairs and tables is the task. That, *after* the false fire alarm."

Lodie laughed. "I heard Big Nick was up to his tricks. I believe the fire department is regretting your gift of that horse."

"He's a fine animal ta be sure, but too darn smart — and they need ta exercise him. He gets bored with no activity. He forces the stable lock with his teeth, goes ta the front of the firehouse, and pulls the bell rope. When I arrived there he was, standing between the shafts of the ladder wagon, waiting ta be hitched."

"Well, you look very distinguished in that frock coat and string tie. I've seen a few women giving you the eye." He spoke loudly to be heard above the music and feet pounding the rhythm of the quadrille.

James finished his punch as he watched Charlotte, out of breath from dancing, giggle her way to the tables with Ella Louise. He muttered to Lodie, "My eye is rather busy."

Lodie shot him a disapproving look. "I'd

think you'd know better than to hold reins too tightly." He greeted the girls with a smile. "Ladies . . . how lovely you do look! Some punch perhaps? You seem to have escaped your partners."

"Thank you, Mr. Glenn," Charlotte said, ducking behind Ella Louise, who then burst into laughter. "We're attempting to give our toes a break . . . too much stomping in a square dance!"

"The polka wasn't any better. Pete crushed my foot at least four times," agreed Ella Louise.

Lodie grinned and spotted his wife at the end of one of the tables. "Matilda! I think these girls are in need of cookies."

Matilda picked up a plate of sugar cookies and hotfooted it in their direction. Huddled together, the girls scanned the room, looking for friends amongst the multitude of revelers.

James suddenly felt grateful he wasn't watching his daughter glued to the side of Drew Hodges. "Has a capable head on her shoulders," he thought. He decided to lighten his mood.

"Having a jolly time, darlin'?"

"Oh, yes, very much. It looks like the whole town is here and half the county," she said looking around. "Oh, there's Althea." Charlotte waved her over.

Matilda offered up the plate of cookies, meeting Althea in their tight little circle in the crowd.

"My, my. Why aren't my belles of the ball out there dancing?" asked Matilda.

"Heavy-footed partners," smirked James.

Charlotte stood gazing at the dancers. "Althea, look at all the gowns! It's a veritable garden of swirling colors out there! How many of them do you suppose we created in the last two months?"

"Goodness, it makes me weary to count."

"Did you see Caroline Williams's gown? It has stunning details. I've been trying to study the bustle in the back to work out how it's done. Do you suppose it's from London?"

Althea turned her head as she watched Caroline breeze by on the arm of her husband. "Paris, I think. Rather interesting — you're right. Her mother-in-law's dress is definitely French." She gave Charlotte a quick hug. "Keep watching; we'll sketch out some of these new trends on Monday."

"Charlotte, that deep-rose color you've chosen is beautiful on you," said Matilda.

"Thank you. I dyed the tatting pale pink as well."

"The way you've placed it on the gown is

434

very flattering."

James gave his daughter a perfunctory look, striving to see what the women discussed.

Lodie rolled his eyes.

"Charlotte, have you seen Justin anywhere?" Ella Louise frowned as she searched.

Matilda and Althea exchanged looks. Seeing this, James was thoroughly confused.

"Not in awhile. He was dancing with Lily Anne earlier."

Ella Louise gave a perturbed sniff and continued looking. Catching on, and amused by the antics of youth, James was relieved to see Charlotte engrossed in watching the room full of women in beautiful gowns. He watched her tap her toe and sway slightly to the music. Then Drew appeared suddenly, blocking her view.

"Are you ready to dance some more, Charlotte?"

"Thank you, Drew, but if you don't mind, I'd like to sit this one out. Would you like some punch?"

"No, thanks." He looked awkwardly over his shoulder. "Say, if you want to rest, do you mind if I dance with Sara Jane?"

She smiled sweetly. "Not at all. I'll wait for the next one."

Matilda winked at Althea while Charlotte was distracted and leaned in to quietly comment to Ella Louise, "You know, if you ignored him, I think he'd come around."

Ella Louise blushed. "How did you know?"

"I have three young boys myself you know — too young yet for the likes of this, but I do know how they think."

Ella looked a bit ashamed. "Do you think he noticed?"

Matilda gave her a level look. "After a time, I think so. You can't wear your feelings on your face. Be gay, laugh, and mean it. You'll have a better time, and he'll wonder what he's missing. All men hate to be out of the loop, dear."

Ella Louise looked at her shyly.

"Come now, you've hardly been lacking in partners. Go and have fun, as young people should. Let the rest take care of itself." Looking up, Matilda loudly cleared her throat. Ella Louise turned to see Howard Simpson waiting.

"Would you like some punch, Ella Louise?"

She smiled. "That would be nice, Howard."

Matilda poured two punch cups, and, as Ella Louise turned away, she nodded ever

436

so slightly her thanks.

Matilda chuckled and turned to Althea. "These young ones, what a stitch they are!"

James shook his head, wondering if he'd ever appeared so foolish and guessing that he had. His eye fell on Althea. She looked stunning. She had chosen an icy-blue silk moiré for her gown, the hue reflecting the lovely color of her eyes. She had woven a matching ribbon through her blonde hair, which she pulled back and gathered under in an elegant chignon. He heard the orchestra striking up a waltz and on sudden impulse stepped up and asked, "Would ye honor me with this dance?"

Startled, she stared for a moment at his outstretched hand and then answered quickly, "Of course."

Lodie rolled his eyes again. "Well, now you're making me look bad." He grinned at his wife. "Matilda?"

Althea took James's hand, smiling as Lodie whisked Matilda onto the floor and teased her until she laughed so hard she could barely keep time with the music. Althea looked up at James, momentarily studying him as he realized he was staring.

"It's turned out to be a wonderful evening. There are friends here tonight I haven't spoken to in ages."

James straightened his posture and held her at a respectable distance. "Yes. Ye know I'm not much for all the hullaballoo, but when it allows ye ta see so many folks ye'd like ta see . . . makes me think we should have events like this more often."

She smiled. "Well, you certainly have relaxed since Drew met Charlotte at the door here."

She possessed a sweet, sincere smile, he thought. He responded quickly, "Och, all this fuss over the lad, and she looks like she cu care less now."

Althea raised an eyebrow as he expertly whirled her around the floor. "It's her first ball. Sometimes it's nice to be asked. Though if it makes you feel better, I did hear her say she thought they should be friends."

James stiffened, annoyed. "Then why did she behave as if the world would end if she couldn't go with him?"

"Honestly?"

He suddenly became uncomfortable. She knew him too well, and he was not sure he wanted to know her opinion. He braced himself as he moved her through the throng of dancers.

"I think she became disenchanted with him when she saw how easily he was spooked by you."

"Good for her! She's too strong for a spineless man."

Althea's gaze latched onto his. "James. As I said, sometimes it's simply nice to be asked. She wanted to go to the party with her friends. She likes Drew, but you can't look at every boy who comes near her as a threat. What concerns me more . . ." she looked away.

Instinctively, he drew her closer. "What?"

"Someday there will be a man that truly strikes her fancy. I don't think you're ready for that. If you treat them all as a menace, she won't listen to you when it's really important."

He grew quiet, feeling caught out by the truth of her words.

She peeked up at him. "James?"

He gazed out over her head as he turned her in time with the waltz. He looked down, feeling drawn in to the crystal-blue depths of her eyes. "There are times I am reminded how long and how well we know one another."

She looked down demurely, and his heart wrenched. Suddenly, he was aware of the feel of her in his arms. His foot stumbled out of time with the music. She looked up, and their gaze locked, as they spun over and over, lost in the music and each other's faces.

Althea stopped abruptly. James looked at the odd expression on her face and followed the path of her stare to a small group of people only a short distance away. They all chatted amongst themselves. All save one. The man stood quietly waiting for acknowledgement. His brown hair was shorter than he remembered it, with a soft streak of gray at the temples. The eye patch he wore hindered recognition. Althea shook her head dumbly and then whispered, "Sean."

James released her. She moved slowly away as if unaware they had been dancing. She gradually closed the distance between herself and Sean. Her outstretched hand rose hesitantly to the side of his face and touched the edge of the eye patch. Sean caught her hand and pressed it to his lips.

"Hello, Thea. I didn't know how to tell you . . ."

"It doesn't matter," she said softly. "It only matters that you are here."

CHAPTER 30

Nevada City

He found it unsettling that he had barely seen Althea since the dance. James fell asleep in a chair by the hearth waiting for Sean to bring her home in the wee hours of the morning and awoke to a soft tap at his door. He rushed to answer it, rubbing the weariness from his eyes to be greeted by Sean's sheepish apology and request for lodging. He welcomed him in and went to bed, figuring he could at least talk to Sean come morning.

When he arose, Sean had already squired Althea out early to church and then on a long buggy ride into the country. Althea, exhausted from the long day and festivities of the night before, retired early. He planned to catch her this morning before she drove in to Nevada City, wondering how she felt about Sean's sudden re-appearance. She overslept, causing her to rush to and from

441

her cottage gathering what she needed to take to work while he hitched the buggy for her. In frustration, he had watched her hasty wave good-bye as she called to Charlotte not to hold supper for her.

Deep in thought and lost in the rhythm of his boots striking the hard Nevada City boardwalk in unison with Justin, he failed to notice his companion come to an abrupt halt.

"James!" Justin stared at him. He jerked his thumb, motioning behind them. "We passed Vicente's shop."

"Och. Sorry, lad. My mind is elsewhere."

Justin smirked. "What's that you're always telling me about 'clearing the cobwebs'? I feel like I'm five again, running after a long-legged giant."

"Aye. Not very good company today, am I?"

"I figure you'd warm up once you're sitting still with a beer in your hand. Let's grab Vicente and go. I want to hear Sean's war stories."

Vicente Sifuentes spent years selling his leather goods through Lodie Glenn's emporium while still working hydraulic mining sites. His saddles remained in such high demand that Lodie found it difficult to keep them in stock. Often, he traveled with James to the horse market in Sacramento to sell his merchandise. Eager to be close to his large family, Vicente decided he was getting too old to work mines. Lodie backed him in his new establishment, repaying the debt of opportunity Vicente shared with them all.

Entering the small, but cleanly organized, shop James felt gratitude for strong friendships. Papa Bear Lodie was nothing if not loyal, he mused to himself. Even though Vicente was widely acknowledged as producing superior work, Nevada City had been slow to embrace a Mexican shop owner in their midst. Lodie nudged their thinking along after he announced that leather goods would no longer be sold at the emporium, only at Vicente's saddle shop.

The aroma of new leather and neatsfoot oil filled the room. Following Justin to the front, James pounded jovially on the counter. "Is the proprietor working today?" he shouted.

He then noticed the small girl quietly sitting on a three-legged stool behind the counter. She stood and turned towards the workroom in the back and called, "Poppy?" Her large, doe-brown eyes watched James carefully.

"Ah. Sorry about the racket; just being silly with yer father," he said to reassure her. "Now, which one would ye be?"

She looked down at her feet shyly. Her thick, dark lashes hid her expression.

Justin poked James. *"Hola, Mariposa."*

She peeked up smiling. *"Hola, Justin."*

Justin said to James, "She's Vicente's youngest, almost eleven I think."

She nodded.

"My apologies for na remembering, young lady."

She looked at Justin in wide-eyed adoration.

Vicente came quickly from the back room, waving his clasped hands in the air.

"So sorry, my friends. Busy, busy before, but now I am ready. It is a happy day." He turned to his daughter and spoke quickly to her in Spanish, reminding her that her older brother working in the back was in charge in his absence. She nodded, *"Sí, Poppy."*

Justin turned to wave good-bye. Once outside, Vicente said to Justin, "I am grateful that you are kind to her and more grateful that she is so young. She has a terrible crush on you."

Justin laughed. "That'll pass soon enough. I remember feeling small and invisible."

James added, "From one father to another, yer worries are only beginning."

"This I know! It is why I worry."

The Silver Moon hosted a pack of miners and townies eagerly soaking up celebratory drinks. They entered to find Sean holding court, regaling the crowd with tales of his journey home. Peter and Rob Stuben pushed several tables together as old friends clustered around. Sean apparently knew enough people to fill his own town, and those listening hovered close with curiosity. He rose from his seat as Lodie went to get more chairs for James, Vicente, and Justin.

James and Vicente each grabbed Sean in a backslapping embrace. Justin shook his hand. Sean stood back, stared, and whistled. "Dang! What happened to the lanky kid I left behind?" Sean sidled up to him as if to prove his point. "Yep. At least as tall as me."

Justin smiled. "It's really good to see you, Sean."

Sean winked his good eye.

"What've we missed?" asked James.

"Only my trek over three states," he quipped, "and I lost the eye at Vicksburg. That's all I'll say about that other than I was fortunate it was only the eye."

"Don't fret, fellows, I'm sure we'll all hear these same stories *over and over* anytime a drink is poured," joked Lodie, arriving with the extra seats.

"Only Rob and I won't be buying after

the first telling!" Peter called out.

There was an outburst of laughter, and then a shout from the back, "C'mon Sean! Let's hear about the Comstock!"

"Yes, let's hear why you came back if there was so much gold *and* silver!"

"Face it, gents, the reason he came back is blonde!" ribbed Clancy.

James glanced at Justin but could not get a read on his calmly composed face.

Sean held up his hands as if to ward off guesses. "True, enough. And now I will awkwardly change the subject back to mining if you don't mind. Eh, ummm . . ." he loudly cleared his throat.

"Before the war started I was quick enough to beat the masses of hopefuls up there. Handy that the first confirmation of the strike came from Ott here in our own assay office."

He chuckled. "Hell, boys . . . they'd never have thought about silver until the heavy blue-black stuff clogged up their riffles and interfered with washing out gold! Hardly knew what they stumbled across. When silver played out in one area, somebody would holler, 'gold!' somewhere close by, and all went running in that direction.

"It's true for a time the strikes alternated between the two metals, making for a

446

stronger payload than we saw here with drought dragging down our production the past four years. Last year's conscription didn't help either. But the heat! Had to get used to working in my underwear."

Clancy balked at this. "Comstock has altitude, don't they? Surely wasn't hot underground?"

"Especially underground! Hot springs everywhere. Like one of them fancy health places Brannan's building in Calistoga. A man could boil his skin right off if'n he tapped an underground spring. I was drenched everyday with either steam or sweat, hard to tell which. I stopped and worked awhile on my way back from Tennessee trying to get used to this," he said, tapping the eye patch. "Like everywhere else, it's getting too organized — big business moving in and taking over. They're making some pretty impressive improvements with shoring up tunnels and such, so I stayed to learn as much as I could." He paused to throw back the rest of his beer. "After awhile I figured I had better reasons to come on home as long as big outfits were pushing folks out."

"But what if you had a claim . . ." began Rob.

"Claims are a tougher and tougher thing

to be grasped. Lawyers change the definition every day," Sean declared.

"Where a man sinks his sweat is his land! His claim!" exclaimed Peter.

"In the beginning, yup," Sean agreed. "Now boundary disputes pop up everywhere."

James asked curiously, "But if it's duly recorded . . . how can it be disputed?"

"Ah, depends on definition. Say a company buys land next to your claim. They argue: is it one continuous vein of ore or many splintered veins underground in that area? If they contend the main vein is on their land and what is on your claim is an extension of what they own, then you're poaching. I can tell you, lads, it's a battle you'll lose. While it's arbitrated, they can keep you from taking ore out. Deeper pockets can survive the wait. If you go in anyway, they throw you in jail over a nickel's worth of dust. Believe me, I saw it all."

"But I thought you made money?" asked Justin.

"I did. I talked to a lot of folks, did a lot of educated guessing, and it paid off some places. I settled in a spot until someone made me move on. After the war, worked for a company for hourly to learn square set timbering to shore up the mines. After a time, I knew it was no better there than here, so I came on home."

James sensed the mood in the saloon turning glum.

Clancy sighed loudly. "Thought maybe it was a fitting place to pack it off to. Hasn't been a big strike to speak of around here in a spell."

"A great place if what you're after is a steady job and a bustling town. That's all there to be sure. After it was clear I was wasting my time digging in pinched-out glory holes, I hung around long enough to see what salaries were going for and learn the organization."

James glanced at Lodie, who was unusually quiet. The big man wore a furrowed frown as though sorting through Sean's details trying to figure out the fit into a master puzzle. Eventually he spoke, asking, "So, what are your plans now?"

"Well," Sean straightened in his chair and looked hesitantly at the faces around the room. "I've taken a foreman's job . . . with the new owners at the Empire mine."

The bar grew unexpectedly still. Men squirmed in their chairs, shooting looks to one another. An uneasy silence fell.

"Come on, lads, it's not a wake. And not so different than working outfits along the ridges," Sean protested.

Rob Stuben spoke first. "But it is different. It's big business. Mines don't hire in the old 'in and out' way anymore — any days they could get a crew, or single man, to work. They like steady employees. It's not so easy to change outfits, because they're so competitive. I like calling my own shots . . . what I work for is mine."

"What about days on end you work, and there's nothing?" Sean countered. "Four dollars a day is pretty good pay."

Clancy sighed again. "We was hopin' you'd learned a few new tricks, new methods. And that you'd throw in with some of us."

"I learned the life we've known up to now is finished. Can't be done without big equipment and even bigger dollars." He met the hush in the room with empathetic tones. "For me, I got serious plans now. I need to count on something steady. Rob, you and Peter got the Silver Moon to live on. Others of you fill in the gaps with odd jobs when you can. How much do you really make anymore?"

A man called Charlie asked seriously, "Are you recruiting?"

Sean nodded. "It's part of my job. The Empire's looking for experienced men.

There's not a man in this room I wouldn't hire. Better the devil you know, lads . . . and you know me."

Peter shook his head. "Nope. Not me. Not yet."

James looked at the faces around him amidst the sound of reluctant grumbling.

"Me, neither. We're still finding pockets in abandoned shafts. There's still a chance there's overlooked veins."

James turned, trying to catch all the comments that melded together like a buzz of bees.

"All it takes is one. Working together, we could find it."

"And if we find just *one*, we could be set for life."

"There's still small finds — only makes sense there's still a big one in there somewhere."

"I'll take my chances with blokes I've been working with all along."

"We're in this thing together, not taking orders from a company that's gonna profit from our sweat."

Someone called out above the hum, "James. You've done the in and out with the mines. What do you think?"

The room quieted again as James contemplated his answer. "I might na be the one ta

451

ask," he said truthfully. "Except for blasting work from time ta time, checking structural safety in tunnels, or helping our 'cousin jacks' with the Cornish pump, I've been out of it for some time now for the day ta day. But I'll say, I was never too proud ta take a salary so my family cu eat on a regular basis. Steady pay got me where I wanted."

Sean nodded thoughtfully.

James frowned and then addressed the room. "But tell me. What bothers ye the most? Giving up on the big strike — 'someday'? Or knowing someone ye trust is saying 'someday' is already over? If ye're honest with yerselves, ye'll realize we've all seen this day comin' for some time now."

"They can't take away our right to try!" groused Clancy.

"Sean's na taking anything from anyone. He's trying ta give ye jobs — if ye want them," reasoned James.

"It's what's right for me, that's all," Sean stated plainly. "I'm happy to talk to anybody interested, but it's for each man to decide for himself."

Lodie stood beside his seat and turned to Peter behind the bar. "Well I'm thinking that's enough talk of business at what's supposed to be a celebration of our good friend coming home," he announced. "The problem is, we're all too dry! Peter! The next round is on me!"

Cheers went up around the tables. As drinks arrived, spirits improved. Soon old friends talked amongst themselves and welcomed their long absent mate home.

As the merrymaking ended and revelers called it a day, Justin decided to walk to Althea's shop and drive his mother back to Thistle Dew. Lodie, Vicente, Sean, and James set out for a return to sobriety and a quiet meal at the hotel next door. Once hunger was satisfied, small talk ended, and Lodie fished about for pieces to his puzzle.

"So . . . foreman with the Empire." He nodded as he spoke as if inviting elaboration. "That's a different way to go."

Sean sat forward at the table, suddenly animated. "They got exciting things happening — new money breathing life into a dying thing — *believe me* it's good. Tunnels need work, need pumping out — even in this drought since production idled. Get this: New management is pouring money into improvements. They're installing Blaisdell mercury amalgamation pans, settlers, and blankets — a terrific system! Besides the old six stamp mill on Wolf Creek, they're building a new stamp mill — thirty stamps powered by steam, all the parts to be made right here at our foundry . . ."

Sean gave Lodie a playful shove. "Which ought to make *you* happy, Mr. Mayor."

James chuckled, thinking Sean's enthusiasms remained as infectious as always. He felt a glow of relief that his friend's spirit remained intact despite grievous injury and his family's sufferings.

Vicente exclaimed, "You have studied greatly, my good friend! You will be very successful here, I am thinking."

Sean grinned. "The whole operation's good for the town, even all Nevada County, because it's not only Empire — North Star's doing likewise. They changed hands, too. Old ownership ran operations off removing the richest surface ore, never put any reserve aside in case they hit a barren zone — and they had to shut down. New management is operating for the future by investing big sums into development." He leaned forward. "You know they got a 750-foot incline shaft and put over fifteen grand into a drain tunnel and sunk a perpendicular shaft 500 feet east of the collar!"

He sat back, looking blissfully content. He viewed all their faces. "This is it, fellas. Where my experience does me the most good. I've spent too many years at this not to let what I do know work for me," Sean stated. "I never had that 'other passion' for anything . . . stores," he gestured to Vicente and Lodie, "or horses," he looked at James. "I know mines. And I can see the hand-writin' on the wall everywhere. It's pretty much over for a man on his own."

Lodie took a hard tone. "The boys over at the Silver Moon seemed to feel differently. They think there's still enough gaps in the system for a man to squeeze out a living. I've seen them . . . working the hills outside of town . . . working like dogs. Like you, when you scraped up at Comstock . . . they're picking at what's been abandoned."

Sean looked uncomfortable. "Yup. And like me in Comstock . . . only until I was asked to move on." He sighed. "I couldn't tell them yet . . . those gaps are going to close. They were nowhere ready to hear me. Same arguments here as Comstock. The day's coming when corporate mines *will* take away their right to try. The Empire means to enforce their holding. I don't know where these boys are digging, but if it's on Empire's land, they'll be asked to leave it."

"What do you mean by enforce?" Lodie demanded.

"Nothing ugly, but they'll bring the law into it. They'd rather see these men working for Empire than to piss 'em off. Bottom line is a lot of what's abandoned ain't safe. James, you've seen how the timbers can rot; you've inspected for companies. Empire intends to go in and fortify the supports in there. They'll clean it up and reopen when ready *and safe.*"

"Is part of yer job ta move the men out?" asked James.

"If it's Empire land. The company figures the message will go down better from one of their own than from management they don't know."

"Is that something ye really want ta take on?"

"They're paying me damn well to do it."

Lodie started aback and stared.

James saw Vicente look at Lodie, as puzzled as he. He caught Vicente's eye, giving him a slight, like-minded nod.

"Look," Sean tapped his finger on the table. "The end result will be the same. It's happening. I'm hoping coming from me . . . they might loathe me for a while, but they won't fight like a stranger is stealing from 'em. There's no sense in anyone getting hurt. I know it's a tough sell, but I *am* trying to help. Those that come aboard now are going to be senior employees in an organization that's only gonna grow. I hope to convince them not to waste their time or money trying to fight. Legally, they won't have a leg to stand on."

"You're right — they're not ready to hear you! A lot of them have got a lot of debt, and they're trying to hang on! I know. I carry a lot of them. They're gonna feel like you yanked a rug out from under them!" Lodie exclaimed.

James shifted in his chair at the edgy tone of Lodie's voice.

Vicente shook his head in disagreement. "It is the times. Sean is not taking from them. They work and work and make no money to take. He tries to give them jobs."

"Thank you!" exclaimed Sean, acknowledging Vicente.

James's eyes narrowed as he quietly studied his oldest friend.

Lodie leaned in across the table. He held up his finger, waving it closely in Sean's face. "One strike . . ." he growled, "even a little one, even one damn lump of ore — and they could clean up their debt! That's what they're waiting on. They're too proud to quit! They don't want to let their families down! Then, and *only* then, they'll walk in Empire's door and ask for their own damn jobs. Do you *know* how long it will take them to get even on a salary? Do you *know* how this affects families?"

"Geez, Lodie, last time I felt this fired upon the other guy was wearing a blue uniform."

Startled, Lodie held Sean's one-eyed gaze until finally he muttered, "Sorry." He looked down. Then he sighed. "It's just . . . that I hear a lot. I know their struggles."

"Yeah, well . . . all I can tell you is, I been there. Remember? And I know I was dumber about going broke than them. But it don't matter *how* you hit bottom once you're there. I fought my way back, and so will they. I took a steady paying job so it don't happen to me again. And I'm offering one to them . . . to help get them started. It's all I know to do."

"It's all you can do," offered Vicente. "In the end they can take it, or no."

Lodie shook his head. "I'm sorry, Sean. It's not the welcome you deserve." He gave them all a hangdog look and smirked. "I guess I bailed on the three of you when the time was right for me." He regarded Sean. "Of course you have to take this job. Better for them to have someone understanding their point of view in a position to help." He offered his hand.

Sean shook it. "When they're ready. Speaking of ready, I'm ready for the sack. It was a long journey home, a late night after the ball, and now drinking with you jokers all day." He rose to leave.

"I walk with you," said Vicente, getting up.

"Congratulations, Sean. Get some rest," said James.

James and Lodie pushed back from their chairs to leave as well. As he turned towards the door, James caught Lodie lightly by the arm and asked lowly, "What is it that ye know?"

Lodie gave him a long look as if deciding. "Not yet. But soon."

CHAPTER 31

While the nation mourned the death of President Lincoln, Dutton Dandridge searched for opportunity presented by change and chaos. The war's end provided reasons enough for upheaval as the country struggled to become whole again. As state and local governments reeled from the shock of loss, Dutton unearthed vulnerability.

The maneuvering of a master such as Collis Huntington intrigued him. During his time in Washington, he absorbed every lesson. Dutton examined the levels of tolerance that government allowed itself to be pushed. He observed Huntington's proficient political timing and connections as unmatched. Prior to the war's end, Huntington circumvented the secretary of war to divert thousands of kegs of blasting powder to tunnel through the Sierras. He bargained and bullied Congress into amending last year's act — now permitting his railroad to release its own mortgage bonds on up to one hundred miles of track *prior* to its construction. Banking on hasty decisions in the wake of Lincoln's assassination, he renegotiated the Central Pacific's proposed route, blatantly flouting its limits specifically outlined in the 1864 Railroad Act. And he stalked senators possessing a propensity to sell their votes.

Inspired by ruthless men with a ravenous appetite for power, Dutton envisioned a limitless future. Today's meeting, marking the commencement of his agenda, he set deep in the obscurity of Sacramento's growing Chinatown amongst rows of merchants, restaurateurs, laundrymen, peddlers, and gambling halls.

He pictured Neil Collier wandering through the Chinese enclave noting local newspapers, various shrines, a joss house, and the rather hopeful Christian chapel run by Congregationalists. Dutton chose one of many small theatres and seated himself such that he maintained his view of the hallway as well as the play in progress. He dipped his cigar in brandy, lit it, and settled in to the unfolding drama.

A bell tinkled as the door opened, and a

small Chinese woman beckoned for Neil to follow her. Trailing closely behind her, Dutton watched him duck his head as he pushed aside the jangling strands of hanging beads in the doorway. Amused, he observed his friend's confused expression.

The low, dim-lit stage placed in the midst of its audience consisted of a small floor holding half a dozen performers; adequate, considering only six tables occupied the room — four of them empty. Dutton quickly stood to shake his hand.

"Neil! Excellent, you're here. Brandy? Whiskey?"

Neil shot him a perplexed look. "I think whiskey will be required."

Dutton nodded to the hostess and laughed. "Here, sit . . . sit." He lowered his voice in deference to the performance and said, "Are you familiar with Chinese theatre?"

"This would be a first. Please . . . enlighten me."

Cigar in hand, Dutton pointed to the stage. "This . . . is Kunqu, the most ancient and refined form of Chinese theatre. Some say it goes back as far as the third century B.C."

Silk-garbed Chinese musicians positioned at the edges of the stage played odd stringed instruments interspersed with flutes and the rhythmic beating of a drum. Costumed performers with exaggerated expressions painted on their faces moved in a highly stylized manner with gestures adhering to ancestral rules of technique and execution.

"Kunqu embraces elements of dance, opera, poetry recital, and mime. Even casual movements are precisely coordinated with the rhythms of orchestration. It includes all facets of performing art," Dutton stated with admiration. "Arias are sung to ancestral melodies called qu-pai. Performances are revered for their riveting collaboration of drama, singing, and dancing — and known for literary sophistication. Plots of time-honored stories are familiar to the audience — much like mythology to the Greeks. As you can see, Kunqu uses little in the way of scenery or props, thus enabling the mind to indulge the imagination for a more cerebral effect."

"That's a weighty collective of art forms." Neil's gaze remained captivated by the stage. After a few minutes of silence, he confessed, "While I appreciate the boundless scope of what they're creating, I admit the intricacies are above my head."

Dutton smiled. "An acquired taste for a sophisticated palate."

"Or a deviant bent in personality," Neil countered.

Dutton laughed.

Neil lowered his voice. "I'm curious. You have a significant grasp of the culture. The choice of venue surprised me to say the least; what sparked this interest?"

Dutton raised his brow with a cavalier air, though quickly answered, "Business. As always." He leaned forward. "The influx of Celestials can't have escaped your notice — an industrious and intelligent people whom I believe are incredibly underestimated in their contributions to society. There's a great deal to be learned from ancient civilizations."

"Hmm . . ." Neil sipped his whisky, fidgeting with the glass. "I know their numbers have caused an irrational panic amongst some of our peers."

"People, like sheep, are frightened by what they don't understand."

"True. Leland Stanford certainly changed his tune. Hard to forget his inaugural speech when he referred to them as the 'dregs of Asia.' "

"A necessary public reversal. Charles Crocker brought in five thousand. The Central Pacific is racing against Thomas Durant and the Union Pacific. He needs

Chinese to expedite progress at the summit of the Sierras to push further into Nevada." Dutton gave him a wry smile. "Now Stanford refers to them as 'a great army of civilization.'"

Neil frowned. "I suppose the worry is loss of jobs."

"Tch. Hardly. They need laborers for permanent work. Crocker advertised months ago for the five thousand, and he got two — mostly Irish. The minute a new Comstock silver rumor hit, they ran for Nevada." Dutton took a large draw from his cigar and blew a long satisfying puff of smoke. "I know what you're saying. And the Central Pacific may need to provide military protection to get the job done."

"Wouldn't surprise me. Like everything else, it's a balancing act. The railroad is crucial to California, and we must aggressively do whatever it takes to bolster its success."

"That's what I admire about you, Neil — you never attempt to bluff your way through anything, and you say what you think. You're forward thinking and stimulatingly honest."

"And yourself?"

"I prefer to think of myself as refreshingly blunt." Dutton swirled his brandy in the glass. He signaled for the hostess to bring another round. "That's why I think we could work amazingly well together."

"I must say, I've given a great deal of thought to the ideas you raised at our last meeting."

"Excellent. I'm pleased to hear it." Dutton leaned in close, his dark brow furrowed in reflection. "As discussed previously, I'm accumulating an interesting array of investments. I need a trustworthy, creative mind to work with — someone with bold energy and drive. You and I teethed on such qualities with successful fathers; it's almost second nature to us both."

Neil raised his glass. "As well as the code of Harvard . . ."

Dutton clinked his glass to it. "Exactly. Neil, you possess the desire to accomplish great things — similar to the way your old man did — same as I do. You want to build the legacy to the next generation. I am the last Dandridge. The task is left to me alone."

"And I'm the eldest son."

"So, our first step is to create capital. It is, after all, the measure the judge most relates to. I want to build my own foundation for future endeavors, not use his resources."

Neil leaned forward, eagerly agreeing. "Royce and I are engaged in massive planning concerning future expansions with the ranch and other holdings. Nothing radical, but we envision development with advancements mindful of the community."

"Yes! The growth of Sacramento and surrounding counties is of utmost importance. I look to back the 'small operation.' Make it possible for expanding businesses to reach their potential. In return, we acquire a small portion of those companies."

"Creating a banking syndicate?"

"Of sorts. Why not bring our Harvard financial educations home to work? Neil . . . your charitable causes and local community efforts are noticed and embraced. You have a touch . . . a rapport with people." He grew serious, watching closely for Neil's reaction.

Neil brushed the compliment aside. "Father expected it. If the successful don't step up, who will?"

"Exactly. There's a connection — you demand better of yourself, and the public knows the Colliers care. Father mentioned he's never witnessed such reciprocal feelings of trust."

"The judge?"

"He's always liked you, Neil; considered you a steadying influence on me." Dutton took another draw on his cigar. "He thinks you're tailor-made for a meaningful career in politics."

Neil laughed.

"No; consider this: is the thought so far from what you'd like to do with your life? As long as I've known you, you've possessed this need to reach out to your fellow man."

Neil frowned as he pondered.

"*Think* about it. If we accomplished absolutely nothing with our lives, we could live off the wealth of our fathers. But that's not your way. It's not my way. There's a higher calling. To leave a mark on this world."

Neil sipped his drink, intently watching the characters on stage. After a few moments, he uttered, "Fascinating."

Dutton enquired, "Finally seeing the merits of something new?"

"Yes," he said slowly. "Indulging my mind. I hope . . . for more than a cerebral effect."

Dutton sat back with satisfaction, re-engaging with the performance. He enjoyed walking on the edge. Neil could not help but be intrigued enough to join him.

Early the next evening, Dutton arrived at the office on Montgomery Street in San Francisco. He jogged up the stairs and entered at a brisk pace, waving off a need for announcement from the woman sitting at the desk. He proceeded down the hallway, pulling off his kid gloves as he went. The portly man standing behind the desk studiously flipped through one of his law books. Dutton tossed his gloves on the desk, plopped into a chair, and put his feet up. He leaned back in the chair with his hands behind his head like a lazy cat stretching. His father looked up over the top of his glasses.

"He's in," Dutton stated plainly.

Judge Dandridge snapped the law book shut and nodded. "Excellent. We'll talk next steps over dinner."

CHAPTER 32

Nevada City, November 1865

Althea fussed about the shop, restless and annoyed. She stopped, placing her hands on her hips, and scanned the stacks of fabric on her worktable. For some reason, she felt unable to concentrate on the tasks at hand. She sighed loudly and turned to an even messier mound of bobbins full of lace.

"Whatever are you looking for?"

Charlotte sat on a high stool behind the counter with a ballooning mass of pale-green silk in her lap. She pulled the straight pins from her mouth and pushed aside the skirt she held.

"You've moved those stacks on the table twice, you pushed the lace to both ends of the counter, and you're pacing like Banshee waiting for a run."

"Buttons! The smallest and simplest little buttons. I had them this morning, and I can't find them anywhere." Althea swatted

470

away the tendril of flaxen hair falling on her face with the back of her hand. "Honestly, I can't fathom what's wrong with me today. I bought the silly things at the emporium yesterday."

"Want me to help you look?" Charlotte watched her curiously.

"No. You just . . . keep working on that. It's me that's useless at the moment." She whirled around at the sound of the door opening.

"Knock, knock!" Sean popped his head through the door hesitantly. "No ladies in here I might offend? I'm a mite dirty." He waved to Charlotte sitting behind Althea.

"Oh, Sean." Althea gave him a tired look. "Truly the break I need. Come in, come in."

"In that case . . ." He entered with an exaggerated shuffling little step. "Hello, gorgeous!"

Althea smiled, then added the frown as she remembered they were not alone. She raised her eyebrows in admonishment.

"Oh, now. Don't scold," he teased. "Greetings, Charlotte. Nothing improper about a fella stopping in to see his gal, now is there?"

Charlotte grinned and returned to her sewing. "Nothing at all. Good to see you, Sean."

"See there?" He waved his finger in the air. "No prattling townies and our own chaperone back there."

Althea shook her head. "I won't even attempt to argue the point. What brings you to town?"

"I dropped by the foundry to order some replacement parts for the old stamp mill on Wolf Creek. Thought I'd see if you're free for dinner tomorrow night. I promise to arrive with less of my work clinging to my clothes." He wiggled his eyebrows at her, then pointed at his face. "You have to admit, that's a pretty charming move for a one-eyed man."

Charlotte burst out laughing, and Althea raised her hand to cover her mouth. "What . . ." she began to giggle, "What has gotten into you today?"

"I don't know." He tilted his head. "Happy to see you. Now say yes so I can go back to work."

She rolled her eyes. "Yes. Now be on your way."

"As you wish, my lady." He bent low in a grand bow, then rose, took her hand, kissed it, and said, "Until tomorrow."

Althea watched him leave, shaking her head. She turned, still smiling as she considered the silliness of a courting man.

"Well *that* certainly improved your mood." Charlotte watched through the front window as Sean turned the corner. "He seems nearly back to his old self. I'm glad."

"Hmm. He's doing very well at Empire — enjoys the work, being in charge."

Within months, Sean became an integral part of the Empire Mining Company. He trained with management, planned with engineers, and Althea knew he worked to build pride, fellowship, and loyalty with his men. New employees found him fair, knowledgeable, and obliging. She smiled to herself, knowing his charisma capable of overcoming obstacles. But now the time to approach those whom he knew only too well drew nigh.

She glanced up at Charlotte. It seemed to Althea the girl's large, misty-green eyes keenly sought clues to her most secret thoughts, as if Charlotte possessed the ability to see straight into her soul. Precisely like her father, she mused. Suddenly she felt a sensation as if a bird flittered across her chest. The impression of looking into James's eyes unnerved her. Her face grew warm, and she became instantly aware that she gazed into the abyss she sought to avoid.

"I . . ." she turned away quickly to break the spell. Althea reached for her blue wool wrap hanging on its peg by the door. "I'm going to the emporium for more buttons. I'll be back shortly."

With that, she bolted out the door, walking quickly down the hill on East Broad. Her jumble of thoughts fought for focus. She hoped the cold, brisk air would numb emotion, allowing her to prioritize her concerns. She *had* dodged conversations about Sean with James. She felt guilty for dumping her doubts in his lap before Sean's return. Absorbed in Sean's homecoming, she ignored the previous hesitations lined up like unwelcome Tommyknockers. The question she most feared loomed large — how long would it last this time?

She could not march fast enough to escape this judgment. Stability and strength, the two qualities she desperately yearned for, the traits she counted on James for . . .

And again, the bird that never lingered fluttered in her breast. Startled, her foot faltered, and she felt her wrap slide off one shoulder. She stopped abruptly to grab it and folded both ends tightly in her crossed arms. A glint of metal flashed in the sun. She looked down the short alleyway beside the New York Hotel in time to see a man step back behind the corner of the building. His companion remained in full view a half-dozen yards away, an odd, grubby looking man she did not recognize. She stared, though remained lost in private deliberations. The stranger's dark, unkempt hair hung in long, oily hanks. He scowled at her, his pockmarked face appearing menacing, and she saw that his earlobes were noticeably mangled, as if they had once been cut. As he took a step towards her, Althea felt threatened and darted on her way.

She shivered and glanced behind her twice, continuing down Broad Street towards Lodie's Emporium. She felt safer with distance and returned to her churning reflections. The last few months Sean exhibited work with purpose matching promises. He openly professed his intent, determined to labor for their future and regain her trust. She *had* missed him, she realized fondly — his humor and his buoyant spirit. Reason told her to let go of past mistakes — his and hers. Her confidence grew. As a peace settled her heart, the image of James waiting for her on the front porch sprang to mind. She felt ashamed of childishly evading her most faithful confidant. His council never failed her. She must speak with him without delay. Deciding this, she walked into Lodie's Emporium and greeted Matilda.

■ ■ ■ ■

"What is *wrong* with you?" He grasped his silver-headed cane in a chokehold and shook it angrily in Tolliver's face. "Why would you go after her like that? She's an important woman in this town and I *know* her!"

"More to the point, chief — she knows you."

"She didn't see me."

"Ya don't know that. You're the one what says no one can know it's you that's been talkin', or the deals fall apart."

The man turned away to regain his composure. Inside, he seethed. Dandridge should never send his flunky here when he'd gladly meet him in Sacramento. In the future he'd insist on it; this was entirely too risky. He received the telegram — another mistake in his opinion — instructing him to meet Tolliver and carry the silver-headed cane he favored for recognition. He planted the cane firmly and pivoted to face . . . what was it Dutton called him? "Father's pet dog"? More like a mangy mongrel, he thought.

"She's on the merchants board! This little

exercise could be over if she suspects any-thing."

Tolliver smirked. "Boss'll be mighty pissed if his information dries up. You bring the list?"

He reached inside his coat for the envelope and hesitated. Mining woes for the locals escalated at a pace even he had not antici-pated. The ore coming in to the assay office looked thin, unyielding, and unprofitable. Without heavy equipment, small mines began a process of slow death. Men ran off to Comstock, which created boom one day and bust the next. North Star, Empire, and North Bloomfield Mining Companies, among others, all engaged in the shuffling dance of investors and acquisition. He held the list of independents, men who couldn't survive without cash to sustain them and possessed some title to land they mined. They needed loans, and Dandridge would supply them — cheap. A win/win, he rea-soned. He waved the envelope in Tolliver's face.

"You tell Mr. Dandridge — no more meetings here. No more telegrams. If he must, he can send you to bid me to come to him discreetly, if you can manage that."

Tolliver snatched the packet from his hand. "Just the courier, mate. Until you gets what you wants I reckon you'll come 'round to his way of thinkin'." He touched the envelope to his head in salute. "He'll be in touch."

CHAPTER 33

Thistle Dew

Hard work remained the only remedy he knew to subdue frustration. Not a cure, but a needed distraction. From his stance inside the corral, James looked at Althea in the rocking chair on the porch, shelling peas for dinner. He felt she dodged conversation with him lately, though he supposed it only natural as she became reacquainted with Sean. Undeterred, he meant to hear her concerns. Last night she lingered on the porch, but now it was too late.

The sorrel stallion snorted, unable to paw the ground with his front feet tied in a quick-release hobble. James watched the animal's white-eyed stare as it shifted nervously, waiting for Justin's approach.

"The toughest of the lot, ye are," James said to the horse in soothing tones. "It's why ye get ta go first. Took a lot of stroking yer ego ta get that saddle on ye, so behave yerself."

Clutching the flour sack, James held it up to the stallion's nose, allowing him to smell it again. Once the animal understood the object in no way threatened him, James tossed it slowly and gently over his forehead, stroking the sack over the eyes. He repeated his earlier movements of rubbing the face, down the neck, and along both sides, relaxing the brute to his touch. He moved to take the lead, gently pulling it to apply slight pressure on the hackamore. "Hop up on the fence Justin; he's as ready as he's going ta be. I'll hold him 'til yer set."

James held him firmly, crooning a constant chatter as Justin eased into the saddle. He watched Justin test the horse's reaction to weight in the stirrups while swiftly crossing the reins in his hand into the correct grip, grasping a portion of mane between his first two fingers.

"I'm good," said Justin, concentrating on his mount.

James leaned down, pulled the rope loose from the horse's legs, and stepped back. Suddenly free, the stallion bolted forward. "Let him feel his space! Let the pole corral do its job."

Instinctively the beast tried to run but

found the rounded enclosure discouraged speed. Exasperated, the animal tried spinning, with Justin thwarting his effort. Combined attempts to flee and rotate both wearied and frustrated him. Justin tightened his grasp as the bronc began to buck.

Though skilled, Justin did not weigh enough to finish the job. The horse leaped, twisted, and slammed back down onto his forelegs. Justin's spine jolted clean into his hips, but he hung on with tenacity. He kept at the sorrel until James figured he'd bounced enough to hear his teeth clatter together. Justin pulled him to a stand, allowing James to step forward and take the reins.

"All right, now! Good job. Ye've worn him down. Now let's see what he thinks about some added weight."

They quickly changed positions. The horse whinnied nervously and rolled his eyes back as James settled in. As Justin released him, he took a half-hearted hop, feeling the solid difference between the two riders. He darted forward with a burst of speed and then spun in tight turns, trying to scrape James into the fence. James's strong legs and the solid kicking of his heel into the animal's flank next to the fence encouraged the beast to trot more for the center. The stallion sidestepped, then blew out a big breath.

"Ha!" James walked him in slow, controlled circles. "I think we've taught him a thing or two."

"He'll be more cooperative next time," said Justin, grinning.

"Can ye handle another one? That red roan is pretty well broken, but he's still got a bad habit of dashing off when he's a mind ta."

"Sure thing. I'll get him."

Justin stopped at the trough and pulled off his shirt. He threw half a bath's worth of water on his lean upper body. The day was unusually warm, so he put on his shirt, allowing the dampness to soak in.

Charlotte stood grooming a tethered Banshee by the barn. She called out to him, "You almost make that look like work. Why don't you try something harder?"

"Yeah. And you go fire up the smithy and pound out some shoes in *your* spare time." Justin knew his way around a forge as well.

James chuckled at their sparring. He patted the calmed sorrel's neck, riding him in an easy trot around the ring. Contentment filled him. He watched Charlotte lean into Banshee's shoulder until he shifted his weight, allowing her to raise his hoof and clean it out with her pick. Banshee's chest had grown deep, and his ribs had filled out, erasing earlier neglect, though he still carried a nasty scar on his shoulder.

Now over seventeen hands, Banshee was big by anyone's standards. James admired the large eyes, his well-defined head, and long, strong neck with big shoulders and a tail set high. He boasted a graceful, floating stride, a wonderfully flowing movement. His proud carriage and build suggested power and speed. James intended to make him the kingpin of his breeding program. The stallion's color had lightened; he was nearly silver now, especially when the sun glinted off his coat. Even his eyes mirrored a deep, yet ghostly, mist gray. Althea found this unnerving.

Banshee's lips tumbled over themselves as he sought the grain in Charlotte's outstretched palm. The circular chewing motion amplified the methodical crunching, and he blew the last hulls out of her hand looking for more. She laughed, scratched his ears, and moved to comb him out.

"Well matched in spirit, those two," James muttered to himself. He dismounted, tied the stallion to the railing, and removed the saddle.

He knew many times Althea cringed at

the sight of Charlotte thundering up to the courtyard with her horse running so hard that it slung froth from its mouth and tossed its head wildly as she reined in to an abrupt halt. From the time she first put her foot to the wheel of the spring wagon to boost herself on to the seat next to him, Charlotte drew complaints from her mother about her lack of gentility. Now Althea took it as her weary task alone to keep her in line.

Charlotte's manners were impeccable — Althea made sure of it. However, she had a limited tolerance for executing said manners. James realized with a jab of guilt that his daughter mimicked his views of politeness and drivel — too much of the former, led to the latter. She learned to excuse herself when she felt in danger of crossing the line in either direction — a compromise Althea learned to live with.

"Ah, Emma," he sighed to himself. As he did at some point each day, he missed her. Where had the years gone? "Ye'd be proud of our girl, ye would, but I cu sure use yer help." Emma would know what to do about Thea and Sean. He was torn.

He opened the gate of the pole corral and led his tired conquest to a holding pen to cool down. He saw Althea rise from the rocking chair to take the bowl of peas into the kitchen. Charlotte would prepare dinner tonight, as he knew Althea was due to dress for her dinner with Sean soon. Worry sat on his shoulders like birds of prey to bedevil him. He needed to hear her state her feelings conclusively; perhaps warn her of the risks she herself fretted over. But he was sworn to secrecy. Sean in all good faith had come to him — his friend — to express his joy and seek his counsel. James freed the stallion of the hackamore and watched it dart through the opening of the pen, shaking its head in defiance, wishing he could so easily throw off his cares.

It would not be right to plant negative ideas in her head at this point, he admitted. The decision after all was hers alone. Justin approached, leading the red roan. Hard work — James focused on his most reliable diversion.

CHAPTER 34

Nevada City, March 1866

The Empire Mine now employed over 130 men working two shifts a day. After striking a new rich vein, their deepest shaft descended over 200 feet. The new system of square-set timbering enabled crews with heavy equipment to penetrate abandoned interests to far greater depths and therefore reach untapped ore. But these veins stretched their spiderlike spread under areas both claimed and poached by independent miners — areas Sean warned months ago nested on lands titled to Empire. As luck would have it, many old friends indeed harvested the dregs of a played-out mine above Nevada City, an Empire mine.

Yesterday James wandered into the Silver Moon to find Sean had gathered a group together to give them the news over drinks. James knew Empire's owners turned a blind eye for a time to encourage men to join the company. But now a general mining slump crept stealthily into Grass Valley, and Empire intended to tighten its grasp. Independent miners struggling before now teetered on the edge of the abyss. He arrived to hear the end of Sean's battle with a belligerent ensemble.

"You fellas are pressing my back against the wall here, you know. It ain't that I don't sympathize, but I've a job to do, and a legal right to do it . . ." Sean's voice strained at the brink of failing patience.

"And you feel good about turning on your old mates, do you?" Clancy scoffed.

"Do *you* feel good about trespassing and pilfering? Nobody feels good about this situation. I've tried to offer alternatives, but so far you say there's no interest. I'm afraid I'm giving notice — you and the men need to clean out your gear and move on. I'll be coming tomorrow to the site with an official eviction notice, and I'm going to expect you to clear out immediately. If not, you'll force me to come back with the sheriff."

Sean met stony silence.

"C'mon lads! If it weren't me, someone else would've come with the law already — someone not offering jobs to intruders and lawbreakers. We're friends! Work with me here." He frowned.

Arms crossed, Rob exhaled loudly. "It's not personal, Sean. We're simply not ready to pack it in. I guess we'll be seeing you tomorrow."

Sean looked to each one with a determined glare. "You bet." He stalked out of the Silver Moon with James following quietly at his heels.

"Sean, wait!"

Sean stopped short. He took an aggravated stance with hands on his hips, shaking his raised head skyward, then looked at the ground. He took a swift kick at pebbles in the dirt.

"There ain't no more I can do here," he growled.

James caught up with him, laying a hand on his shoulder. "Ye're doing fine."

Sean glanced back as if he'd expected a lecture and took a deep breath. "Why, then? We all know how this has gotta end. Why make me the bad guy?"

"I think Rob meant it when he said nothing personal. They aren't pushing ye, not really. They're pushing Empire, and that's who ye represent." James smirked. "Ye have ta stand yer ground; ye're the boss."

Sean sighed. "I thought they'd be more reasonable. I tried to present everything fairly. I've played the patience game. There's men that needed work but wouldn't speak up in the group. I kept at 'em, talking to them one on one, and they took jobs. Some took jobs with other outfits, and that's okay. I realize a lot of them boys are supplementing other endeavors and ain't interested, but I didn't expect 'em to stand against me."

James shrugged. "Human nature. Like you, they want ta know they tried everything before givin' in. Company mine is a bad word ta them. It's disappointing they drag it out ta the last, but they're squatters, and they know it. Let Sheriff Shaw be the bad guy." James pushed his shoulder in jest. "Besides. Ye got much better things to keep yer mind on, eh?"

Sean gave a wistful grin. "Yeah, but I want 'em dancing at my wedding, not throwin' rocks."

James smiled. "It'll blow over by then."

Sean cocked his eyebrow over his good eye, meeting James's gaze. "I guess. Thanks. Reckon I'll go have a chat with the sheriff."

Charlotte hardly noticed that her father drove to Nevada City mostly in silence. He grumbled as they left Thistle Dew, something about a full day and not the type he liked. He couldn't have squeezed a word in edgewise, for she peppered Althea with

489

questions about the wedding. The two of them worked madly together on a beautifully embroidered blouse, laden with lace and seed pearls. The project kept her eager to get to Althea's shop.

Lodie wanted to meet with James on town business, so her father decided to make the most of the trip by stocking up on supplies. He figured Justin might as well come along, too, to load and unload at the Emporium. Charlotte thought the day felt like a joyful family outing.

James pulled the wagon over in front of the dress shop to let the women out. He nodded back towards the Emporium. "I'm likely ta be tied up with Lodie for at least an hour; Justin can take care of the supplies. I thought then I might head up ta the ridge ta see how Sean's getting on. I imagine he'll have a tough day of it. It's a hard thing ta draw the line with mates. Might be helpful ta see at least one friendly face."

Althea smiled. "I know he's grateful for your support, James. I can't tell you how much it means to me."

"It's what families do," he said simply, as he slapped the reins on the team.

Althea turned to Charlotte. "Well, come on. We've got orders to work on before we can even think about working on your dress for the wedding."

The morning passed quickly with a steady stream of patrons in and out of the shop. Charlotte brought two bundles of fabric to the table where Althea worked with Peter Stuben's wife. She paused at the sound of a chime off in the distance. She stopped and tilted her head as she listened. Suddenly, her look of recognition turned to alarm as she opened her mouth to speak. By then, the bell sounding in the hills was amplified by the clanging of the bell at the firehouse.

Mrs. Stuben shrieked, "It's a cave-in!" She bolted from the shop in a panic.

Althea went pale. She stared wide-eyed at Charlotte. "Sean's on the ridge. And your father."

"We've got to get up there." Charlotte dropped the bundles to the floor and hurried for the door. "I'll find Justin; we'll take the wagon," she called.

Charlotte ran into the streets. People poured from homes and shops like ants from a mound. Some milled about in confusion, others dashed by on horseback and in wagons rolling out of town. Charlotte sprinted down the sidewalk, dodging panicked townspeople as she went. She saw Lodie throwing picks, shovels, and rope into the back of their wagon. Justin leapt into the driver's seat.

"Justin!" she screamed.

Lodie looked up and snatched the reins. "Hold up, Justin."

Charlotte rushed up, panting. "You've got to take us up there. Althea's coming, too."

Lodie grabbed her arm to boost her onto the bench. "You go with Justin, now! I've got to grab some medical supplies; I'll bring Althea."

"But . . ."

"We'll be right behind you, but they need that equipment up there now! Go, Justin!" Lodie smacked the horse's rump, and the wagon lurched forward.

Justin whipped the reins furiously, forcing the team to a breakneck pace, and the wagon hurtled precariously down the road. Charlotte yelled, "Out of the way! We have supplies!" to men running for the site. Justin had barely pulled into the clearing where a horde gathered when Charlotte scrambled out of the wagon and dashed up the path to the head of the mine. Men from the crowd swarmed the wagon and grabbed available tools before running to the entrance. The bell continued to sound the frantic alarm.

Aftermath in the Schoolhouse

Exhausted, every inch of uncovered flesh smeared with a paste of grime and sweat, Sean sat head in his hands on the schoolhouse steps. "I should've read them the riot act like you just did." He looked at James wearily. "It's what I should've done before the damn thing collapsed."

James shook his head, the dusty residue of failed dreams coating his russet hair. "But ye took control, man. Ye arrived ta deliver a message, and instead ye jumped in leading the rescue. By virtue of that alone I think ye'll see a number of them looking for jobs now. Perhaps they'll think how close they came ta ending their lives through their own stubbornness."

Lodie added, "They knew it was dangerous. You told them it was unsafe. No excuse."

They sat silently for a few minutes — physical and emotional fatigue claiming its due.

Lodie pondered aloud, "I think perhaps there might be some merit to picking up on a conversation James and I had earlier today . . ."

James stood abruptly. "No. I'm spent. And I'm going home ta the family."

493

Sean looked up at him with a puzzled look. "Leave it. We've all been through enough today. It's nothing won't keep until we have clearer heads." James patted Sean's shoulder and took his leave.

CHAPTER 35

San Francisco, April 1866

At the junction of Washington, Montgomery, and Columbus Avenue stood the imposing center of the political universe, the Montgomery Block. The audacity of its four-story construction by General Halleck intrigued the citizenry of San Francisco in 1853. The populace had flocked along the docks to witness the unloading of every conceivable part — bricks, plaster, windows, and even doorknobs from the gale-battered ships arriving from the East Coast via the Horn. Clucking like disapproving hens, they watched the building rise on top of a raft of redwood logs and ship's planking bolted together in a deeply excavated basement on the edge of the bay. Naysayers opined it would sink in the tidal mudflat and dubbed it "Halleck's Folly."

The Montgomery Block boasted a 122-foot frontage and was hailed as the tallest building west of the Mississippi. As it rose in splendor, the sculptured heads ornamenting the keystones of its windows peered down with mocking looks at the crowds. The doubting public, first reacting as though Halleck had built an ark, now acclaimed the daring Montgomery Block as the showplace of the business community. To be one of Halleck's tenants was to bask in prestige, and Judge Dandridge became one of the first.

The building attracted a collective of lawyers, judges, engineers, scientists, politicians, and businessmen and emerged as the political and professional beehive of San Francisco. Offices aside, Montgomery Block's two gracious inner courtyards, salons, libraries, billiards parlors, and even The Bank Exchange Bar on the first floor promoted the location as a premier meeting place.

Dutton relished this backdrop of preeminence and felt well in command of today's meeting. A dozen representatives of the investment community elite filled the seats surrounding the boardroom table. His well-received presentation created a buzz and piqued their opportunistic interest. Beaming with confidence, he studied their faces as they reviewed the fat proposal packets.

Most had attended the clandestine site visit below ground at the Empire Mine itself. The judge sat at the far end of the table, looking pleased. Dutton surveyed their handpicked players — cards in his deck, to be shuffled and dealt as he chose.

A hesitant tap at the door caused his father to rise. The judge gave him the nod to begin again and exited quietly. Dutton cleared his throat. "Gentlemen. This is for all intents and purposes, our board. To re-cap . . .

"Step one — discover *location* of the ore." He laughed. "Well, some drunken prospector did that part for us.

"Step two — *exploration* — to define the extent and value of the ore — also done, because our drunken sot of a friend couldn't keep his mouth shut, and the hills became infested with fortune seekers.

"Step three — an ambitious friend in Nevada City's assay office is *very* helpful providing information on value, density of the ore, the richest veins found, and on whose claim. Our humble independents made modest fortunes and are running out of exposed ore that they can physically reach."

For emphasis, Dutton held up his right hand, raising his fingers in a rapid one, two, three fashion. "At this point, the project needs money, equipment, and manpower. In short, it needs organizational skills and collaboration these 'all in for self' miners are incapable of producing.

"So," he smacked the table lightly. "We need to send in *experts* for step four — to estimate the *extent* and *grade* of these deposits — before we send in our own 'government officials'; not to alarm anyone, but to check safety and value in order to 'help' miners make better decisions . . .

"Once accomplished, we go to step five: we evaluate what portion of the deposit is *economically recoverable;* that is, advise our entrepreneurial friends on the hill that only big machinery will reach the ore. We offer to buy out their claims, give them jobs."

The judge re-entered with a slight frown and reclaimed his seat, giving Dutton his full attention.

"*So,* where do our investments come in? Our final step is to conduct a *feasibility study* determining which area, which holdings, are of most interest and scoop them up. To begin digging we'll need engineers to plan the shoring up and path of the mine itself.

"We need to *sell shares,* gentlemen — shares to friends and neighbors interested in sound investments for the future. Our approach is in both surface mining and subsurface mining. For sub-surface, we begin square-set timbering. For surface, recent advancements in a more powerful head and hose for hydraulics utilize greater force to break up the stubborn barrier layers of dirt and rock in the way of our prosperity." Dutton stopped, smiled, and scanned the intrigued faces in the hand-selected group before him. "Questions? Yes, Mr. Redmond?"

Caleb Redmond, ex-foreman of the Brunswick Mine in Grass Valley, smiled. "From my experience, this plan looks right on target, no question. I understand, though, that William Bourn owns a substantial part of Empire Mine. How does he fit in?"

"Ah." Dutton raised a finger in the air as if he had forgotten an important point. "To clarify, Mr. Bourn is an investor of great magnitude. He is president and director of the board of The Fireman's Fund Insurance Company and holds in his portfolio shares of the combined Imperial-Empire Mine in Gold Hill, Empire and North Star in Grass Valley, and the Comstock Lode. He develops city lots here in San Francisco, timberland in Michigan and Washington Territory, and has invested in ranches in San Bernardino and Napa. His accumulated mining interests go back years and, for the time being, yes, he is a major investor with many ventures demanding his time and attention. We welcome him to take as large a role as he sees fit."

Judge Dandridge spoke up. "Dutton, I imagine our friends would like time to go over the materials and perhaps present us with their ideas at the next meeting." He raised his bushy brow in question and was answered with agreeable murmuring and nodding of heads. "Good! I propose we adjourn to the bar downstairs for a round of their famous Pisco Punch."

Caleb seconded with a "Hear! Hear!" and the enthusiastic assembly gathered their business plans and departed for The Bank Exchange Bar.

As Dutton moved towards the door, his father called out, "We'll meet you down there, gentlemen." The frown returned, darkening his mood as the judge said lowly, "Tolliver is in your office. It seems we have a pretty little problem in Nevada City holding sway over your contact. Take care of it — before your meeting with the Colliers."

Dutton nodded, irritated that Tolliver had not come to him directly. The two Dandridges split off, the judge to the bar to entertain and Dutton to his office to contain.

He found Tolliver leaning against his desk in a casual slump, arms crossed.

"What's going on?" he demanded.

"Having a bit of trouble with your friend." He handed Dutton the envelope.

Dutton scowled. "He gave you the list? Then what's the problem?"

"He don't want to give no more. A woman — *an important woman,* he says — saw us. Said the whole business ends if she talks."

"Did she get a look at you?"

"Me, definitely. Him . . . not sure how much she put together."

Dutton turned away, rubbing his jaw in frustration. "This is a complication I don't need."

Tolliver began smugly, "He's making demands. Says no more telegrams like he's callin' the shots. I'm thinking somebody's forgot his place . . ."

Dutton whirled around. "You're not paid to *think*!" He paced, wanting to jerk the leash tighter on his cur. "Just . . . make sure she's not a problem in the future."

Tolliver took on the look of a mongrel sizing up prey. "I can . . ."

"I don't want details! Get out."

Dutton watched him slink towards the

501

door. He called out over his shoulder, "Done."

CHAPTER 36

Nevada City

James intentionally busied himself at the farm for weeks. He found respite in his created world where his fights were limited to the land, the weather, and the animals he raised. He found reasonable compromise with all of these and had no desire to be drawn into the discussions of unions or the part Lodie selected for him to play. Mining showed every sign of evolving into big business, and the hierarchies of such rankled his soul.

He despised the systematic classification of people according to relative importance and status — the inevitable drive for success that led to an absolute addiction to power. He knew firsthand the sting from men so consumed with prestige they no longer noticed whom they crushed. He witnessed the inclusiveness of wealth lead the rich to conclude people on lower rungs of their system were theirs to rule and toy with. He had been held under the thumb once and vowed — never again.

Lost in this steadfastly embedded mind-set, he tied up his big bay to a hitching post outside Vicente's saddle shop. He heard someone behind him clearing a throat and turned to find a contrite looking Clancy standing with his hands stuffed in his pockets.

"Eh . . . em . . . a word?"

James inclined his head. "Certainly. What's on yer mind?"

Clancy winced. "I'd like to thank you . . . officially . . ." he looked momentarily away and then met James's eyes with an apologetic look, "for pulling my worthless arse out of the hole. You were right. There now, I've said it."

James chuckled. "No need. I don't suppose any of the others feel the same?"

"Some. But for myself . . ." he sighed. "I'm looking for steady employment. On my way to find Sean now."

"Good man. He'll be happy ta have ye. What of the others? I guess some are checking out some of the smaller mines for higher positions?"

"They won't find any more than I did when I went."

"What do ye mean?"

"Very odd, the whole business. The small outfits are folding."

James frowned. "Surely not all?"

Clancy gave him a direct look. "I went to seven of them. The others might as well cut to the chase and go directly to Sean. They're all flyin' the Empire flag now."

The Silver Moon

Their cordial meeting for drinks turned into a solemn gathering. Lodie sat with his arms folded. James brooded. Sean was perplexed.

"I told you . . ." began Lodie.

"It's na as though any of us cu do anything about it," James snapped. "It isn't my concern."

"Then why are you here?"

"I suppose to tell you, since ye're making it a concern."

"Whoa." Sean held up his hands between them. He gave them both stern looks. "The question is — what does it mean?"

"Ye're right. That is the question. And it looks as though ye're the one closest ta the source and closest ta answering what Clancy claims. What have ye heard?" asked James.

Sean scratched his head. "Whew. Not a lot. There's talk of various expansion projects. And I only know that because they've told me they'll be moving me around from site to site — as I help teams get organized and underway — then I'm off to the next. In between, I circulate — inspect operations; check on safety issues." He was quiet for a moment. "But . . ." he hesitated.

"But what?" asked Lodie.

"There is a man . . . that . . . judge. Oh, what's his name? Dandridge. Judge Dandridge — out of San Francisco, that's it. He's been around a lot talking with the top brass. The word is he's been looking for interests in the area for some time. I only know who he is because I recognized him from the flood meetings in Marysville."

"Wait, he was there?"

"Yeah, you might remember him . . . short, real heavy-set guy . . . bald on top with really fuzzy eyebrows. He wore a fancy suit, so he sort of stood out at the time."

James shook his head. "I don't know that I recall."

"From what I hear, he's got a load of money. And brings more of his type with fortunes behind him."

They sat quietly absorbed in their own thoughts of what this might mean.

Lodie looked at James. "What are you thinking?"

James looked troubled. "I don't know. I

have this gnawing in my gut. I think I know what my great-great-grandfather must ha felt like when he was told there was a dragon in the village."

Lodie looked away. "All right. Let's get back to current needs. Sean: Who's come to you for jobs?"

He shrugged. "Most all of them, now. Though Peter and Rob decided to hang it up."

"And you feel good about the jobs?"

"I wouldn't be there if I didn't. It won't be without risk. As we know, some of these shafts are in a terrible state, not helped by the gopher tactics of our friends. There's rotten timber from dampness and seepage at deeper levels. We'll be investing more in the Cornish pumps and keep them running non-stop as we dig deeper."

"There!" Lodie pounded the table with his fist. He looked at James. "This. This is why we need to organize the union. Here's an entity we know little about, with a lot of money to call all the shots. Someone's got to look out for these men."

"Sean can do it," James answered stubbornly. "He's sitting right in the middle of it, and he knows better than anyone what's needed."

"Union? *That's* what this is about?" asked Sean.

"Lodie thinks it is."

Sean pondered this for a minute. "I can't be mixed up in the union as a company man. But I'd support it for the men's sake on a personal level — maybe as a company representative. I learned a lot watching operations at the Comstock, and they do have a union. Being an Empire employee, I know my place. Lower management or not, I'm expendable as soon as I displease someone at the top."

He hesitated. "So, I got to play this thing smart. Like James, I'm uncomfortable with the wheeling and dealing behind the scenes. If the control goes too far from home — to a bunch of speculators in San Francisco — we all suffer. I'm only a project foreman. They can squeeze me down to nothing like everyone else, only I'm the one that's supposed to make it palatable for the rest."

James grumbled. "Hard medicine never goes down easy . . . especially when ye know its snake oil."

Lodie looked first at Sean. "I like the company representative idea. At least the thinking of the man in the middle is friendly. And, as I've said all along, James should head up the union."

Sean looked as though he'd been struck by a thunderbolt. "Of course!"

Lodie grinned. "See?"

"No. No, see?" said James. "They've no reason ta follow anything I have ta say; I have na worked the mines in years."

Sean began to laugh. "Oh, no? Face it my friend — you're an authority figure whether you like it or not. Who else could've marched those men into the schoolhouse after the cave-in and verbally spanked them like you did? And they took their licks and fell in line. Oh, ho, ho," he laughed. "Lodie. You're a damn genius."

Lodie grinned. "I've often thought so."

James remained frowning.

Sean placed his hand on top of James's clenched fist. "I can see us working together for this. I can be your counterpart on the other side."

James sat stonily.

Lodie grew serious. "James. A lot of years have passed since we came to this place. We've watched it grow up around us . . . and with us. Nevada County's the sweat and vision of all of our friends. This concerns *all* of us. What else will outsiders want to buy up and control? If we don't stand up for ourselves, protect ourselves . . . well, we might as well hand over all we've worked for, because none of us is really safe."

James glared at him.

Lodie's calm blue eyes pierced through the barrier James put between them. "It isn't that you believe there's no problem. You're hoping the dragon will stay in its dark corner and not bother anyone. You know that it won't."

James rolled his eyes heavenward. "I'll do this. I'm going ta the horse market in Sacramento soon. I'll go ta the state court-house and see if I can learn anything. For now, that's all I'll promise. Agreed?"

"That might help," offered Sean.

Lodie nodded. "It's a start."

Thistle Dew

Little peace awaited James when he arrived home. As he reached the front door, it flung open, and Charlotte stalked past him as if she had not seen him.

He turned and called, "Well, that's a fine hullo."

"Going to work the colt!" She called back without turning.

Althea appeared in the doorway looking after her and shaking her head.

"Dare I ask? Quarrel?"

"Not with me. She's frustrated."

"Oh? Before I ask any more questions, I

don't suppose there's coffee in the kettle?"

"Yes, come in and sit. You look a bit frazzled yourself."

"Och. I'd rather talk about her issues and forget mine for awhile."

He sat at the kitchen table, and Althea poured him a cup of piping hot coffee.

"How about a scone with that?"

"Ah, Sean's a lucky man. My loss, but it was bound ta happen."

Althea smiled. "I've dinner to attend to . . . but I think I'll sit with my dear friend and share the coffee."

"I'm going ta miss our talks, Thea."

She looked down. "That won't end. It will simply move to a dinner table in town with my husband. And we have the added good fortune you are best mates. I'm so grateful, James . . . for everything . . . for giving me and Justin a home . . ."

"Stop right there, because it's nonsense. Charlotte and I cu na have done without the two of ye. We're family. All of us, such as we are, and however we grow and spread out." James sighed. "I don't know that I'm ready for this conversation yet — perhaps after I've given the bride away, eh?"

Althea sipped her coffee. "Agreed."

"So," he inclined his head towards the door, "what's all the fuss about?"

Althea rolled her eyes. "Girls. And fickle boys."

"What? Perhaps ye better start with the girl part."

"Ella Louise. Apparently, she set her cap for young Drew Hodges. It appears she felt she couldn't compete with Charlotte for his attention, so she began saying unkind things about her to persuade him."

"I thought the infatuation with Drew was over."

"Yes, for Charlotte — though they're still friends. Drew still harbors a great deal of admiration for her. I've noticed Ella Louise hovering in the background for some time, always managing to be present, as if afraid for them to spend time alone. I've watched her invite him to church functions, trying to keep him to herself . . . and her parents make a huge fuss over him. Of course, Charlotte cares nothing about any of this; she's perfectly happy to see them as a couple. But Ella Louise . . ."

"Was jealous. Hmph." He bit into his scone. "Hard for any lad not ta be dazzled by my girl's beauty," he said with some pride. "Makes a father's job damn hard, though."

Althea spoke up resentfully. "There is *no* advantage to beauty — what will it bring her? It attracts the wrong sorts of men with the worst of motives and the begrudging bitterness of other women. There's no resting place. It just makes life harder."

James proceeded cautiously. "And what of the fickle boy part?"

Althea huffed with anger. "Nothing we haven't seen before. A young man from a family with means — spoiled, as it were. His attitude is deplorable. He shuns her as if she were the problem."

"Are we still speaking of Drew?"

Their eyes locked in this moment, but they were frozen in thought of times past.

James said softly, "You are a beautiful woman, Thea. And ye're right. Life has na treated ye kindly because of it."

She stiffened. "I was naïve and unprepared. Edward led me in an elaborate game of cat and mouse. Of course, it never occurred to me that the mouse can *never win,* and the cat will toy with it until it tires, or languishes and dies."

Unsure which avenue to pursue, James chose the safer one. "It is not always so. There are those dangers ta be sure, but let's not forget that her mother found it otherwise."

Althea sighed. "Emma was lucky it was you, James. And she possessed enough

513

Presbyterian stiffness about her to make other women wary about crossing her. But it didn't make them like her any better. Charlotte has a kindness that reaches out to people. She'll be eaten alive for her trouble."

"That's why it's good she has the two of us. All of life is a lesson. We've got ta point out the thorny parts, for both the children." He paused. "It's not an easy time I'm having saying this ta ye . . . but at some point . . . ye've got ta talk ta Justin about this."

She quieted. She fingered the tablecloth as she thought. Finally, without looking up Althea said softly, "I know. It's weighed on me for some time. It's hard to admit he's a man, now . . . and certainly old enough to know the truth. If I could only bear telling it." She could not bring herself to look at him.

James stood and bent over her. He kissed her lightly on top of the head. "Any help ye need . . . I'm here. I best go out and see if I can cheer up my girl."

He left Althea to her thoughts and walked out to the corral. As he approached, he watched Charlotte put Banshee through his paces. The girl had an instinctive skill with horses, and the bond with this one was nothing short of enchanting.

"Now *there,*" he bellowed, "is a thing of beauty." He rested his arms on the top of the fence.

Charlotte smiled and trotted up to her father. She stopped, patting Banshee's neck affectionately. "He really is, isn't he?"

James winked and laced his fingers together, holding them up for her to see. "I was talking about the pair of ye. I think he's ruined for anyone else now. Good thing we aim ta keep him around . . ."

"To begin a dynasty!" She laughed. "We'll breed a dozen like him."

"Only a dozen? I'm thinking that dozen will each sire a dozen and so on. He's a champ, all right. And I see he's lightened your mood?"

She wrinkled her nose. "I needed to take my mind off some things."

He climbed up on the rail and threw a leg over so he could sit and talk to her, eye to eye.

"Althea tells me there's a bit of trouble amongst friends?"

A brooding look crossed her face.

"So young Hodges is a fair-weather friend and Ella Louise pulled a fast one, eh?"

"Boys are pinheads."

James smirked. "Granted. I'd like ta say it's a passing phase of manhood but admittedly . . . not for some. Best ye know that now."

"I didn't *have* to be friends with him, and it's not the first time he's been rude. He's *not* that smart . . . even though he thinks he is. I guess because his father is smart. And they know a lot of people. And now . . . now he acts like I offend him somehow."

James nodded. "Well, his father has a sterling job, yes. I believe his biggest accomplishment is that he inherited very well. But I understand Drew's sudden behavior reflects some bad information?"

"Ella Louise has always been my best friend. She would never say anything bad."

"Has she turned her back on ye as well? She has feelings for him?"

"Well . . ."

"And ye heard, perhaps, some of the things said?"

She frowned. "Mean things. She would never . . ."

"Oh, no? Ye've noticed whom the boy clings ta? Who's always there whispering in his ear? Pay attention, love. It doesn't matter that ye deny any interest in the lad; she thinks ye're the competition. Ella Louise's mother, God bless her ignorance, is pushing the girl on him. Tim approves because he wants what he thinks is security for his daughter. It's a step up in the world as they see it. A match is being made, and she thinks ye're in the way."

Tears filled Charlotte's eyes. "I would never do that to her."

"There's where ye do yerself a disservice, my girl. To assume others will do as you would in a situation." He tapped her nose. "Many times ye'll be disappointed for counting on it."

She looked at him glumly. "She does talk a lot about getting married. She thinks life on the farm is too hard. She wants to be a society lady."

"There's no ease in this life, girl. If ye want ta believe in fairy stories and riches as happiness, ye'll always see them with money as living charmed lives. But, be forewarned, ye might as well look for honey in a sea of brine."

"But what do I do now?"

"She let ye down. Yer friend let ye down. First, make up yer mind ta not depend on her ta that level again. Next, ye forgive her as a human being that also makes mistakes. Finally, ye ignore the slight and be happy and supportive as her friend. Ye can na control her actions, only yer actions in return. Then move on from it. It's only when ye're bumped that what's really inside spills out ta tell what ye're made of. And I happen ta think ye're made of some pretty grand stuff."

Charlotte leaned out of the saddle and put an arm around her father's neck.

"Thanks, Da."

"Now then." He reached out to rub Banshee's forelock. "How about if I see ta settling our friend here back in his stall, and you go help Althea with dinner? Our dinners are quickly coming ta close."

She sighed. "I know. I'm trying not to think about how lonely it will seem without her. We'll still be together at the dress shop . . . but it'll be different."

"At least Justin will be back and forth. It'll help the transition."

"I suppose."

"Just life moving forward. One day ye'll be leaving me . . . for some pinhead," he teased.

"Oh, stop, Da," she laughed. "I have a feeling you'll make sure no pinheads make it past your door."

CHAPTER 37

"To Coleridge Sierra!" declared Neil Collier.

"Hear, Hear!"

The melodic ring of six champagne flutes touching resounded within the tight circle in Adele Collier Hensley's drawing room. Dutton surveyed their faces, relaxing as he read the family's enthusiasm and relieved at his ability to bring good news quickly. Profitability only helped accelerate next steps.

"To our continued success," added Dutton. "And . . . many thanks to my gracious hosts! Dinner was fabulous, Adele." He lifted a glass in salute to Dr. Stanley Hensley standing proudly with his arm around his lovely wife.

Stan beamed. "Please . . . let's all sit. Dutton, what you and Neil have accomplished in a short amount of time is nothing short of astounding. Eleven mining operations added under the Empire banner in less than a year — I'm impressed. It bodes well for the future of our joint family venture."

Dutton chose a yellow, silk, tufted chair by the fireplace. Its rosewood trim encircled a high, round back, giving it a throne-like feel. The chair suited him. He gave a swift mental appraisal of the Hensleys' home outside Sacramento. Stan loved a rural setting, so he bought a small, picturesque dairy farm. He worked as a physician in Sacramento but found the farm relaxing, gentlemanly — particularly since he hired others to run it for him. The property's stately two-story home — not too large, with a grand front porch — featured elaborate rose gardens, pathways, benches, and arbors enhancing its pastoral beauty. Dutton recognized this as Adele's touch.

"An auspicious start," added Neil, sitting in the butter-colored counterpart flanking the opposite side of the marble hearth. Adele and Celeste settled into an elaborately curvaceous settee to Neil's right, while Stan fetched the champagne bottle from its stand. Royce waved off Stan's attempt to refill his glass and opted to exchange it for whiskey. He hovered at the table behind the settee, seemingly too restless to sit.

Neil hesitated before finishing his thought.

"While our investment shows excellent growth . . . the actual acquisition of the mines was not what I envisioned."

Royce frowned. "What are you saying?"

"I worry that perhaps we foreclosed a bit quickly."

Dutton deflected the comment. "When there's nothing left, how can it be too quickly? We don't make decisions for them. They didn't come to us for advice, but for cash. Why, we gave them every opportunity to make those mines thrive."

Stan deposited the empty champagne bottle upside down in its bucket. He turned, glass in hand, to Dutton. "Of course. Everything was executed according to the terms of the loan agreements, correct?"

"Without question."

"Well . . . some of those men possessed absolutely no business acumen at all. They flaunted more ambition than they were suited to pull off," Neil countered.

"With interest half the going rate? They had every chance. Where else could they acquire that kind of loan? Aw . . ." Dutton flicked his wrist in dismissal, "I know what you're saying, Neil; their failure wasn't the goal here . . . but fail they did. It was inevitable, apparently. The ones *able* to survive didn't come to us at all."

"Not a way to keep friends or allies," said Royce.

Neil thought for a minute. "We need to address these concerns . . . Do we have employees reaching out to these folks, at least offering them jobs? I can't see leaving these people with nothing . . . especially when they represent knowledge and experience useful to us."

Dutton sat back with a conciliatory look. "You're absolutely right. Done. I'll delegate a member of my management staff to reach out to them." He smirked. "Spoken like a true public servant."

Royce scoffed. "That's a bit slick, isn't it?"

"Royce!"

Celeste flinched at the sharpness in Adele's tone. She had been sitting quietly after arranging her skirts just so and now peered at Dutton as if looking for offense. The two women made very attractive, though opposite, bookends, thought Dutton wryly. Adele's dark tresses arranged in a tasteful chignon seemed to contradict sister-hood with Celeste's strawberry-blonde curls pulled pertly to the side. Both stared at him with the brilliant-blue Collier eyes.

Dutton addressed the girl. "I imagine you're thinking of a million things more

interesting than listening to us drone on."
He winked. "Afraid I can't promise it will
get any better."

"I'm used to it in this family," she stated.

"You're fortunate to be exposed to the
education of life at such a young age," said
Stan brusquely.

Celeste replied, ignoring Stan's remark,
"You see, Mr. Dandridge, what happens
when you lose two parents at a young age
— suddenly I have four of them." She
cocked her head.

He gave her a lazy smile. "You may call
me Dutton."

"Thank you. For including me as an
adult."

Adele broke in. "I believe we were about
to discuss Neil's running for senator?"

Royce set his whiskey glass on the table
with a thud. "Since we're destined to have
our names linked together in this *Coleridge
Sierra* entity, Dutton, let me tell you what
our name means." Dutton felt the heat of
Royce's glare.

"Garth Collier wasn't a highly educated
man, but he was cunning. He derived power
from an unbending will to accomplish what
he put his back and his mind to. And he
had the guts to carry it out. He came to
California with a small inheritance long

523

before statehood and worked as a ranch hand for a prestigious Spanish family. Spanish *vaqueros* are experts with cattle and horses, and he absorbed every aspect of the trade. He became an indispensible and respected member of the household. When a small parcel of land came available, what's now our north forty, he purchased it and sent for Mother.

"Grandpa Dylan sold all he had in Texas for a place at their table. With the proceeds, he and Pap took advantage of the changing loyalties of government. The end of the Mexican war brought Spanish titles to land into question. With gold discovered and statehood imminent, Spanish land grants became absorbed by the United States. Grandpa Dylan had rallied his neighbors to join General Zachary Taylor on the Nueces River defending Texas from Mexican invasion. His loyalty found favor with the new California government. They could've scooped up newly available lands for a song and, with unclaimed land, they did. But they did the honorable thing — they sought out Spanish owners willing to sell and paid a fair price."

"That's some recitation," said Dutton.

"Because it's important! I'm telling you this because the Collier name means something in this community. I don't want it sullied by bad politics or shady business practices."

Neil protested. "For heaven's sake, Royce! Do you think I do?"

He turned to his brother. "I know what you think. I want Dutton to understand what our expectations are. Pap held a personal creed that whatever he did was to be done well. Never embarrass the family with half an effort. He'd accept failure in a project so long as every life's breath went into the attempt. He backtracked mistakes to see what he could learn in every situation."

Royce pivoted around to face Dutton. "We were raised on hard work, humble beginnings, and lending a hand to our neighbors. I don't expect that to change."

"Well . . . at least I got the terminology right — public servant, I did say." Dutton spoke in smoothly soothing tones. "Let me tell you what I know from the judge. As early pioneers, Garth's successes were nearly legendary, and Eugenia possessed the rare combination of grit and charm. Father says Eugenia could have milked a bear to feed her children if necessary and then gone on to serve tea in the most elegant manner on the most humble tree stump. He told me that, as the Colliers grew prosperous, they never forgot their neighbors and never forgot a deed of kindness or bravery unless it was their own. Why do you think the judge and I have such confidence in Neil?"

Dutton smiled charmingly. "Politics is the long-term goal. It plays well to your brother's sense of community. As you point out, Royce, you Colliers like to build things. It only seems natural that, while you're growing the ranch, he should share in growing the state. Takes a man with vision; Neil certainly has that. For my money, he's exactly the kind of man I'd like to see running things."

Stan agreed. "I can't argue with you there. Neil tells us you have an ambitious career path laid out for him. But business and politics? Seems like they'd be at odds with each other."

Dutton continued knowingly. "Don't be too sure about the two being at odds. Look at our friend President Lincoln. He pushed Nevada's statehood through so quickly the state constitution had to be telegraphed to Washington. He needed another free state and access to the riches pouring out of it — never mind the lack of inhabitants to qualify for statehood. I think at some point he began counting gold nuggets instead of men. How better to finance the defeat of the confederacy?" He paused. "Pity he didn't live long enough to see his dreams come to fruition. At any rate, don't think political decisions aren't linked to industry. Symbiotic friendships exist — good ones get things done."

"What about bad ones?" countered Royce.

"That is precisely why we need a man like Neil." Dutton hesitated. "Believe me, Royce, your questions of me are no different than ones voters will raise of Neil. It's why it's so important that the entire family is involved. When you have concerns, I expect you to challenge me. Iron sharpens iron, my friend."

Royce stood, arms crossed over his broad chest, studying him. "It's all I'm asking."

"Good! Now, Neil . . . I did bring campaign appearance schedules in my valise if you'd like to look at timing with the family? It'll be important to get up to the mining districts soon, especially with our interests there. They need to see a face they can trust." He reached into the leather bag.

Neil shrugged. "Certainly. It'll let Royce know how much of my slack he'll need to pick up."

Adele rose. "Celeste, I think coffee is in order. Would you help me?"

Celeste stood to follow, but Dutton held up his finger. "Wait — I'll do that. Here . . ." He handed Celeste the schedules. "You go over these with the family; I want everyone involved."

As they proceeded down the hallway Adele asked, "Is this part of the campaign manager's duties?"

"Everything but kissing babies," Dutton said lightly. He pushed open the swinging door to the kitchen for her. The room was spacious and cheery. "Your home is beautiful, Adele. It suits you." He walked over to stoke the stove while she filled the kettle. "An ideal setting for a local political fundraiser, perhaps?"

She laughed. "I wondered when we would get to that. I'd be honored, of course. I appreciate your patience with the family. We all tend to look at a topic from different angles."

"Not at all. I expect there will be questions at many phases. Cups?"

"The shelf to your right — the small floral ones, please. There's a silver tray over by the door."

Dutton arranged six cups and saucers on the tray. "Adele? It's none of my business, but . . . did I sense a bit of tension with Stan and Celeste?"

She sighed. "Stan is suffering from a little wounded pride. We had lively debates amongst all of us about where Celeste should live after Mother and Father died. She chose to stay in the family home. She said it would be too traumatic for her to be torn from what's left as familiar."

"And you don't agree?"

"In part. Celeste savors a penchant for drama. She's very . . . boisterous, Dutton. She needs firm supervision, and I fear she thinks she can control her freedom living with Neil and Royce."

Dutton laughed. "With those two?"

Adele pursed her lips. "Neil is far too tender hearted to scold her for anything. Royce leans to the rambunctious side, so he hardly sees the need to rein her in — he likes a free spirit. They're both so busy all the time . . . I worry she needs stricter guidance."

"Ah. She lives to escape eagle-eye Adele?"

"She would have a more stable home environment here with me and Stan. Mother certainly restrained her more. I try to stay on top of it, but I have the two little ones here. She *is* nearly grown . . ."

"Sounds like good training for you . . . wait until yours get to be that age."

"It's so much easier when you can hold

them and hug them."

Dutton smiled as she placed the silver coffee pot on the tray. "I'd say she's in good hands. Shall we?"

Adele led the way, carrying cream and sugar on a smaller silver tray. Dutton caught a faint trace of her perfume above the aroma of the coffee. He allowed himself a quick moment of regret as he followed her. Adele possessed a grace, an understated elegance, that few women had. But he realized early on she was too intelligent, or at least far too discerning. He could never maneuver without her seeing through the shadowy façade he erected for the world — though he often thought it might be fun to try. If only it wasn't for that unrelenting morality of hers, they might have made a nice couple. "Ah, well," he thought, "all men need an unfulfilled dream to drive them harder towards success."

CHAPTER 38

Nevada City

Mrs. Hodges arrived at Althea's shop with a dress draped casually over her arm. Charlotte addressed her warmly. "Well, Mrs. Hodges! We haven't seen you for a while. Is there something I can help you with?"

"Thank you, dear, but Althea promised to have a quick look at this dress I bought in San Francisco. There's something not right about the fit in the shoulders. Is she here?"

"She left for a few minutes to check on the workmen at the new home. The wedding is only a few weeks away, you know. She shouldn't be long."

"Everyone is delighted that the Millers decided to take a house in town." Mrs. Hodges put her hand to the side of her mouth as if imparting a secret. "It was a worry that Sean would carry her off to settle somewhere else. We're very fortunate to have someone so talented. And you, Char-

531

lotte — how lucky to have such a teacher!"

"Indeed," Charlotte beamed. "Let me take that dress from you until she gets here. Care to look around?"

Mrs. Hodges gratefully handed over the heavy dress. She murmured, "Well, it never hurts to look." She glanced over Charlotte's shoulder at a table in the corner. "Oh, are those new brocades?"

"Yes, some lovely colors there. I'll put your dress in the fitting room until Althea arrives. I'm sure she'll want to see it on you when you're ready." With her customer well occupied, Charlotte disappeared behind the curtain of the dressing area.

At that moment, Althea crossed the muddy street on her way back to the shop. She pulled up her skirts and gave a little hop to dodge the puddle before her. As she cleared the murky furrow, she was vaguely aware of a sudden thundering sound and a wild jangling noise. Shouts arose from alarmed bystanders on the sidewalk. She looked up just as the driverless team of a whiskey wagon was upon her.

Justin emerged from the tack room, his tally in hand, as well as three worn out halters. He found James as he rounded the side of the barn.

"All cleaned out." He tossed the halters to the ground. "These three are beat; they'll need replacing. As far as leads and lariats go, with the increase in the stock we'll need at least half a dozen from Vicente. Bridles all looked good; I cleaned them up. We're running low on liniment as well."

"Sounds like a trip inta town is warranted . . ." James looked off into the distance, his reddish-blonde brow knit together in a frown. He could barely make out a horse barreling down the road at breakneck speed.

"Someone's sure riding hell for high ground. I don't recognize the horse, do you, Justin?"

"No, but . . ." The rider suddenly came into view. "It's Charlotte," he said with surprise.

"Och, perhaps yer mother was right," James muttered.

He stood with his hands planted firmly on his hips. "Ridiculously reckless speed." He began to stalk towards her as she reined in her mount to a skidding halt. He stopped short, seeing her wildly disheveled hair and her face streaked with tears.

She dismounted, shouting, "Quick! Get horses. You've got to come at once, both of you!" She choked on sobs. "Althea's hurt . . . terrible accident."

Justin leapt forward. "Where is she? What happened?"

"They took her to Dr. Wyndem's house. There was a runaway team. She was in the street . . . it's bad."

They froze for a moment, not comprehending. As if awakening from a nightmare, James shoved Justin's shoulder. "Take the bay . . . quickly, lad, go ta yer mother. *Go!*"

Justin ran to the fence where Rusty was tethered. In a matter of moments, he tore down the road towards town.

"Charlotte, that horse is spent. I'll saddle two others. Go inside, wash yer face, and pull yerself together. Althea needs us. Justin will need us ta be strong as well."

He stopped, grabbed her shoulders, and looked hard into her face. "Did ye see her?"

She nodded, fresh tears running down her face. "I heard yelling in the street. I looked out of the shop as the wagon lurched around a corner out of sight. I looked back the other way. She was crumpled up in the street. The next thing I knew, Vicente was there picking her up. She wasn't moving. She's alive, but . . . it's bad, Da."

James closed his eyes as she continued. "Vicente is still with her and the doctor. They sent someone for Sean."

■ ■ ■ ■

Lodie and Vicente waited outside on Dr. Wyndem's porch as they arrived.

"Any news?" James asked tersely.

"Not yet. Matilda's inside with Justin. The doctor's still in with her. He hasn't let the lad see her yet."

"Vicente, was she conscious at all?"

He shook his head. "Not while I see her. She spit up blood when I put her on the bed."

Charlotte fought for control. "I'm going in to be with Justin."

"What about Sean?"

"It could be a few more hours before he gets here. God, he'll be frantic."

As Charlotte opened the front door, James glimpsed the doctor enter the parlor. They rushed inside.

Dr. Wyndem wiped his hands on a towel. He took a deep breath. "She's not out of the woods yet, I'm afraid. I won't know more until she regains consciousness. She was trampled pretty severely. There's a couple broken ribs, which I believe punctured a lung. Her right hip is broken, and there are multiple contusions and lacerations. She'll require someone with her around the clock until she wakes and I can reassess. I'll sleep in the office until we know more. All I can do is keep her comfortable and quiet. Justin, you can go in to her now."

Charlotte squeezed Justin's hand. He glanced back at her. "I want to go alone. Give me a few minutes?"

She nodded.

Dr. Wyndem looked at the group. "I'll be in the back of the house. Make yourselves comfortable. Fetch me if there's any change at all. I'll check in every hour or so."

They murmured thanks with heavy hearts.

It was nearly dawn when a bleary-eyed Sean shook James on the shoulder. He awoke with a start and bolted upright, as he feared the worst.

"Shh." Sean pressed a finger to his lips and pointed at Charlotte and Justin asleep on blankets stretched out on the floor.

"She's awake and in a lot of pain. I'm going to get the Doc. She asked to see you."

James nodded and rubbed his hands over his face. He got up quietly and slipped into the sickroom without disturbing the others.

She lay so still he thought at first she had relapsed. He sat in the chair beside her bed and placed his hand gently over her smaller one. Her face was badly bruised. Her eyes opened, just barely, as she struggled to speak.

"James?" she whispered.

"I'm here, Thea."

She tried to nod. "I need you to do something for me."

"Anything. Try not ta talk. Save yer strength."

"Need you . . . to tell Justin for me. Just in case."

A chill tingled his spine. "There will be plenty of time for that."

"I couldn't find the right time. I confess . . . I've been too afraid. I've tried hard . . . to raise them well . . . both of them. I thought that should be enough."

"A steadier hand they cu na have known. Emma cu na have wanted more than ye've given her girl."

Althea gave the weakest hint of a smile. "I'll tell her you said so . . . when I see her."

He blinked hard. "It's na yer time," he said hoarsely. "Ye're na going anywhere yet. I'll not allow it. Do ye hear me, Thea?"

"I hear. Promise? He needs to know. Now."

James's eyes burned with tears he would not let come. "Ye're going ta feel damn foolish when ye're well."

"Something to hope for."

James blew out a heavy sigh. "I promise ta tell him . . . if ye promise ta fight. Justin still needs ye. I . . . I need ye. Will ye fight, Thea?" He sounded almost angry.

"Very tired, James." She was succumbing to sleep. She wrapped two fingers around his hand. "I . . . know. And my Justin has always been my whole heart."

He sat by her side and watched the slight rise and fall of her chest, afraid to look away lest it should stop.

Sean came in with the doctor, and James stood, feeling drained. Sean put a hand on his arm and whispered, "I know what she's asked of you. She told me the whole story when I asked her to marry me. It's important to her." James nodded and left the room.

He stopped and closed the door behind him. The sun began its rise. Both Justin and Charlotte sat up, eyes wide open, waiting expectantly.

"She woke for a short time. Sean took Dr. Wyndem back in. She's in a lot of pain."

Charlotte spoke first. "Is she going to be all right?"

"She woke up; that's an encouraging sign. But she's very weak."

Justin stood. "Can I go in?"

"Perhaps when the doctor comes out.

We'll see what he says." James paused hesitantly.

Justin was immediately alert. "What is it?"

"Truly, it's all I know." James took a deep breath and studied him. "She asked me ta do something."

Justin's gaze never left James's face. James walked over and slumped into a chair. He rested his head wearily in his large hands. His red and tired eyes stared sightlessly through his fingers. He seemed for the moment to be somewhere else.

"Justin . . . come sit. Yer mother has some things she wants ye ta know . . . well, she hasn't the strength ta tell ye herself right now. She always meant to; it didn't seem ta serve any purpose before. Charlotte, come, too, lass. It's time ye both knew about the past."

Justin warily took the chair across from James. Charlotte pulled a footstool over from the fireplace.

"I met yer mother and Emma while we worked on the Vernon estate in England — those stories ye already know." In his mind's eye, he saw them both as they were then. "They were young and pretty. Both hard workers and well respected by the master and mistress of the house. And they were best friends. Justin, yer mother was always a romantic, more of a dreamer. If it were na for her matchmaking, I doubt Emma would ha given me a second look.

"As well as duties ta the mistress, they were largely in service ta the daughters in the household, Margaret and Virgilia. Not bad sorts, either of them. Pampered and spoiled they were, but not unkind. Althea and Emma grew up with them so ta speak and were devoted servants."

James's eyes began to take on a hard look as his mind reached back.

"There's an inherent problem with becoming too close ta those above ye. Ye can never allow yerself to believe ye're more than a servant, no matter how many confidences ye keep, no matter how many assurances of affection."

His eyes latched onto Justin's face, willing him to understand.

"Yer mother was caring and light-hearted. She has a natural gaiety about her that drew people in. Lord Vernon also had a son. Edward. A sullen brute. He took no amount of advice or criticism from his father. He rebelled, complained, looked for sympathy — largely from yer mother. He cu tell her any whiny version of the truth he liked. She gave him solace, made him laugh, and she made him feel better without having ta face

540

reality or responsibility. She . . ." James's voice caught in his throat. Justin began to shift uneasily in his chair.

James's face grew grim. For several minutes, he did not speak. He fought anger. He closed his eyes as he heard the voices from that fateful, ugly night. He saw it as clearly as if Emma whispered it in his ear.

Virgilia had suspicions. She made accusations to the mistress, who summoned Althea at once. Emma had rushed to her side. The mistress tried to be firm but helpful, not being in possession of all the facts.

Lady Vernon had begun. "Althea, I'm trying my best to be understanding. Surely you know what kind of position you've put me in. In these cases, a girl in your circumstances would be dismissed. You've always been a pleasant, hardworking servant in this house . . ." She paused.

Althea was terrified, looking down at the floor. Emma stood as if shielding her.

"Althea, if you are truthful with me, perhaps I can help."

Althea could not look up. "I'm afraid no one can help me now."

Emma held her hand.

"You are with child, then?"

Althea nodded.

"Can you tell me who the father is?"

The question met with stony silence.

"Althea, if the man works for us, it is highly possible the master can make this man live up to his duty and marry you. I would like to make it possible for you to stay on with us," she said kindly.

Althea began to weep openly. Emma put her arm around her.

Lady Vernon was deeply unsettled. "Of course this is distressing for you, dear. Emma?"

Emma looked up and met her questioning gaze. She was not defiant, but she was not subservient either.

"Do you know the father?"

Emma never looked away, "Yes, Madam."

"Nooo!" Althea sobbed.

Emma and the mistress remained with eyes locked. " 'Tis Edward, Madam," she said quietly.

Many closed and slamming doors echoed in the halls that evening. First Lord and Lady Vernon. Then the master and Edward. Margaret and Virgilia were sent to their rooms. Althea, Emma, and James waited in the kitchen. Then Lord and Lady Vernon were again in conference. Finally, Althea was called. She was allowed to

542

bring Emma, while James paced in the kitchen.

Lady Vernon was silent. She had been crying. She seemed detached and hurt.

Lord Vernon began to speak, sadly, but with authority.

"You've been a very foolish girl, Althea."

Emma bristled; her lips pursed, she began to speak.

Lord Vernon held up his hand. "Now be still, Emma. Don't get yourself into trouble here." He continued sternly. "I cannot begin to tell you how my son's reckless behavior grieves me. For that, I take responsibility. We will not throw you out, girl."

Althea's relief showed visibly by the slump in her shoulders. Emma squeezed her hand.

"But it is obvious that you cannot remain here." Both girls froze.

"As difficult as it is for me to say, I have to remind you that you have allowed your present circumstances to happen."

She nodded tearfully. She would not explain herself or grovel.

"How many people know the child is Edward's?"

She opened her mouth to speak, but couldn't. Emma held her friend tightly and answered, "Only myself and my husband, sir." She guarded her own feelings carefully, not wanting to hurt Althea's chances for generosity with the master. "Several of the other servants are aware she is with child. Some may speculate as to the father, but they'll not get any verification from us."

"Good." Lord Vernon relaxed a bit. "As long as I can count on your discretion, I am prepared to help as best I can."

"We understand, sir," she said evenly.

"Good. We think it best if we find Althea a position away from here as quickly as possible."

Emma was alarmed. "How far away, sir?"

"That depends on the two of you," he said seriously. "We realize she will need the support of those around her. So we thought a few hours from here, in the village."

Althea looked up, frightened. "But what will I do, sir?"

"You will be an apprentice in the dressmaker's shop there. The owner has been indebted to me for some time. They do business for the gentry for some distances. My wife tells me you have talent in this area. If you apply yourself, you could do well for yourself and the child. I will set *you up myself in a small cottage so you won't starve. But . . ." he held up one finger in warning, "there are conditions."*

Emma spoke up, "Yes, sir."

"None of you are ever to speak of the child's father. Make up whatever story you like, but do not involve this family. Second — Emma, you and James are free to visit on your own time as often as you like, but Althea — you will never set foot on this property again, understood?"

Althea nodded miserably. The mistress sat in the back of the room, silently dabbing her eyes.

"If any part of this agreement is broken, then all support on my part will be withdrawn, understood?"

"Yes, sir."

"Then you are dismissed." Lord Vernon turned his back to them.

Emma gently guided Althea to the door, but, before they left the room, she stopped and turned. "Pardon, sir?"

"Yes?"

"Meaning no disrespect, sir . . . but what of Edward?"

She saw the flare of temper in the master's expression. Hurriedly she added, "I mean, I imagine this is difficult for him as well, and I assume you have asked him to

have nothing further to do with Althea?"
She found herself half bent in a bow of
humility.

The master noted her manner and said
stiffly, "Edward will soon begin a military
career."

"Da?" Charlotte began softly. "You aren't
saying anything."

James opened his eyes and returned to the
present.

He said quietly, "She let her heart rule
her head. She knew better. But she fell in
love. He was na worthy of it, nor did he
stand by her."

Justin shook his head, struggling to com-
prehend. "What are you saying?"

James put a hand on Justin's shoulder.
"Yer mother felt it's time ye knew . . . that
Edward Vernon was yer father."

Justin stood abruptly. "Then, who was
Edward Albright? My father drowned."

"No, lad. Albright is yer mother's name."

"She has a picture of him."

"She has a picture of Edward Vernon. She
took it from the house in Boston so someday . . . ye would know."

Justin's face turned red. He ran his fingers
through his rumpled, blond hair and looked
from his mother's closed sickroom door

back to James.

"You know what that makes me?" His voice became louder. Bitterness rose in him like the burning taste of bile. "Do you know what that makes her?"

James sprang quickly from his chair and, mindful of Althea convalescing in the next room, shouted in a fierce whisper, *"No!"*

He poked his finger in Justin's chest. "I know it's a shock, but ye don't get ta judge her! Ye'll find . . ."

James sucked in a deep breath and dropped the accusing hand to his side.

"Ye'll find the older ye get, the more ye'll have ta make yer peace with." He looked at Justin sternly. "Ye put that anger aside now, lad. Ye mustn't let her see it. It isn't her ye should be angry with. She needs ye ta understand. Ye can be mad at the likes of him all ye want. It's no bloody secret I hated the man."

Justin glared at him. He turned and bolted from the house.

CHAPTER 39

Nevada City

Lodie fumed in a highly unusual temper. A suitcase lay open on the bed, and he tossed articles of clothing out of the closet as he searched.

Matilda ran up the stairs as she heard the commotion.

"What on earth is all the fuss about? Everything will be fine."

"This is the worst possible time to leave town!"

"I know, but Althea's going to recover." She smiled gently. "I'll be here to help out."

Un-mollified, he ranted on, "I'm going to be late for the meeting. I still have to give the boys instructions about the store."

Matilda put her hands on her hips. "The boys are pretty much in charge of the store other than your accounting books and have been for months now — nothing they aren't used to. And, again, I'm here."

He slammed the suitcase shut. "I'm sorry. You're right. There's a lot riding on this," he said nervously. "Stupid, unnecessary mistakes have been made." He sighed and sat on the bed. He looked around the well-furnished room and then up at the wife he adored. "We've done really well here, haven't we? I wish Father had lived to see all this."

"He'd be *so* proud."

"Hmph. He was always too important in his own right to be impressed with me. I think he thought I was a fool to drag you out here and leave both thriving family farms behind."

"Don't be hard on yourself. You have a beautiful, loving family, a successful business, and the title of mayor, of all things! If the meeting goes well, who knows the limits of what you can achieve? Remember, *I'm* proud of you always."

He stood and kissed her lightly. "Invariably, you have the right words. Thank you, darling."

She patted his arm as he turned for the door. "You'll be brilliant," she encouraged. "Ah, wait. Is this what you're looking for?" She reached behind the door. "You don't want to forget your lucky charm." She handed him the silver-headed cane.

CHAPTER 40

Thistle Dew

"What?! No! When?" She felt her heart tumble.

Her father spoke firmly. "Right now."

"Well, he can't!"

Charlotte flung open the door to the house and darted onto the front porch, her eye and direction set firmly on the barn. She halted, seeing Althea sitting in the farthest corner of the porch, a blanket covering her lap, her gaze distant and sorrowful. Charlotte walked quickly to her and hovered in a partial kneel, compelled to stay, but wanting to run. She took Althea's hand and squeezed it. The perfumed bloom of lilac bushes surrounding the porch seemed to smother her ability to think clearly.

Althea's recovery was slow. It took her weeks to get back on her feet, and even now, the pain in her hip made walking difficult.

She leaned heavily on a walking stick, forcing her right leg forward with every step. Though the doctor promised improvement over time, she refused to marry Sean as an invalid and postponed the wedding. In light of revelations from the past, she was not the only one in need of healing. Justin's reluctance to approach the subject of his father with her drove an uneasy wedge between them.

Charlotte received no acknowledgement from her now. She stood and kissed Althea on the cheek and promised, "I'll talk to him." She hastened down the steps and across the courtyard to the barn.

Passing through the tall threshold, she blinked, trying to adjust to the dim lighting. She turned as she heard Justin's movement near one of the stalls. As his form came into focus, she saw him tying a bedroll behind the saddle of the sorrel stallion.

"Is it true?"

He looked up, grimly determined. "Yes." He returned his attention to readying his mount, checking the security of his rifle in its scabbard.

She fought through her own feelings and weighed them against his. She knew he struggled with how to come to terms with information that changed everything about his life, and yet nothing at all.

"You weren't going to tell me?"

He checked the saddlebag one last time and turned to her. "I didn't plan on leaving this quickly. It was only fair to talk with Mum first. Once I got through that, I needed to get on with it."

She nodded her understanding. "But where will you go? What will you do?"

He looked at her plainly. "I'll head towards Sacramento. Look for ranch work."

"There's plenty of that here. Da counts on you. He's taught you everything."

"I know. Kind of thought I'd always be here." He looked around the familiarity of the barn as if memorizing it. "I've spent my whole life in a mixed up clan of MacLarens and Albrights. I need to try things on my own. James understood."

Justin sucked in a breath in disbelief. "He gave me Baron, here." He put his hand on the horse's rump. "I told him it was too much, but he insisted. And the saddle's brand new, one of Vicente's best." He looked at her earnestly. "It really means a lot . . . to have his support."

"Justin, please wait awhile longer."

"It was all I could do to wait until James got back from his trip to Sacramento."

"And Althea?"

He looked at his feet. "It's hard." He was quiet for a time. "She'll have a new life with Sean soon. I'll be back for the wedding. All men have to leave home someday, Charlotte. My someday is now."

She swallowed hard. "And me?"

He smiled sadly. "We're still family. Nothing's changed. I know I have to go."

The tears glistening in her eyes seemed to magnify their greenish hue. She looked at him with her fiercest face. "If you don't write . . ." She shook her fist at him and wiped away an errant tear. ". . . I'll come wherever you are and make such a scene . . ." She smothered a sob. "Well, no one'll let you work for them after that!"

He stepped closer and gave her a hug. She clung to him, and he kissed the top of her head. "Just life moving forward."

They walked into the sunlight of the courtyard arm in arm, with Justin leading Baron. Althea remained in her corner of the porch staring blandly. James stood beside her.

Charlotte looked up at Justin and insisted, "This is not good-bye. And I'm not going to stand here and be the pathetic face watching you leave." She embraced him tightly and said, "Until I see you."

He smiled fondly and then looked up at

the porch. "Take care of Mum? We've already said our good-byes." She nodded and walked up the porch steps, passing James on his way down. She lingered on the top step, watching.

James approached and patted the stallion, giving him a visual once-over. "Ye check his shoes?"

"Yes, sir. Gear's secure as well. I . . ." he glanced at the horse. "I can't tell you how much I appreciate . . ."

James merely shook his head and said, "Ye've earned him many times over."

They stood silently for a few awkward seconds until Justin nodded, tugged on the reins, and walked Baron forward.

James caught Justin's arm lightly as he passed and held him no more than a few moments. He faced towards the barn; Justin faced the road ahead with his horse. Charlotte could see the swell of emotion between them. Their eyes did not meet, but the connection of just two fingers upon Justin's arm provided the link they needed.

"Ye can na truly appreciate all that is good without teetering on the edge of the bad," James said in a low voice. "And when ye feel chased away by some grim thing, it makes ye run . . . towards something more noble. Pace yerself lad. Work at forgiving —

Mercy drives winged horses, while wrath's footsteps are slow and heavy. Don't carry this weight. Leave it here, lad."

Justin gave a short nod. Without looking back, he patted James's arm. Then his rigid demeanor broke and he threw his arms around the only father figure he'd ever known. They clasped one another tightly until Justin turned abruptly and mounted his horse. He did not speak but looked down upon James in such a way that words were not necessary.

James raised his head and met his gaze. He murmured, "Aye."

Justin kicked Baron to a start and rode off with a burst of speed.

James watched him until he disappeared around a small grove of trees.

ABOUT THE AUTHOR

Kalen Vaughan Johnson is a historical fiction writer living in Raleigh, North Carolina. She graduated from UNC–Chapel Hill with a BA in mass media and worked in television for eight years. Together with her husband, Gary, she raised three children on the move in Chicago, Tokyo, Sydney, and New York before returning to her southern roots. Visit her website at kalenvaughanjohnson.com.

The employees of Thorndike Press hope you have enjoyed this Large Print book. All our Thorndike, Wheeler, and Kennebec Large Print titles are designed for easy reading, and all our books are made to last. Other Thorndike Press Large Print books are available at your library, through selected bookstores, or directly from us.

For information about titles, please call:
  (800) 223-1244

or visit our Web site at:
  http://gale.cengage.com/thorndike

To share your comments, please write:
  Publisher
  Thorndike Press
  10 Water St., Suite 310
  Waterville, ME 04901